Margaret Wolfe Hungerford

A Maiden all Forlorn, and Other Stories

Margaret Wolfe Hungerford

A Maiden all Forlorn, and Other Stories

ISBN/EAN: 9783337280604

Printed in Europe, USA, Canada, Australia, Japan

Cover: Foto ©Andreas Hilbeck / pixelio.de

More available books at **www.hansebooks.com**

A MAIDEN ALL FORLORN
AND OTHER STORIES.

A MAIDEN ALL FORLORN

AND

Other Stories.

BY

THE AUTHOR OF

"PHYLLIS," "MOLLY BAWN," "LOYS, LORD BERESFORD," ETC.

NEW EDITION.

WARD AND DOWNEY,

12, YORK STREET, COVENT GARDEN, LONDON.

1885.

CONTENTS.

MOONSHINE AND MARGUERITES (*continued*).

A PASSIVE CRIME.

CONTENTS vii

A MAIDEN ALL FORLORN.

CHAPTER I.

"But, what will your uncle say?" asks Mrs. Rivers, nervously.

"My uncle will say just what the Major says," replies Ronnie, shrugging her shoulders.

"Wouldn't it be a comfort if the Major died?" says Cecil, from her low chair in the chimney-corner—her own special corner, in every house wherein she may go. As she makes this charitable speech, she sighs profoundly.

"My dear," says her mother in a tone that is meant to be full of rebuke, but is only fond.

"Well, I know that," returns Miss Cecil, saucily; "I am perfectly aware that I am dear to you. What's the good of telling me the same thing over and over again? Only that it would be naughty to one's own sweet mother, I would give you a pinch for stale news."

"I suppose even uncle Gregory can't expect us to live in London all the year round," remarks Ronnie, a frown darkening her pretty little baby face. It is the funniest little frown, and certainly has no right whatever to be in its present resting place. "I suppose he can't control our every action."

"He can, however, keep us comfortable or reduce us to absolute want—at least, to something very near it," answers Mrs. Rivers in a trembling tone.

"My mind is made up," says Cecil, lightly. "Rather than

be reduced to absolute want, I shall marry a Marquis—a Duke even—if need be.   Let nobody try to dissuade me; I shall do it, or die."

"Then, I'm afraid you will die," returns Ronnie, who is the least bit of a cynic.

"You sha'n't discourage me," says Cissy, gaily.   "Even down in the 'deserted village,' where you and mother are bent on burying yourselves, I dare say I shall meet my fairy prince."

"I hope he will be a prince worthy of you?" says Mrs. Rivers, somewhat wistfully gazing at the lovely face smiling up at her, from the chimney-corner, out of its tangle of golden hair.

"You hope for too much," replies the owner of the golden locks merrily.   "The prince was never yet born, I am convinced, who would be worthy of such peerless charms as mine."

"But really, mamma, when we are all so tired of town life, why should we not go into the country, and especially to this pretty place the Freres have written to us about?" asks Ronnie.

"I am sure uncle Gregory ought to think better of us, for preferring the dulness of a country life to all the glittering dissipations of the town," observes Cecil, laughing.

"Your uncle likes nothing he doesn't suggest himself," says Mrs. Rivers.

"Then make him suggest it.   Let us go to him in a body and tell him how we are enjoying ourselves here, and ten to one but he will order us into solitary confinement, without delay.   He is such a perverse old dear."

"Cecil, you talk too much," murmurs her mother, mildly.

"I'm like the brook," says Cecil, unabashed?   "I go on for ever.   After all, I am better than a stupid girl who can't talk at all.   Ronnie, how silent you are!   Don't you like this country scheme?"

"Yes," returns Ronnie, very deliberately.   "It is my greatest desire to leave town forthwith."

As she says this, her mother raises her soft eyes and regards her curiously—nay, indeed, sadly. But Ronnie's face, whatever she herself may be thinking, is staunch to her, and betrays nothing.

"Yes, yes—country air will be good for us all," says Mrs. Rivers, hastily. "It must be arranged. I wish the Major could be brought to speak to your uncle about it."

"If you mean that I am to conciliate, and play up to the Major, I simply sha'n't," answers Cecil, with a vicious little nod. "I detest him. It is my belief he wants to marry that daughter of his—Maria, to uncle Gregory!"

"Oh, no!" says Ronnie, quickly. "He may live in the fond hope that uncle Gregory, growing disgusted with us and our frivolities, will leave Maria the bulk of his property; but I know he intends her to marry a much younger man. Lady Marsden told me all about it the other day. It did not interest me, so I have forgotten the minor details, such as names and places. But I know this young man has been abroad for years; that he has a tremendous amount of money; that he lives somewhere in the country, in a house beautiful as a dream; and that the Major was a friend of his father's and has been a sort of agent over his estate for years."

"You remembered a great deal considering your want of interest," observes Cissy. "Well, if it comes off, I wish this poor young man joy of Maria!"

"This poor young man, as you call him, will probably not marry to order. But the Major has quite made up his mind to it; and he is a man of many resources."

"How I should like to frustrate Maria!" exclaims Cecil. "If ever I meet this misguided youth she intends claiming as her own, I shall make violent love to him."

"Cecil!" says Mrs. Rivers again."

"Well, then, I shall let him make violent love to me. Is that better?"

"It is not amiable either way. I am sure, darling, you would not like to interfere with any other girl's lover."

"Well, fortunately, I can't," says Miss Cecil, in a tone of resignation, "as I have made up my mind to marry a Duke.

Therefore this excellent young squire will be beneath my notice."

"I think we had better go and speak to your uncle Gregory about this move," remarks Mrs. Rivers, presently. "You will both come with me, girls?"

This is said so hopefully that neither girl can find it in her heart to refuse.

"Oh, yes, of course, dearest!" replies Ronnie.

"Well, I do hope, mamma, he will not be primed and loaded with evil thoughts of us this time," says Cecil. "Do you remember our last visit—how he stormed and raved until Ronnie and you were nearly in tears, and I was in a wicked rage? And all about a very innocent little trip to the Kensington Museum with Sir Sydney Walcott?"

"I remember," answers Mrs. Rivers.

Ronnie grows a shade paler, and beats her fingers impatiently against the edge of the table near her.

"He is burdened with a terrible sense of propriety," she observes, after a moment or two. "He is a male prude. And the Major is always telling him stories about us in the hope Maria may be preferred to us at last. You know she is some sort of distant connection, and might be easily magnified into a second cousin with a claim to any loose money that might be going."

"I shall fall upon Maria some day, and rend her in pieces," says Cecil. "I shall indeed, mamma. There is little use in appealing to what you are pleased to call 'my better self.'"

"Let us go and see uncle Gregory to-day, and speak to him, and get it over," says Ronnie, decisively.

"Yes, do let us," cries Cecil.

And so it is arranged.

About five years before, the Honourable Mrs. Rivers had been left a widow, with two little girls, and inconsiderable fortune. When only seventeen she had married the younger son of an impecunious Earl, and therefore, on her husband's death, found herself possessed of few worldly goods beyond her pension and a small sum bequeathed to her by a maiden aunt. Her uncle, Sir Gregory Growle—an old bachelor holding eccentric views of life generally, and the possessor of a large fortune that had been amassed in India—had come to her rescue, and, though a crotchety, disagreeable old fellow in many ways, had settled upon her a rather handsome allowance, to be continued or discontinued at his good pleasure.

This allowance, however, was embittered to her by sundry scoldings, delivered at odd intervals, and much uncalled for advice about " the girls," who, as they grew up, were frequently declared by their grand-uncle to be too much for their mother, who plainly did not go the right way to control them. He furthermore gave it as his opinion that they ought to be kept in subjection.

All these hints and innuendoes did not help to endear Sir Gregory to his grand-nieces, though there was still another person, who, if possible, was more objectionable in their sight. This was an old friend of their uncle's—a swarthy Anglo-Indian, named Major Jervis, about sixty years of age. He had been a so-called friend indeed of the whole family for many years, and under that name had managed to make himself particularly obnoxious both to Ronnie and Cecil Rivers, who had taken little pains to disguise their dislike, and, by chilling replies and remarks, which sometimes bordered upon impertinence, had let him know what they thought of him. These signs and tokens of ill-will had of course been noticed by the Major, and treasured up in his memory, to be repaid fourfold should occasion offer. He had one daughter, a certain Maria Louisa, on whom he had centred all his ambitious hopes. She was tolerably good-looking, and to marry her to rank and wealth, or even wealth without the rank, was the dream of the Major's life.

Just at this time he had for her in his mind a *parti* unexceptionable in every respect, and only awaited the opportunity to throw her in his way. Maria Louisa, who was well known to the Rivers girls, was very distasteful to them, principally perhaps because they attributed to her father the meanness of retailing to their uncle Gregory all the stories he heard of them —simple stories enough in themselves, but, when distorted and exaggerated, black as Erebus.

To-day, as Mrs. Rivers and her daughters enter the library in the handsome house in Cromwell Road that calls Gregory Growle master, they find their uncle stretched upon a sofa, with one leg well bandaged and a rather sour expression upon his cadaverous countenance.

"Glad you felt it your duty to come to see me, even at the eleventh hour," he says, unpleasantly. "One might be dead and buried for all one's relations would care! Perhaps, indeed, you would prefer seeing me buried. But beware, beware!"

"'Trust her not, she is fooling thee,'" quotes Miss Cecil, in a low tone, to Ronnie, who can hardly suppress a smile.

"Dear Uncle," says Mrs. Rivers, who is really distressed, not having heard of his illness, "I had no idea you were laid up again with your old enemy."

She is plainly alluding to the gout, which is a devoted adherent of uncle Gregory's. Indeed, he is a perfect martyr to it, and it does not help to sweeten his temper.

"If we had known of it, the girls and I would have been here long ago to inquire after you," she continues, in a conciliatory tone.

"That may or may not be," returns uncle Gregory, uncompromisingly, though somewhat appeased by her gentleness; "I only know you never did come. Well—eh! And what news, eh?"

He is, as every one knows, the most notorious old news-monger in town, and is just now utterly disheartened because he cannot attend his club, where the choicest *morceaux* of scandal are disseminated daily.

"Very little news anywhere just at present," answers Mrs. Rivers, absently. She is anxiously wondering how she shall bring in the subject of the country scheme.

"I hope you have not been letting those girls out again without yourself," says uncle Gregory, irascibly. "I heard about that Kensington trip from Major Jervis who saw them there. Wrong, very wrong, my dear Elinor; young women should never be allowed to go anywhere without their mother or guardian."

"Sir Sydney Walcott is such an old friend," responds Mrs. Rivers, nervously, "that I thought they might safely go with him."

"Old! Pooh! Seven-and-twenty, I suppose! A boy indeed! And no doubt dissipated too."

Ronnie's eyes flash fire.

"The present generation," pursues Sir Gregory, "knows no boys. They are all grown up from their cradles; and girls should not be trusted out of one's sight. You can't be too careful, my dear Elinor."

"I should wish to be careful, of course," says poor Mrs. Rivers, in a depressed tone.

"Then make Sir Sydney discontinue his visits. I hear from a certain quarter how frequent they are."

At this Ronnie grows pale, and, lifting her blue eyes, fixes them beseechingly upon her mother. Her mother, though she refuses to meet her glance, still feels deeply for her.

"I think any young man who keeps philandering after two girls for months together without coming to the point—you see, I know everything, my dear Elinor—should be summarily dealt with. I have heard a good deal, and I think this Sir Sydney should get his *congé*. If he is not going to marry the girls, he ought to be forbidden the house."

"He can't well marry us both, poor soul!" remarks Cecil, demurely. "The law forbids."

"Eh? Eh?" says uncle Gregory, irritably.

"And, at all events, he certainly can't marry me," Cecil goes on suavely, in spite of a warning glance from her mother, which she pretends not to see. "Because the Duke wouldn't hear of it!"

"The Duke! What Duke?" demands old Sir Gregory, rais-ing himself from his recumbent position, to stare blankly at her,

"My Duke," replies Cecil, boldly, though her eyes are sparkling with laughter. "Didn't you know of it? I have made up my mind at last, and nothing under strawberry-leaves will content me!"

"It is only Cecil's nonsense," says Mrs. Rivers, in an agony.

Her dearest Cecil, she tells herself, is so inconsiderate, and so thoughtless; and if the old man should be offended——

But the old man is not offended. On the contrary—strange to say—he is amused, and gives way to a prolonged chuckle.

"Eh? Eh?" he says again. This is his favourite ejaculation. "So you are flying high, are you? Well, I wish you luck. But,"—with a relapse into his former tartness, and a glance at Ronnie, who is sitting calm and pallid as an early snowdrop—"don't have your Duke dangling after you for months, making you a laughing-stock for all your friends."

Ronnie sighs, and grows even a shade paler. Her mother, seeing this, turns hastily to Sir Gregory.

"I agree with you," she says, though the words almost choke her. "And to prevent any further nonsense of the sort you speak of I think of taking the children "—they are always children to her—"down into the quiet country, that is, if you approve of the move."

"To the country?" repeats uncle Gregory, taken aback. Then he tells himself she has taken to heart his advice about avoiding the sullying influence of town life, and he is flattered. "Well, I'm sure I'm glad you have at last determined to act on my suggestion," he says, in a gratified tone. "Come to me again to-morrow, and we shall see what can be done about your removal into the country. You are a very sensible woman, Elinor—very sensible indeed!"

By which they know he will put no obstacle in the way of their going to the new abode on which they have so set their hearts.

*　　*　　*　　*　　*　　*

That night, as Ronnie and Cecil are brushing their hair, preparatory to going to bed, Cecil, turning suddenly to her elder sister, lays down her brush, and places her arm around her.

"Dearest," she says, tenderly, "how is it you want to leave town now, just when he has returned home again?"

"You mean Sir Sydney Walcott, I suppose?" answers Ronnie, in trembling accents. "I leave town because—because I want to test him. It is all quite true what they say. He has been coming here for months and months, as you know, and yet he has not spoken to me about——. He has not"—with a violent effort—"asked me to marry him!"

"And what of that?" says Cecil, valiantly, patting her shoulder, with a reassuring touch. "He will ask you some day, I know very well."

"And, in the meantime, I am to be a laughing-stock to my friends," returns Ronnie, bitterly.

"Don't mind that cross old man, darling; such a speech as that only meant an additional twinge of gout."

"Nevertheless, I shall be glad to leave town; I cannot bear it longer," says Ronnie, earnestly. "If he honestly loves me, he will follow me to Branksmere; if not—well, then, if not"—with a little heart-broken sob, "I shall know he never loved me at all."

"You will never know that," is the consoling answer—"never. He will follow you. He adores you. I feel it—I know it."

At this Ronnie, turning suddenly to her sister, kisses her warmly.

"At all events, this visit to the country will decide all things," she says, with some renewed hope in her voice. "I trust uncle Gregory will not put any obstacles in the way of our going, at the last moment."

"He won't—Major Jervis is out of town," says Cecil, significantly.

Time proves her words true. Before another week has flown, they find themselves established in a pretty old-fashioned house, in the quiet country.

CHAPTER II.

THE snow is falling fast at Branksmere.   All the air is full of
it.   The wintry wind, coming with a rush round the angles of
the house, catches it and floats it towards the windows, where
it clings to sill and pane.   The laurels at the end of the lawn,
and all the evergreens in the shrubberies, have lost· their indi-
viduality, and have changed from green to dazzling white.
Far below, in the bay, the sullen ocean rushes inland with a
roar, and dashes against the giant rocks, which take no heed
of its passion.   Above is a sky all dull and leaden-hued, below
a world monotonously white—a world in which the trees, bereft
as they are of leaves, and gaunt and bare as skeletons, show
black against its chilly purity.

Cecil, standing at the window, contemplates this dreary
picture with a slightly discontented expression on her usually
smiling face.

"Just like my luck," she says, in a plaintive tone.

Presumably she is addressing her mother and sister, who are
sitting before a glorious fire, piled high with fragrant pine-wood;
but her eyes are fixed with mournful reproach upon the
descending snow.

"What, darling?" questions her mother, rousing herself from
a pleasant reverie to ask the question.

"I am alluding to the snow," replies Cecil, still in the same
melancholy tone.   "In my heart I am calling it bad names.
Here we have been for two whole, long, interminable days in
this new neighbourhood, and I have never yet been able to get
out to explore it, as would be my delight.   Yesterday it rained.
To-day it snows.   What bitter lines!   I shall go out of my
mind if I am 'cribbed, cabined, and confined' much longer."

"It is hard on you—my 'red rover,'" observes Ronnie, with
a smile, glancing up from the piece of coarse ugly ticken she is
embroidering.

"No aspersions on my ruddy locks, if you please," says

Cissy, putting up her hand to her hair, which is really charming, and of that very rare colour where brown melts into amber and amber into a still warmer shade. "To-day my spirits are too low to admit of my taking it amiably. What an irritating thing snow is! So slow and would-be meek, yet so determined. And how brown it makes one look! I feel just like a Zulu or a North American Indian when I compare myself with it."

"Certainly it is not becoming," admits Ronnie, reflectively, gazing pensively at her own dear little face in a mirror near her. "It puts one out of conceit with one's self."

"It is downright spiteful," says Cecil, vindictively.

"Yet I think one never thoroughly appreciates a good fire, until the snow is on the ground," puts in Mrs. Rivers, sleepily, at which remark both the girls laugh in concert.

"I never saw the day or hour you didn't enjoy it," says Cecil, saucily, whereupon her mother laughs too.

Silence follows. Mrs. Rivers dozes. Ronnie stitches. Cecil commences a low-spirited and dismal tattoo upon the window pane. To say the least of it, it is a depressing noise. Ronnie bears it patiently for many minutes, until indeed her nerves are quite unstrung, and then she says, meekly—

· "I dare say it is musical, dear, and that my want of taste is unpardonable; but whenever I hear that noise I feel I want to die."

Cissy foregoes her melancholy amusement, and mourns that even this poor consolation is denied her.

"I really think it is clearing," she says presently, with some faint show of animation. "It looks ever so much brighter, doesn't it Ronnie? After all, it can't hurt much; so I'll put on my things, and get even one small scamper before it grows dark."

"My dear child, do not dream of such a thing!" exclaims Mrs. Rivers, sitting quite upright this time, and looking dismayed. "It is a terrible day; you will catch your death of cold!"

"I wouldn't be guilty of such a thing for worlds," returns

Cissy, gaily, " and, besides, I shouldn't dream of interfering with Ronnie's special *rôle*. She catches cold for all the family"— glancing fondly, even regretfully, at her fragile sister, who looks younger than herself, but is in reality her senior.   " The village is only a mile away ; I shall walk there, and see what is to be seen, and, if I am snowed up beyond hope of return, I dare say that fat little woman at the inn will give me shelter."

"You mean the woman who was so kind to us, when one of our horses came to grief the day of our arrival, the day before yesterday ? " asks Ronnie.   "Mrs. Stilton they called her.   I never forgot it ; she did look so like a cheese."

"Yes.   Don't look as if this was to be our final farewell, mamma !" cries Cissy, with an irrepressible laugh.   "You haven't a chance of getting rid of me so easily.   'I will return ; you know me well ! ' But in case I shouldn't "—she has her hand by this time on the handle of the door, and is looking back mischievously at her mother—"if it be my lot to be discovered stiff and stark and frozen in some picturesque hollow, remember, I leave my debts to Ronnie and my kittens to you.   Don't let them starve."

" I wish you would not jest on such horrid subjects," says Mrs. Rivers, in a nervous tone that fills Miss Cissy with delight.   " And I wish too——"

But the door is shut before she can disclose her second wish, and Cissy is beyond reach of eyes and ears.   Of course she carries the day, and presently comes downstairs, and starts for her walk half-smothered in furs, and with the daintiest of little otter-skin caps upon her head.   The whole costume suits her to perfection, and, with a light heart and a quick step, she runs up the avenue, through the feathery snow-flakes that fall all round her, and passes the entrance gate.

Oh, the joy of being in the open air again—however cold— after two days' confinement to the house !   And the rapture of having " fresh woods and pastures new " before her !   All is still unknown.   Such a short time has elapsed since Mrs. Rivers and her daughters took possession of this, their new home, that as yet their present world is an unexplored territory, full, it may be, of delightful possibilities and golden treasure.

To-day the spirit of adventure is rife within Cecil's breast. She moves briskly, with a buoyant air, up the road; past the wall that bounds her own place, past a gate that leads no doubt to some near neighbour's dwelling, and straight on until she comes to the open highway beyond. Here she comes to a standstill, and ponders a while. A broad road stretches to her right, a large common to the left; yet she has been told that both will bring her to the village, and that the common is the shortest route by a full mile. Which shall she take? After a short but severe struggle with prudence, she pushes it into the background, and decides on speed and the common. It looks vast—nay, even vague; but, taking the little well-beaten path that lies through it, she walks on bravely, with her head held high, and a delicious sense of freedom, light, air, youth, pervading her whole being. As she goes, and as the road grows dim behind her, she even breaks into song, and carols as sweetly as any bird that flies the air.

So passes a long hour, and then—then—slowly, and without any undue misgiving—it occurs to her that the village must be farther off than she has been told. Surely it is a good mile that she has travelled, and that was the distance specified! At this time she is not frightened; but presently, as the storm rises, and the snow falls ever faster and faster, and she finds she has unconsciously quitted the path, and is walking upon grass, a little feeling of nervousness gains upon her. How can she know where the path may lie, when all is so even, so covered with an unbroken shroud of purest white?

Rough Boreas has awakened, and, ever and anon rushing at her, seizes her in his strong embrace, and, shaking her slight frame with rude violence, leaves her breathless and unstrung. The darkness is growing rapidly. Already a veil of sombre hue is overshadowing the land. Twilight deepens, yet no village is within sight, no road can meet the eye; the bare wide common seems vaster, more interminable that ever. She is alone upon a desolate waste, uncertain where to go, which turn to take !

The horrible thought that she may be lost—really lost, like one of those unhappy people one reads about, but hardly believes in, comes to her with unpleasant force. But she fights against it, and walks on, determined to overcome the sensation of fatigue that, in spite of all efforts to subdue it, is asserting itself.

Another cruel gust of wind, arising suddenly, and sweeping boisterously past her, unnerves her, and reduces her almost to despair; and it is at this moment, luckily, that she finds herself once more on the edge of the common, with a road on her left hand—a road well covered with snow, beyond question, and leading she knows not whither, but still a veritable road.

With renewed hope she quits the unfriendly common, and walks on, wearily but determinedly, for quite another half-mile. Her feet are growing painful; an increasing longing to sit down and indulge the miserable drowsiness that is creeping over her, if only for a short while, frightens her. Clenching her poor little frozen hands, and forcing back the tears that are dimming her eyes, she still struggles on, though hope within her is again almost dead.

So another quarter of a mile is conquered; and then, when she is least expecting succour, what is that she sees through the gathering gloom? A light—a lodge—a gravelled avenue, and two big pillars on which rest dragons' heads that grin defiance on passers-by. Yet never did tender lambs seem sweeter in Miss Rivers's sight than these threatening beasts.

Not waiting to summon the lodge-keeper, with her own trembling fingers she undoes the fastening of the gate; and, forgetful of fatigue and fear, runs swiftly all down the curving avenue, never drawing breath until she reaches the hall-door, and knocks with eager haste.

It is opened by an old man in irreproachable livery, with a pock-marked skin, but a benign expression.

"Can I—see the—lady of the house?" begins Cecil, anxiously, almost timidly. "I have lost my way. I am a stranger here; and—I don't know my way home."

The old man looks concerned; and, stepping back, entreats her respectfully to enter.

"Pray, miss, come in! Dear me, dear me, what a night to be abroad!"—regarding with deep compassion the little woe-begone figure before him, with her furs all covered with snow and her blue eyes bright with tears. "There is no mistress of this house as yet," he goes on gravely; "but, if you will follow me, ma'am, Mrs. Richards, the house-keeper, will do what she can for you. Dear me, dear me, what a night!"

Cecil, hardly knowing whether she is relieved or sorry at the news that she must trust herself to the tender mercies of a house-keeper instead of a châtelaine, follows him through two brilliantly lighted halls, down a corridor, and into a warm, cosy room, where sits an elderly woman, knitting by a fire.

"Beg pardon, Mrs. Richards," says her first friend, in a mysterious whisper; but this young lady has lost her way in the snow, and has come to ask shelter here."

"Bless me!" exclaims Mrs. Richards, looking over her spectacles. She rises, advances a little, and, having satisfied herself about Cecil's appearance, drops a slight curtsey.

"I'm so sorry to trouble you," says Cissy, quickly, with a rather nervous laugh, beginning to think that, after all, genuine adventures are not quite such enthralling delights as she has hitherto imagined. "But I don't know the neighbourhood. I left home intending to reach the village; but I lost my way, and don't know what would have become of me, but that fortunately I found this place. The snow was so blinding, and the wind so strong, and—I am so tired."

Her voice quivers perceptibly, and two tears that will not be repressed steal down her pale cheeks. Sinking into a chair, she looks piteously at Mrs. Richards. That kind-hearted woman is not proof against so much beauty and distress combined. The little break in the voice does wonders—the tears still more; but the piteous, appealing glance makes a conquest of her for ever.   Then and there she falls in love with Miss Rivers.

"My dear young lady, you are quite worn out!" she cries, coming quickly to her side, and hastily removing the snow-crowned hat and the damp jacket. "Peters, bring some brandy directly."

"Oh, no!" says Cecil faintly.

"But, indeed, my dear, I insist," returns Mrs. Richards, putting up one hand authoritatively, as though to prevent further discussion; and Cissy, being too weak to do battle, she has her own way, and soon has her young charge ensconced in a large arm-chair before the fire.   She has bathed her feet and hands, and has even unearthed from some old family chest upstairs a tiny pair of quaint black velvet slippers that suit Cissy wonderfully well.   Indeed, after a little, Miss Rivers declares herself quite recovered both in mind and body, and not a bit the worse for her fatigue and anxiety.

"I felt so strange," she says, presently, with a languid smile, "when Peters said there was no mistress in the house.   Is there no one here but you?"

"There's the master," replies Mrs. Richards, looking up from her knitting.   "But he has been here only four days.   I lived with his uncle, the old master, for twenty years, and when he died six months ago, Mr. Craven fell in for the property; but he was abroad then, and only returned to England a few weeks since.   I believe he knows as little about the neighbourhood as you do, miss; indeed, I am the only one in the house who does know it, as the old lot except myself left in a body on the master's death, and Mr. Craven brought all his present staff of servants with him from his other place in Kent."

Cissy flushes and looks distressed.

"If nobody here knows anything about the neighbourhood," she says, nervously, "how am I to let mamma hear where I am, and that I am safe?"

"May I ask where you live, miss?" demands Mrs. Richards, quietly.

"At Branksmere. It must be a long way from this. You know it?"

"Branksmere! The Whitleys' old place—and this is Oaklands. My certie, but you have had a walk!" exclaims the housekeeper, lifting her hands in dismay. "Why, it is four miles from here by the common, and eight by the road! And what an evening for such a journey! See—how dark the night has grown!"—drawing aside the curtains to peer out. "I fear no human being could find his way to Branksmere at this hour, in such weather, unless he knew the road well, and even then it would be dangerous to make the attempt. Hear how the storm rages, and the wind howls; and the snow comes thick and fast! It is a wild time, I'm thinking, we shall have before the morning. But rest easy, miss; if, as you say, you told your mamma you were going to the village, she will believe you are safe there with Mrs. Stilton of the inn."

"I hope so," says Cissy, with a sigh.

At this moment there is a knock at the door, and somebody, without waiting for permission, opens it and walks boldly in. The new-comer is a young man of about twenty-nine, tall, and finely formed, with a well-shaped head. So much can be discerned in the shadow; and then he comes quickly up to the table, right within the ray of the lamp, so that Cissy can see him distinctly.

He is evidently "the master," the hero of the hour, the one ingredient indispensible if she would throw a touch of romance into the adventure; and therefore it is sadly dispiriting that at first sight Cissy must acknowledge him disappointing. In spite of his fine figure and commanding height, he is like anything in the world but a Greek god. In fact he is decidedly plain. His mouth is large, his nose is long, his eyes—his only redeeming feature—are a dark gray, kindly and honest. His hair does not admit of description, being cropped so closely to his head, in the prevailing fashion of the present day, as to be almost invisible. His forehead is somewhat too square, yet there is a gentleness, a brightness, and withal an amount of strength about his face that redeems its want of beauty.

"May I come in, Mrs. Richards?" says the young man, with a smile that lights his whole face—perhaps he is smiling at the absurdity of his question, delivered from the middle of the room.

Mrs. Richards curtseys and bids him welcome. Then he comes a little nearer, even to the hearth-rug, and addresses himself to his unexpected guest.

"Peters has just told me of your unlucky walk," he says, politely. "I am so sorry about it, but glad more than I can say that you found your way here."

He is gazing with suppressed, but evident curiosity at the pretty girl, who appears half lost in the embrace of the big arm-chair, and who has raised herself and is gazing back at him shyly, with heightened colour, but clear, earnest eyes.

"I hope you are quite comfortable," he goes on, with increased cordiality, now he has seen her. "I know Mrs. Richards has done all she can for you; but"—hospitably—"dinner is ready, and you must be hungry, you know, and I thought I would come in myself and ask you to dine with me. There is nobody but myself.

This wind-up to his speech is so naïve that Miss Rivers has much ado to suppress the smile that lurks in the corners of her mouth, threatening every moment to betray her. This is an adventure with a vengeance ! She begins to feel like a heroine in a novel, all but in one point. He is right; she is hungry, disgracefully, most unromantically hungry, and thinks with a pleasure not to be subdued of the dinner beyond.

An hour ago, when first she arrived, she had felt too exhausted to partake of anything Mrs. Richards had laid before her ; but, now that recovery has set in and warmth and rest have done their work, she cannot help remembering that she has eaten nothing since two o'clock, and that it is now almost seven. Yet will it not be rather a strange thing to dine *tête-à-tête* with her unknown host? And yet again, will it not seem prudish to refuse, as evidently he sees nothing in it ? In her perplexity she glances appealingly at the only other woman in the room.

Mrs. Richards is equal to the occasion.

"I think, Miss Rivers, some dinner will do you good," she says, respectfully. "You have eaten nothing since you came. And, if you will permit me, I shall have a cup of tea for you directly dinner is at an end."

Now this last is a master-stroke on the part of Mrs. Richards! It gives Cissy a feeling of protection, a sort of conviction that she belongs to Mrs. Richards, and that—though parted from her for a little while—she will ultimately be expected to return and deliver herself up to her rightful owner.

She smiles at Mr. Craven—Cissy's smile is "a thing of beauty and joy for ever"—and, rising, accepts the arm he offers her, and walks away with him demurely to the dining-room. With the utmost gravity, yet with a good deal of pleasant converse, they both get through a capital dinner; and, by the time it is ended, they discover they both know almost everything it is necessary to know about each other.

Cissy has had a little claret, has eaten all the walnuts Mr. Craven has broken for her, and an unlimited supply of candied fruit, when an ormolu clock somewhere behind her tinkles softly. She starts a little, and turning, sees it is on the chimney-piece, and that it is half-past eight.

"So late!" she murmurs. "Who could have believed it?"

She glances at her host, her face full of genuine surprise; and he feels intensely flattered.

"I am so glad you haven't felt bored," he says, politely, carefully suppressing the warmth he could willingly have thrown into his tone.

"Bored! No, indeed!" But here memory whispers in her ear. Her expression changes, and she glances involuntarily towards one of the windows. "I could quite say I have enjoyed myself," she says, with a rather pensive smile, "if I were positive mamma is not at this moment enduring agonies of fright on my account."

She rises from her chair; so does Mr. Craven from his; and, as though divining her thought, he goes to the window, opens the shutters, and, throwing up the sash, they both gaze upon the thick darkness without. It is still snowing. Upon the sill the flakes have grown and mounted, until they have reached the first pane. With a shiver he pulls down the sash, and they return to the grateful fire

"You may be sure she believes you safe in the village under Mrs. Stilton's care," he says, soothingly, anxious to restore her to peace of mind.

"She may, if she has not sent a messenger to the village to inquire," is the doubtful answer.

"Oh, no! She wouldn't do that, you know, such a severe night. Who would go? I'm quite convinced she hasn't done that," he asserts, earnestly, though it would have puzzled him to give a reason for his assertion.

"You think she has not?" asks Cecil, still doubtfully, though longing to feel as convinced on the subject as he— apparently—is. Some hope revives within her as she remembers that the servants in her house are as ignorant of their way to the village as the servants in this!"

"I know it," returns Mr. Craven, with considerable force; "she would of course wait until the morning. Why, it would be inhuman, actually unsafe, I think, to send any one abroad on such a night as this!"

"And mamma is not inhuman!" murmurs Cecil, with a slight smile, staring thoughtfully into the glowing coals beneath her.

Over the chimney-piece is a large picture, finely painted. It represents an elderly lady with a charming face, with brown hair arranged in little curls on either cheek, a handsome bust generously displayed, a waist well under her arms, and a small foot protruding from beneath the satin gown that partly covers her. It is the foot that attracts Cecil's attention. It is very small, and clad in black velvet. She laughs.

"I hope you are not making merry over my elderly relative," says Mr. Craven, severely.

"Far be it from me; she is much too uncomfortably digni-fied to excite mirth in any one. I was only thinking of that old adage, 'It is ill waiting for dead men's shoes,' and wonder-ing whether it is as 'ill' to wait for a dead woman's, because I am sure I am at this moment wearing your——" She hesitates.

"Great-grandmother?" he prompts.

"Great-grandmother's slippers," concludes Cissy, laughing again, and looking down at her velvet shoe, the very fac simile of that worn by the dead and gone grand-dame.

"What miraculously small feet my great-grandmother must have had!" says Mr. Craven, solemnly, regarding her foot with interest.

"Oh, no! These shoes are quite loose on me," she replies, innocently.

"I can see that," he remarks, unwisely, and regrets his speech a second later, when to his chagrin the pretty foot is hastily withdrawn.

A silence follows, and then Miss Rivers, as though the thought has just occurred to her, says gently—

"I must now bid you good night, and go to Mrs. Richards; she has promised me tea at nine."

"But it is not nearly that yet. It wants quite a quarter to it," protests her host in a somewhat injured tone. "Pray do not hurry yourself. Do you know"—warningly—"that from the moment you join Mrs. Richards until you elect to go to bed, she will spend the time telling you old tales about the family. I know it, because I have been through it. And it is no joke. Every story is thirty minutes good; not a second less."

"How nice! I adore old stories," says Miss Rivers, sweetly.

"You won't adore hers; there's not a bit of go in them, not a murder, or a ghost, or a suicide, or anything amusing from start to finish. We are a wretched lot, you know, when all is told"—alluding apologetically to his ancestors. "Don't let yourself in for it, if you love yourself."

"You greatly relieve my mind," says Cissy. "I couldn't sleep in a house where a ghost walked."

"Couldn't you? I should find even that poor excitement welcome, so dreary is my present existence. You can't think"—dejectedly—"how slow I find it here, with no society. Your coming to-night has been such a relief. Up to this I have had to endure the Major; and, though I'm generally considered rather good-natured than otherwise, he is much too much for any fellow. He was agent, you see, in my uncle's time—who never attended to anything—and now, before retiring from office—thank goodness, he is retiring—he insisted on coming down here with me to see after things, and behave uncivilly, and harass the very lives out of my unfortunate tenants."

"Why do you let him?" reproachfully.

"I'm afraid to interfere; and besides, it doesn't matter much, because he can't stay long; and I'll make it up to them afterwards. The gout overtook him yesterday. I'm devoutly thankful that it came down upon him heavily, as I have been spared his inane twaddle for a few hours at least."

"Poor man!" says Cissy, vaguely, leaving it doubtful whether she intends her sympathy for the Major or his wearied friend.

"I have often wished I hadn't come here at all," continues Mr. Craven; "my place in Kent is so much prettier and far more comfortable; but I was obliged to do so. He talked me into it. But now"—warmly—"I feel I owe even the Major a debt of gratitude, as my coming has enabled me to be of some slight use to you."

"Even that miserable solace is denied you," returns Miss Cissy, with a calm smile, "if you reflect that, even if you had remained in Kent, Mrs. Richards would still have taken me in, and been very good to me."

"True," rejoins her crestfallen host; "I have not been of much service to you, after all—have I?"

Cissy is conscience-stricken.

"Yes, indeed you have!" she says impulsively. "It wasn't

civil of me to say that, was it, when you have been more than kind to me?" Then, as though ashamed of her amiability, she goes on hurriedly, with a rather brilliant colour—"Good night, Mr. Craven; I must go, or Mrs. Richards will think I have vanished in as mysterious a manner as I came."

"You consign me to solitude?"—half jestingly, half in reproach.

"A cigar will no doubt console you effectually."

"And Mrs. Richard's company will be a relief to you. I shouldn't, of course, dream of doing combat with a woman of Mrs. Richards's attractions. May I show you the way to her room? As yet the house is strange to you. She has tea at nine, I believe you said"—with a calm glance, but a faint accession of colour that betrays itself even beneath the bronze that Egypt has lent to his face. "Do you—do you think, if I asked her, she would give me some? If there is anything on earth I covet, it is a cup of tea at nine."

"You know Mrs. Richards four days longer than I do," answers Miss Cissy, coolly; "you can ask her."

So he does ask her after a short preamble about nothing in particular. Mrs. Richards makes her Sunday curtsey, and assures him she will feel it a great honour to entertain him; whereupon he thanks her gracefully, and, telling Miss Rivers he has some letters to answer, but will be back again in no time, he leaves her for the present. And indeed his promise holds good; because the time that elapses before he again makes his appearance is scarcely worthy of record.

· CHAPTER III.

CECIL falls into a sound sleep that night almost as soon as her head touches the pillow

All through the silent, darksome hours she lies, scarce stirring, until morning forces itself rudely through her chamber windows, morning so-called; but it is dull, and dark as twilight.

Springing from her bed, Cecil runs bare-footed to the window, and pushing back the curtains gazes eagerly on the outer world. Nothing but the same uniform white meets her eyes. Through the whole night the snow has fallen unceasingly—even now is falling, thickly, steadily, as when she last watched it yesternight.

The drive below is on a level with the grassy banks on either side; the fir trees are bending to the very earth, so weighty is their dazzling burden. Upon the window-sill a little brown bird lies dead, pathetic in its stiff and mournful quiet.

Cissy, putting out her hand, raises it, and tries to warm it into life again within her hands and bosom, but to no avail, and sadly she lays it where she found it, and heaps a tiny mound of snow upon it. And then, shivering, she closes the window and rings her bell for one of the maids.

She dresses rapidly, though with a mind pre-occupied. The prospect of having to spend another day at Oaklands, with no chance of letting her mother know of her safety, fills her with anguish. Depressed, but pretty, perplexed, but indescribably charming, in her soft, navy-blue serge gown, with some old lace ruffles, borrowed from Mrs. Richards, or rather from her host's ancestors, at her throat and wrists, she goes dejectedly downstairs in the direction of the housekeeper's room.

Being obliged to pass the library on her way thither, she encounters Mr. Craven emerging from it, some letters in his hands. He bids her good morning in his most genial tone, hopes she has slept well, and that she has not suffered from yesterday's imprudence. Miss Rivers thanks him sweetly, and tells him she has slept well, and that, so far as she can judge at present, she has not succumbed to cold. Then the lachrymose expression returns to her face, and she says mournfully—

"Did you ever see such a day! Worse than yesterday. What shall I do about mamma?"

"I have arranged all that," answered her host, pleasantly. "The post-boy—wretched youth—ploughed his way up here as usual, this morning, in spite of wind and weather, and he

undertook to show one of my men the way to Branksmere.
So I wrote your mother a polite and reassuring note, to say
you were all right with Mrs. Richards, but that I feared you
could not return to day, as no horse could travel."

"Oh, how good of you!" says Cecil, gladly. "How can I
thank you enough! You have taken quite a load off my mind,
and made my heart as light as a feather. But I wish you had
told me before you sent your messenger, as I too should have
liked to write mamma a little note."

"It was so early"—gently—"and I hoped you were sleeping.
And I would not for worlds have had you disturbed after all
the fatigue you experienced yesterday."

Miss Rivers is touched by his kindness and thoughtfulness.

"How well you can think for other people!" she says, a
little vaguely, but gratefully, giving him the cool, slim hand she
had wilfully withheld when wishing him good morning. Only
for a moment, though. Hastily withdrawing it, almost before
his willing fingers have closed over it, she says, gaily, "How is
your friend, the Major?"

"Better—much better," he returns, in a tone that would lead
one to imagine he had said, "Worse—much worse." "He
even spoke of being able to get down this evening in time for
dinner. But "—with mock solemnity—"the day is long, and
gout is not trustworthy."

"Then I shall dine with Mrs. Richards," says Cecil, reflectively, and as though, little hypocrite that she is—the idea is
rather pleasurable to her than otherwise. "And that reminds
me "—quickly—"I shall also breakfast with her. Good-bye "
—nodding to him brightly, and moving on a step or two, until
he stays her by an imploring gesture.

"You won't breakfast with me, then? How rash of you!
Peters, I am positive, can provide twice as good a breakfast as
Mrs. Richards. Don't sacrifice yourself on the altar of duty."

"I sha'n't. I, for my part, believe firmly in Richards. She
looks like a good breakfast. By-and-bye, when we meet again,
if indeed "—with a quick glance from under her long lashes

which is full of coquetry in spite of all her stern resolves—"we ever do meet again—I expect you will be consumed with envy when I tell you of all the nice things I have had to eat."

"Well, rush upon your fate if you will," he replies. "But at least let us make a bargain. If Peters outdoes Richards, will you promise to throw yourself on his tender mercies to-morrow? · The old gentleman "—waving his hand upwards to where the Major's room may be—"never enchants me with his society before noon."

"A bargain it shall be," rejoins Miss Rivers, promptly. "But, if you lose, you sha'n't get any breakfast at all. That is my amendment."

"I'll risk even that for the chance of the alternative," he says, gallantly. "I think, Miss Rivers, you expressed a wish to see the picture-gallery—didn't you?"

"I should like it so much," answers Cissy. "It is now "—drawing out her watch—"a quarter to ten; at twelve I shall be ready to pay my respects to the old people. Will that hour suit you? Yes. Very well then "—with a backward glance, and a smile charming because swift. "Be sure you are not late!"

He is not. Indeed, it still wants fully five minutes to the appointed hour when he presents himself at the door of Mrs. Richards's parlour, to find his guest awaiting him.

The picture-gallery proves a complete success. Miss Rivers, her mind at rest about her mother's anxiety on her behalf, is in her gayest mood, and declares herself, and is in very truth, enchanted with the endless rows of simpering dames and dauntless knights that line the walls. She insists upon hearing every dark legend connected with the grim warriors, every romantic and eerie tale about their wives.

"This gaunt spinster," says Mr. Craven, indicating a withered damsel of sour aspect, " was a lady of advanced notions. In our days she would have gone in heavily for woman's rights. Perhaps "—hesitating—"you agree with——"

Here he stops, abashed by her reproachful look.

"How could you so misjudge me?" she says. "Do I look like one of those awful people?"

She stands a little back from him, as though imploring him to assure himself now and for ever that she is not of the abhorred race. She certainly does not look like it—not in the least like anything awful or abhorred; and he tells her so mildly, as far as words go; but with considerable warmth if she can read his eyes aright.

It is a pleasant morning, in spite of the wind and the never-ceasing snow; and when luncheon is at an end Mr. Craven proposes a game at billiards, to which Cecil, who plays as badly as most women, willingly assents. In the middle of the third game she grows absent, and forgets to play; and her host, looking at her, sees a smile creep over her face.

"What is amusing you now?" he asks, smiling too out of pure sympathy.

Miss Rivers starts, and looks a little ashamed of herself.

"I have a horrid trick of laughing when amused," she says, demurely; "and it came to me just now that the whole thing is so absurdly funny. Don't you agree with me?"

"I am positive I should," he replies, "if I had even the faintest idea to what you are alluding."

"Why, my presence in this house. Here you are, doing all you know to amuse me—an undesired guest."

"Certainly not that," he says, with rather more earnestness than the occasion demands.

"Well, at least, an uninvited one," she corrects impatiently, the smile fading.

"I am afraid you are growing tired to death," says the young man, with some pain in his voice, laying down his cue and coming to her side. "Of course you are; it is only natural. It is so slow for you here, being locked up in a place against your will, with nothing to amuse you. That is the worst of being a bachelor. If now," he continues, dejectedly, "I had a wife, you might be so much happier, and could talk about dress, you know, and that."

"Yes; and bonnets, and servants. How well you understand women ! " says Miss Rivers, curtly, turning away. "Perhaps if you had a wife I should hate her."

"Then I'm downright glad I haven't, as that would make your enforced stay even more unpleasant to you than it is," he returns, a little bitterly.

"Did I say I was bored, or found things slow, or that I found anything here unpleasant? " she demands, slowly. "I don't remember making such remarks."

"Well, you looked it, you know," he replies, still somewhat aggrieved.

"What, all that ? Bored and slow—and unpleasant ! "— softly. "How rude you are ! "

"You misunderstand," he begins, warmly.

"Nobody ever made me such an uncomplimentary speech before. I think you needn't call me bad names," she interrupts, meekly, turning a red ball round and round between her pretty white hands.

"You know I didn't mean that," he exclaims, eagerly, and is probably going to say a good deal more, when she raises her eyes, and he, seeing the mischief lying in them, foregoes further explanation and joins in her merry laugh.

"Shall we finish this long-suffering game," she asks, lightly, "and put off our discussion till another day ? Go on; it is your turn."

So he goes again to the table, and, by the most flagrant bad play and an evident determination not to hit anything whatever, compels her to win the game.

"Shall we play another ? You should give me my revenge," he says, seeing her lay down her cue, and fearing lest a thought of Mrs. Richards may be again possessing her.

"No, you play too badly," she answers, calmly.

Now he is the best billiard-player at his club, and is, moreover, rather proud of the fact, yet he bears this aspersion on his skill with the most exemplary patience, making not the smallest protest.

"Time may improve me," he says, with an impassive countenance. "Give me one more chance."

"What a hypocrite you are!" returns Miss Cecil, with startling promptitude. "Don't you think I read your determination to give me that game? And I thought it so silly. No, I shall not play again with you until practice has made me more perfect. Will you come and show me the china in the small drawing-room? Richards says it is lovely, and that it is locked up in the ebony cabinets."

"I am not very well up in china, but they say my uncle's collection is rather fine," he replies, delighted at the prospect of having her with him for at least another hour.

And together they go to the drawing-room and ransack the cabinets. Some tiny tea-cups of the reign of Queen Anne raise in Cissy's bosom feelings of the most intense admiration.

"What a darling!" she says, taking out a cup and laying it on her palm. "Such a little pet, and so pretty!"

They are both kneeling before the cabinet, and are therefore close together. In his heart Mr. Craven thinks every word of praise she has uttered to the cup might be applied to herself.

"Keep it," he says, genially, alluding to the cup. "Take anything you like. There's any number of them. And it is a pity to leave them there, you know, when I don't care about them."

"Oh, no, thank you!"—colouring hotly, and putting back the tea-cup hastily. "I would not spoil the set for anything."

"Then take the whole set if you fancy them," he entreats. "I really wish you would. Nobody here ever looks at them."

"Not now. But"—mischievously—"that wife you spoke of so confidently a little while ago, she will like to look at them by-and-bye."

"Will she?"—thoughtfully. He stares intently for a moment or two at Miss Rivers as she kneels beside him—perhaps the attitude suggests visions of a possible altar; and then he says, rather irrelevantly, "You are very fond of china, are you not?"

"Well, yes, rather," she replies; and then, conquering an inclination to laugh, she rises to her feet and goes over to the fireplace. "I think you said this morning your friend was much better," she says, presently, more from a desire to make conversation than from any overpowering interest in the Major. "Is he still growing towards perfection?"

"Yes"—in a mournful tone—"he is decidedly better. There is no hope. He is coming down to dinner. Nothing would prevent him, though I sent several messages, beautifully worded, to say I thought it foolish to make too free just at first, and that draughts were dangerous."

"Messages never succeed. Why did you not go in person?"

"He wouldn't let me in—wouldn't see me at any price. I made one or two noble efforts to carry his chamber by assault when first he was laid up—thinking it inhuman not to show some interest in him—but was repulsed with great slaughter. 'No admittance to strangers' should be posted on his door, as no one dares enter it but his own man."

"How mysterious! But why?"

"That is just what I am not in a position to tell you, never having been there. I suspect"—solemnly—"that he gets himself up—goes in heavily for paint and powder, wigs and teeth, and so on; and, when in bed, without all these attractive appliances, is a complete wreck—'sans teeth, sans eyes, sans taste, sans everything?'"

"What a glowing picture!" says Cissy; and then again—"What an unpleasant old person!"

"Oh, he's all that," assents Mr. Craven, agreeably, "and a good deal more! When a fellow is pretty well on in years, and certain portions of him have dropped away, such as hair and teeth, why can't he confess it? The Major would die first. He abhors wrinkles, and thinks grey hair rude. When he shows up in all his war paint, he is perfectly ghastly."

"You make me long to know him. Your description reminds me of a friend of my own," says Cissy with an amused laugh. "May I ask this hero's name?"

"You shall have all the information in my power. He served in the—th Lancers some few centuries ago. He lives at a place called Lynn Hall, in Kent—oh, that he was there now!—and he rejoices in the name of Jervis."

"What!" cries Cissy, faintly. "Lynn Hall! Jervis!" Her breath comes quickly, and she pauses as though the news just imparted has been too much for her. Then she goes on hastily—"You say he is coming down to dinner; he may come here, to this very room. Mr. Craven, forgive me; but I must run."

"But why?" demands her puzzled host, detaining her.

"He is my uncle's dearest friend. And my uncle is to leave us all his money; and he is as particular as you please, and so old-fashioned; and, if he heard through this dreadful old man of my being here for two days, snowed up alone with —without mamma, or any one, he would disinherit me," winds up Miss Rivers, breathless and incoherent.

"But does Jervis know you—personally, I mean?"

"Yes, intimately, and he owes me many a grudge, because Ronnie and I can't bear him, and have often been very rude to him," acknowledges Cissy, in a distressed tone. "He used to worry so. There is no end to the mischief he would make out of this if he knew of my being here. I do hope he has not heard my name mentioned by the servants."

"He sha'n't hear anything," says her host, reassuringly; "but——"

At this moment a heavy step in the hall outside, drawing every instant nearer and nearer, fills the hearts of the two within with dismay."

"He is coming," he whispers.

"Oh, what is to become of me?" she murmurs, looking wildly around in search of sanctuary—trying to discover some faint chance of escape. No such chance presents itself. Already the owner of the heavy step has touched the handle of the door; but not before a bright idea has dawned in Mr. Craven's mind.

"There is an ante-room, a large closet—come with me, quickly," he says, grasping her hand, and leading her across the fire-lit room to where some crimson curtains hang, apparently without aim or purpose, Pushing them aside he discloses a door. Opening it hurriedly, he entreats her to enter the tiny room beyond.

She obeys him instinctively, but whispers nervously as she sees him going—

"Do not leave me here long. It is dreadfully dark, and I do so hate being without light."

He can only look a reply, which she does not see, and has barely time to close her in, and get back to the fire, before the Major comes slowly up to him.

"Horrid cold house!" says the new arrival, in a grating tone. "Ugh, ugh "—coughing—"reminds one of a vault!"

"I am afraid you have come to the very coldest room in it, the library is much more comfortable; you don't take half care of yourself," says the young man with great concern, wondering wildly how he shall get him out of the room again.

Night has fallen, and only the glow of the brilliant fire throws light upon the sombre apartment. All the corners lie in shadow, only the hearthrug and part of the carpet stand revealed.

"I've been there," returns the Major, irritably. "It nearly froze me. Barely got off alive. And there isn't a chair in it fit to sit on."

"The dining-room," begins Craven, weakly, at his wits' end, but the Major stops him.

"And dinner preparing"—in disgust. "If there's one thing I hate, it is being in a place where servants are fussing and rattling plates and silver. One has eaten one's dinner in anticipation long before one gets it. No, thank you. I shall stay here until the gong sounds; it's a degree less depressing than the other rooms."

Driven to this pass Mr. Craven falls to thinking, and happily remembers how Richards, when showing him the house, had

told him of a second door leading from the closet where Cissy
is immured into the dining-room. If only the key of this
door can be produced!

Making some frivolous excuse, he forsakes the Major, and,
rushing headlong through the hall, bursts like a whirlwind into
Mrs. Richards's parlour, and asks her, with incoherent anxiety,
if the key he hopes for is still in existence.

She thinks so—with maddening hesitation—but is afraid
she cannot lay her hand on it at this particular moment, that
is, unless——

Here she pauses, and meditates for some time, unconscious,
dear soul, of the torments her master is enduring. When she
has thought it out carefully, and when the young man is almost
on the verge of lunacy, she recollects all about it, and, with a
smiling countenance, delivers the key to him.

Seizing it joyfully, he speeds towards the second door, cries,
"Open sesame!" and enters eagerly—only to find the ante-
room empty and the bird flown!

Horrible visions of discovery, and consequences of the most
unpleasant nature, crowd upon his brain as he goes back to the
small drawing-room, expecting to find the Major irate and indignant, and Miss Rivers in the midst of angry argument.
But no. The Major is in his chair, serene, sleepy. There is
no sound of discord, not the faintest sign of Miss Rivers's
presence anywhere!

CHAPTER IV.

WHEN Cissy—who, in her enforced concealment, could hear
all that passed in the next room—had listened to the Major's
spoken determination not to quit his seat until dinner was
announced, her heart died within her. The ante-room—closet
rather—was stuffy, above all things, dark; and if there was
one thing in the world to which Cissy strenuously objected,
it was the dark.

Yet even at this pass she put her faith in the man who had beguiled her into her prison, trusting to him to bring her safely out 'of it again, and that without delay. But when this man coolly left the drawing-room—and left her to her fate—and she heard his footsteps dying away through the hall, her faith melted like the morning dew the poet sings of, and her indignation knew no bounds.

To calmly forsake her, desert her in her hour of need! Could anything be more abominable, more base, than such conduct! She knew nothing of the second door and Craven's eager efforts to release her, and therefore abused him heartily whilst standing, cold and half-frightened, in her detested shelter. Would she have to stay there in " durance vile," until dinner was served? She supposed so ; unless, indeed, something very unforeseen—nay, marvellous—should happen, now he had so cruelly abandoned her.

Even as she so decided, the unforeseen, the marvellous, did actually occur. A noise outside attracted her—not that it was very attractive in itself—a breath, a snort, a—— Was it, could it be, a snore ? It was. A veritable, undeniable, prolonged snore.

Miss Rivers laid her hand upon her bosom. Emancipation seemed near. Opening the door cautiously, she peeped out, and saw the Major in the sullen glow of the firelight wrapped in innocent slumber. " Now or never" was her motto. Still cautiously she came forth, and began her journey through the long, unlighted room, hoping to make her escape without discovery.

Two doors lay before her, one leading into the hall, one into the conservatory. Keeping well in the shadow, she skirted the wall, and passed the first window in all safety.

The Major still snored on tranquilly, enchantingly—sweeter music Miss Rivers had never heard—but, alas, as she reached the second window, her heavy serge gown caught in one of those fragile abominations of the present day—a weakly chair done in gold and ebony, a woven seat of rushes—and the delicate article came to the ground, dragging with it a flower-stand

and a few other things of little value, but undoubted china manufacture, to judge by the crash that followed.

With a loud snort, the Major awoke and turned his head in her direction. The malicious fire blazed brightly, and she knew she was seen, indistinctly, yet distinctly.

To fly was the one thought uppermost in her mind, and, the conservatory door being nearest, she made for that. The Major followed in hot pursuit, crying " Thieves ! "—cowardice, unfortunately, not being one of his many vices. She had her hand on the handle of the desired door ; it resisted her ; in her agitation she had turned the handle the wrong way ; and, in spite of his gouty foot, the Major was gaining on her.

Here the kindly gods came to her aid ; the Major stumbled over the prostrate chair, the broken flower-pot, and the other trifles, and came heavily to his knees. Picking himself up however from amongst the *débris*, he continued his chase, nothing daunted, muttering an imprecation. Cecil, having turned the refractory handle by this time and entered the conservatory, got hurriedly behind a huge shrub, rich in leaves, that adorned one corner, and with the calmness of despair awaited Fate.

It came in the shape of the Major—mumbling and grumbling. He too entered the conservatory, looked eagerly around him, and found it, as he believed, to his consternation—empty !

No sign of any human thing betrayed itself to his astonished eyes, and the door leading to the steps and the open air was locked on the inside ; yet surely it was this way the figure— the—whatever it was—had passed a moment since !

"Ugh ; nobody after all !" he growled, in disgust. "Nothing to show for my trouble. Must have been a ghost. Couldn't have been dreaming, as I never sleep before dinner, never. Ghost, of course ! These wretched old houses are always full of 'em—at least, so I'm told. Haven't seen one till to-night.' Well, it's a new experience ; but I can't say I think much of it. Tame, very tame. Ugh, ugh, what a draughty hole !"—and so back, still grumbling, to his arm-chair and Morpheus again, leaving Cecil, terrified, but safe, behind her friendly shrub.

When Craven comes up to the drawing-room fire—puzzled, and uncertain how to proceed—the Major so far rouses himself for the second time as to ask languidly—

"Whom have you got in the house besides the servants?"

Craven is somewhat taken aback, but has sufficient presence of mind left him to enable him to ask blandly, in turn—

"How do you mean?"

"Well, my dear fellow, the most extraordinary thing has happened. A few moments since some one, who refused to answer me, walked deliberately through this room."

"This room!" repeats Craven, innocently.

"Yes; here—there—over on that spot," answers the Major, testily, but disconnectedly. "I saw it with my own eyes. I wasn't asleep, you know"—sternly. "I never do that sort of thing out of my bed; but I confess I was in deep thought about—about your affairs, when a noise attracted my attention. I looked up, and there was a figure just beyond, near the curtains—a dark figure"—reflectively. "It couldn't have been a winding sheet, because it was quite dark."

"The housekeeper, no doubt," says Craven, with an air of settled conviction.

"Eh?"—incredulously. "Is your housekeeper a very slim young woman?"

"Well, not so very slim," admits Mr. Craven, suppressing the fact that both his arms would not meet round Mrs. Richards's waist.

"Has she fair hair?" catechises the Major.

"Not exactly, though it might be considered so by this light," says Craven, suppressing the second fact, that every hair in Mrs. Richards's head that is not white is of the raven's hue.

"Does she always," demands his inquisitor, anxiously, "wear a dark, noiseless gown?"

"Always," returns Craven, unblushingly, even as he calls to mind Mrs. Richards's favourite dress, a wine-coloured silk of curious texture, that literally crackles as she goes.

"Oh, well, it wasn't the housekeeper! It was a lady, in my opinion "—mysteriously—" the ghost of a lady. It reminds me strongly of somebody." The Major pauses, and Craven's blood runs cold. "No doubt "—thoughtfully—" it was the ghost of one of your grand-aunts, who both died here." Craven breathes again.

"You don't surely believe in ghosts ? " he says, laughing, feeling intense relief, and imagining Cissy safe in Mrs. Richards's parlour.

"Why not ? " retorts the Major. "Nothing is impossible. And I tell you I watched her minutely, and, as I watched, she reached that door over there, paused a moment, and then disappeared. I searched every hole and corner in the conservatory "—the Major firmly believes he has done so—" but could discover no sign of living occupant; and the door leading to the garden was locked on the inside. She must have gone through the key-hole, or else melted into thin air; that's the usual thing, isn't it ? The only thing that staggers me," he adds, "is the colour ; she ought to have been in white, oughtn't she ?—grave-clothes and that—eh ?"

"Sometimes they vary," answers Craven, gravely. " I suppose even our defunct relatives have their fancies ; and I have heard of people appearing after many years in the garments they last wore, or at least most affected, when in life. Perhaps my grand-aunts looked with scorn upon gaudy raiment. It went into the conservatory, did you say ?"—carelessly. "Very curious! No doubt you are right; most old families have their skeletons; it is rather respectable than otherwise, and pride feels no pain. I think, do you know, I shall just take a look in there myself."

He saunters slowly down the room, lest the Major should guess at his inward anxiety, and has hardly got through the glass door when two cold nervous little hands fasten on his arm and a voice whispers with tremulous eagerness—

"Let me out of this at once—at once."

"How imprudent of you," he whispers back, "to come here!"

"How unkind of you," she retorts, "to leave me there!"

He begins a vehement explanation, still in a whisper; and, peace being restored, he draws her to the door opening on to the steps that lead to the ground beneath; and, having passed through, they bolt the door, this time on the outside, and once more feel free.

The reaction agrees with Cecil; she stops short on the top step, he standing a little below her, and laughs aloud.

"If he had found me then," she says, "after his hard run, nothing would have cleared me. What should I have done?"

"I know what I should have done," returns Craven. "I should have strangled him then and there. It would have been the only way out of it, and I should not have hesitated for a moment."

"Poor old man; he little knows what a violent death he has escaped! But are you sure he has heard nothing about me?"

"Certain. He does not allow his man to say even 'good morning' to him—thinks it *infra dig.*—so of course he hears no gossip; and, as you know, he is leaving here the first moment it is practicable."

Whether this last remark suggests other thoughts, who can say? But on the instant Miss Rivers turns her face heavenwards, pauses a little, and then lays her hand upon his shoulder.

"What, have you noticed nothing?" she says, with suppressed excitement. "See, see—it has ceased to snow!"

"So it has," he returns slowly, the enthusiasm that ought to belong to the occasion being absent from his tone.

"What a way you say that!" she exclaims, severely, scrutinising his face in the dim light. "Just as if you did not care, as if you were not a bit glad. Why"—after a pause—"I actually think you are sorry!"

"Don't think of it; be sure of it," responds the young man, gloomily.

Perhaps at this point it occurs to Cecil—who in some matters is a wise child—that his tone is dangerous. At all events, she declines to continue the conversation, and begins again to descend the steps slowly. But presently they become aware that the snow has risen as high as the second step from the bottom, and the portico of the hall-door is thirty yards distant; and how shall velvet shoes and silk stockings and dainty little feet wade through it all without getting wet ?

"What is to happen next ? " she asks, making a comical gesture of despair with her hand. "I forgot all about the snow, and that I must walk through it to get indoors again. Oh, that tiresome Major ! "

"Can I—— Would it—— May I carry you across ? " he demands, with a proper amount of hesitation.

"Oh, no ! "—shrinking back. "I shouldn't like that at all."

"Well, I didn't suppose you would, you know ! " he returns, somewhat aggrieved. "But I see nothing else to be done, and it will only be for a moment."

"Dear me, it isn't that ! " says Cissy, honestly, divining his thoughts. "I don't mind that so much as—— Are you sure —positive—you would not let me fall ? "

He laughs.

"Let you fall," he says—"a child like you ! I am not such a puny fellow as you seem to imagine."

He draws himself up to his full height, which is magnificent, throws up his chin rather scornfully, and in this attitude cer tainly looks as fine a specimen of manhood as one need wish to see. Miss Rivers, though piqued, has to admit this fact.

"Child ! " she says, indignantly. "I'm not a child. I was eighteen last month. How long does one continue to be a child, I wonder ? "

"I beg your pardon "—meekly. "I retract my words. Let me say rather that I think I am sturdy enough to bear the weight of a middle-aged lady of your size."

"I'm heavier than you think "—doubtfully.

"How do you know what I think ? But indeed you need

not be afraid; I have often before carried women over the snow and swollen streams and that, and never yet broke down beneath my burden."

"Oh, indeed, have you?" says Cissy, with just one flash from her violet eyes. "How considerate of you! You remind me forcibly of one of your own stalwart knights in the gallery upstairs. Do you really spend your winters then in carrying distressed damsels over stony and snowy places? How slow you must find your summers!"

"Well, not quite! I do a few other things," answers Mr. Craven, mildly. "I mean, I have helped my sister once or twice, you know, when she was in a dilemma, and——"

"And your cousins and your aunts, no doubt," interrupts Miss Cissy, still wilful.

"I'll tell you what it is!" he exclaims briskly, refusing further discussion. "You will catch your death of cold if you stay here arguing any longer. Your hands"—touching one of them—"are already nearly frozen. Come."

"Well, then, if I must"—still wavering. "Remember, it is only out of regard for your great-grandmother's velvet slippers that I give in. And indeed, after all, if I took them off, could I not——"

"No; you could not"—decisively; and, as though to end all controversy, he here takes her bodily up in his arms and bears her safely over the snow into the warmth and light of the grand old hall.

As she regains her feet, Cecil laughs a little and shakes her head, as though to rearrange the soft bright hair that a moment since brushed across his cheek as he carried her. Then she leans against the side of the inner door and sighs profoundly, as though thankful the journey that has seemed so unkindly short and so cruelly sweet to him is at an end. After which, with her most matter-of-fact air, she says sedately—

"Now go at once and change your boots. It will be quite as bad for you to catch cold as for me."

"Not quite. You have a mother, a sister, and"—with a

slight contraction of the brows—"of course many others, to whom your sickness would be pain."

"Well, yes !" returns Cissy, slowly.

"But I—— There is no one in the world, I believe, who would feel very much regret if I died."

"Oh, don't say that !" she exclaims, earnestly. "It is not true."

"Is it not ? I know of no one."

"I do." She colours crimson, stays a moment, and then, as though compelled to finish her sentence, goes on calmly—"I know some one who would be very sorry indeed."

"Do you mean yourself ? " he asks, quickly.

"Yes." She answers him honestly, because she can see no reason why she should not do so. He has been very kind to her. Surely she would be ungrateful to feel no sorrow at his death ! Then she smiles carelessly, and says, with her most unsympathetic air, "So now you are bound to go and make yourself comfortable, as it would be an act of unpardonable rudeness on your part to make me 'very sorry indeed.' Was not that what I said ? "

She has moved into the second hall, and is now standing within the full glare of the lamplight. Craven, who has followed her, thinks she is the most charming picture his eyes have ever seen ; and it may be that his eyes tell her so.

"One moment," he says, seeing she is about to disappear. "You allowed just now that, if anything were to happen to you, your mother and sister and—some others—would grieve for you. Are there—do not think me rude ; I have no right to ask the question, I know—but are there many others ? "

"Yes, a great many," she responds promptly, some surprise in her tone and in her large eyes, which she has opened to their fullest extent and has fixed upon him. "Why do you ask ? "

"'There is safety in a multitude,'" quotes the young man, with a rather forced smile. "Is there no one in particular ? "

"Do you mean a lover ? " she asks, slowly, blushing again, a

soft sweet blush, yet evidently much amused.   "Dear me, no!
I have any number of friends, but not one lover—at present.
My last was a dear old thing of about sixty, excellently pre-
served; but he died eight months ago, and ever since I have
been the actual 'Maid forlorn.'   Ronnie"—regretfully—"has
two lovers just now; but I have none."

Mr. Craven does not appear to sympathise with her affliction.
On the contrary, he grows more cheerful with every word she
utters, and at her last positively beams.

"And you—do you care for no one?" he asks, forgetful of
everything but his intense desire to know.

Miss Rivers, who is still palpably amused, thinks this question just a little too much, and telling herself it is her turn now,
determines to punish him for it.   So she hesitates, opens her
lips as though to speak, checks herself suddenly, looks down,
turns a ring round and round upon her finger, and finally says,
very consciously—

"I am afraid I do."

This is a crushing blow.   All Craven's content dies on the
spot.   He glowers, knits his brow, and looks utterly miserable.

"Somebody, then, is very fortunate," he answers, rather unsteadily.

"But there are two of them," explains Cissy, shaking her
head in a perplexed fashion, "and I cannot quite decide which
I love best."

"Love!" he echoes, in a desperate tone.

"Yes; I feel I adore them," she confesses, with unaffected
and growing ardour.   "So would you if you knew them.   I
sometimes tell myself it is unlucky to love them as I do, with
all my heart."

"But you cannot love two men equally!" he exclaims,
aghast at this daring declaration.   "It is impossible!"

Cissy, as though thoroughly confounded by his words, moves
back a step or two and raises one hand in bewilderment.

"Two men!" she says, disdainfully.   "Of what are you
thinking?   Are you so behind the times as to imagine I should

do such a *rococo* thing as to love a man ! No, indeed ; I was but thinking of—mamma and Ronnie."

As though aware of her victory, she finishes this saucy speech with a merry laugh, and moves away from him in the direction of Mrs. Richards's parlour. She looks so arch, yet so provoking, so mischievous, yet so charming, that Craven, while acknowledging himself shamefully taken in, laughs too in spite of himself.

" Listen to me," he says, hastily. " If the Major goes to bed early—which of course "—in disgust—" he won't do, because he ought—may I hope for a cup of tea from Mrs. Richards ? "

" I am sure "—demurely—" she will be delighted to give it to you." Then, seeing the disappointment in his face, she adds kindly, and with a pretty smile, " Yes, do come. You will be quite welcome ! "

And for once in his life the Major—though unconsciously— does the right thing, or rather the gout does it for him; he goes to bed early, and leaves his grateful host to follow his own devices.

*   *   *   *   *

The next morning, what a change appears ! Yesterday the world was white but dull. To-day it is white too, but sparkling, as though with innumerable diamonds. The snow has ceased to fall, the sun is shining bravely, lighting up with a million rays each spray and bough, on which the snow still lingers. The fir-trees have shaken off a little of their chilly burden, and now show again in parts some evidence of green. A few birds, though in a somewhat weak and melancholy fashion, are chanting a hymn of praise, and preening languidly their draggled plumage.

Cissy is so delighted with them that she opens wide her bed-room window and throws out to them the thin slice of bread and butter sent up to her with her tea half an hour before. They fly down to it, to her intense satisfaction, and chatter about it, and fight a little over it, before it comes to an end.

At the foot of the staircase, as she runs down to breakfast, she encounters Craven, who had been waiting for her.

"Was I not right?" she says, gaily, giving him her hand. "The weather has changed. See what a delicious morning it is! No doubt about my being able to get home to-day, is there?"

"I hardly know if the horses can travel yet—the snow is so deep in some parts," he replies, avoiding her eyes.

"I shall walk if I cannot go any other way," says Cissy, with quick determination and some faint doubt of him expressed in her tone.

"If it comes to that, and you must go, you certainly sha'n't walk," he returns. "I suppose, with care, a horse can be induced to go so far." Then reproachfully—"In what haste you are to be gone!"

He is looking so honestly grieved at the thought of her departure that her heart smites her.

"Only in haste to see the two at home," she says, gently—"not to leave this house, where every one has been so kind to me, and where I have been quite happy. You must not for one moment think me ungrateful."

She says this so sweetly that he is comforted; and, when she has so far given in to his wishes as to breakfast with him, and has made herself specially charming throughout the meal, he is almost himself again. Directly breakfast is at an end, because he sees and understands her hurry to be gone, he orders the dog-cart to be brought round; and Cissy, once more enwrapped in her furs, is handed into it. Craven, seating himself beside her, takes the reins, the groom jumps up behind, and together they start for her home.

The drive, though slow, and in parts difficult, is a rather silent one; but, just as they enter the gates of Branksmere, she, turning to him, says impulsively—

"What a long time it seems since last I was here—weeks almost!"

"I told you you were bored to death," he replies, with a

curious smile, "though you were too good-natured to acknowledge it.   See how heavily the time dragged."

"Nonsense! You know I did not mean that. I was only
trying to explain to myself how in so short a time I could learn
to regard you in such a friendly light. It seems absurd, doesn't
it? Two short days—hardly two—and yet I feel quite as if
you were my brother."

"Not in the least like your brother," says Craven, hastily.
"Your brother would be far handsomer a fellow than I can
ever hope to be. I don't feel a bit like your brother."

"Well, then, you seem to me like a very old friend"—
smiling.

"I am glad of that. It tells me I am not quite out in the
cold," he answers, heartily; and then they pull up at the hall
door, and the groom jumps down, and Cecil has barely time to
reach the ground when Ronnie comes running out and, catch-
ing her in her arms, holds her until her mother releases her.

The liberated prisoner is embraced and kissed and examined
with tearful eyes; and then, turning, flushed and smiling,
towards Craven, she says, brightly—

"This is Mr. Craven, mamma. You must thank him for all
his kindness to me."

Mamma is secretly rather taken aback, as she has been
picturing an imaginary Mr. Craven to herself as a stout middle-
aged gentleman of fatherly aspect, not in the very least like the
tall, fashionably-dressed young man who stands smiling genially
down upon her now, hat in hand.

She conceals her surprise very successfully however, and
murmurs a few words of earnest gratitude ; and then they all
go into the house and up to the drawing-room fire, where explanations follow, and where Cissy—who is in wild spirits—
makes them all laugh a good deal at her version of the adventure—especially Ronnie, who has found it intolerably dull
without her.

"You will, of course, stay to luncheon," says Mrs. Rivers, pleasantly.   "Your man can put up your horse for an hour or two."

She rings the bell; and Mr. Craven, who is singularly amenable to pressing on this occasion—hardly indeed requiring it as he gives in at the first request—stays on for many hours, only tearing himself away with open reluctance as the daylight fades, and thoughts of the Major and his duties as host crowd heavily upon him.

CHAPTER V.

WHEN the young man has gone, Ronnie turns to her sister, and placing her arms round her, gives her a good hug.

"I couldn't half do it while he was looking," she says, "though I think him very nice, nevertheless."

"He was very kind, at all events," says Cissy, gratefully, "Wasn't it a wonderful adventure?"

"It might have been a terrible one," replies her mother, with a shudder.

"Oh, mamma, and who do you think was there besides me?"

"Who?"

"Major Jervis!"

"Major Jervis! And he saw you?" asks Mrs. Rivers, in a horror-stricken tone."

"Yes—but—— And yet he didn't see me!" continues Cecil. And then she gives them the entire history of her escape from the Major and her terror on the occasion.

When she has finished her recital, her mother draws a breath of deep relief.

"You are sure Mr. Craven won't betray you?" she asks, still a little nervously.

"Quite sure! Mamma, how could you think him a traitor?"

"I didn't, my dear. I was merely anxious," answers Mrs. Rivers, hastily. Then she rises and quits the room for some domestic purpose.

"What nice eyes he has!" says Ronnie, when the girls are

alone again. "And how he uses them—though only on one object, I grant! I firmly believe, though he has been here to-day for nearly two hours, he would not, if put on his oath, know me from mamma, or mamma from me."

"I don't think he is such a stupid young man as you seem to think," returns Cissy, mildly. "And it is folly what you say, dearest; any one can see that mamma is at all events a year or two older than you."

"I am not accusing him of stupidity. I have no doubt he is a second Socrates," rejoins Ronnie, meekly. "I merely meant to say he never took his eyes off you from the time he came till he went away. I was but as dross in his sight. Well, never mind! I wonder, by the bye, when we shall see him again?"

"Some time next year, perhaps." It is now close on Christmas.

"Some time to-morrow, I should say."

"Ronnie, how can you be so absurd! What could bring him here again so soon?" says Cecil; but she blushes vividly as she puts the question.

"Well, you, I suppose," rejoins Ronnie, unabashed. "Little hypocrite that you are, why don't you confess what you know in your secret heart? What do you think he meant by asking mamma if she wanted some books to read? Simply an excuse to put in an appearance here early in the morning. Now, mark my words, it will be early. And I shouldn't at all be surprised if he ordered up the whole library, book-shelves and all, for your delectation. My own opinion is," adds Miss Rivers, laughing, "that this poor young man is head-over-ears in love with you."

Cecil leans back in her chair and laughs also.

"And what do you think his name is?" she asks, still laughing. "It is Duke!"

"Then you are bound to marry him," says Ronnie, merrily. "You always declared you would marry a Duke if you ever met one. You certainly can't go back from it now."

"I have another idea, too," remarks Cecil. "I think— indeed I feel sure—he is Maria's young man !"

"No !" cries Ronnie. "But yes, of course. He is *un bon parti*, and just all we ever heard of the happy man who has been laid aside for her. Poor Maria ! I am afraid it was a luckless day for her when you lost your way in the snow."

"Well, it is all mere supposition about Maria," says Cecil. "Of course, Mr. Craven may not be the man assigned for her by the Major."

"Of course not. But I prefer thinking he is the man. It makes it all so comfortable. You said you would like to cut out Maria, if only for vengeance' sake ; now you can do it. You said you would marry a Duke ; now, too, you can do it. It is all like the fulfilment of a pretty dream."

"But what about you, dearest?" asks Cecil, softly. "Have you heard from him?"

"I had one letter from Sir Sydney," answers Ronnie, slowly.

"One? Well, of course you could hardly have had more. To me it seems a long time since we came here. I feel indeed as if I had been away from you and mother for a twelve-month—— But go on, Ronnie; tell me about your letter."

"It was short, and not particularly sweet. It began, ' My dear Miss Rivers,' and it ended, ' Always yours most sincerely.' It was filled with London gossip, and that is all I can tell you of it until we go upstairs ; then you can see the original of what I have been telling you, if you will."

"I think ' Always yours most sincerely ' was very nice indeed," says Cissy. "' Yours sincerely ' would be commonplace, and quite nothing ; but the ' always ' and the ' most ' make such a difference ! "

"I am so glad to have you back !" returns Ronnie, gratefully, throwing her arms round her sister. "Do you know, Cissy, what is your principal charm ? You always know just what is the right thing to say."

Ronnie's surmises prove true. The very next morning brings Mr. Craven again to Branksmere ; and for the matter of

that every other morning sees him there too—until a week has
passed over their heads.

The day is lovely—clear and bright, and full of sunshine.
All sign of snow is gone from the ground; only a thin sparkling frost, that sits lightly on tree and shrub, makes one certain it is winter still, and not early spring. From the sea comes
up a moaning—sad, but sweet. A few birds, taking courage
from the calmness of day and the warmth of the welcome god
of light, who, up above in the blue heavens, sits enthroned,
"diffusing radiant bliss around," hop from bough to bough on
the bare trees, and twitter meek little songs, as though half
afraid of their own temerity.

Indoors the fires are burning brightly. The logs are crack-
ling on the top of the coals; the great white Persian cat is
blinking lazily on the hearthrug, and pretty Cecil, with a huge
black fan in her hand, is sitting on the rug too, her head resting against her mother's knee.

It is now the seventh day since her return home, and they
are all sitting in the small morning-room—the room in the house
they most affect, it is so snug and cosy—with Duke Craven in
their midst, but as near to Cecil as circumstances will permit.

"By-the-bye," says Craven, suddenly, *à propos* of something
just said by Ronnie, "the Major is with me again, in spite of
his dread of that awful ghost he encountered some days ago.
He has heard of your having taken up your residence here,
Mrs. Rivers, and declared his intention, this morning at breakfast, of calling upon you without loss of time. Shouldn't
wonder if he came to-day."

"Old Horror !" says Ronnie, irreverently.

"If he knew he was going to encounter his ghost face to
face, I don't believe he would be in such a hurry to call,"
continues Mr. Craven, smiling at Cissy, who smiles back at
him, and says, with affected fear—

"Ah, if he had found me substantial flesh and blood that
night instead of barren bones, what should I have done?"

"I know what I should have done," says Ronnie, viciously. "If he had caught me on that occasion, I should have beaten him black and blue. Death would have been his portion that night. He should never, with my consent, have lived to tell the tale."

She looks such a ridiculously fragile creature to be the author of this awful speech that every one laughs.

"I don't think even the Major would be afraid of you," remarks Craven. "Do you know, I'm not sure why I think it, but it seems to me that Jervis is rather put out at your settling down here"—he is speaking now in a low confidential tone to the girls alone, Mrs. Rivers having gone into the next room to write a letter. "He appeared disconcerted when he spoke of your being here, though why I can't imagine."

At this both girls exchange glances; the glances mean, "Ah! didn't I tell you so? He *is* Maria's young man!"

"However, he is such a grumpy old chap always, I dare say it was imagination on my part thinking so," Craven goes on, carelessly. "Miss Cecil, did you really mean it, the other day, when you said you adored honey? Because Mrs. Richards—I can't fancy how she knew of your love for it—desired me to tell you this afternoon she has·more than she knows what to do with, and wants to know if she may send you some."

"Did she really say that?" asks Cecil, eagerly. "Now isn't she an old dear? Give her my love, please, Mr. Craven, and say she may send me some honey as soon as ever she likes; and tell her, too, I shall give her a kiss for it the very next moment we meet."

"Happy Richards!" says Mr. Craven, in a low tone, with an indescribable glance that is half amused, and half earnest, and wholly loving.

Ronnie laughs; and then, Mrs. Rivers returning to the room, Craven rises and takes his departure. He has not been gone half an hour when the servant announces—"Major Jervis."

Mrs. Rivers, rising, receives him very courteously, and the girls give him their hands with a passably good grace.

"Had no idea until the day before yesterday that you and the young ladies had come to reside down here," begins the Major, when he has ensconced himself in the most comfortable chair in the room, and drawn himself close up to the fire. He always calls the girls the "young ladies," to Ronnie's intense disgust.

"We rather tired of town life," says Mrs. Rivers, finding she must say something.

"Ah, yes! It is disappointing at times," replies the Major, with a meaning glance at Ronnie, who takes no notice of it or him. "By-the-bye, I saw our common . friend, Sir Sydney Walcott, in Piccadilly last week, looking uncommonly well and happy. You will all be glad to hear good accounts of him; he was such an intimate friend of yours."

"Very intimate. I know few people I like so well as Sir Sydney," says Mrs. Rivers, calmly, but she colours as she says it.

"You have made the acquaintance of Mr. Craven, I hear," remarks the Major, presently. "I am staying with him, you know."

"Yes. He himself told us so just now."

"Ah! Been here already? Sharp work!" says the Major; and Cecil, who is earnestly regarding him, sees that he starts a little, and that a slight frown contracts his forehead. "Early visiting; wasn't it—eh?"

"Is it early?" asks Mrs. Rivers, languidly. "We hardly thought of that. You see, we know so few people down here as yet that we make more than usually welcome any one who is kind enough to break in upon our monotony."

"And he is just the sort of person to make 'more than usually welcome,'" returns the Major, with an unpleasant smile. "He is about the best catch down here, or anywhere else that I know of; but yet not to be caught, I think—not to be caught. Ha, ha!"

"I have heard he is very well off," says Mrs. Rivers, coldly.

"Heard it before you came down, I dare say"—chuckling.

This is almost too much. Cecil grows as red as a rose and bites her lip. Ronnie turns as if bent on annihilating their enemy then and there; but Mrs. Rivers checks her by saying blandly—

"You know all about him, of course, Major Jervis. His father was a great friend of yours, I believe."

"Ye-es," says the Major, so doubtfully that Ronnie and Cecil both decide that the late Mr. Craven suffered him more than he regarded him.

"Have any of you seen his place yet?" asks the Major, turning as if instinctively to Cecil. She colours hotly.

"We have been hardly anywhere yet; the weather has been so terrible," replies her mother, coming quickly to the rescue.

"Splendid old place," says the Major—"antique, picturesque —pure Gothic, you know, and all that sort of rubbish! The drawing-room is a study in mediævalism, and the old china is priceless."

"Oh, yes, those beautiful old Queen Anne cups with the tiny gold tracing!" exclaims Cecil, leaning forward, and forgetting in her eagerness all her words may convey to the Major.

"Eh? What!"—suspiciously. "I thought you said you had not been there. Then how did you see the china, Miss Cecil—eh?"

"I heard of it," replies Cecil, blushing nervously.

"Heard—eh? Very accurate description from mere hearsay."

"Really, Major," says Mrs. Rivers, half smiling, yet wholly angry, "Cecil will not be pleased with you if you doubt her word. Some day we are all going over to see those wonderful things. Mr. Craven has kindly expressed a wish that we should go and look at the old place."

"Ah, yes, no doubt!" growls the Major. "Not that I think it would be an advisable step on your part, my dear madam.

If you will allow an old friend of the family to give his opinion on this subject, I should say young ladies are better out of bachelors' quarters! They are hardly suitable for young unmarried ladies, I should think. Better at home, eh? But, of course, my dear madam, you are the best judge of all that."

"Yes, I think so," returns Mrs. Rivers, a little haughtily; but this terrible old man is not to be rebuked.

"No offence," he says. "A word in season, you know; and —er—my young friend Craven is rather a gay fellow—nothing very much against him, you know, my dear madam, only young men will be young men to the end of the ·chapter! Ha—ha!"

His words mean nothing, his manner a great deal. A vague shadow as of coming grief falls upon the heart of Mrs. Rivers as she turns almost instinctively to look at her pretty Cecil.

Her pretty Cecil is looking utterly unconcerned, and is simply regarding Major Jervis with a glance suggestive of indifference and contempt. Mrs. Rivers sighs, and wonders inwardly whether she is doing a wise thing in allowing this acquaintance with Duke Craven to ripen into a friendship—nay, into something that may prove even warmer than friendship, and more capable of bearing fruit either of joy or sorrow—what if it should be sorrow? After all, what do they know about this young man Craven? He has fallen into their lives by the merest chance, and is literally unknown to them beyond the fact that he is of good family and has a house and some considerable property. Of his character or his usual habits they have learned absolutely nothing. And even now is not the Major throwing out hints of a most unpleasant nature about him?

Meanwhile Ronnie is cross-questioning Major Jervis about Craven Court.

"Yes, it is a capital place," he says, "but draughty—very, and haunted into the bargain."

"Haunted! How delicious!" Cissy cries, clasping her hands. "Do tell us all about it, Major?"

Whereupon the Major, who dearly loves the sound of his own voice, gives them a most extraordinary account of his pursuit of Cecil on that memorable evening now more than a week ago. He has hardly finished his highly coloured recital when, to the surprise of all, Craven again enters the room.

"I really must beg your pardon," says that young man, blushing ingenuously. "But not until I had reached home, Mrs. Rivers, did I remember about that address for which you so wished. I have it with me now. As I was going to Carbery"—a village some three miles away—"I thought I might as well drop in again and leave it with you."

"Much better," answers Ronnie, graciously.

"Ah, Major; knew I should find you here!" says Duke, genially. "I hope you are making yourself agreeable."

"What an absurd question!" cries Ronnie. "When is the Major anything else? Just now, too, he is making himself more than usually charming, because he is telling us ghost-stories. Think of that!"

"Just that little adventure of mine the other evening," says the Major, airily. "Nothing much, you know; but of course it is something to have been face to face with a real ghost."

"Something! Everything!" exclaims Cecil. "Weren't you frightened to death, Major?"

"Not I, indeed! By Jove!" he says, looking fixedly at Cecil, "I have it! There was a certain familiarity about that ghost that puzzled me at the time; I thought it resembled somebody, but could not make out whom. Now I know. It was you."

Mrs. Rivers looks a little nervous, and Cecil and Craven break into merry laughter, instantaneous and irrepressible.

"I think it is very unkind of you," says Cissy, presently, with a little laugh, "to compare me to a horrid ghost!"

"But the figure was marvellously like yours," persists the Major, in a puzzled tone, "and the side-face too."

"The story grows more thrilling every instant," observes Ronnie. "I do hope, Cecil, that you will not imitate your ghostly fetch and dissolve away into a gentle dew."

" Don't you feel very uncomfortable, Miss Rivers ? " asks Craven, addressing Cissy.

" No—rather flattered than otherwise.. A very little more thought on the subject would make me imagine I was the actual heroine of the story the Major has so kindly told us."

"Well, I must be going," says the Major, rising. "You will come with me, Craven ? "

" I am going to Carbery," returns Craven, evasively.

" So am I," says the Major, determinedly; and so, sorely against his will, the young man is compelled to rise from his comfortable lounge, and follow him.

CHAPTER VI.

A MONTH has flown swiftly by. Already the earth is whispering of spring, the trees are budding, the grass is throwing out fresh green shoots; and, indeed, all Nature is lifting up its head and rejoicing as "Spring comes up this way."

To Cecil this past month has been one of intense happiness ; to Ronnie one of unrest, though perhaps not altogether painful. Sir Sydney Walcott has been abroad, summoned there to attend the death-bed of a rich relative, but his letters have not ceased, and though calm as the first she received from him at Branksmere, have been at least undeviating in their constancy.

Mrs. Rivers, however, has been seriously uneasy. The hint dropped by the Major about Duke Craven's not being all one could desire in the way of steadiness has lingered in her mind ever since, and tormented her by day and by night. This doubt, too, has been confined perforce to her own breast, as the Major returned to town the day after he had sown the seeds of distrust in her breast, and to Cecil or Ronnie she would not talk on such a subject.

Craven's evident admiration for Cecil is apparent to all eyes

—so apparent that Mrs. Rivers longs daily for the hour that will see him present himself as her open suitor. But that day has not yet come, and misgivings oppress her in spite of her determination to have patience and let things take their proper course.

By nature a nervous woman, she is now doubly so, on account of her dependence upon her uncle, Sir Gregory. She would gladly see her girls married comfortably and beyond the power of any whim of his to hurt them. She is anxious, too, about Cecil. The girl, she can see, has given her whole heart to this acquaintance of only six weeks. She is blindly, utterly happy when with him—which is dangerously often—and plainly trusts him entirely.

Just now Craven is with her in the drawing-room, and both are standing in the big bay-window counting the pretty snow-drops that are coming up one by one. Duke is not talking. He is, indeed, almost deaf to what Cecil is saying, so rapt is he in contemplation of her own fair self.

She is dressed in a gown of dark-brown velvet, trimmed with coffee-coloured lace at the throat and wrists, and is looking more than usually lovely. Presently she becomes aware that he is not listening to her, and, turning to him, tells him so, with a pretty show of petulance.

"I confess my crime," he says, quickly, his voice full of eager passion. "How could I think of anything but you when you are there opposite to me? Your voice, indeed, is sweet; but you are even sweeter. No, I heard nothing. I could only see."

"See what?" she asks, with an attempt at gaiety, though she has grown a little pale because of his manner, which is strangely unlike his usual calm self.

"You, my 'dainty Ariel'—my darling!" he whispers, quickly. The words come from him almost involuntarily; almost unconsciously too he takes her hand and holds it closely. Cissy colours faintly, and then grows even paler than she was before.

"Why do you call me that?" she says. "Why? You have no right to—no——"

He interrupts her by a gesture, and draws her even nearer to him.

"Give me the right," he says, eagerly. "You know—you must know by this time—that there is nothing in the world I love so well as——"

"Major Jervis" announces a servant at this supreme moment, throwing wide the drawing-room door.

With a smothered exclamation, Craven lets Cecil's hand drop, and, turning aside, steps through the open window on to the small verandah outside, which by stone steps leads to the ground.   Descending these, he goes quickly out of sight, but not before the Major has had time to catch a glimpse of his departing coat-tails.

"Hum! Hah!" says the Major.   He has hardly had time to return Cecil's somewhat cold greeting when Mrs. Rivers and Ronnie enter the room.   There are signs of very distinct irritation about the Major.   He blows his nose somewhat effusively and refuses to let his eyes meet those of any one else present.   "I think I saw Craven going out of that window just as I came in," he says, staring at Cecil.

"Yes," she returns, slowly; her mind is still full of Duke, and she is wondering what it was exactly that he was going to say when interrupted by this troublesome Major.

"He didn't expect me down to-day," the Major goes on. "Thinks me safe at home at this moment, no doubt."

Again he looks at Cissy, as if expecting her to answer.   He is in truth curious to know if Duke saw him coming or heard him announced by the servant, and, if so, whether he ran away to avoid the bore of having to speak to him.

"He will be all the more delighted to see you at the Court, of course," says Ronnie, ironically.   "Surprises of that sort are so pleasant!"

"Quite so ;" and the Major directs a withering glance at her.   "Fact is, I hardly knew I was coming down myself until this morning. But business must be attended to, you know. Business for the fair sex especially—ha, ha ! I've come indeed to carry Craven back to town with me. I bring a letter from his cousin, Lady Maud Esterdale, demanding his immediate attendance."

"Who is this cousin Lady Maud ? " asks Cecil, quickly.

"Oh, don't you know ? " inquires the Major. "It's not quite settled, I believe; but——"

"What is not quite settled ? " demands Cecil again. She is quite calm, but deathly pale.

"His marriage," says the Major, quietly. It is true that he shifts a little uneasily in his seat as he says this, and refuses to lift his eyes from the carpet; but nevertheless he says it.

A dead silence ensues—a silence short in reality, but of intolerable length to some in the room. Then Cecil laughs—quite a natural little laugh too ; so natural indeed that both her mother and Ronnie turned involuntarily to look at her.

"He is rather a scamp in some ways," continues the Major, in a genial way. "Now if you ask him about this marriage it is as likely as not he would deny all knowledge of it, and declare he was never farther from matrimony in his life. But don't you be taken in by him. He is a disgraceful fellow in the way of flirtations ; makes love all round, you know, to every woman he meets, and makes some of 'em believe him too. But he's not a bad young fellow at heart. No, no—far from that. But this marriage now will be a good thing for both of them ; she with title, he with money."

"A charming arrangement indeed ! " says Cecil, without so much as a quiver of her eyelids.

"Well, it is rather premature yet to speak about it," pursues the Major. "Craven mightn't like it, you know ; so don't mention my name in the matter as having been the one to tell of it. You see, he is such a great friend here that I dare say he will wish to be himself the first to tell you of it."

"Of course he would like to tell us himself," returns Cecil, smiling calmly. "As you say, he is a great friend of ours, and he knows we will be glad to hear of anything likely to add to his happiness."

The Major watches her closely as she makes this set little speech, and she as closely returns his fixed gaze. Then, with a somewhat puzzled and baffled expression on his face, he rises and bids them " Good-bye " for the present. When the door has shut behind him, Ronnie turns vehemently to Cecil.

" I don't believe one word of it," she says, hastily—" not one ! He looked as if he were telling a falsehood."

" I saw no trace of falsehood either in his look or tone," answers Cecil, in a strange tone, " and as for the rest, I believe every word he said."

She moves towards the door ; her mother, with tears in her eyes, rises as if to follow her ; but, with a gentle gesture, the girl prevents her.

" I want to be alone, mamma," she says, entreatingly, "just for a little while ; I shall be all right then. But there is one thing you can do for me," she cries, breaking suddenly out of her terrible quiet. " Never—never—never mention his name to me again ! "

Poor Mrs. Rivers is thoroughly cast down, and Ronnie scarcely less so.

" How shall we receive him if he calls to-morrow ? " asks her mother, when poor Cecil has crept away from them up to her own room to cry her heart out on her bed.

" Just as if nothing had happened. Cecil, of course, will not appear. I will make her go for a walk at that hour, so that we can truly say she is not in. Mamma, if only for Cecil's sake, do not let him see we care about this thing."

So the next day, when Craven calls at his usual hour, Mrs. Rivers is as nearly as possible the same to him that she has been during the past month. Perhaps some subtle change in her manner might be noticed by a very acute observer, some vague irrepressible shrinking from all more open cordiality ; but beyond this her demeanour is perfect.

As for Ronnie, she is a degree more sad than angry. She

maintains an almost utter silence; but every now and then Craven, glancing at her, wonders vaguely why her eyes are so large and mournful, her whole manner so full of an uncertain depression.

His wonder on this point, however, is indeed vague, as his whole mind is filled with a longing to see a particular lounging-chair near the fire occupied by a little lissom figure whose smile is wont to beam at him, half-roguishly, half with a tenderness not to be described. Where is she now—his little sweetheart?

"Where is Miss Cecil?" he asks at last, unable to restrain his impatience any longer.

"She has gone for a walk, I think," replies Mrs. Rivers, stooping to poke the fire.

"Let me do that for you," says Craven, taking the poker from her. "She has gone to the garden, perhaps." He is kneeling on the hearth-rug, and is looking very earnestly up into Mrs. Rivers's face, with his pleasant, honest eyes.

"I think not—certainly not—she did not say exactly where she was going," returns Mrs. Rivers, evasively.

Ronnie at this sighs audibly, and Craven, turning, looks at her sharply. Something in her expression evidently strikes him as being peculiar, but he says nothing, and presently turns the conversation into another channel.

"I have a friend coming to stay with me next week," he says; "a friend of yours, too, I think. I met him in London, and he almost asked me to invite him down. He said he knew you all very well."

"I dare say. We lived some years in town," responds Mrs. Rivers, indifferently. "One gets to know so many people there."

Ronnie evinces no curiosity either about the new arrival at the Court; so Mr. Craven goes on—

"I'm rather sorry he is coming just now, as I am bound to be in town in the morning, and sha'n't be able to be back for a fortnight. I am afraid, therefore, he will have only a slow time of it."

He rises to go ; as he does so, Ronnie rises too, and follows him into the hall.

"I think," she says, in a tone that falters slightly—"I think Cissy went in the direction of the beech-wood."

Before he has time to thank her for this hint or wonder at the strangeness of her manner she has disappeared ; and, somewhat puzzled, Craven makes his way towards the wood she has mentioned.

Just as he enters it, he encounters Cecil coming towards him, her head slightly bent, her face rather paler than usual.

"How d'ye do?" she says, quite calmly, but without an accompanying smile. She lets her hand lie in his unsympathetically, and then draws it away almost before he has time to know it was there.

"I was unfortunate to-day. I thought I should have found you within"—with an attempt at cordiality, though some inward misgivings have cast a shadow on his usual light-heartedness.

"For the future I think you must not expect always to find me in," she replies, with a faint smile.

"Why?" he asks, astonished at her whole treatment of him.

"Because winter is at an end, and the fine weather tempts one to go out," she says, coldly.

"For that reason one loves the fine weather," he returns, striving against his growing anxiety. "May I not sometimes accompany you in your rambles?"

"No, I think not. When I go for a walk in these quiet woods I prefer my own company to any one's. A strange fancy, and rather egotistical, is it not?"

"It is very unlike you"—gravely ; then, unable to control his uneasiness any longer, he says, anxiously, "What has happened that you treat me like this? What have I done to you?"

"Done to me?"—haughtily. "Nothing!"

"I am going to town this evening, Cecil. I shall not be back until——"

"I must ask you not to call me 'Cecil,'" says the girl,

quietly, and with a certain amount of dignity. "I must always be 'Miss Rivers' to gentlemen-acquaintances."

"Am I only that? Only an acquaintance?"

There is a world of reproach in his tone.

"Yes, only that "—remorselessly.

"And yet yesterday——"

"Do not speak of yesterday!" she exclaims, putting up her hand impulsively, as though to ward off something that is hurting her.

"As you will, of course," he returns, in a tone nearly as cold as her own. "I have no claim, of course, to be considered even a friend. May I say good-bye to you, and let you finish your walk in peace? I am going away this evening."

"Where are you going?"

"To my aunt—Lady Eton."

"Ah, to your cousin, Lady Maud!"

"Yes, if you like. Who was telling you of it? The Major?"

"Yes, the Major. He told me everything."

"I don't know when I shall be back."

"Soon enough, no doubt. What are you going for—the wedding?"

"Yes, for the wedding." He speaks in a very low, depressed tone, because of her cruel coldness. To her his depression means only shame at the discovery she has made.

"When is it to be?" she asks, slowly.

"Next week."

"So soon? It is sudden, is it not?"

"Not very; I have known of it for some months."

"You knew of it before we came here?"

"Oh, yes; long before that! I wish you knew Maud—she is a very nice girl, and I am sure she would be a great friend of yours."

"I am equally sure she would not. I hate nice girls!" says Cecil, with sudden and most unlooked-for vehemence.

"Surely they are better than nasty ones, at all events!" he returns, somewhat aggrieved.

" I don't know. At all events "—defiantly—" I don't care to hear anything more about either you or Lady Maud."

Silence follows this outburst—a silence that lasts until they reach the small path that leads to the avenue.

" I think you are hardly kind to me," he says then, gently. "And I don't understand you at all."

"No "—in a very low tone—" I don't wonder at that. There are times "—bitterly—" when I cannot understand myself. Well, shall I say then that I wish your Lady Maud joy ? "

"Thank you. I shall give my cousin that message," he answers, gravely; then, holding out his hand—" Good-bye."

"Good-bye "—stonily.

" I shall not see you again for some time," Craven goes on, wistfully.

" Don't let that trouble you," she returns, with a little heartless laugh that certainly has no mirth in it.

" Does that mean that you do not care ever to see me again ? " he demands, his face darkening.

" It means whatever you like," she answers, icily, though at this moment she would have given half her life to be able to fling herself into his arms and cry her heart out upon his breast.

" No ; you shall tell me what you really mean now—at once ! " he declares, sternly, compelling her to face him. " Is it that you honestly hope never to see me again ? "

"Yes, that is my honest hope," she returns, calmly, her face deathly pale.

" Ah ! " He draws his breath quickly, and for a moment his own face rivals hers in pallor. "You shall not be bored by me in the future," he says, slowly. "I shall not trouble this part of the world much again as long as it shall please you to remain in it."

So saying, he turns from her, and, with bitter anger in his heart, strides rapidly through the woodland, and is soon lost to sight amidst the shadows of the coming night.

CHAPTER VII.

AND LAST.

A MISERABLE week, fraught with bitter grief for Cecil and even bitterer disappointment, goes slowly by. No one has said a word to her about her faithless lover, no one has even ventured to mention his name in her presence; but just now, when she and Ronnie are standing alone in the pretty morning-room, Ronnie goes up to her and places her arm around her neck. The girl is impelled to do this because of the forlorn expression upon Cecil's face and her disconsolate attitude. She is leaning against the shutter of the window, and great tears are shining in her mournful eyes.

As Cecil does not repulse her, Ronnie is emboldened so far as to lay her soft cheek against her sister's; and, being still further encouraged, as no rebuff has followed on this overture, she whispers, tenderly—

"Do not be so sad, darling. It will be better by-and-bye. Time cures all things."

"Has it cured you?" asks Cecil, with a little catch in her breath.

"Nearly, I think," replies Ronnie, with a heavy sigh that belies her words.

"Do you mean to tell me "—glancing reproachfully at Ronnie—"that you have ceased to long and hope and pray for Sydney's return?"

"I think so—I hope so," answers Ronnie. But as she says this there are tears in her voice and eyes.

"It is not true," says Cecil, regarding her fixedly. "You love him still in spite of everything."

"Why should I love him?" demands Ronnie, with much agitation. "Why should I let one thought of him find harbour in my breast? He has forgotten me—has rubbed me out of his life without even a passing pang. I hope," she cries, earnestly, "I shall never see Sydney Walcott again."

"Sir Sydney Walcott," announces a servant, almost as she ceases speaking, and then both girls become aware that the door is open, and that the young man upon the threshold has in all probability heard every word of Ronnie's passionate little speech.

Cecil, advancing to cover her sister's confusion, greets him kindly. Ronnie, who has turned first pale and then red, and finally pale again to the very lips, comes towards him now, and gives him her hand in silence; then, summoning all the courage she possesses to her aid, tells him in a conventional tone that it is really quite a pleasure to see him again.

This remark is so palpably insincere that the young man she addresses forgets to make any immediate reply, and only stares at her in a reproachful fashion.

He is of middle height, with a quiet, kindly expression, and a manner pleasant, if a little languid. When they have all seated themselves, he makes no attempt at promoting conversation, and even while answering the questions put to him appears very far away from them all in spirit. It is quite evident to Cecil that his thoughts are elsewhere, and that he is in the very lowest of low spirits.

Presently she rises, with the expressed intention of seeking her mother, and, in spite of a beseeching glance from Ronnie, deliberately quits the room.

Almost as the door closes behind her, Sir Sydney, rising from his seat, goes over to the hearthrug, and, standing opposite to Ronnie, leans his arm upon the mantelpiece and gazes down at her.

"I hope Cecil will not return for some time," he says, slowly, "because I have a great deal to tell you. What was it you were saying just as I came in? That I had forgotten you—rubbed you out of my life—eh?"

"Well, was it not true?" asks Ronnie nervously, twining her fingers idly together.

"There could hardly be anything less true; but let that pass. You said also—if I remember rightly—that you hoped you would never see me again. Was that also true?"

"If you won't believe me in one instance, I suppose you won't in another," says Ronnie, evasively. "And yet I think —it ought to be true."

"Well, it isn't," returns Sir Sydney. "I don't believe a word of it. I won't; so you need not say it again." Then, suddenly —"I've been abroad, you know. My uncle is dead."

"I am very sorry," begins Ronnie.

"Don't be. I'm not," answers Walcott, calmly. "He was as disagreeable an old beggar as any one could possibly meet. However, I forgive him. He died—and left me all his money."

"I congratulate you," says Ronnie, icily.

"It is a case for congratulation, certainly," he replies, coolly. "And yet something is lacking to me that damps all my prosperity. That time last spring, when we were in town together, I was miserably poor. Nobody knew it, I think—at least, I hope I didn't look poor. But there were any amount of debts that should have been paid off, incurred by my—— Well, never mind that; I paid them—they were debts of honour; but the paying crippled me so much that I was afraid to ask you to marry me in those days. Now I am not. I have got the title, you see, and the estates, and—and that."

"The title !" repeats Ronnie, in a low tone.

"Yes. My uncle was Earl of Errington, and there wasn't any son to inherit. That was my luck, you know."

"I suppose I ought to tell you again how glad I am of your——"

"Say nothing of the kind ; say only you are glad to see me. Ronnie "—with an utter change of tone—" my dearest love, tell me you will marry me as soon as you can."

When Mrs. Rivers and Cissy come into the room, a few minutes later, they find Ronnie standing on the hearthrug with Lord Errington's arm round her, and a smile upon her mobile lips that has been absent from them for many a day. A few words explain everything, and then the future Countess is caressed and made much of by her mother and sister for a little while.

"I had no idea that you were the friend who was coming to stay at the Court," says Mrs. Rivers, presently, smiling at Errington.

"No? Didn't Craven tell you? I chose a rather peculiar time for my visit," he adds, with a little laugh—"just then Craven was absent about this wedding."

"Yes, yes," says Ronnie, in an agony. In vain she tries to think of something to say that will turn the conversation into another channel.

"Very pretty girl, Lady Maud," he goes on, suspecting nothing; "and enormous fortune. I think myself she is rather throwing herself away upon McGregor !"

"Upon whom ?" asks Ronnie, breathlessly. Cecil, who has placed one hand upon the back of a chair to support herself, is looking at Sydney with all her soul in her eyes.

"McGregor," he repeats, carelessly. "He's a sort of distant cousin of hers, and really nothing much in any way. But she likes him, and has married him—the wedding took place on Thursday—in spite of every one."

"This is dreadful !" says Ronnie, in a frightened tone. She would perhaps have said a great deal more ; but Errington, with a smothered exclamation, goes quickly forward, and catches Cecil in his arms. She has not quite fainted, but for a minute or two is compelled to lie passive in his arms, her breath coming and going in little fitful gasps.

After a while she opens her eyes, and tries to smile, and murmurs feebly that it is only the heat—nothing more ; that she is very foolish, and so on.

"You are not foolish, and it is not the heat !" cries Ronnie, with tearful indignation. "It is only that hateful Major !"

After this, everything is explained to Errington, who looks as concerned and is really as distressed as any one could possibly desire.

"Do not let us talk any more about it, Ronnie," says poor Cecil, at last. "It is all over, and it was all my own fault, and I will not have Sydney worried about my grievances. I shall

go for a walk in the beech-wood and try to leave my troubles
there behind me."

She smiles a little wintry smile as she says this, and, softly
beckoning to her mother, they both go out of the room, leaving
the lovers alone.

Down the bare leaf-strewn path goes Cecil, her mind full of
bitter thoughts. Entering the wood, she strays deep into it,
thinking always of that last day when she was there with him,
and when she had so wilfully put from her the one chance of
happiness she most desired. Two tears spring into her violet
eyes and linger there. They do not fall, but shine like twin
stars in the last beams of the sinking sun.

She has now reached the very spot where last she saw
Craven. Up to this she has been walking with bent head;
but now, lifting her eyes, she looks around her. As her glance
slowly travels from tree to tree, her sadness increases. Now
she is looking wistfully at the little babbling brook in the
distance, and now at the mossy hillock beyond, and now——

Who is that coming towards her? Her heart stops beating
for a moment, and then throbs frantically. It is Craven, looking sad and careworn and full of dejection. As he sees her, he
checks himself for an instant, and then comes resolutely onward.
Flinging away the cigar he has been smoking, he stops just
before Cecil. He does not offer to shake hands with her, but
stands regarding her fixedly.

"You!" he says at length. "What has brought you
here?"

"I don't know; I wanted to come here—I——" She feels
a little choking sensation in her throat, and stops, unable to
proceed.

"I didn't mean to come back again so soon," says Craven,
who has never once removed his eyes from her face, while
she, on the contrary, has not had the courage to lift hers
to his.

"I thought you meant never to come back," she answers, in
a low, husky tone.

"So I did—but"—bitterly—"you see I could not help myself; you ought to be proud of that, ought you not?'

"Oh, do not speak to me in that tone!" she entreats, at last letting her eyes meet his, and he can see the heavy tears lurking in their soft depths.

"How would you have me speak to you?" he asks, reproachfully, but not so coldly as a moment since. "When last we met, you scorned my advances, and told me that you hoped never to see me again; and that too at a time when I was consumed with a desire to tell you how I loved you—how that every thought of my heart was yours."

"Ah, if you could only understand," she murmurs, desperately.

"Understand what?"—eagerly. "Cecil—speak to me, tell me what you mean."

"Major Jervis said you were going to be married to your cousin, Lady Maud," says Cecil, in a stifled tone.

"The old scoundrel!" he mutters. "Was that why you behaved so cruelly to me on that wretched afternoon?" he asks presently, when his wrath has somewhat subsided.

"Yes"—shyly.

"And—and now you know the whole truth—do you love me, Cecil?"

"I do"—still more shyly.

"My dearest heart!" murmurs Craven; and then somehow she finds herself in his arms with her head against his breast, and knows that she is utterly and entirely happy.

"What misery I have endured since we parted!" says Craven, after a little while. "It is quite a year ago now; isn't it?"

"A year! A week," she corrects, lifting her brows.

"Oh, nonsense! It might be a century at least," he says. "Well, you shall never know what unhappiness means again, if I can help it," he adds, tenderly.

Then they wend their way slowly homewards. In the hall they meet Mrs. Rivers, who regards them, naturally enough, with astonishment; and they have hardly explained matters satisfactorily to her when Ronnie and Errington join them, when it has all to be said over again on both sides.

Whilst they are in the very midst of their double congratulations, one of the servants, coming into the little morning-room where they have seated themselves, tells them that Major Jervis is in the drawing-room.

"I'll go to him," says Ronnie, rising; "you are too nervous to-day, mamma, and Cecil's eyes are pink—she has evidently been enjoying herself excessively with Duke."

With this, and a little laugh, she rustles out of the room and into the next by a folding door, which divides the two rooms from each other. There she finds the Major.

When he has gone through the ordinary questions about her own and her mother's and sister's health, he says, somewhat jerkily—

"Seen our friend Craven lately?"

"Yes, to-day. But he is not so interesting, I think, as he used to be."

"Ha! How is that?" asks the Major, in a delighted tone.

"Well, he is engaged, you see," answers Ronnie, as if reluctantly, "and young men engaged are young men lost, so far as their being entertaining goes. You know you gave us a hint about his being bent on getting married without delay when last you were down. We have discovered since that your surmise was correct."

"Eh—eh?" he says, fidgeting anxiously in his chair. "But I was wrong then. I alluded to his cousin, Lady Maud; but she has married McGregor since that. May I ask whom Rumour has given him to now?"

"Well, to Cecil, I believe!" returns Ronnie, with provoking unconcern.

This is a death-blow. The Major turns pale, and blows his nose violently to cover his chagrin.

"Ah, Rumour is a worthless jade!" he says, with a miserable

attempt at disbelief in her news. " As a rule, she tells more lies than truth."

" This time she has varied it," returns Ronnie, " by telling more truth than lies. My sister and Mr. Craven have quite made up their minds and are engaged to each other."

" I don't believe it !" cries the Major, rising to his feet.

At this instant the folding doors are flung open, and Craven, appearing on the scene most unexpectedly, enters, leading Cecil by the hand. He draws her gently forward, until they both stand before the discomfited Major.

" Major Jervis won't believe you are going to be married," says Ronnie, with a little laugh.

" Oh, yes, I am ! Am I not, Cecil ? " asks Duke, glancing down lovingly at his betrothed, who laughs a little too and blushes deeply.

" You will come to their wedding, won't you, Major ? " asks Ronnie, mischievously.

The Major, though overpowered by numbers, still lets his evil humour have full sway.

" With pleasure," he replies, with an ill grace. And then, maliciously, " Only sorry I can't come to yours too, Miss Ronnie."

" Don't be sorry another instant, Major," says Lord Errington, pleasantly ; he has come up to them unnoticed by Jervis. " Ronnie and I will be only too glad if you will promise to dance at our wedding also. It will be quite simple, you know, as we all intend to be married on the same day from the same house."

" Very charming arrangement, I'm sure ! " returns the defeated Major. " It would be quite superfluous to offer you my congratulations. You all know exactly how I feel towards you."

He smiles grimly as he says this.

" Yes, we all know that," rejoins Errington, with emphasis.

" Dear me ! " says the Major, pulling out his watch. " It grows very late. I shall miss the up-train if I don't make haste. Good-bye, good-bye ! "

"Stay and sleep at the Court to-night," says Craven, hospit·ably, if a trifle coldly.

"No, thank you—no. I am bound to be in town to-night."

"Why, where are you going in such hot haste?" asks Craven, curiously.

" I'm—I'm going abroad !" declares the Major, desperately; after which he shuffles out of the room, and is lost to their sight for many a day.

"Poor Major !" says Cecil. "How disconcerted he looked ! I know he deserved anything bad, but I couldn't help feeling sorry for him."

" He is unworthy of your pity," answers Craven, drawing her away from the others into the deep embrasure of the window. " Did he not very nearly take you from me ? "

" Would that have been such a terrible thing ?" she asks, with an upward glance, and a very pardonable touch of coquetry.

" Cecil, what a question ! " he returns, reproachfully.

" I think you put it wrongly," says Cissy, softly. " I think he meant to take you from me."

" Would that have been such a terrible thing ? " he asks, in his turn, with a little smile.

" I don't know. Would it ? " she questions, tremulously.

" My love — my life — it would have been death ! " says Craven, with passionate earnestness. Turning to her, he takes her into his arms and holds her close clasped against his heart, where indeed her proper home most surely is.

MOONSHINE AND MARGUERITES.

CHAPTER I.

"MY LOVE SHE'S BUT A LASSIE YET."

"It's a tremendously good thing for her," says Mr. Wilding. "She's got the match of the season. There she is, standing over there. Do you see? Little girl in white, with daisies all over her."

"Eh? Oh, yes," says Sir George, looking in quite the contrary direction at an overblown young thing of thirty or thereabouts—not to be uncharitable.

"Not there, my dear fellow. *There!*"

"Eh? Oh, yes, of course," says Sir George, in exactly the same tone. "Why, she's a child!"

"Barely seventeen. But her people put her up first chance on account of her remarkably fine eyes and the six sisters yet to come. Ponsonby's got a lot of money, and *looks* as if he adores her."

"He *does*," says Sir George, staring at the young beauty's present partner—a stalwart Mephistopheles, who is decidedly *épris* with her; "but she don't *look* as if she adored *him*—eh?"

"*That* isn't her *fiancée*. He is lounging against the doorway on your right, talking to that tall dark girl in yellow—Miss Nugent."

"Why on earth can't he talk to his *own* girl?" says Sir George, testily, who is growing angry at his many mistakes.

Mr. Wilding laughs. " Miss Nugent was very near being that," he says. " She is his cousin, an heiress in her own right, and, I dare say, the girl he *would* have. married but for the *beaux yeux* of that little baby over there. The Ponsonbys had it all arranged. It's just another case of 'man proposes,' you know."

" You haven't told me the baby's name," says Sir George, who has never taken his eyes off her since first they fell on her.

" Disney—Alys Disney."

" Her costume suits her. Is she a Marguerite ? "

" Not Goethe's Marguerite," says Wilding, coldly and with a half-frown.

" I meant nothing half so indelicate, believe me," says Sir George, with an amused smile : " you need not ruffle your feathers like that. I meant only one of those charming, innocent field-flowers one sees sometimes in—er—Birket Foster's pictures, and that. I'm told they grow in meadows ; but I never saw a meadow : beastly bumpkins always cut 'em down before one can get to the country. There's something—er —very special about her mouth, isn't there—eh ? "

" I really don't know," says Mr. Wilding. " Come into the supper-room and have something. I feel awfully used up."

Taking forcible possession of the little baronet, he pilots him successfully through massive dowagers and languishing wall-flowers to the room beyond without making a mistake. Mr. Wilding is a young man of much merit, whose manner ladies call "invaluable" and girls "charming." By these last he is regarded as a general favourite—principally, perhaps, because, though now twenty-nine, he has never yet selected from among them a *particular* favourite. He is still all their own, and belongs to everybody because he belongs to nobody.

By the time he and his companion have gained the happy land of chicken and champagne, it occurs to Sir George Grande that he had not wanted to come.

" I wish you hadn't shown such senseless haste," he says.

"I hadn't half done looking at that little girl in the daisies. She's pretty."

"Don't give yourself airs," says Wilding. "Pretty! She's *the* new Beauty! with a great big B. Don't make a mistake about it. You are to rave whenever you hear her name mentioned, or they will argue you unknown."

"I wish they would," says Sir George, with a faint grimace. "I've put in my year abroad, like a good little boy; but the welcome accorded me by the duchess on my return could hardly be called scorching."

"One's own people are always the hardest on one's little peccadilloes," says Mr. Wilding, staring at his glass.

"I call it real nasty of her, anyway," says Sir George, "considering it was to please her I cleared out and lost my season last year."

"Well, you know you *had* been going it a bit," says Wilding, apologetically. "Two fortunes, by Jove! before you were twenty-six; and—and that other little affair. But I think, now your banishment is at an end, open censure should be at an end too. I gave your sister credit for better feeling."

"She's one of the goody-goodies. Never expect anything from them but a scandal in the long run. And when they do give place to the devil, it is with a vengeance. Charity, because it is the greatest, is the rarest of all virtues, and the duchess lacks it. However, I am independent of her and all since I came in for the Trevor estates. I wonder how long this third fortune will last me! Eh, Wilding? Never mind; let's talk about that pretty child upstairs. Know her?"

"She is my cousin," says Wilding.

"Then she is 'a dangerous thing,' as some old rhyme says— and justly so in this case, I should say; though I believe *you* are fire-proof. Take me back to the ball-room and introduce me to her."

"You have proved yourself anything but fire-proof, and she is a forbidden sweet," says Wilding. "Better keep your fingers out of the blaze."

"But, alas! she is another's, and she never can be mine! that is what you mean—eh?" says Sir George, laughing with exceeding light-heartedness. "Well, I'll risk even that; and if I fall beneath her chariot-wheels, my blood be on my own head."

Still Mr. Wilding palpably hesitates.

"Not moral enough for sweet seventeen; is *that* it?" says his friend, with a very faint sneer. "Don't try to disguise the fact, old man: one can read it on your ingenuous countenance. You will never reach the wool-sack, Wilding, if you give way to your emotions like this."

"You go something beyond the mark," says Wilding, reflectively.

"Do I? I am willing—nay, *anxious*—to believe you. Make me known to your cousin, then. I swear"—half mockingly—"I will be as good as gold in her sainted presence, and never once cease to remember that she has been labelled as 'a *good* man's bride.'"

"Come, then. A promise is a promise," says Wilding.

And presently they find themselves face to face with Miss Disney and her intended, in a small conservatory, and Sir George has the pleasure of knowing that Miss Disney is now in full possession of the fact that his name is Grande.

He has taken her card, and now says, "May I?" standing before her with pencil uplifted, waiting her permission to engrave his name thereon.

"With pleasure," says Miss Disney courteously, but indifferently. With the young, however, it is as natural to smile as to breathe: so she smiles at him.

Having made his own of this careless concession on her part, Sir George lets his eyes wander back again to her programme. "It sounds incredible," he says at length, "but it seems as if you are disengaged for *this* dance. I can see no name before it. If so, may I have it?"

"*Am* I disengaged?—then yes," returns she, thoughtlessly.

"You are engaged to *me* for the next," interferes Ponsonby

at this moment, in a dull but hurried tone which he strives hard to relieve from a suspicion of offence.

"Yes? Is it? But of *course*. I quite forgot. The next, then, Sir George, for which I am free, which will be the fourteenth—if we stay so long. You see," bending slightly toward him with a childish, restless movement, " I *never* put down Mr. Ponsonby's name.

" I quite understand," says Sir George, with a gesture of the hand and a smile. And then the interview is over, and Miss Disney is in her lover's arms, waltzing languidly to the strains of the band sent down to the castle from town.

He cuts the dance somewhat short, and draws her, not unwillingly, to the open window of a room that, leading to the balcony, is suggestive of an easy descent by stone steps to the *pleasaunce* beneath.

Into the night and into the slumberous garden he leads her, where mignonette and late sweet roses give forth unconscious perfume to the drowsy air.

A pale young moon is hanging in the heavens above, her beams falling tenderly upon the sleeping earth. Ever and anon a fleecy cloud glides over her, threatening to blot her from her place ; but again, ere doubt has time for growth, it hurries on, and—

> Melting like a wreath of snow, it hangs
> In folds of wavy silver round, and clothes
> The orb with richer beauties than her own,—
> Then, passing, leaves her in her light serene.

"Do you feel the softness of the air ?" says the girl, turning to him with a touch of impulsive gladness in her tone. " I like a garden at midnight, and I like the country better than the town. The season wearied me. It was always the same. Monotony, some say, belongs altogether to fields and woods and streams; but it is not really so. Here everything speaks to me ; it is only those others who cannot understand—— " Here she checks herself, as though some sudden recollection returns to her. " Are you laughing at me ?" she says. " I am, I *know*, in one of the moods auntie calls funny. Well, even if you do smile at my folly, I sha'n't mind *you*. Look at these garden-marguerites; are they not lovely in the moonlight? Wait. Let me try your fortune with one." She plucks it petal by petal, murmuring, as she does so, the old refrain, " He loves me—a little—indifferently—passionately—not at all." As the last leaf comes, it brings her "indifferently." "Oh, you bad boy!" she says; "and after all your protestations."

" It is a lying prophet," says Ponsonby, who is a tall grave young man of twenty-seven, with very loving grey eyes, sensitive lips, and an earnest expression. He looks decidedly older than he is, whilst she, who is only seventeen, looks decidedly younger.

" Well, it is only natural you should make out a good story for yourself," she says, with a mischievous glance. " Now to see how *she* regards *you*." She picks another marguerite from the group near her as she speaks, and as she flings its mutilated remains away, says gaily, " She loves you."

" There ! that is more than you deserve : you have got the best assurance of all, to *my* thinking. ' Passionately ' is such rubbish. Don't you think so ? "

" I am not sure," says Mr. Ponsonby, with his eyes on hers.

" No ? Well, I hope you don't love *me* passionately, because I should hate it. There is such a pretence about it. It is mere sound. One can't pass perfection, you know. I know *I* couldn't love any one to distraction, as they call it, to save my life. Oh, *listen* to that nightingale ! " She turns from him and gazes with eager eyes in the direction whence comes that heavenly music, while her lover gazes at her with eyes into which a certain sadness has fallen.

There she stands, a flower among her fellows, radiant, beautiful, in the clear light of the pure moon—such a child !— with her little curly head and smiling lips and large, dewy eyes. Already where are her thoughts? flying—flying ever, now to sweet Philomel, now perchance to——

She has given herself to him, but is she *really* his? The body minus the soul is but a sorry bargain, and whether he has ever honestly touched her heart has been a question with the young man ever since that first day when she promised to be his.

"Your cousin looks as if *she* could," she says, turning, not so much suddenly as with a certain sense of vitality, toward him.

"Could what?"—with a start.

"Love passionately. Katherine Nugent, I mean."

"Oh! Do you think she could?" His manner is still a little vague.

"Yes. Do you know, Frank," coming a little nearer to him, "sometimes I have thought she is in love with *you?* '

"Nonsense, darling!"

"I *have* thought it. *Is* it nonsense?"

"Utter. If you were right, you must confess she has a singular way of showing her attachment. Only yesterday," with a light laugh, "something cutting in her manner made me tell myself I was an object of positive aversion to her."

"Still, I *thought* it," says Alys, with all a child's wilful persistence. "But, of course, I was wrong." Then, "*Why* didn't *you* fall in love with *her?*"

"Because you came to me."

"Was that your only reason? See, now, what mischief I have done. She would have suited you better than I shall."

"That is the one point on which I will not give in to you."

"She is clever, and handsome, and——"

"Dear heart, you are all that, and a thousand other things besides."

"A thousand bad things, I dare say; whereas she—she seems to lack nothing."

"Beyond the crowning imperfection that she is not—*you !*"

"And yet——" She pauses, and casts at him a glance swift but anxious from under her long lashes. "Sometimes I vex you, don't I?" she says, dropping her lids again.

"No——" he is beginning, but she stops him with a merry little gesture.

" Let us have the whole truth, and nothing but it," she says, with a charming smile. "You were angry with me only twenty minutes ago."

"When, my dearest ? "

"When I forgot my dance—*this* dance—with you ; and again when I promised Sir George Grande one later on. Deny it if you dare."

" How did you know that ? "

"Your eyes told me. Ah !"—laughing softly—" I can see things sometimes."

"You are a little witch. I confess all. Your forgetting grieved me sorely; but, besides that, I didn't like you to dance with Sir George."

" But why ? "

" For many reasons—— " He hesitates. Why raise un-lovely thoughts in the mind of this tender child ?

" He looks as if he could be amusing," says she, carelessly ; "and he is staying here with us, you know. He came this morning, and will be here all the week. And auntie says Lady Fanny Davenport is very anxious to marry him."

" Is she ? Well, never mind. Let us forget him. *You* are going to marry me, are you not ? And soon, darling ? "

" I think so," says Miss Disney, with the utmost serenity. " Mamma says Maudie can't come out until I am got out of the way : so it is unfair to her to delay *too* long. And it is all the same to you, I suppose, isn't it ? "—anxiously.

The humour of this naïve remark might have struck the young man but for something else that strikes him still more keenly, and that has *no* humour in it : a shade saddens his face.

" Is it to please Maudie or me you give so ready a con-sent ? " he says, a tinge of bitterness in his tone. It may be that the girl marks it and resents it. At least she turns from him with a gesture that is petulant.

" Perhaps to please myself more than either," she says ; and, though the words might be made to convey a compliment, the delivery of them spoils the effect.

"You love me?" asks Ponsonby, suddenly turning to her and taking her hand.

" Still a sceptic ?   Has not this mystic flower assured you of my truth ? " nodding her small head at the marguerites hard by.   "*I* should be the one to doubt, considering the dreadful tale it told me !"

" If ever," says Ponsonby, drawing her close to him, " you should feel that the—the affection you now bear me is less than you imagined it, and that you could "—growing very pale—"give your heart more entirely to another, promise me you will let me know of it in some way, by some word, or sign, or token."

" I couldn't promise to be as rude as that," returns she, mischievously.

" Be serious for once," entreats he.   Something in his tone touches her.   The smile fades from her lips, leaving only a certain sweet reflection of it behind.   Coming closer to him, she lifts one bare round arm and with very tender little fingers smoothes back the hair from his brow.

"There is no need for me to make such a promise," she says, " because I shall never have to tell you *that.*"

"Nevertheless, promise !"

" 'A wilful man must have his way.' You have my promise, then; but not in words shall I redeem it. When I have learned to hate you, I will send you one of *these*"—again pulling a marguerite from the tall bunch growing near—" with 'not at all ' as its last petal.   Poor flower !" compassionately apostrophizing it, "what a sad mission I should send it on ! Do you know, I never invoked my fortune with one of these until I tried it to-night with you ?"

"I am glad of that ; and "—eagerly—"you never will again, will you ?"

"Why, how *can* I now ? " says Miss Disney, with uplifted

brows. "My fortune is told: *you* are it. How funny that sounds ! it puts you in the neuter gender at once !"

"I sha'n't see you again for a week," says Ponsonby, suddenly. "I go to town by the early train. You will not forget me during my absence ? "

"No. Take this with *you*, to remind you of *me*, every moment, until we meet again "—she places the marguerite in his coat as she speaks—"and, when you look at it, remember the message it brought you," she says, coquettishly.

"For that reason its whole tribe shall be sacred to me for evermore," says Ponsonby, with a smile that lights his face into actual beauty.

CHAPTER II.

"WHOSE TONGUE OUTVENOMS ALL THE WORMS OF NILE."

IT is mid-day, and all the world is mad and merry with excess of sunshine and the myriad harmonies of nature's gigantic choir. Even through the carefully-closed curtains of Indian muslin that shade the morning-room at Moorlands, great Sol is penetrating, rendering the air hot and languorous.

"I have come to a conclusion," says Miss Disney, suddenly, sinking back in her huge arm-chair, that might easily entomb her, and flinging her arms with lazy grace above her head.

"Yes ?" The answer, which is half a question, comes in low soft accents across the misty, hazy heat that fills the room, yet with a suspicion of veiled insolence about it. It comes from a beautiful mouth, however, and Katherine Nugent, as she utters the unpleasing monosyllable, turns calm, dark eyes upon her cousin's *fiancée*.

The *fiancée* moves restlessly, and a faint colour creeps into her *mignonne* face.

"I suppose," she says, with a rather shy laugh, "that a

conclusion coming from me (involving, as it must, some thought) may be regarded in the light of an eighth wonder. Is that what your tone meant ?"

"And the conclusion?" asks Katherine, tranquilly, and with all the air of one who has heard nothing of the foregoing protest.

"Is—that to-night will never come. Was there ever such a long, long day ?"

"You miss Frank"—shortly.

"No: do I? Perhaps so. I am not sure. I was not thinking of him."

"Yet he is a man to make himself remembered even when out of sight."

"You think so ?"

"I know it."

"Katherine," says the younger girl, suddenly, "how often you get me to speak of Frank ! Sometimes I have thought— but of course it was only fancy. You never *did* care for him in *that way*, did you ? "

"The way *you* care for him ? Never."

"I am so glad I asked you, now. If you had given me a different answer it would have made me very unhappy."

"That is a very kindly speech. But you need suffer no generous pangs of regret for me. Frank is as little to me as I am—to him." She shades her eyes with her hand for a moment, perhaps to conceal a smile, for presently she breaks into a low laugh, suggestive of amusement to her listener. "What put the silly thought into your head ? " she asks.

"I hardly know."

"Somebody must have done it." Again there is the carelessly-veiled insolence of tone, the contemptuous disbelief in her companion's sagacity or penetration.

"Somebody, I dare say," says the girl, musingly. "Perhaps——" she pauses.

"Was it *he* ?" The words come from her with exceeding sharpness, as though forced to her lips by some terrible thought that has just pierced her brain and brought with it an agony too keen to be silently endured.

"Oh, no!"

"You are *sure?*"—still fiercely, with pale lips, and dark eyes alight with passionate fear.

"You will see how sure, when I tell you that Frank believes you positively dislike him. He told me so last night. Now"—laughing—"I think he was right. How angry your eyes have grown at the bare mention of his name!"

"Ah!" says Miss Nugent. It is a sigh of relief that escapes her. She leans back in her chair, and a great wave of colour sweeps over her white face. She unfurls her huge black fan with a little crashing noise.

"You haven't told me how you enjoyed last night," she says quickly, as a means of covering her confusion.

"*So* much!" says the young girl, smiling, and throwing some animation into her air.

"I saw you dancing rather frequently with Sir George Grande toward the close of the evening."

"Twice I danced with him, I think. Do you know, I quite like him, though Frank doesn't?"

"Men like Frank, who have been through a good deal, are always inclined to be jealous. Experience has taught them how transient a love-affair *may* be."

"You mean"—emotionally—"that Frank has loved so often that——"

"I mean nothing. There is really no occasion for any excitement. But of course you will understand that a man cannot grow to Frank's age without having played with fire. There is nothing to render you uneasy in anything I have said."

"I am not uneasy,"—flushing warmly.

"No? But of course not. There is really nothing in it."

"I know that," says the girl, loyally, yet even as she says it her heart grows heavier within her. There *is* really nothing in it; but *why* had he *told* her she was his first and only love? Perhaps men always said that to the object of their latest fancy.

"Once last night when you were dancing with Frank," she says, turning to Miss Nugent, and recovering her self-possession by an effort, "I looked at you, and both you and he were looking at me. Was he talking of me then?"

"Does he ever talk of anything else? A man *freshly* in love is the most selfish thing on earth. Later on they grow more considerate, and can afford to forget the beloved angel now and then."

"Can they?"—wistfully. Will Frank indeed learn to forget her at times?

"Yes. What were we saying just then? You asked me if he was talking of you? Yes, entirely. He was telling me of something you had said—I forget what now—and he was laughing. He called you 'such a child,' I remember. It was some silly little trifle, amusing because of its crudity. He is very devoted to you."

Again the sting is in her tone. It makes the girl's lips quiver and brings the light of rebellion to her beautiful eyes.

"At seventeen one is not a child. You make me think he spoke of me as a doll, a baby, a mere plaything."

"Oh, *no!* Merely as a *very* young girl. You *are* young to *him*, you know : he is quite ten years your senior."

"The advantage there is on my side, surely,"—haughtily. "If *I* don't mind it, he need not."

"Quite so. I think every woman should be ten years or so younger than her husband," says Katherine, who is just six months younger than Ponsonby. "And as for him, I *know* he prefers extreme youth. It is easier to mould and form."

She closes her fan with another click, drops it languidly into her lap, and smiles faintly.

"'To mould'!" The girl's tone has grown strangely cold and calm. "I am to be educated to his will, you mean?"

"Well, that was what he said——"

"*Said?*"

"My dear child, I can't remember the exact words, but he told me last night he had gained a treasure—one of those rare beings to whom the world is unknown. He dreaded no rival, he said, because—I really forget the ‘because,’ but it was something to the effect that, as you had not dreamed of lovers until he came on the scene, they were not necessary to you, and all that. I told him not to be too certain ”—laughing— “ but he quite scoffed at the thought that you could prefer any one to his royal highness. After all, I doubt if it is a wise thing to let a man feel *too* sure of one.”

“ Is *that* how he talks of me to you? ” says Alys, with a glance of cold disdain from her heavily-fringed eyes. To really know any one is difficult ; and to view one’s dearest friend in a different light is to regard him as a stranger. “ We have been prosing a good deal, have we not? I am afraid I have made the day even duller for you than it really is.”

“ Perhaps it is my fault,” says Miss Nugent, politely.

“ Impossible ! You have tried your best to enliven me, and if you have failed it is *my* fault. It is the heat, I suppose. Who could have believed in so hot a sun in September ? ”

Miss Nugent, as though scenting sarcasm in this speech, glances at her sharply ; but the girl has risen and has averted her face, and, after a languid attempt at further conversation, quits the room.

When the men come in from shooting, however, she reappears in a charming pale-pink tea-gown, and as Sir George flings himself upon the lounge close beside her she turns to him with new graciousness, and lets her lovely eyes smile into his, and draws away her skirts that he may nestle even nearer to her.

“ She is rehearsing her new *rôle*,” says Katherine Nugent, taking in all this from afar, with a curl of her lips, and a shrug of her handsome shoulders, and a most unlovely smile of devilish gratification.

CHAPTER III.

"LOVE! THOU ART CRUEL!"

AT the end of the third day Sir George Grande is as much in love with Miss Disney as his nature will permit. At the end of the week, and when the night is come that is to see the return of Mr. Ponsonby, he has overstepped that limit, and is making an open ass of himself about the youthful beauty—*not* without encouragement! For Mademoiselle l'Ingénue during these seven days has developed into a subdued but dangerous coquette.

Ponsonby, who has arrived barely in time to change his clothes for dinner (but who has been nevertheless bitterly disappointed that no gracious childish form has met him on his arrival to bid him welcome), coming into the drawing-room twenty-five minutes past seven, is somewhat taken aback by the tableau that there presents itself to him.

Upon a couch, half shrouded by the lace curtains of the window near it from public view, sits his promised wife, looking lovely as a dream, in Indian muslin and filmy laces, Sir George Grande beside her. The latter is stooping forward, gazing intently into her eyes. Upon every line of his good-looking face hopeless infatuation is written.

Ponsonby, advancing slowly as one walking in his sleep, knocks inadvertently against a spider-legged chair and sends it to the ground with some noise.

Miss Disney starts, looks round, and, seeing who it is who is coming toward them, colours deeply. It is only a momentary emotion, however, and, conquering it, she rises swiftly, but with inherent grace, from her seat, and goes to meet him. Her self-possession is complete.

" You have come ? " she says, with a smile most lovely, but studiously indifferent.

" Yes." If his life depended upon it, Ponsonby could say

no more. He is feeling stunned, bewildered, lost! Here is this girl, whom he had left believing her his own, standing before him now in all her radiant beauty, clothed in careless smiles, and with a touch of something new (is it triumph?) upon her parted lips. He turns away, sick at heart.

Finding her alone later on in the evening, he says quietly, "You and Sir George seem to be quite good friends."

"I like him very much," she says, gently enough, but with a grain of defiance in her tone which he is not slow to mark.

" *That* I can see for myself," he says, with a rather forced smile. "What an atom out of eternity is a bare week! and yet——"

"You found it short, then?"—glancing at him with a half-frown.

"Never mind me," he says, impatiently. "What of *you* ?"

"Why should *I* submit to an examination from which *you* shrink ? " retorts she with some *hauteur*, throwing up her dainty head, and making a smile from Lady Newport, who is sitting directly opposite, an excuse for leaving him.

"What a heavenly night ! " says Miss Nugent suddenly, as, drawing back the curtains, she lets a rush of glorious moonlight flood the room. "And the air—how soft and warm ! Why not come into the gardens and enjoy it, as we have done every night for the past week ? You and Sir George, Alys, used to be the first to propose it. Now"—smiling—"you basely throw the responsibility upon my shoulders."

" Far be it from us," says Sir George, lightly. "Class us not among the backsliders. There is something about Miss Disney that always suggests to me a kinship with Diana ; not for one moment, therefore, would she, I feel convinced, dream of casting a slight upon her illustrious relative. You will come and pay your accustomed court to her, will you not, Miss Disney ? "

For a moment she hesitates ; almost a refusal is on her lips, when her eyes chance to fall on Ponsonby's. In his there is open though unconscious rebuke, and it turns the scale in Sir George's favour.

"Come," she says, holding out her hand to him with a sweet smile prettily tinged with coquetry, and together they step lightly from the drawing-room to the balcony, and from thence to the gardens—lit by the "wandering moon" to a transparent brilliancy—that lie beneath, wrapt in sleep. The others follow.

Ponsonby, as though compelled thereto by some iron demon, moves in their train, speaking such idle trash as society demands, even from the heavy-hearted to Katherine Nugent. But his whole soul is centred on the form of the little wilful girl flitting before him, now nearer, now a long way off, now fading away altogether in the embrace of some amorous shadow, only to reappear again in a patch of purest moonlight.

At last he really loses sight of her. Two or three people coming up to Katherine engross her in some merry argument and will not let her go. Glad at heart at this chance of being once more alone, Ponsonby moves away from the group, stepping out from it silently.

Seeing this, Katherine says gently but hastily, "Go and see the eastern end of the gardens, Frank : it will reward you; it is lovely in this light. You know it?—that little bit apart, where the old statue of Apollo stands half shrouded in ivy?"

Does he know it? How well he remembers how he stood there with *her* a week ago and had a sweet but lying tale told him by a marguerite ! No, he will *not* go there again ! And yet some fascination draws him through the scented dews and glittering beams to the spot where, seven days ago, he had at least been happy in the thought that he was without a rival ; and now——

Now ! He had reached Apollo's shrine with downcast eyes ; but the sound of voices near compels him to lift his head. As he does so, he starts, and turns deadly pale. There, in her clinging white gown, scarcely less fair than the moonbeams that riot round her, stands the girl he loves, a freshly-plucked marguerite in her hand, and beside her Sir George Grande.

Is it a ray from her high-born kinswoman, or what is it, that makes her appear so pale? She is plucking the flower, petal by petal, and once again the old-world refrain comes to Ponsonby across the fragrant sward, borne upon the wings of the night-wind, " She loves you a little,—indifferently,—passionately——"

"Ah! cruel flower! why will it not stop there?" says Sir George, sentimentally.

At this moment the hand that holds the flower droops, and the girl, raising her head, looks calmly and defiantly into Ponsonby's eyes. There is no surprise in her glance, no shrinking: it is as if she had known he was there even before she looked.

Thus for an indefinable period they gaze at each other, and then he lowers his eyes, and turning, walks slowly away.

"That was Ponsonby," says Sir George, screwing his glass into his best eye the better to discern the retreating figure.

"I know it."

"Ah! you saw him before I did?"

"I saw him as he came."

"Yes?"—airily,—"you would, you know: there's such a lot of him. Modern Hercules, and all that sort of thing. Good fellow, Ponsonby, though. Capital fellow, don't you think,—eh? but a trifle dreary. Looks as if he has the tooth-ache just now, don't he?"

"No, he '*don't*'!" says Miss Disney, answering him in his own sweet English, but with a sudden and unexpected change of tone—from lively to severe.

"Very good, then: he *don't*," replies Sir George, totally unabashed. "Let's forget him. I've set my heart on hearing my fortune told me to-night by you, and beneath these mystic moonbeams, and as yet you have only got half-way. Try again."

"No,—*never* again!" cries she passionately, crushing the poor flower in her slender grasp and flinging it far from her. There is such startling vehemence in both her tone and gesture that Sir George loses his glass and his self-possession simultaneously. Before he can recover either, she has run away from him, and is lost among the shadows that lie lurking in the secret places of the laurels.

"By Jove! what a small tornado!" says the baronet, staring after her with uplifted brows. "A good deal of temper, no doubt, but all round—charming!"

Panting,—hopelessly out of breath,—Miss Disney gains her chamber and locks her door. Whilst running in, she has made up her mind she will not appear below again to-night. She is tired,—yes, yes; she will go to bed. With hurried fingers (as though action is necessary to her in her frame of mind) she undresses herself, says her prayers, looks into her Bible (a very little look to-night, I am afraid), and finally, finding herself standing in her dainty night-gown, goes up to a tall cheval-glass in the corner of the room and gazes at her own lovely image therein.

Her cheeks are still flushed by her run; her lips are red and parted, her soft eyes full of a defiance that is most foreign to them.

"At last I have shown him I am not a mere baby, to be moulded as he wills, and that a rival is not an actual impossibility," says this silly child to herself; all the while her heart is breaking with suppressed pain, and a wild desire to run to "him" and throw herself into his arms and confess to him how eagerly she longs to be friends with him again.

Yet bravely she keeps back the emotion that threatens to overpower her, and, still encouraging vengeful thoughts, slips into her lavender-scented sheets—a thing as white as they.

CHAPTER IV.

"TREASON DOTH NEVER PROSPER."

BUT calm sleep, and morning, bring a more heavenly frame of mind. The extreme nervousness she feels at the thought of being obliged to meet him soon again face to face, and the painfully distant greeting accorded to her by him when they do meet at breakfast-time, both combined, reduce Miss Disney to a state bordering on tears and penitence.

Yet luncheon and dinner-hours arrive without action of any sort having been taken ; and it is only when the first *entrée* has gone round (which, though excellent, has been discovered by her to be utterly tasteless) that a way of escape occurs to her.

To tell him in simple English that she is sorry has long been found to be out of the question ; but there is another very graceful little plan that suggests itself to her, and is carried *nem. con.*, and passes from a thought into a resolution.

That little episode last night he will surely forgive her. He must have *felt* she only did it through childish spleen. She will send him a carefully selected marguerite that will finish with "she loves you."

Going to her room directly she gets out of the dining-room, she selects from among a large bunch of flowers upon her table a giant daisy, and counts it eagerly. Plucking off those that mar her design, she leaves it with the desired reading for the last petal, and then goes slowly downstairs again. But at the last step her courage fails her. He has looked so cold, so unloving, all day, that she dares not give it to him herself. Even as she hesitates with this new trouble at her heart, Katherine Nugent crosses the hall below her.

In a flash it occurs to her that *here* is a way out of her difficulty. "Katherine !" she calls, softly. "Katherine !"

" Well ? " says Miss Nugent, pausing.

" I want "—hurriedly—" to *tell* you something—to *ask* you to do me a great favour. You are *his* cousin and *my* friend, are you not ? And—and I *must* speak to somebody, and auntie is so impossible."

"Well?" says Miss Nugent again.

"Will you listen to me for a little while ?"

"Certainly." The word is uttered with studious politeness. "What is it ? "

What it is—the primary cause of all the disturbance, the enlargement of the quarrel, and the means to be now employed with a view to restoring the old harmony existing between them —is soon laid bare to Miss Nugent.

"And now I want Frank to know it was all a mistake, and that I still love him dearly—*dearly*. You know I do."

"I know nothing," says Miss Nugent, stonily. "Well, go on."

"He once called this flower *sacred* to *us*—for—for a certain reason," goes on Alys tremulously, her eyes bent sadly upon the marguerite in her hand. "And I thought if I sent him one with 'she loves you' coming on the last petal it would tell him everything. Would it not?"—wistfully.

"You know him so much better than I do that you can answer that question more satisfactorily for yourself. He is in the billiard-room. Are you going there now to give it to him?"

"I—I *can't*," says the girl, with a sudden accession of shyness, colouring violently. "Katherine,"—desperately—"will *you* give it to him for me?"

"Me! You ask *me!*" says Katherine, growing deadly pale and recoiling from her.

"If you will, dearest," says the girl, timidly.

"Ask *any* one but me," says Miss Nugent in a low but vehement tone, throwing out her hands with a passionate gesture. Then, the necessity for composure recurring to her, she makes a supreme effort, and in some measure regains calmness. "Take it yourself," she says, slowly ; but her tone is harsh and strained. As yet she cannot altogether command herself.

"I—I should be ashamed to go to him now," says the young girl, with a blush and an abashed laugh. "Katherine, *do* help me. He is in the billiard-room : take him this flower, and tell him I shall be in the library in five minutes. I am going there now."

"You persist in asking me to do this?" says Miss Nugent in a strange tone.

"I don't *insist*,"—gently—"I only entreat you. There, go,

like a dear girl ; and—and be sure you take the flower with great care, as the loss of a petal would be fatal. You think me foolish, don't you ? " she says, blushing again as she misconstrues the fixed expression on her companion's features.

"I think you are mad," says Katherine, slówly. "Give me the flower, then. I will take it—if I can." The last words, uttered in a falling tone, are unheard by Alys as she moves away to the library, there to wait with beating heart the coming and the pardon of her lover.

Left alone in the large, hall, Katherine stands motionless, staring vacantly at the pale marguerite. There appears to be in it some horrible fascination for her. Her eyes are riveted upon it; her lips twitch; slowly (as though deterred by some hidden power) her other hand creeps toward it.

Almost as she touches it she pauses, and a shudder passes over her. With a heavy sigh that is almost a sob, she resolutely throws up her head, thus withdrawing her eyes from the flower, and at the same time places the hand that holds it behind her back, as though to remove it from her gaze.

A struggle short but sharp goes on within her. So powerful is it that her whole frame trembles beneath it. Then a face, childish, trusting, pleading, rises before her, and she moves with hurried footsteps in the direction of the billiard-room, still with the flower hidden from her view. But, almost as she turns the handle of the door, a voice from within, reaching her, kills the good so lately born. It brings before her another face,—the face of the man she loves passionately though hopelessly,—and, with a groan, she falls back from the door, and, her nerves ceasing to be under her control, the arm so persistently heretofore kept behind her falls again into its usual position, so bringing her eyes once more on the fatal flower.

Is *she* to be the one to give this baby to his arms ?—she, whose vaguest thought of him contains more passion than the warmest this petulant child has ever known? Again the half-shy, half-tender, girlish face comes before her; but this time she shakes the apparition from her with a frown. Pshaw! she would forget in a month this mawkish love of hers, and would be ready to love again in her poor fashion. And yet—there was something in those large blue eyes that——

She hesitates for one heaven-born moment, and then is lost.

Deliberately plucking one white petal from the marguerite, she opens the door of the billiard-room, and, with a smile and a calm word or two to some man who addresses her, moves with languid grace to where Ponsonby is standing somewhat apart from the others.

"Do you remember that book of James's we were discussing last night?" she says. "I can't think where I put it. Have you any idea?"

"I think you took it upstairs with you."

"Oh, did I? I dare say. It is just the most possible places one never searches. Thank you. The fact of not being able to get it has made me long for it with the greater intensity for the last hour." She turns, as if to go away, then turns back again, as though in sudden remembrance of some trivial thing. "I had nearly forgotten," she says, carelessly, "but your little *fiancée* asked me to give you this as I met her on my way here just now." She holds out to him, as she says this, the frail blossom in her hand, now drooping as though sad at heart because of the treachery of which it is the unwilling agent.

"From Alys?" says Ponsonby, a flush born of emotion darkening his face in spite of his desperate resolve to show none.

"Yes. She desired me also to tell you she would be in the library any time from this. A lover's tryst,"—with a light laugh.—"To take my revenge *now*, Captain Sartoris? Well, I don't mind. Sir George to play with me against you and Lady Newport? Charming! Consider yourselves beaten before you begin. I feel that victory rests with me to-night."

There is an exultant ring in her voice as she takes up her cue with a hand steady as marble, and as cold. It is the hand that a moment since held the mutilated marguerite.

The flush has died from Ponsonby's face, leaving only a deathly pallor in its place, and a smile replete with scorn for his own weakness. In eager, hopeful anticipation he had plucked the petals one by one from the flower sent by the love he now deems false, only to find the bitter assurance that she loves him " not at all " at its end.

How had it ever come to pass that he had given the entire happiness of his life into the keeping of this girl, who as the hour changed went with it and in a few short days had discovered a new lover ? That she should have chosen a marguerite, the flower he had consecrated as sacred to her and him, as a means of conveying to him her altered sentiments, has hurt him in a terribly cruel manner. There is a lack of refinement in it that strikes a chill to his heart.

Still holding the flower in his hand, he crosses the billiard-room to the door, as blind to Katherine Nugent's keen glance as he is deaf to Lady Newport's honeyed speech, and goes straight to the library, where, by her own word, " *she* " is awaiting him to have her liberty restored to her. Surely it is not *his* part to delay the restoration.

Entering the library, he walks like one in a dream to the upper end of it, where, near the fireplace, Miss Disney is standing with a beating heart and all her soul in her eyes.

But her eyes grow dim and her heart dies within her as she marks the expression of his face, and as he draws even nearer she palpably shrinks from him. To him this shrinking is a fresh proof of her inconstancy. " There is still some grace left in her, some pity for the forlorn wretch she has betrayed," he tells himself grimly, mistaking her nervousness for remorse.

" I have come to you at your own request," he says, sternly. " Though I think this appointment—*made by you*—is a mistake. It is useless to talk of even a *friendly* feeling between us again, after all that has come and gone. There is nothing I so keenly desire as a formal separation between us."

Stunned, bewildered, she gazes at him in a speechless astonishment too fresh as yet for grief.

"I have come to set you finally free," he goes on. "I say nothing. I do not accuse you ; and it is too late, we *both* know, for hope or expostulation of any kind. It is impossible to misunderstand *that*, at least. I have now to return you *this* "— laying the innocent instrument of their undoing upon the table near her—"and *this*." By its side he lays a faded bit of nature's handiwork that a week ago was the marguerite's gay sister, plucked among the moonbeams and given him by the girl standing before him, pale and mute, and, in his eyes, most false.

A terrible sense of utter desolation falls upon him as he turns away undelayed by any word from her. Even at the door, though inwardly cursing his own weakness for so doing, he pauses, as though in a wild hope that she yet may call to him to come back to her; but no sound breaks upon the heavy stillness that seems to have fallen on the room, and, opening the door, he goes out quickly, closing it firmly behind him.

The click of the lock rouses Miss Disney from the spell that has taken her into full possession. With a little gasping cry, she sinks into a chair and covers her face with her hands. What does it all mean ? What has happened ?

Slowly—slowly—the thought dawns upon her that he has *rejected* her—has spurned her overture and treated her poor attempt at reconciliation with ignominy. He had not *wanted* to be reconciled. He was perhaps *glad* of the chance of escape she had first afforded him by her senseless encouragement of that *hateful* Sir George (alas ! how the great are fallen !) ; and she had tried to force herself upon him, and he had come himself to tell her he would none of her. Oh !——

She starts to her feet and clasps her hands together to prevent herself from bursting into tears of cruel mortification. She walks rapidly up and down the room, planning deep thoughts of vengeance, but no help, no comfort comes to her. For a long half-hour she so ponders in fruitless search after a calm that will not come, and at the end of it her courage forsakes her. She confesses to herself that she is unhappy, miserable, that all men are detestable, and that above and beyond all his fellows Mr. Ponsonby is *the* most detestable, and that she hates him, and she doesn't care ; and then she flings herself into a huge arm-chair, and, letting her face drop upon her lovely naked arms, breaks into bitter weeping.

Mr. Wilding, entering the room a few moments later, finds her in this condition.   She tries, indeed, to rise suddenly, and turns her face from him ; but to conceal the fact that she is in great distress is impossible.

"Never mind me," says Mr. Wilding, going up to his poor little cousin and patting her shoulder tenderly.   "I'm sorry it has come to this; because he's an uncommon good fellow. He has just told me all about it."

"He is a wretch !" says Miss Disney, with startling fervour.

"You ought to be the last to be down upon him," says her cousin, reprovingly.   "Even supposing he *did* give you a piece of his mind, I think you should be the one to make allowances for a slight display of temper.   No fellow likes being done in that sort of way."

"*Done ?* "

"My dear child, what's the good of keeping it up before me ?   I *know* all about it, from start to finish."

"Oh, you *do !* " says Miss Disney, in a tone of bewildered resignation.

"Yes ; and, though I am not, as a rule, one of the obnoxious ' *I-told-you-so* ' sort of people, still I foresaw that when you *did* do it you would be sorry for it."

"Ah, you saw that ? " says Miss Disney, in a tone of even greater bewilderment and resignation.

"*Certainly*, I did."

"Yes ?   And what was it you saw, dear ? " asks she, meekly.

"Oh, I say, you know," says Mr. Wilding, in high disgust— "that is no way to treat a fellow who is almost your brother, you know.   If I *must* be plain, I think it is excessively foolish of you to throw up Frank Ponsonby for the sake of an empty title."

"Is *that* what he told you?" exclaims she, flushing with indignation. "Now, hear the truth from me. It's — it's a *horrible* thing to have to confess; but I'll trust *you.* I tried to make friends with him, and I sent him a flower, and he wouldn't *have* it; and he came here and told me he wished to set me '*finally free*' (*such* a way of putting it!); and "—her cousin's arm is round her by this time, and she is sobbing her heart out on his shoulder—"I am the most unhappy girl in all the world!"

"Bless me! there must be a mistake somewhere," says Mr. Wilding, at his wits' end.

"You won't betray me, will you?" sobs his pretty but deeply afflicted cousin.

"Nonsense! Of course not. But tell me about that unfortunate flower."

She tells him.

"Show it to me," says Mr. Wilding, at the close of her confession, assuming the barrister air that gains him daily commendation from the bench. Together, and with the utmost caution, they count the petals again, and at the end look blankly into each other's face.

"How *could* it have happened?" says Miss Disney, in an awe-stricken tone.

"One petal is missing," says Mr. Wilding, still before the bar. "One of two things must have occurred—either *you* counted wrongly the first time, or else it was removed by——"

At this moment Katherine Nugent enters the room.

"Oh, Katherine!" cries Alys, and, running to her, throws her unsuspicious arms round her and tells her all. "My cousin, Mr. Wilding, tells me, he, Frank, is suffering as much from this wretched mistake as I am. You gave it to him yourself—with your own hands?"

"Yes," says Katherine, calmly.

Wilding, who is watching her closely, tells himself she does excellently well indeed. "It is a very unfortunate affair," he says, still with his eyes on Miss Nugent.

"Very."   Her eyes meet his calmly, unwaveringly.

"Something ought to be done about it at once."

"I quite agree with you.   But who is to do it? and what is to be done?"

"I know," says Alys, very quietly, and with a strange amount of determination for her.   "I shall explain all to him myself— *to-night.*"

"*You!*" says Miss Nugent, an unpleasant amount of astonishment in her tone.

"Yes.   Why not?   I think it only due to him," says Mr. Wilding, slowly.   "*You* see an objection to this course?"— turning to Katherine.

"I?   Oh, *no!*   Why *should* I?   It is really nothing to me. I have no *right* to an objection.   Besides, there *isn't* one. Frank Ponsonby"—here she compels the girl's eyes to meet hers by the very intensity of her own regard—"is of too generous a nature to see any *indelicacy* in this act of hers."

"Indelicacy!" repeats Alys, growing very pale.   "If I speak to him on this subject, can I be accused of *that?*"—turning piteously to her cousin.

"Being a man," says Mr. Wilding, slowly, "I can tell you all the more surely what *his* answer would be to that question. It would be ' *No.*' "

"There, dear; Mr. Wilding knows," says Miss Nugent, with a faint smile.

"But, oh, if he should be *wrong!*" says the girl, in an agony of doubt.   "Perhaps if some one else were to tell him it would be better; but who?"

"Shall I?" says Katherine, softly.

Wilding, still with his eyes on Katherine, makes no move-ment.

Katherine, stooping forward, lays her hand on the girl's arm.

There is a long pause.   And then the girl, lifting Miss Nugent's hand, holds it for an instant in mid-air, and then gently drops it.   Some divine instinct at the same moment makes her fall back, as though to ward the other off.   "No *no.* I will tell him myself," she says, with nervous haste and a profound sigh. She walks away from them, and, reaching the door, is soon beyond recall.

"A very impulsive girl," says Miss Nugent, turning to Wilding.

"A very good girl when under no evil influence," returns he, coolly.

"Sir George's, you mean ? "

"No."

"Frank's ? "

"Certainly not."

"Whose then ? " asks Miss Nugent, with the softest smile.

"To be discourteous is to lose a point," says Wilding, unmoved. "But,"—confidentially—"if I were *you,* I should—*chuck it up.*"

"Slang has always been a buried language to me," says Miss Nugent, politely. "You mean——? "

"So very little already unknown to you that it is hardly worth while my explaining it," says Wilding, genially. "Still, I would repeat my former words, because——" He pauses. Miss Nugent looking to him for a continuation of the sentence, he says mildly, "Because you haven't the ghost of a chance."

CHAPTER V.

"By some degree of woe
We every bliss must gain."

FINDING herself once more in the silent hall, Miss Disney stops short and sighs again. Then a great longing for fresh air overcomes her, and, passing quickly through the now deserted dining-room, she steps on to the balcony outside, and presently finds herself in the garden.

A silvery light hangs over it. The moon, that "goddess excellently bright," is hanging amid trembling fleecy clouds, like a great lamp lent by the heavens to shed a glow upon the despondent earth.

Again its rays pierce the gloom of the eastern corner of the gardens and shed a mellow lustre upon the forced modesty of Apollo—ivy-clad—and upon the dazzling bunch of marguerites, nodding and drooping in their sleep.

Only a week ago she had stood just here with her *true* love, —happy, yet hardly aware of the depth of her happiness ; and now with what a different gaze she looks upon the world! Knowledge has come to her *too late.* Only with the *loss* of it has come the full appreciation of the thing she has lost.

Something in the scene before her brings prominently forward a doubt that ever since her last interview with Ponsonby has been weighing heavily upon her. Now, as it asserts itself fully, it sends a little chill to her heart.

In spite of all her cousin has said, may not her late reckless encouragement of Sir George have killed the love once felt for her by Ponsonby? This terrible thought grows stronger the more she dwells upon it, and at length grows into such tremendous proportions that her heart dies within her.

If she now seeks a second explanation with—with Mr. Ponsonby, will he not be justified in thinking she is seeking to throw herself upon his mercy, and that she is desirous of renewing old associations with him at any cost ?

She grows crimson as this thought comes to her, and tears of mortification rise to her eyes. No ! she can never speak to him on this subject—*never !* She *will* not ! She puts up her hands to her face, as though to hide her shamed eyes even from the tender moonlight, and in so doing hastily decides that she now for ever abandons all idea of seeking an interview with Ponsonby.

She will not speak to him ; she will not *see* him again, if possible ! Deriving some mysterious comfort from this resolution, and feeling therefore somewhat better, she takes down her hands from her eyes, and in so doing finds herself face to face with Ponsonby.

She turns as white as death; but with the necessity for speaking comes a rush of womanly dignity that reduces her to instant calm and adds tenfold to her girlish grace and sweetness.

"Let me speak to you for one moment," she says, impulsively, with a slight motion toward him. His sudden presence has convinced her that her late cowardly resolution had in it no element of *right*, and that an explanation is due not more to her than to him.

"Certainly," he says, very gently. All the sternness is gone from his tone, a settled melancholy having taken its place. Encouraged, though weakened, by this change in him, she goes on hurriedly.

"There is something I *must* tell you," she says, tremulously. "But first"—throwing up her head with a little proud gesture that becomes her infinitely—"I would have you understand that what I have to say cannot in *any* way alter the relations now existing between us. We are separated *for ever*. No one, I am glad to think at this moment, can know that better than you."

"No one," corroborates Mr. Ponsonby, in a tone that has acquired even a deeper dye, so far as misery is concerned.

"I am glad of that," says the girl, readily. Yet an intelligent observer might have failed to see where the gladness lay: certainly not in voice, or lips, or eyes. Mr. Ponsonby, I regret to say, proves himself on this occasion (only) wanting in intelligence, as he openly accepts her statement at her own value, and grows in dejection thereby. "I am *very* glad of it," repeats Alys unsteadily, and with now averted eyes and a paltry assumption of content, "because I can now safely tell you, without fear of misconception on your part, that it was all a mistake about that marguerite I sent you an hour ago. At *that* time" (by her manner it might reasonably be supposed again by the intelligent listener that the time mentioned is a year agone) "I was troubled, and—and ashamed of myself (I am neither now), and anxious to let you know that—that I had not changed toward you in any way, in spite of anything foolish in me that might have induced you to think otherwise."

There is something in this rebellious speech so sadly regretful, and so very near to tears, that instinctively Mr. Ponsonby goes a step closer to her, and puts out his hand as though to take hers; but she waves him back imperatively.

"When I sent you that flower," she goes on, her voice taking a still prouder ring as she feels the humiliation of her confession, and with her soft eyes suffused with tears of childish grief and agitation, "I thought,—I *firmly believed*,—it was conveying to you the message 'I love you!' I counted the petals carefully; I made sure not one was missing; but I suppose I counted badly. I tell you this now, for no motive but the natural wish that you should not believe me altogether heartless. You understand me? You *must* know"—passionately—"that for this reason alone I have spoken to you to-night."

"I *do* know," says the young man, earnestly. Again he goes nearer to her. There is suppressed hope and growing excitement in his face and manner.

"Not that it matters now," says Miss Disney, her voice trembling more and more. Nothing matters any more at all! We have both learned to be indifferent to each other, and—and—I hope I shall never, *never*, NEVER see you again after to-night!"

Here the voice passes beyond all trembling, having broken down and given place to bitter weeping.

She has lifted her hands to cover her face, and so stands before him, a little, slender, grief-laden figure, on which the gentle moon is shining, lighting up the pretty rounded arms and the gold-brown tresses of the bowed head. But for not half so long as it takes to write this does she so stand. In a moment she is in his arms, and is sobbing out the remainder of her grief upon his breast.

He has drawn her close to him, and closer still, until their hearts beat almost in unison.

"My darling," he says, with passionate fondness, "my dear, *dear* love, do not cry like that. I think,—I never thought it until to-night,—but now I *do* think that you love me. Alys, tell me I am not deceiving myself."

She can find no words, but, still with her face hidden upon his breast, lifts her arms and slips them lovingly round his neck. It is an answer all-sufficient.

Never before has she so abandoned herself to him, and for the first time the gladness of possession enters into his soul.

"You are mine now," he says, tightening his clasp round her, "now, and for ever! Let us go back a week in our lives, and forget that these last miserable seven days have ever been. You—you don't *care* for that fellow Grande?"

"There is only one person on earth I care for, and that is *you!*" says the girl, clinging to him.

"And yet——"

"Yes, yes; I know all that. I should not have believed her, but she told me you thought me a baby,—a mere silly child,— who could have no lover but you."

"*Who* told you all this?" demands he, with darkening brows.

"Katherine, your cousin. But "—dissolving into tears again —"it wasn't *true*, Frank, was it?"

"It was not, indeed," says Mr. Ponsonby, grimly. "These last few days have proved it. I cannot help feeling that I am depriving you of a title."

"You *said* you would forget this past horrid week," says Miss Disney, reproachfully, "and now you are scolding me about it."

"Well, it shall be my last scolding," says Ponsonby. "And as for the other things, you say I thought of you as a child. I tell you now, with your heart against mine, that I thought of you only as the woman I loved beyond all this earth contains."

"I know it now; I was mad to doubt you," says Alys, remorsefully; "but she *said* it; and, knowing you are superior to me in every way, I felt it easy to believe her."

"And it was she, too, who brought me the marguerite," says Ponsonby, musingly, in a low tone.   A sudden thought occuring to him, he tightens his grasp on her arm.   Then he recovers himself.

"Why think of *anything?* " he says, placing his lips to hers. " Let us only remember that we belong to each other by the divine right of love.   All else may readily be forgotten."

"No," says the girl, leaning back in his embrace so as to look into his eyes.   "I shall never forget this, our first and last quarrel.   I don't *want* to !   I am *glad* of it !"

" *Glad*, my soul ? "—regretfully.

" Yes,"—triumphantly,—"*very* glad.   Because," a smile fighting with the tears that still linger on her lashes, " but for *it* I should never have known how entirely *you* love *me* and *I you*."

"My beloved !" murmurs he, with ineffable fondness.

A PASSIVE CRIME.

CHAPTER I.

THE MOMENT APPROACHES.

FROM its site upon the high rocks that overhang the sea, Penruddock Castle, in all its Gothic and somewhat savage grandeur, frowns down upon the vale beneath ; upon plain and upland, park and winding stream; and the pretty cottage far below, that lies half-hidden by the spreading foliage.

Although belonging to sunny June, the day is dark and lowering.

The ocean, with a sudden roar, is rushing inland, to break out with furious hisses upon the long, low beach.

The sky is overcast ; no faintest gleam of sunshine comes to lighten the gloom, or throw some brightness on the scene, so replete with heaviness and a vague melancholy.

" And such a winter wears the face of heaven," that all the happy birds lie cowering out of sight.

Upon the castle walls the flag waves fretfully in the breeze. A sense of desolation and of coming evil is over all the place. The servants go softly to and fro, as though waiting solemnly for death's messenger, who comes with hurried feet. The moaning winds and drifting clouds murmur of misery, and plainly tell of dawning grief.

Beneath, in the valley, upon the grass plot that belongs to the cottage, a man is walking slowly up and down with lowered head, and a heart filled with envy and vain longing. His face, though handsome and suggestive of good breeding, is dark, stern, and impenetrable. His arms are crossed behind his back. Just now an expression, almost evil, mars the beauty of his features. His thoughts, busy with the past and the present, are full of discontent.

Sometimes, as though unconsciously, he lifts his eyes to gaze upon the crimson flag floating so high above him, marking the spot where his sister-in-law, the lady of Penruddock, lies at the point of death, very certainly to follow her husband into the land of shadows.

Within twelve months they will both lie buried, and all this goodly heritage, these swelling fields and softly undulating plains, will pass into the hands of a child, a feeble girl—a creature scarce fit to combat with the winds that blow ; whilst *his* boy, his treasure beyond all price, must through all his life toil for daily bread.

At this moment a merry laugh rings out upon the air, and from the house, with fair hair flying, a lovely boy of seven runs eagerly and joyously, with arms extended, to the man so deep in envious thought.

As the sound of childish gaiety smites upon his ear, his whole expression changes, and he lifts his head, and gladly welcomes the child with word and gesture, as he flings himself, breathless, upon the man's breast.

The boy clings to him, murmuring a joyful story of his escape from nurse and tutor without fear of reproof, and with no dread of the dark features and gleaming eyes above him, that betray some sense of cruelty.

Perhaps his little son is the one thing in all the world that does not shrink from George Penruddock, and is, therefore, doubly dear to him on that account.

He holds him now closely clasped against his heart, as though the contact were sweet to him, and whispers in his ear words of fond endearment that are almost womanish in their tenderness.

Yet even as he holds the youngster in his arms dark thoughts come again, and take fast hold of him.

But for the puny baby in the Castle above, all these lands around him might be the boy's, and wealth and position be assured to him.

That thought it is which is now torturing, and which has long driven from his heart every feeling save only one that should inspire a human being.

He loves his little son; for him it is that this man is ambitious, and would enrich even by a crime.

The daughter of Alice Penruddock (once so vainly loved, now so long detested) will soon be in possession of all, whilst his little son, his pretty Dick, must for ever remain portionless. It is this thought that constantly tortures, that poisons and lays waste his every hour.

The boy has darted off again, chasing from flower to flower a showy butterfly; and once more Penruddock looks up sharply to where the crimson flag should be. But it is no longer there; and almost it seems as though a faint cry comes to him upon the rising wind.

He shivers, and then cries shame upon his superstitious fears, and tells himself it is but the shriek of the sea-gulls flying inwards from the storm.

The click of a latch makes him turn his head. The garden gate is thrown wide, and a tall woman, of servant's rank, but finely formed, and of the gipsy type, comes hurriedly up to him. Her eyes are peculiarly large and dark, and there is a determination, a stolidity, about her lower jaw somewhat re-markable. Perhaps the touch of Romany blood is rather more discernible in carriage and complexion than in eyes and hair, though both are dark as midnight.

Penruddock grows a little pale as she approaches, and acknowledges her presence, not with speech, but by a slight gesture of the hand.

The woman takes no notice of his greeting, but, drawing herself up to her full height, for several moments gazes at him thoughtfully.

"Well?" he asks, at length, as though unable longer to endure her scrutiny.

"My lady is dead!" says the woman, slowly, rather than curtly, and with a difficulty which is very apparent to him.

Penruddock starts, and moves back a step or two. However prepared we may be for such news, the plain telling of it must occasion a shock.

"Ay," says the woman, quietly.

"Dead!" says Penruddock, in a low tone. "So soon—so very suddenly!"

"Yes, it is always so," returns she, moodily, gazing at the green sward; "the young and the gay go soonest. She is clay now, though a week ago she could chatter with the best; nay, so lately as an hour ago she called me by my name, and held my hand—so. I can feel the pressure still. But it is all over, all over; she is still and cold now, poor soul! And it may be happier, for her heart was broken!"

"How dreadful it all is—how depressing! I feel it as though——"

"No more, Penruddock," says the woman, suddenly, raising her head, and flinging up her hand with an uncontrollable and almost haughty gesture. So standing, she is quite beautiful; and though wearing the garb, loses all the aspect of the menial. "Hypocrisy is a vile sin; and why try to deceive *me?* There was no love lost between you. Even at the last, the very last, when life was nearly over, she——"

There is a pause, and Penruddock, in an agitated voice, says, with some excitement, "Go on! Do not hesitate—tell me the worst, Esther! At the last she spoke of me! What was it? Did she forgive?"

"Never!" says the woman, firmly. "No, not even then. You know how she disliked the master's will, and your being left sole guardian of the child in the event of her death. *I* say nothing," slowly, and with averted looks. "The dislike may have been—nay, must "—with a curious contraction of the brows—"have been unreasoning, but still it was there ; and at the last she alluded to it. As I knelt beside her she laid her hand on mine, and whispered a few words. They were not many, but they were of you and the child. If you command that I should speak those words, of course, I must ; but better not hear them, sir——"

"Speak, woman !" replies he, roughly. "What could she say of me in death that would be harsher than that which she said in life ?"

"Nay, then, if you *will* hear, of course, you must," returns she ; yet she pauses as though somewhat reluctant to proceed. "It always seemed to her a strange thing that Miss Penruddock (the little one) should by the will be compelled to live here in this small spot until her eighteenth birthday, when in reality she is mistress of *it*, and all the lands around, and the great castle up yonder."

"Tell me what she said of me as she died?" says Penruddock, impatiently.

"She mentioned no names, but bending towards me, said, with her poor eyes wild and frightened, as it were, ' Now that I am torn, and for ever, alas ! from my sweet lamb, she must walk beside the *wolf!*'"

"Ah !" says Penruddock, drawing his breath quickly, and colouring darkly ; "is that the truth, or is it only that which you have yourself invented ?"

"It is true. You would have me speak. But "—lowering her head—"it may have been but raving. When death is near, how few know light from darkness !"

"What more did she say ?" demanded he, as though deaf to her last remark.

"She made me swear that I would never forsake the little one ; that as I had been its nurse for three long years, so I would still cherish and keep a watchful eye upon her. I swore it," says the woman, solemnly, raising her eyes to the dull sky above her, as though in memory of her " oath in heaven ; " " and I shall never break that promise, come what will, and cost me what it may to keep it."

She pauses then, and looks keenly at Penruddock, who meets her gaze as firmly as though his heart was frank and true, his mind without a single thought of evil.

" When will it please you, sir, that I shall bring the child down ? " she asks presently, in a subdued tone. " This evening ? Already she pines for her dead mother, poor bairn ; but if with Master Dick, I think the feeling of loneliness might be lightened, and, no doubt, in a very little time would cease to exist altogether."

" Very well.   Let her be sent this evening," says Penruddock, slowly, unwillingly, as it seems to the ears of his attentive listener.

" Perhaps I hurry you ? " she says, with a certain new-born nervousness in her manner. " It is too hasty an arrival. There will be our sleeping-room to arrange, and the preparations for it may——"

" There need be no trouble," says Penruddock, slowly. There is nothing to arrange. My niece can sleep in the nursery with Wilkins."

" Miss Penruddock always sleeps with me, in my room," says the woman, growing terror in her eyes. " Wilkins is nothing to her ; I am all the world to her."

" For the future many things will be changed," says Penruddock, speaking coldly and with singular precision. " It is better you should understand at once that your services in this family will no longer be required. My son's nurse will be sufficient for both children."

The woman's face alters as he speaks until it is almost unrecognizable.

A gray, leaden pallor discolours her lips ; her eyes grow strangely dark.

By a supreme effort, she so far controls herself as to speak with some appearance of calmness.

"You would separate me from the child?" she says, in a low, anguished tone.

Her hands are clasped behind her back, well out of sight, lest he shall see how the fingers, closing on each other, leave white marks upon the knuckles.

"Yes; it will be better so. I shall keep no one near my niece who may prejudice her against her uncle," replies he, with a slight sneer; "her guardian, too, according to her father's wish."

She makes a quick gesture, as though she would dispute the insinuation; but he prevents her.

"It is useless arguing," he says. "Your manner betrays you. It is distrustful, and touches on insolence. From your mistress you have, I know but too well, imbibed a hatred of me strong as it is unjust."

The woman, pale now as death, makes a step forward.

"I was her nurse," she says, desperately. "She is like my own—nay, more to me than the one I lost. All through her young life I have borne with her, cared for her, loved her. She is part of myself. At this bosom"—crossing her hands passionately upon her breast—"she was fed. She is all on earth I care for—my *last* tie. And will you now compel me to part with her? Penruddock, have pity!"

"I have spoken," returns he, unmoved; "and tragic scenes have no charm for me. I shall give you a character, and any wages that are due you can have whenever it may suit you to come for them."

"Then it is all over!" murmurs she faintly, pressing her hand to her heart, and turning away.

But when she has gone a yard or two, she comes back again, and confronts him with a look upon her handsome face ill to meet.

She is very white, and her large, unearthly eyes burn with a revengeful fire.

"I had forgotten," she says, slowly. "My lady sent you

one more message. 'Tell him,' she said, 'that surely *he* shall be dealt with as he deals with *mine!*'"

So saying, she moves away into the leafy recesses of the wood, and presently is lost to sight.

CHAPTER II.

THE GUARDIAN.

JULY is come. The hot sun is pouring down its scorching rays on tree and drooping flower, on waving meadow, and the cool and smiling river, with its "water, clear as beryl or crystal," that, flowing through the cottage garden, rushes onward to the illimitable ocean.

Amongst the great roses, heavy with scent and bloom, the children are playing merrily, chasing each other in and out, and hither and thither, through countless rows of gaudy-coloured beds.

Hilda Penruddock, the little heiress, with her yellow locks and pleasing countenance, fair as an angel's, and eyes, "coloured with the heaven's own blue," is racing madly over walks and closely-shaven grass, looking like some "milk-white blossom of the spring."

Her cousin, tall and slender for his age, and handsome as an Italian cherub in spite of his golden-brown hair, is swiftly pursuing her, whilst merry laughter from both their lips ascends into the summer air.

"Ah, take care, Hilda!" calls the boy, as his cousin runs dangerously close to the deep shelving bank that overhangs the river. "Do not lean over. You know how strictly nurse has forbidden it."

"The river is shining—shining!" cries she. "See the little stars that dance on the top of it, and the pretty white lilies! I wish I had a lily!"

"Come away," returns he, coaxingly, "and I will get you prettier lilies from the lake outside by-and-by. Come, let us finish our game. Now, I am the robber chief, and you are my prisoner, and this is my castle."

Penruddock, sitting in the oriel window of the library that looks out upon the garden, watches the children at their play with moody brow and lips compressed.

Upon Hilda more especially his gaze is fixed. What a frail life—a mere breath, as it were—to stand between his and (what is far more to him) the boy's advancement!

That this baby should inherit what, but for her unwelcome birth, would by law have been his, embitters and makes wretched every moment of his life.

What a little, fragile thing she looks, flitting about in the sunshine, in spite of her merry laugh and joyous disposition— a thread that might be easily snapped!

Yet how slow is the great King of Terrors in claiming those whom we would wish away—how swift to clutch at those we would give our heart's blood to retain!

At this moment he sees the children leaning over the bank (perpendicular and utterly unprotected), at the base of which the water runs so rapidly.

The boy's warning to stand back comes to him upon the air.

What if the child, stooping *too* far, should overbalance herself, and sink into the foaming depths beneath—swollen with last night's rain—and be carried onward to the cruel ocean? Whose fault would it be? Who would be to blame? Such accidents happen very frequently.

Idly the awful thought presents itself, bearing with it a fascination hard to combat. Heart and brain it fills, to the exclusion of all other thoughts.

Meantime, Hilda has stopped short, and in her shrill, sweet treble has ordered Dick to go indoors and bring her out the dolly that shall represent another unhappy captive to his powerful and daring arm.

Dick, engrossed in the reality of his game, departs for the

fresh prey, nothing loth, leaving her alone in the quiet garden, with no eye upon her save his who watches with disfavour her every movement.

At first, when left alone, she stands, her little finger in her mouth, as though uncertain what next to do. Then a butter-fly, blue as the skies above her, crossing her path, she gives chase, and runs until it is beyond her reach, and she herself is once more close to the fatal bank before described.

She is singing softly a little gay song all about that silly Bo-peep of ancient memory, and the song is borne inwards, even to the ears of Penruddock, as he sits behind the curtains, cold and motionless, waiting for he hardly knows what.

Whatever fiendish thought has taken possession of him, he is, as yet, scarcely aware of it, but tarries, with white lips and distended eyes, that follow eagerly and glaringly each footstep of the child outside.

Hilda, with all the youthful longing for forbidden fruit, gazes eagerly down upon the water-lilies that are rocking to and fro on the disturbed breast of the agitated river.

Stooping over, she examines them minutely, longingly, her eyes intense, a faint smile of pleasure on her lips.

Presently, kneeling down, she suspends half her small body over the sloping bank, as though to gain a nearer knowledge of the coveted flowers.

Penruddock, shrinking back, with one hand grasps the curtains, and trembling violently, whilst great drops of dew lie thick upon his forehead, that already in anticipation seems red with the cursed brand of Cain.

Eagerly he gazes on the little one. She is barely balanced; the slightest touch, the faintest motion may send her over into the river.

Prompted, it may be, by his good angel, he makes a step forward, as though to stay the catastrophe so imminent. Then he suddenly stops.

A wretched memory that but belongs to his vile desire comes to him, and crushes all good within him.

Has he not somewhere heard that to speak, or call, or cry aloud to a child when in a dangerous position is but a swift and sure means to cause its sudden destruction? Therefore. will *he* not speak.

And, as though virtuous feeling alone prompts him, he holds his peace, and tries to believe that his non-interference may yet save the child.

Yet in reality, and he knows it well, he does not so believe. No, he cannot so deceive himself.

The little heiress creeps still nearer to the brink, always with her soft and tender song upon her lips.

She sways suddenly, seeks to recover herself, and then the poor baby—filled with her childish longing for the unattainable, and with all her little soul wrapt in admiration of the fatal lilies—falls forward.

For a moment she clings convulsively to the slippery bank, then, with a sharp and bitter scream, rolls downward, and is instantly snatched to the bosom of the greedy river as it rushes onward to the sea.

The whole awful tragedy has occupied scarcely more than one short minute.

Penruddock, rousing himself when it is too late, springs through the window, out into the garden, past the roses—that still smile and tremble coquettishly beneath the touch of the fickle breeze, as though no horrible thing had just been done— and gains the fatal spot.

Gazing with wild and too late remorse into the river, he fails to see sign of white frock, or whiter limbs, or small face pale with terror.

The river has caught the little body, and hurried it along, past the curve of the rock, through the meadow, perhaps already—so deadly swift it is—out into the open sea. No tiny, struggling mass, still instinct with life, can be seen—nothing but the turbid waters.

Penruddock, with a groan, sinks upon his knees, and falling each second lower, soon lies prone, an inert and unconscious heap upon the grass.

How long he remains there, prostrate, and mercifully lost to time, he never knows, but a voice, sweet and loving, rouses him to life again.

"What is it, papa?" says Dick, bending over him. "Are you ill? You will catch cold, so get up. Nurse is always saying that Hilda and I are sure to catch sore throats if we lie on the grass."

As the little one's name passes his boy's lips, Penruddock starts and shivers, and after a few seconds, by a supreme effort, raises himself to his feet.

Never shall the boy know how evil has been this deed he has committed.

He moves very feebly indeed towards the house; but Dick follows him.

"Where is Hilda?" he asks, standing on tiptoe, to bring his face nearer to his father's. "I can't find her anywhere, and I left her just here. She is a little imp, and is always hiding from me; but she will come back when I want her. Hilda," raising his voice to a shout, "I shall pick the eyes out of Miss Maud" (the doll) "if you don't come soon. One would think she was *dead*, she is so silent. Why, papa, how pale you are!—and how ill you look! Has any one been vexing you?"

"No," says Penruddock, harshly; and pushing the boy, for the first time, roughly from him, goes indoors.

Many years afterwards, Dick Penruddock remembers how that day his father, for the only time in all his life, treated him harshly, and without the accustomed tenderness.

CHAPTER III.

AT THE OPERA.

It is the height of the London season. All the world is alive and eager in search of amusement, and to-night, as Patti is to sing, each box and stall in the Italian House is filled—over-flowing, indeed.

One box alone on the second tier is empty, and towards it numerous lorgnettes from the stalls beneath, and from boxes opposite, are anxiously directed.

The Diva has appeared, has sung her first solo, has been rapturously received and applauded to the echo, and the house is now listlessly paying attention to a somewhat overdone tenor, when the door of the empty box opens, and a woman, pretty, and with a charming expression, if slightly *passé*, comes slowly within the light of the lamps.

She is followed by a girl, who, coming to her side, stands for a moment motionless, gazing down and around with a care-less calm upon the fashionable multitude with which the vast building is crowded.

So standing together, the elder woman sinks into insignifi-cance, whilst the younger becomes the centre of attraction. She is of medium height, with a clear, colourless skin, and large blue expressive eyes. Her hair is not golden, but light brown, through which a touch of gold runs brightly. She is aristocratic, almost haughty, in appearance ; yet every feature, and, indeed, her whole bearing, is marked with a melancholy that seems to check even the smile that on very rare occasions seeks to dissi-pate the sadness on her lovely countenance.

She is dressed in a somewhat strange fashion for so young a. girl. Her gown is of black satin, relieved by some heavy, golden chains that encircle her neck; she wears black gloves. to her elbow, and an enormous black fan flecked with gold. Upon her fair hair a tiny Indian cap of black satin, embroidered with gold, and hung with sequins, rests lightly.

She is whimsical, old-fashioned, what you will, but perfect in every look and movement.

Having completed her slow survey of the house, she turns and says something in quite a languid fashion to her companion, who laughs, taps her with her fan, and motions her to the chair opposite.

What a success you are, Maud!" says the elder woman fondly. "Even royalty has taken notice of your entrance! Did you observe that?"

"Royalty, as a rule, is very rude!" says Maud, slowly, after which they both fall into line and turn their attention to the divine Adelina.

Two young men in the stalls beneath, who up to this have been engrossed with the new beauty, at this instant turn to each other.

"Who is she?" asks the youngest, eagerly. "I have been in town some time—quite three weeks—but anything like that has not——"

"Dear child, don't—don't say it!" interrupts his companion, sadly. "It isn't like you! Not to know *her*, argues yourself unknown! I thought better of you! She is our beauty *par excellence*, our modern Venus, and licks every one else into fits! She is the very cream of the cream where beauty is concerned, though somewhat shady, I am reluctantly compelled to admit, in the matter of birth!"

"Birth!" repeats the young man, with a start. "But look at her—look at her hands, her profile! Who can dispute the question of birth?"

"No one! It is indisputable! That charming girl up there, with the most irreproachable nose, and the haughtiest mouth in Christendom, was picked off the street by her chaperon, Mrs. Neville, when a baby, and is probably—at least, so I hear—the daughter of a woman, poor, but strictly honest—they are *always* strictly honest,—who lived by infusing starch into limp linen! I really don't like to say coarsely that she was a washerwoman, it sounds so vulgar!"

"It sounds as horrible as it is impossible!" says the younger man, still gazing dreamily at the box that holds his harmony in black and gold.

"Most impossible things are horrible," says his companion, lightly. "They grate; they are out of the common. Perhaps that is their charm. Miss Neville charms. Yes, that is her name; her adopted mother wishes her to be so called. Don't look so excessively shocked, my dear Penruddock; it is rather a romance, if it is anything at all, and should create in your mind interest rather than disgust."

"It is not disgust I feel, it is merely a difficulty of belief!" says Penruddock, vaguely. "Is *that* her adopted mother?" shifting his glasses for just a moment from the calm and beautiful blue eyes that have so bewitched him, to the faded pretty woman who sits near them.

"Yes. *She* is all right, you know—quite correct! She is George Neville's widow, son to Lord Dulmore, you may remember, who broke his neck, or his head, or something—I don't exactly know what—when out hunting."

"Yes; I remember. He was a friend of my father's. By the bye, that Mrs. Neville must be a sort of connection of ours —at least, her sister married my uncle. But all friendship there ceased with my aunt's death. I don't recollect anything about it myself, but I believe a coldness arose after my poor little cousin's unhappy accident. You heard all about that of course?"

"A very fortunate accident for you, all things considered. Other fellows' cousins don't drop off like that," says Mr. Wilding, in an aggrieved tone.

"My father was awfully cut up about it," says Penruddock; "he has never been the same man since. Moody, you know, and that; and goes about for days together without speaking a word. It preyed upon him. And the Wynters—my aunt's people—said ugly things about it; that sufficient care hadn't been taken of the poor little thing, and all the rest of it. But of course it was nobody's fault."

"Of course not! Some people—especially law relations— are never happy except when making themselves disagreeable! That's their special forte! The fact that your father minds them betrays in him a charming amount of freshness!"

"And so she adopted that lovely girl!" says Penruddock, presently, returning to his contemplation of Beauty's box, and referring to Mrs. Neville.

"She might have done worse, might she not?   I shouldn't mind adopting her myself," says Mr. Wilding, genially.   " And nobody seems to mind about the linen ; she is received every-where, and has refused several very good men."

" Tell me all about it ; do, now, there's a good fellow," says Penruddock, leaning back in his seat, and beginning to look profoundly interested.

"There isn't much of it.   It is a romantic story, certainly, and a very Quixotic one, but it can be told in a word or two. Brevity is the soul of wit.   To begin with, you must try to master the fact that Mrs. Neville adores dogs, and driving in the Park one day about fifteen years ago, she drew up her car-riage at the railings and proceeded to gratify the appetite of her Pomeranian by bestowing upon him a cracknel.

" Even as she broke it, a faint cry from the world outside her carriage attracted her attention, and glancing up she saw a very lovely child in the arms of a tall, rather peculiar-looking woman.   The child was gazing at her imploringly, its little hand extended, as though desirous of the biscuit the dog was devouring.

" Mrs. Neville is tender-hearted.   The child, as I said, was beautiful ; a very model for an angel or a love.   Mrs. Neville, who even *now* is nothing if not emotional, gazed entranced ; the pretty baby pouted, and cried again for the biscuit.   The cry went to her listener's heart.

" ' She is hungry,' she said to the woman, who leaned against the railings in a picturesque attitude.

" ' She is often hungry, madam,' returned the woman stolidly, yet far from brutally ; indeed, the apparent hopeless resigna-tion in her tone must have been very perfectly done, from all I have heard.

" Mrs. Neville, an unaccountable pang at her heart, pressed all her remaining biscuits into the baby's hands ; told the woman to call upon her next day ; heard next day the child was an orphan ; and the end of it was, took her to her house and heart, to the intense disgust of numerous nieces and nephews, who had looked on Mrs. Neville as their joint prey. There you have the whole history, I believe."

"It is a very strange story; she must have seen a great many pretty children besides this particular one. Why did she choose her?"

"Fancied she saw in her some resemblance to a dead sister, that was very fondly, and even extravagantly regretted—your aunt, Mrs. Penruddock, I suppose, as she hadn't another sister that I ever heard of."

"If she—the young lady above—is like Mrs. Neville's sister, Mrs. Neville must be very unlike her own people," says the young man, slowly.

"Yet, strange to say, that girl is most absurdly like a portrait of Mrs. Penruddock, that hangs in the small drawing-room in South Audley Street, where Mrs. Neville lives. Not that there is anything so very remarkable in that; one sees chance resemblances every day. But you, being one of the family, should see this likeness yourself."

"No; I have no recollection of aunt. My father and she were always on bad terms with each other during her lifetime, and there is no picture of her at the Castle. The one you mention was sent to Mrs. Neville at her death. I have been so much abroad that I am quite a stranger to the Wynters, and all their set. You know Mrs. Neville?"

"Intimately; and Beauty, too," with an amused smile. "And every Tuesday afternoon Beauty gives me a cup of tea with her own fair little hands."

"Indeed!" exclaimed Penruddock.

"Yes, indeed; you did not think such bliss could be on this miserable earth, did you? And sometimes, *not often*, I take a nice boy, when I find one, and introduce him to Mrs. Neville."

"Am *I* a nice boy?" asks Penruddock, with a laugh. "Wilding, if you will introduce *me* to Mrs. Neville I shall never forget it to you as long as I live!"

"And a great deal of good that will do me," says Wilding,

mildly. "However, I consent, and on Tuesday you shall make your bow to Mrs. Neville, and worship at Beauty's shrine."

"Oh, thank you, my dear fellow, thank you !"

"But one word of warning—don't go and fall in love with her, you know; it wouldn't do at all. I am responsible for you to your father, and it would be the worst possible taste on your part to bring down his condemnation on my head !"

"Do not make yourself unhappy about that," says Penruddock, quietly. "It may be *my* fate to be miserable about Miss Neville—I feel inclined to believe that—but I am not sufficiently vain to flatter myself that she will ever take the trouble to make herself miserable about me."

CHAPTER IV.

IN THE ROW.

ALL yesterday the rain fell heavily. Not in quiet showers, but with a steady downpour that drenched the world, rendering the Park a lonely wilderness, and the Ride deserted.

To-day the sun, as though weary of yesterday's inaction, is out again, going his busy round, and casting his warm beams on rich and poor, simple and wise, alike.

The Row is crowded—filled to overflowing with the gaily-dressed throng that has come out to bask in the glad warmth of the sunshine, and revel in the sense of well-being engendered by the softness and sweetness of the rushing breeze.

> " The heaven shows lively art and hue,
> Of sundry shapes and colours new,
> And laughs upon the earth ! "

A faint languor, born of the increasing heat, pervades the air.

But for the gentle wind that dances gaily hither and thither, wooing with its tender touch each thing it passes, the heat would be almost insupportable.

The occupants of the chairs seem drowsily inclined, and answer in soft monosyllables those with energy sufficient left to question them.

One old lady, unmindful of the carriages that pass and re-pass incessantly, has fallen into a sound and refreshing slumber, made musical by snores low but deep.

The very loungers on the railings have grown silent, as though speech is irksome, and conversation not to be borne, and content themselves with gazing upon the beauty that is carried by them as the tide of fashion ebbs and flows.

A dark green victoria, exquisitely appointed, and drawn by two bright bay ponies, claims, and not at all unjustly, the very largest share of attention.

Not so much the victoria, perhaps, as Mrs. Neville, to whom it belongs, and who is now seated in it, with her adopted daughter beside her.

Miss Neville, as usual, is faultlessly attired in some pale fabric, untouched by colour of any sort, and is looking more than ordinarily lovely.

Her large dark eyes, blue as the deep Czar violet, and tinged with melancholy, are in perfect harmony with the cream-coloured hat she wears.

A little suspicion of crimson adorns each cheek. Her lips are parted.

She seems indeed a very phantom of delight.

> "A lovely apparition, sent——"

not so much to be a moment's ornament as a lasting joy.

"There is Dick Penruddock," says Mrs. Neville, suddenly. "I want to speak to him."

Leaning forward, she says something to her coachman, and presently the carriage is drawn up beside the railings, and, with a smile and a nod, Mrs. Neville beckons the young man to her side.

It is quite a month since that night at the Opera, where Penruddock first saw Maud Neville—a month full of growing hopes and disheartening fears.

At first Mrs. Neville had been averse to the acquaintance altogether, bearing a strange grudge to the very name of Penruddock, as she held it responsible for all the ills that had befallen her beloved sister.

She had scolded Wilding in her harmless fashion as severely as she could scold any one for having brought one of "those people," as she termed them, within her doors, more especially the boy who had succeeded to the property that should by right have belonged to the little Hilda, her dead sister's only child.

But time and Dick Penruddock's charm of manner had conquered prejudice and vague suspicion ; and Mrs. Neville, after many days, acknowledged even to herself that she liked the young man—nay, almost *loved* him, in spite of his name and parentage.

Just now he comes gladly up to the side of the victoria and takes her hand, and beams upon her, and then glances past her to accept with gratitude the slow bow and very faint smile of recognition that Miss Neville is so condescending as to bestow upon him.

"Such a chance to see you in this confusion !" says Mrs. Neville, kindly. "And can you come and dine to-night ? It is short notice, of course, for such a fashionable boy as *you* are ; but I really want you, and you *must* come."

"If you really want me, I shall of course come—your wishes are commands not to be disputed," says Penruddock, after a second's hesitation, wherein he has decided on telling a great fib to the other people with whom he is in duty bound to pass his evening. "But your dance——"

"Is later on—yes. But I have two or three old friends coming to dine, and they are very charming, of course, and I quite love them, you will understand ; but old friends, as a rule, are just the least little bit tedious sometimes, don't you think ?

And I want you to help me with them. I may depend upon
you ? "

" You may, indeed."

" Ah, so Maud said ! " says Mrs. Neville, with a faint sigh of
relief.

To know that this pleasant boy will be on the spot to make
conversation and carry it on when her own powers fail is an
inexpressible comfort to her.

" Did Miss Neville say that ?. I did not dare to believe that
she had so good an opinion of me.   To be considered worthy
of trust is a very great compliment indeed," says Dick, glancing
past Mrs. Neville again, to gaze somewhat wistfully at the
owner of the cream-coloured hat.

But she, beyond the first slight recognition and somewhat
haughty inclination of her small head, has taken not the
slightest notice of him.

She has even turned her head away, and is apparently lost
in contemplation of the brilliant and constantly increasing crowd
around her.

" Seen the Princess, Miss Neville ? " asks Penruddock at
length, in despair, filled with a sudden determination to make
her speak, and to compel her large, thoughtful eyes to meet his
own, if only for a single instant. " Rather nice, her ponies,
don't you think ? "

" Not so highly bred as Mrs. Cabbe's, nor so perfect in any
way," returns Miss Neville, unsympathetically, letting her eyes
rest on him for a very brief moment, and making him a present
of a grave, pleasant, but cold little smile.

After which she turns her head away again, as though
desirous of dropping out of the conversation.

Penruddock is piqued, almost angry.   Already he has
learned the value of position, money, the world's adulation ;
yet this girl alone treats him with open coldness and something
that borders on positive avoidance, though she herself is utterly
without position, and only indebted to the popularity Mrs.
Neville enjoys with both sexes for her admittance into society.

Two or three men coming up to the victoria at this moment stay to speak to its occupants, and to all Miss Neville gives the same cold greeting, the same frigid, but undeniably entrancing, smile.

Perhaps her somewhat insolent indifference is her chief charm ; or it may be that it lies in the half mournful dignity expressive of an everlasting if silent regret that marks her every glance and movement.

A tall, dark man, pushing his way through the others, makes his bow to Mrs. Neville, and then raises his hat deferentially to the beauty of the hour.

Maud acknowledges his presence with a salutation that is certainly somewhat colder than those accorded to the others to-day.

"How full the Row is this afternoon !" says Mrs. Neville, genially, who has made the same remark to all the others straight through.

"Is it ? " says Captain Saumarez, the new comer. "Really, I dare say ; but once I had caught sight of your unapproachable ponies I could see nothing else. It seems too much luck to meet you this afternoon with the certainty of meeting you again this evening. Thanks so much for the card ! May I venture to hope for one dance to-night, Miss Neville ?—or do I, as usual, ask too late ? "

"Quite too late. Every dance is promised."

She barely looks at him as she speaks.

"What, *all ?* I am indeed unfortunate—there is no denying that ! Is there nobody you could throw over to give me even one poor dance ?"

"I never throw over my partners," says Miss Neville, distinctly ; "my conscience is opposed to that, and will not allow me to break my word—once given."

"Yet I think—short as is our acquaintance—I remember *one* partner ignominiously consigned to the background for no particular reason," replies he, meaningly.

"Do you ?"—innocently. "My memory is not my strong

point, so I shall not discuss the subject. But,"—with a flash from the violet eyes,—"I think I may take upon myself to say that you are wrong when you say there was no 'particular reason' for my so acting."

"Unless caprice be a reason," retorts he, saying it in quite a low tone.

"I do not understand you," says Miss Neville, with some haughtiness of look and manner; "nor do I desire to do so."

"''Tis folly to remember,'" quotes he from a song she herself is in the habit of singing, and with a short, unmirthful laugh. "You are right. To encourage forgetfulness should be one of our greatest aims. But to return to our first discussion. I am indeed the unhappiest of men. Is there no hope that you will change your mind, and let me live in the expectation of being favoured with one waltz?"

"I can offer you no such hope," returns she, with so much pointed decision in her voice and expression, that Saumarez, turning sharply on his heel, takes off his hat with a frowning brow and a somewhat vindictive glance, and next minute has disappeared amongst the crowd.

There is a slight but perceptible pause after he has gone. The other men have melted away before this, and only Penruddock remains.

"I hardly think I shall stay on for your dance," he says, presently, with some hesitation, looking disappointed, and speaking in a very dejected tone.

That little bit of information just given by Miss Neville to the effect that all her dances were disposed of has checked his ardour for the Audley Street "small and early," and has, in fact, reduced him to a state that borders on despair.

About a week ago, Miss Neville had almost promised him a waltz at this particular dance, but doubtless she has by this time forgotten all about such a promise, and has given the waltz in question to some more favoured individual.

"My dear child, why not?" asks Mrs. Neville, kindly, struck

by the sudden melancholy of his appearance. "I do hope, my dear Dick, you are not given to moping. So many young men mope now-a-days. I believe they call it by a finer name, but it really comes to the same thing. Now why won't you stay on for my dance to-night?"

"It sounds rude, and it is rude," confesses Mr. Penruddock, with some contrition; "but the fact is, I know I shouldn't enjoy it—I—I couldn't stand it," says Dick, with a reproachful glance at Beauty, who sits apparently careless and unmoved, looking before her.

But at this moment Miss Neville sees fit to join in the conversation.

She turns her head slowly, and letting her handsome eyes meet Penruddock's, chains him to the spot by the very power of their beauty.

"Then I suppose I am at liberty to give away that third waltz that I promised you at Lady Ryecroft's?" she asks, slowly, without removing her gaze.

"You remember it? I thought perhaps you had forgotten," says Penruddock, eagerly. "No, do not give it away. Dear Mrs. Neville, do not think me unstable, or fickle, or anything that way, but the fact is nothing on earth should keep me from your dance to-night."

He flushes a dark red, laughs a little, raises his hat, and, as though unable longer to endure the rather mischievous smile in Miss Neville's blue eyes, beats a hasty retreat.

"He is a dear boy—quite charming," say Mrs. Neville, who is feeling puzzled, "but certainly a little vague. So very unlike his father, who was the most unpleasantly matter-of-fact person I ever met. What were you saying to Captain Saumarez, Maudie? I saw that you were talking to him, but you did not seem very genial, either of you."

"He is very distasteful to me," says Maud, quickly. "I don't know what it is, auntie, but I feel a horror—a hatred of that man. His manner towards me is insolent to a degree. It is as though he would compel me, against my will, to be civil to him, and I never shall!" concludes Miss Neville, between her little white, even teeth.

"I don't think I care much about him myself," says Mrs. Neville. "He always seems to me to be something of an adventurer; and, besides, he is a friend of all the Penruddocks, and, except Dick, I never liked any of them. Not that he is much of a friend there either, as he never speaks of them, and even if drawn into conversation about Dick's father, as a rule says something disparaging. But he has money, and is received everywhere; and I really think, my dear child, he is very devoted to you."

"Oh, do not, pray, try to make him even more detestable in my sight than he is already," says Maud, with a shiver that may mean disgust.

"Oh, no! Of course I meant nothing. And he is the last man that I should care to see you married to. But some time or other you must make a selection—you can but know that—and I am always thinking for you, indeed I am. Dick Penruddock is very much in love with you, I really believe, though you always deny it."

"I deny it because I think he is not. I hope with all my heart and soul that he is not," says Maud, with sudden and unlooked-for energy.

All the colour has fled from her cheeks, and her lips tremble slightly.

"Well, my dear, perhaps so. I own I am stupid," says Mrs. Neville, who, though the best and kindest of women, is certainly in no danger of setting the Thames on fire with her cleverness. "Though I can't see why you should dislike the idea so much. He is quite charming in my opinion, and *so* handsome! Then there is Lord Stretton; you can't tell me that *he* does not adore the very ground you walk on!"

"Oh, Stretton!" says Miss Neville, disdainfully.

"But, my dearest, you *must* marry some one!" says her "auntie," in an aggrieved tone. "Dick, as I say, is all that one could possibly desire; but Stretton has a title, and that always counts.   As that dear man in *Punch* said some time ago, ' Beauty and goodness may fade and pall, but a title *lasts*.'   There is certainly a very great deal of sense in that remark, and it *is* nice to have a duke for a brother-in-law."

"I don't think Wolfhampton would be nice as a brother-in-law were he fifty times a duke," says Maud, with a curl of her short upper lip.

"He might be improved on, certainly ; I don't dispute that," Mrs. Neville admits, sadly.   "His manners are positively distressing, so redolent of the stable ; and his nose is out of all proportion !"

"It is so like Lord Stretton's that no one could possibly know one from the other," says Maud, wilfully.

Mrs. Neville sighs.   The case is beyond argument.   It is indeed only too true that Lord Stretton's proboscis bears a painful resemblance to his brother's.

"Dick Penruddock is, of course, in many ways far preferable," she says, presently, shifting ground.   "He is quite as rich, and is younger, and has prettier manners.   But, then, you say you object to Dick also."

"No, I don't object to Mr. Penruddock," says the girl, with a soft, slow blush ; "that is not it.   You mistake me, Mimi." (This is the pet name she gave to Mrs. Neville when a child.) "I only mean that I shall never marry."

"But why—*why ?*" impatiently.

"Can *you* ask me that?" returns she, with a glance full of the liveliest reproach.

"But the thing is not a secret—all the world knows how I adopted you, and that you are the daughter of some poor mechanic, dead before I ever saw you.   But they know, too, that you are the most beautiful and the most charming girl in town !   Yes, you *are !*" in answer to a deprecating shake of Miss Neville's head ; "and if these men love you, and choose to overlook such a little fault, why, then, I cannot see——"

"A *little* fault !" repeats she, sadly.   Then, with a touch of pride, "Nay, it is no fault at all, but it is a great misfortune ;

and though Stretton—or—or Mr. Penruddock may, perhaps, foolishly wish to marry me, do you honestly believe their families would receive me with open arms? Do you think it at all likely that Dick's father would be glad to see him married to a girl without name? It is impossible, Mimi!"

"I know not what they might think or say, but I know that if he were my son I would gladly see him married to you," says Mimi, maintaining her cause stoutly.

"That is because you love me, and because you are different from all the rest of the world," says the girl, gently, looking at her through a soft mist, that dims the beauty of her eyes, and is born of tenderness, and gratitude, and deep affection.

At this moment the carriage draws up at their hall door, and, alighting, they pass into the house.

CHAPTER V.

AFTER THE DANCE.

IT is many hours later, and the dance is at its best and gayest. The sound of music and the delicate perfume of dying flowers are in the air.

The rooms are filled with all that London can afford of its brightest, and highest, and best, and pretty women in toilettes almost as desirable as themselves are smiling and waving their fans, and doing all the damage that soft eyes and softer speech are supposed to do.

It is the third waltz, and the band is playing " Mon Rêve." In Dick Penruddock's opinion it is the waltz of the evening, as his arm is round Maud Neville, and her perfect head is very near his own.

He is as happy as a man can be who holds all he deems most precious for one moment to his heart, knowing that the next might separate them for ever.

Presently they pause to rest, and find themselves near the door of a conservatory.

"Are you tired?" asks he, seeing she sighs, and raises one hand in a half-wearied fashion to smoothe back some loose hairs that have wandered across her forehead. "Come in here, and sit down for a little while."

He tightens his arm on the hand resting upon it, and moves towards the cool retreat before them.

"If you wish it," replies she, uncertainly, and with some slight hesitation in her manner.

Yet she goes with him into the dimly-lighted conservatory, where a little fountain is splashing, sending forth a cold, sweet music of its own, and where green leaves are glistening calmly beneath the beams of the subdued lamps.

The time—the hour—the very drip, drip of the fountain— all bespeak loneliness; and to feel oneself alone with a beloved object, as a rule, kills wisdom.

Penruddock, who all day long has been enduring suspense and an uncertainty that borders on hope, suddenly loses his head. Laying his hand on Maud's, he bends down to her, and whispers something in a soft, impassioned voice.

The girl appears neither startled nor surprised, and when she speaks, her tone, though perhaps a shade slower than usual, is firmer than ever.

Only she changes colour, and grows pale until her very lips are bloodless.

"You speak without thought or reflection," she says, gently. "You have considered nothing. No, no; do not interrupt me! I am sorry this has occurred; but there is no reason why we should not forget what you have just said, and be good friends as we were before."

"There *is* a reason, and a strong one," returns he, very quietly now; "and as to our being mere friends, that is quite out of the question. Do you imagine me an impulsive boy to say a thing one moment and regret it the next? I have dared to say to-night what I have wanted to say for many days.   And I must have my answer now."

" And my birth—have you forgotten that ? " demanded she, looking at him fixedly.

" I have forgotten nothing.   But to me it makes no difference.   Princess or peasant, how can it matter?   I love you. Darling," says the young man, very earnestly, taking both her hands and holding them closely, " I implore you to believe in my love !   Take time for reflection, consider well !   I entreat you to give me no hurried answer ! "

" I do not hurry," returns she, in a strange tone ; " I will not even argue with you.   Let us say no more about it ; and please let my hands go, Mr. Penruddock.   I cannot marry you— indeed, I cannot ! "

" But why ?—at least, tell me that ? " demands he, desperately, refusing to release her hands.   " Maud, answer me !   Do you—is it true that you love another better, and that is why you cannot care for me ? "

" No ; that is untrue," replies she, with quick pain in voice and eyes.   " I love no one better than you ; which means, of course "—hurriedly, and with a sad little quivering laugh— " that I love *no one*.   You will understand me ? "

" Only too well," returns he, sadly.   He lifts her hands, and kisses them separately, in a forlorn, lingering fashion.   " And yet there is some talk of Stretton," he says, miserably, his face haggard and unhappy.

" That report is false," she says, slowly.

Then, after a faint hesitation, she raises her head and regards him with earnest attention.

Her eyes are full of unshed tears, and her voice, soft and low as it always is, trembles a little as she speaks.

" Believe nothing you hear," she says, impressively ; " only this—that I shall *never* marry."

Turning abruptly from him, she moves towards the ball-room, and standing in the doorway, gazes, without seeing anything, at the swaying crowd before her.

Presently she becomes conscious that two dark eyes are fixed upon her; she turns restlessly, and Captain Saumarez stands at her side.

"Not dancing, Miss Neville?" begins he, lightly. "And all alone, too!" Then, with a change of manner, and throwing some concern into his tone, he says quietly, "You look over-tired. May I take you out of this to one of the smaller rooms beyond, or in here?" pointing to the conservatory she has just quitted.

"Oh, no; not in there!" exclaims she, with some distress. "But I shall be glad to get away for a little while."

Taking his arm, she makes her way slowly through the dancers and the lingerers at the doorway, and presently sinks, with a sigh of relief, into a low chair, in a small room that opens off an ante-chamber.

The music seems so very far away that the noise and confusion could almost be forgotten. Oh, that she could now get rid of her companion, and find herself, if only for one short half-hour, alone!

"Something has annoyed you. Can I help you in any way?" says Saumarez, in his gentlest manner.

"You are very good. No; it is nothing. I am only slightly fatigued," returns she, listlessly.

"May I get you something? A glass of wine—some iced water?"

"Thank you—nothing."

Her evident determination not to be friendly, her extreme coldness of voice and gesture, pique him beyond endurance. What has he done to her that this proud girl should treat him with such open disdain?

"I saw you go into that conservatory about ten minutes ago," he says, after a slight pause, some reckless desire to rouse her from her apathy, and bring anger, if he cannot summon love, into those beautiful eyes below him, inciting him to this speech. "You seemed greatly disturbed when you came out again. Was that boy rude to you?"

He has certainly gained his point. Miss Neville's blue eyes literally flash with anger.

"That boy?" repeats she, in an impassible tone.

"I am speaking of Penruddock," returns he, with cool persistence. "Was he rude?"

"I hardly know how to answer such a question," says Miss Neville, frigidly. "I never knew until now—to-night—that any man could be rude to me."

"Ah! then I am to understand he did offend?" says Saumarez, insolently, his evil genius at his elbow.

"I was not alluding to Mr. Penruddock—he is incapable of any act of ill-breeding; I was alluding to you!" says Maud, in a clear tone, rising as she delivers this retort.

She would have swept by him and left the room, but with a smothered exclamation he seizes her hand, and detains her against her will.

"Stay!" cries he, with some passion. "I have something to say to you, that I have too long withheld, and that you shall hear now or never."

"Then it shall be never!" says the girl, quickly. "I decline to listen to anything you may have to say. Release me, sir; your very touch is hateful to me!"

"Ay, since Penruddock came upon the field. Do you think I am so blind that I cannot see how he has gained favour where all others have been treated with studied coldness? Do you think I have not noticed how he——"

"I decline to discuss Mr. Penruddock with you," says Maud, throwing up her head with a gesture full of graceful dignity that might have adorned a queen.

"Is he so precious in your sight?" says Saumarez, with a sneer. "And is this new lover prepared to overlook the fact of your humble birth?"

"Take care, sir; do not go too far!" says Maud, her voice vibrating with indignation.

"I don't care how far I go now," declares he, all the evil blood in his heart surging upwards to the surface. "I love you too! Yes; you *shall* listen to me, though it be for the last time!" tightening his fingers on her wrist. "I love you, as that boy can *never* love you—with all the strength of a man's deepest devotion!"

"Hush! *your* mention of love is but an insult!" says she, in a withering tone.

"My voice is not so silken as his, no doubt," replies he, driven to madness by her loathing. "Nor do soft words trip so readily from my tongue. But will his love stand the test of time? Will he never regret that he has married one who is——"

He pauses.

"Lowly born."

She supplies the words; speaking them bravely, and not flinching from the stroke.

"Ay, and *basely!*" says he, between his teeth.

It is a lie, and he knows it. But at this moment he would have uttered any false thing to lower the pride of the woman whom—strange paradox—he loves, yet hates!

A terrible change passes over Miss Neville's countenance as the words cross his lips.

"No, no; it is not true!" she cries, all her courage forsaking her. "I will not believe it! What can *you* know more than all the others? Ah! is it for this reason I have dreaded you? Have pity, and unsay your words!"

"I do not speak without authority," replies he, quickly, stung again by her admission that she dreads him. "I know all about your birth"—there is an air of undoubted truth about these words that strikes cold to her heart,—"and I tell you again, that you are not only humbly but basely born!"

She shudders violently.

A low cry escapes her, and with the hand that still remains free she covers her face.

At this instant, Penruddock, followed by Mr. Wilding (with whom he is earnestly conversing), enters the room. He is unfortunately in time to hear Miss Neville's agonized cry, and to hear Saumarez's last words.

Going up to the latter, he pushes him backwards, releasing Maud from his grasp.

"Who has dared to apply such words as 'basely born' to Miss Neville?" he asks, in fiery tones.

"I have said so, and say it again!" says Saumarez, with his usual evil sneer.

"You are a coward!" says Penruddock, losing all command of his temper; and, raising his gloved hand, he strikes him across the face.

There is a second's awful silence; then Saumarez—who has instinctively raised his hand to his cheek, on which a pink line may be traced—says, quietly, turning to Penruddock, "When, and where?"

"The sooner the better," says Dick, still white, and wild with fury.

Maud, who has shrunk aside, and who is now standing close to Mr. Wilding, says to him, in a nervous whisper, so low as to be almost unintelligible, "What does it all mean?"

"Fighting, I think," says Mr. Wilding, who is a plain-spoken man at times, and given to electrify the judges in court on certain occasions. "They are arranging a duel, unless I am greatly mistaken."

"But it must be prevented!" says Maud, wildly. "Something must be done!"

Going up to Penruddock, she lays her hand upon his arm,— "Let me speak, Dick!" she says, in trembling accents.

The word—his Christian name—has unconsciously escaped her; but he has heard it, and proudly, gladly, takes the little hand upon his arm between both his own, as though this un-expected mention of his name had made her his—had been an informal confession of her love.

"There is no need that you should quarrel," she goes on, with lowered eyes and pallid lips. "He is right; he has but spoken the truth. I *am* lowly born, as all the world knows;

though, sir," confronting Saumarez, and gazing full at him with terrible grief and reproach in her glance, "it has yet to be proved how you came to use that word ' basely.'"

"My conduct to you has been unpardonable, madam," says Saumarez, bowing and drawing back, with set lips and a stern expression. "I ask your forgiveness. To your friend, Mr. Penruddock, I shall give every satisfaction necessary—the very *strongest* satisfaction !" concludes he, with a grim smile ; after which he bows again, and withdraws.

Miss Neville bursts into tears, and sobs bitterly for a few minutes. Penruddock, with his arm round her, supports her head against his breast for some time unrebuked. Presently, however, she checks her emotion, and, drawing away from him, wipes the tears from her eyes, sighing heavily.

"You have got your work cut out for you, you know," suggests Mr. Wilding, in a low tone to Dick, who had forgotten everything but Maud's grief.

"I am quite aware of that," mutters Dick.

"If you are going to cross to the other side, you will have but very little time to arrange matters before starting."

"There is little to arrange," says Penruddock, absently. "My cousin George falls in for everything if I come to grief in the encounter."

Then he goes up to Maud, who is still silently crying, and takes her hand again.

"Tell me the truth now," he says. "At this last moment, it would be a solace, a comfort to me. That time—a few minutes since, when you called me ' Dick '—your tone, your whole manner thrilled me ; it almost caused me to believe that I was not quite indifferent to you. Was that presumption, madness, on my part ? Speak, darling !"

He bends his head, and she whispers something in a voice half broken.

It must have been some word of encouragement, as Penruddock's visage brightens, and his whole manner changes.

"And if I return ? " he begins, eagerly.

But she interrupts him.

"Oh you must—you *will* return !" she says, painfully.

"If I do, you will marry me ?"

She shakes her head.

Even at this most solemn moment her great resolve is not to be broken.

"My dear Penruddock, this is out of all bearing," says Mr. Wilding, who has been engaged in an engrossing examination of a bit of old Chelsea, but now feels it his duty to come to the rescue and deliver Miss Neville from her embarrassment. "Let us discuss what you have got to do."

"That is simple," says Penruddock, with a frown. "If luck stands to me, I shall shoot him through the heart."

"No, no !" says Maud, faintly, putting up her hand in quick protest. "To kill him, that would be murder ! Do not have his death upon your conscience."

"Would you shrink from me because of that?" asks he, wistfully.

"It would be so terrible," she falters.

"Yet, remember, it would be in your cause."

"For that very reason,"—earnestly,—"I should feel it all the more. And later on, when you had grown cool, it would be to yourself an everlasting regret, and I should be the author of it. Oh, let him live !"

"Well, I dare say I shall," says Penruddock, in a curious tone; "for this reason—that I suppose he will kill me."

"He splits hairs, and sixpenny-bits, and all sorts of thin things, at any number of paces that you like to name," says Mr. Wilding, pleasantly.

Miss Neville shudders, and turns a shade paler even than she has been through all.

"After all, there is not so much in life that one should regret it to any intense degree," says Dick, who takes it rather badly that she objects to his killing Saumarez.

"My dear boy, there you err," says Wilding, briskly. "There is a great deal in life, if you go the proper way to find it, and

if you don't expect too much; that is the great secret.   Life
is a first class thing in my opinion—nothing like it.   I never,
you know, fight duels myself—nothing would induce me; but
if you *must*, my dear Penruddock, aim low, and cover him well
with your eye.   I'll see you through it, and stick to you, my
dear boy, whatever happens."

"Thanks, old man; I knew quite well that you would not
desert me," says Dick, gratefully.

"Can nothing be done?" says Maud, clasping her hands.
"Oh, Mr. Wilding, do try; surely something may be effected
if you will only try!"

"Of course I shall try," says Wilding, promptly.   "I'll stand
to him all through—I have promised that.   By Jove! I
wouldn't advise that fellow to do anything unfair when I am
on the field!   And if"—impressively—"anything unfortunate
should occur, I'll——"

"Oh, Mr. Wilding, how I hate you!" interrupts Miss
Neville, with a sudden burst of wrathful tears.   "If no one
else will help me," cries she, going hurriedly towards the door,
"I shall try, at least, what a weak woman can do!"

She opens the door, closes it behind her firmly, and runs
upstairs to her own apartments.

CHAPTER VI.

AN ENTREATY.

IT is an hour later; and in his library Gilbert Saumarez is
sitting with folded arms, on which his face lies hidden.

The table is strewn with papers.

A crumpled, faded flower and a little, six-buttoned black-kid
glove are on the desk close beside him; how procured, he
alone knows.

Certainly, they were never given to him by their rightful owner.

The lamps are lowered, until a half-gloom, that is almost darkness, envelops the apartment.

Ghastly shadows creep here and there, unchecked, unnoticed by the man who sits so silently in the armchair beneath the centre lamp.

He is lost in thought, in vain regrets, that belong to the present and the near past, but have no connection with the morrow, that may bring death in its train.

But not to him.

No fear of being " done to death " in open fight need harass him.

He is too expert a shot ; has too often earned his reputation as a skilled duellist to feel nervous at the prospect of an encounter with an amateur—a raw schoolboy in the art of duelling, as he rightly terms Penruddock.

He has killed his man before this ; and having made up his mind to shoot this present rival as he would a dog, has dismissed the subject from his thoughts.

Other considerations crowd upon him—other remembrances, sweet and bitter ; and so absorbed is he in his inward musings, that he does not hear the door open, nor the sound of the light feet that advance across the floor, until the owner of them is almost at his side.

He raises his head then, and looking up, starts to his feet with an exclamation that is caused by a surprise which for a moment completely overpowers him.

It is Maud Neville who stands before him, pale as " the snowy lily pressed with heavy rain."

Her eyes are large, half-frightened, and full of grief. Beneath them dark circles show themselves. No faintest tinge of colour adorns her cheeks. Her hair, under her swan's-down hood, has loosened, and strays across her low, smooth forehead at its own good will.

She is pale, nervous, thoroughly unhinged, yet never perhaps has she looked so lovely.

To Gilbert Saumarez, gazing at her, some old lines occur that seem to apply to her as to none other—

> " To see her is to love her,
> And love but her for ever,
> For nature made her what she is, .
> And ne'er made sic anither ! "

"You here, and alone ! " he stammers, moving from her rather than towards her.

"Yes, here," returns she, in a low tone tremulous with emotion. "Esther waits for me outside. I have so far forgotten my own dignity and self-respect as to come here to you at midnight, compelled by a sudden necessity. The more reason, sir," with an upward glance of mingled entreaty and pride, "that you should respect both ! "

"Speak ! " returns he, coldly.

She throws back her hood and cloak **as** though half-stifled, and stands before him in all the bravery of her satin ball-dress, on which the pearls gleam with a soft, subdued light.

" I have come to ask you to forego this duel—to give it up," she says, faintly, discouraged by his manner, yet not wholly dismayed. "I entreat you to hear me, to listen to what I have to say, not to turn a deaf ear to my prayer."

" Yet to my prayer not an hour since you were deaf," retorts he, quietly.

She is silent.

" You would ask me to spare your lover—that boy, Penruddock," says he, with a mocking smile, " and so proclaim myself a coward, as he called me ? Impossible ! Why, he struck me across the face with his open hand—here ! "

He raises his hand to the cheek that still bears the mark of the blow, but was paled as the remembrance of the deadly insult returns to him.

His eyes blaze with wrath. Involuntarily he clenches his hand.

To the girl watching him there seems indeed but small hope of mercy.

She draws nearer, and by a sudden impulse lays her hand upon his.

"At least, do not kill him!" she says, despair in her tone, an awful look in her great gleaming eyes. "Do not murder him! He is young, and youth is precious. You will have mercy on him, will you not?"

Overcome by fear, and utterly unnerved, she sinks at his feet and gazes up at him, speechless, but still with imploring look and gesture.

There is a childish grief and anxiety in her lovely face that touches the world-worn and almost utterly callous heart of the man before her.

"How you must love him," he says, bitterly, almost scornfully, "to bring yourself to do what you have done to-night! That you—you, proud child—should come here where no woman could be seen without injury to herself, convinces me of—— But, no!" He interrupts himself, and his voice grows suddenly tender. "I will take care that no evil shall be spoken of you; you need not be afraid of that!"

He stoops and raises her gently from the ground.

"You will promise me," she entreats, in a whisper, "to spare him? I know how skilful you are—what an easy matter it would be to you to place a bullet in his heart. But you will spare him? And who can say but this one deed of mercy may save your soul at last?"

"My soul!" says he, with a haunting laugh. "And supposing that at your earnest instigation I do consent to spare your lover—what then, I pray?"

"I have no lover," says the girl, simply. "I never shall have one. You should know that—you, who told me in plain language not an hour since of my lowly birth and breeding."

"Pardon me," says he, lowering his eyes, shame covering his brow with crimson. "If I could recall that last hour I would. I lied when I spoke of disgrace."

"You do not deceive me now—you tell me truth?" asks

she, with agitation. "Yet you said that you knew of my birth —that I was base-born."

"This is no time for such discussion," says he, evasively; "but if ever you want a witness to prove your birth, send for me. And now, am I forgiven my offence?"

"I have forgotten everything," says she, eagerly, "only this —that I want your promise. Swear to me Dick Penruddock's death will not lie at your door?"

"And if I give this promise—if I tell you I shall fire over his head instead of straight into the centre of his heart, what shall be my reward?"

"Name it," says she, thoughtlessly.

"It is a simple request. I ask but one kiss, and my oath shall be given."

She starts, and shrinks from him perceptibly.

"You are no man to ask me that!" she says, white to the lips again, and with her small hands tightly clenched.

"Yet that is my bargain—the only one I will make!" returns he, doggedly.

Within her breast fierce battle reigns.

All a woman's innate modesty fights with love's self-sacrifice.

The struggle is severe, but lasts not very long. Love conquers.

"For his sake!" she murmurs, brokenly.

And then she goes up to Saumarez, and stands before him, her face like marble.

"You shall have your reward!" she says, faintly.

He lays both his hands upon her shoulders, and regards her earnestly.

Then he pushes her somewhat roughly from him, and laughs aloud—a very unpleasant laugh, and one by no means good to hear.

"Look here," he says; "*I* can be generous, too! Keep your kisses!—keep" (bitterly) "your lips unsullied for him! And keep my promise, too; I give it freely, without reward, just for love of you! Perhaps in the future you will confess that I loved you at least as well as *he* does, or any man could ! Do I not prove it ? For *your* sake—to please *you*—I spare the life of the only man whom I envy, and when I could shoot him as easily as I could a dog ! "

"You are generous, indeed !" she says, below her breath. "I cannot thank you as—— "

"I want no thanks !" he says, shortly. "This is our last meeting—unless," with meaning in his tone, "you *want* me, you shall never be cursed by the sight of me again ! This country has grown hateful to me ! And your fair face has been my ruin—not that *that* counts now-a-days ; a life more or less is of little moment ! Nay," with an effort, "I do not blame you ! It was not your fault ! And now good-bye ! You must not stay longer. At least, before parting, you will give me your hand in token of good fellowship ? "

"Good-bye ! " she says.

" Nay, it is not only that ; it is an eternal farewell !" corrects he.

She gives him her hand, and, taking it, he holds it closely for a moment only, letting it go almost immediately.

Then, drawing her hood once more over her head, she moves to the door.

But at the last instant, even as her hand is on the lock, he follows her, and, falling at her feet, catches and presses a fold of her dress passionately to his lips.

It is all over then ; and, rising, he turns aside, and covers his face with his hands.

A moment later, he finds himself alone.

CHAPTER VII.

FATHER AND SON.

Not even to Mrs. Neville does Maud tell of the terrible anxiety that weighs down her spirits, and reduces her to a state that borders on distraction.

She makes no mention of the quarrel that has occurred between Dick and Captain Saumarez, or of her midnight visit to the house of the latter.

But she is restless and miserable, and Mrs. Neville, watching her, knows that something is amiss.

As all next day goes by, and Wednesday dawns, and still no tidings reach her of Dick's welfare, the suspense and terror she is enduring prove almost more than she can bear.

That she loves Penruddock she no longer seeks to deny even to herself, though in her firm determination never to marry him she is altogether unchanged, has not wavered in the least.

It would undoubtedly have been a comfort to her during all these lonely hours of uncertainty to have had some one near her with whom she could discuss her trouble, and to whom she could breathe out all her fears and longings, but that solace is denied to her.

Mrs. Neville, as she knew, entertained a sincere affection for Penruddock, and to apprize her of his danger would be to raise feelings of grief and direst apprehensions of evil in her kindly heart, and she would herself need comfort, rather than be able to afford it.

So, by a supreme effort, Maud conquered all selfish desires for sympathy, and waited alone for tidings that might bring her joy or sorrow.

" Has Saumarez really and truly kept the promise so strangely given ? "

This is the thought that torments her, sleeping and waking, causing her to grow pale, and place her hand upon her heart, if the door should chance to open suddenly, or any servant make a hurried entrance.

May he not bring with him a telegram or message that shall reduce to an unhappy certainty all the vague fears that now distress her?

She is leaning back in a low chair, in the smaller morning-room, making a poor pretence at reading, whilst Mimi sits writing letters at a davenport near, humming gaily, as her pen runs lightly over the paper, a little soft melody, heard last night at the Opera Bouffe.

The door opens slowly, and a tall woman, dark and careworn, but with all the remains of great and striking beauty, comes quietly into the room.

"Mr. Penruddock is in the drawing-room," she says, in a trained voice, that expresses emotion of no kind, though, as the name passes her lips, a faint quiver contracts her beautiful features.

"Mr. Penruddock !" cries Maud, with a little gasp, springing to her feet.

"Then why not show him in here, as usual?" asks Mimi, glancing round the pretty boudoir to see what can be wrong with it, her thoughts running on Dick.

"It isn't young Mr. Penruddock ; it is his father," says the woman, with sullen looks fixed upon the carpet. " He wishes to see you, madam?"

"To see me? Dear me, what can George Penruddock have to say to me ?" says Mrs. Neville, shrugging her shoulders. "I would rather not see him alone. Indeed, I do not think that I could muster courage for that. Will you come to the drawing-room with me, dearest?"

"Oh, no !" says Maud, turning an agitated countenance upon her friend. "Why should I? He knows nothing of me—at least," with a sudden pang of doubt, "I hope not! *If* he should mention me, Mimi, say I have a headache. It will be the truth ; my brain seems on fire !"

"What an excitable child you are !" says Mrs. Neville, soothingly. "There, lie down on this couch, and keep yourself quiet, for I promise that you shall not be disturbed. Esther, throw one of those soft Eastern shawls over Miss Neville, and fan her for a little while."

Esther arranges the shawl carefully as Mrs. Neville leaves the room, and pouring some eau de Cologne upon a handkerchief, applies it to her young mistress's temples.

She is a swarthy woman, with a visage full of suppressed

power, and with a suspicion of revengefulness in its cast; but her whole expression softens and grows unspeakably tender as she bends above the girl and ministers to her.

When, many years ago, she had brought the baby to Mrs. Neville's house, by her desire, she had so played her cards that she too had been taken in by the soft-hearted, romantic woman, and kept on as nurse to the destitute child, and had never since quitted her.

That undertaking, last night but one, was too much for you," says Esther, in a low tone. "You have not been yourself since. I greatly blame myself, and am very sorry that I ever had hand, act, or part in it."

"Do not," says the girl, wearily; "though I fear that hazardous step has availed me nothing. I doubt if he has shown mercy to Dick Penruddock."

"Was it to crave mercy for *him* that you sought Saumarez's rooms that night?" asks the woman quickly, a frown contracting her brow.

"Yes; I asked and obtained his promise that he would spare Dick. But this long silence terrifies me; what if he should break his word?"

"Had I known *that——*" says the woman, between her teeth, and said it in such a strange tone that Maud glanced anxiously at her.

"What do you mean, Esther? How strangely you speak!" she says, a little sternly. "Would you rather that Mr. Penruddock met his death? You are cruel, very wicked. What harm has he done you?"

"I would spare none of the breed," says the woman, slowly, her looks fixed on vacancy.

"You speak as though you knew them. Were you ever connected with them in any way?" asks Maud, curiously, sitting up and bending eagerly forward closely to watch her nurse's troubled countenance.

"Connected—no," says Esther, in a tone of cunningly-acted surprise, awaking as though to a sense of danger—"how should I? My head is full of fancies to-day—you must not mind me. And Mr. Penruddock—I hope he will come home safe, my dearie, for he is a brave young gentleman and a handsome one; but not so handsome as my Lord Stretton; no, nor in any way whatever so worthy of you."

"When did Mr. Penruddock come, nurse?" asks Maud, after a pause.

"Almost as I came in. No doubt he is here to speak about his son."

She chooses her words carefully, and marks well the effect produced by them.

"He has heard, it may be, of his constant visits here, and deems you unworthy of an alliance with *his* house. But he need not fear, need he? You have rejected Mr. Dick—you assured me of that the other night?"

"Yes, it is true. His fears are groundless. I do not desire to marry his son!" says Maud, proudly.

"So best," says Esther. "His blood is bad; at least"—hastily—"so I have heard."

Maud is silent.

After a little while she says, in a rather depressed voice and with averted looks, "What is he like, Esther?"

"Who?—Penruddock? Stern and forbidding, cold and haughty, as of old," returns the woman, absently;—"not bowed and broken with the weight of time and memory, as, if he had a conscience, he should be!"

"Why, how you say that!" says Maud, raising herself on her elbow. "For the second time you make me think you know him."

"Nay, child—how should I?" says nurse, impatiently, yet in a half-frightened manner. "It is from all I have heard I judge, and that was no good. The old, too, should not be high and mighty; they should remember the grave, and how it yawns for them—they should repent them of the many sins that they, in the past, have committed."

"How ghostly!" says the girl, with a slight shiver. "Do not talk like that ; it almost unnerves me. To hear you, one might imagine that Mr. Penruddock was nothing less than a murderer ! "

The woman smiles disagreeably, and covers her face with her hand, perhaps to hide the change that passes over it. Then taking up the bottle of perfume again, she pours out some more, and applies it, but with a trembling hand, to Miss Neville's forehead.

"Nurse," says Maud, presently, in a nervous tone, "I have been thinking of something, and I cannot get it out of my thoughts.   Perhaps some one has told Mr. Penruddock of this fatal quarrel with Captain Saumarez, and he has come up to town about it, and has come here to accuse me to auntie as being the cause of it ; and "—starting to her feet in her agitation—"if that be so, what shall I say or do ? "

"Tut, nonsense," says Esther, calmly—"that cannot be. Ill news should 'fly apace' indeed to carry itself down so far to the country in such a hurry. And, besides, who knew of it ? There, my dear child, try to sleep," she says, softly ; "and ring for me if you want me again."

So saying, she goes to the door, opens it, and crossing the passage outside, walks lightly downstairs, and seats herself in a room off the hall, from which, with the door just a little way open, she can command a view of any one going to or coming from the drawing-room.

Left to herself, Maud for some time lies quietly upon the couch, thinking sadly of all that has happened during the last two days, and of all that yet may happen.

The blinds are pulled down, and the dusk of evening has descended and is creeping everywhere, making odd shadows in far corners, and rendering even near objects indistinct.

The day has been dark and cloudy, and the rain has fallen —now steadily, anon in fitful gusts.

The evening is as gloomy as the day, and at this moment the raindrops are pattering drearily against the window-panes with a sad, monotonous sound that chills the heart.

The usually pleasant room looks dull and cheerless now in the uncertain light—dull as her thoughts, and cheerless as are her hopes !

The moments fly ; the ormolu clock upon the mantelpiece chimes the half-hour.

And then there is a noise of footsteps outside, a word or two quickly spoken, and the door is thrown open to admit Mrs. Neville and a tall, gaunt man, who follows her closely and quickly into the room.

Maud, springing to her feet, gazes breathlessly at George Penruddock, though she can barely judge of his appearance in the growing twilight.

She herself, standing back in the extreme shadow, is in such a position that he can scarcely, perhaps not at all, discern her features.

"What have I heard, Maud ?" says Mrs. Neville, in great distress. "Is it true that Dick has been led into a quarrel—has, in fact, risked his life in a duel for your sake ? Tell Mr. Penruddock yourself that this story is a vile fabrication—a shameless, wicked untruth !"

"I cannot !" begins Maud, huskily.

"You hear her !" says the tall, gaunt old man, in accents that vibrate with anger. "She acknowledges everything. She alone is to blame ! This adventuress, this young viper, madam, whom you have taken to your bosom, has wilfully led my unhappy son into a quarrel that has in. all probability brought him to the grave !"

"Silence, Mr. Penruddock !" says Mrs. Neville, with an air of offended dignity foreign to her. " This girl that you so ignorantly accuse is in reality as good and true a child as ever breathed, and I shall listen to nothing against her ! She herself shall tell us all the truth ; but I forbid you to annoy or frighten her with your coarse speeches !"

"Yes ; let her speak quickly—let me hear," says Penruddock, brutally, and scowling at Maud.

In a broken undertone, Maud tells them of all that took

place between Dick and Captain Saumarez the night of Mrs. Neville's dance, suppressing only her visit to the latter's house and the promise there extracted.

When she has finished her recital, she bursts into tears, and sobs distressingly.

Mrs. Neville, going up to her, takes her in her arms, and presses her head down upon her kindly bosom.

For a few minutes no sound can be heard in the room save the girl's bitter weeping, as she fondly and gratefully clings to her faithful Mimi.

"Ay, weep!" says Penruddock, cruelly. "You may well waste an idle tear upon the man you have killed—upon the hearth you have left desolate! It was a cursed hour when first he met you! I have heard of you and have been told of your studied coquetries, though I have never seen you, nor do I desire to look upon your fatal face! I thank the friendly darkness now that prevents my seeing one who has blighted my remaining years! I know all! I have heard of the unfortunate infatuation entertained for you by my unhappy son, and I now live to see its sad results! Rest satisfied. Your vanity must surely be satisfied when you know that he died for your sake!

"Oh, Mimi, do not let him say that! He is *not* dead! He will come back!" says Maud, in an agony of grief and despair, appealing in a heart-broken manner to her friend and mother. "And it was not all my fault! And—and I will not believe that he is dead! It would be too cruel!"

"What a gloomy room, and what a gloomy topic! Who is talking of death?" asks a gay, glad young voice from the doorway, that thrills the listeners to their heart's core.

It is a voice that makes the old man start and tremble violently, and hold out his arms in expectation, with a suppressed but thankful cry.

Yet for the first time his loving greeting is overlooked, is cast aside.

A slight figure, half hidden by the dusk, but discernible to the eyes of a lover, has chained the new-comer's attention, and, oblivious of his father and of all things, Dick Penruddock goes eagerly up to it.

At the sound of his voice, Maud has raised herself, and breaking now from Mrs. Neville, goes quickly to him, and, with an impulsive gesture, lays her hands upon his shoulders.

"It is indeed you!" You have really come back to me!" she gasps, in a little, tremulous whisper, that plainly tells her love and gratitude.

"Yes; to *you!*" responds he, gladly. "But there was no danger—none. He fired right over my head, and refused to fire again. No one knows why. I really think he must have had a sneaking kindness for me all through, or else he has tired of killing. So you see I was bound to come back, like that inevitable bad coin, you know. Why, what is this? Are those tears, my love—and are they shed for *me?*"

She is looking up at him with eyes full of tears, and pink lids, and pallid cheeks; yet never has she appeared to him so beautiful as now, when decked with these signs of woe that are worn for love of him.

"My dear Dick, what a fright you have given us!" says Mrs. Neville, with a deep sigh, half of relief, half of annoyance. "Why, we have been mourning you as past all help in this world, during the last hour; and now here you are, safe and sound! I really think you ought to be ashamed of yourself, and ought also to offer us a profuse apology."

"For being alive," smiled Dick.

"Yes—no, I mean, no—— Dear me, I hardly know what I am saying; but you really ought to feel sorry for all the trouble that you have caused."

"Have you nothing to say to your father?" says Penruddock, at the far end of the room. "That young lady,"—pointing to Maud—"if all I hear be true, you saw only two nights ago; *me* you have not seen for two months! Yet it seems that you have nothing to say to *me*, though much to *her*. Has"—and this was spoken very bitterly—"has an acquaintanceship of weeks obliterated the affection of years?"

"My dear father!" says Dick, deprecatingly.

Then he kisses Miss Neville's hand, and, leaving her, goes up to where his father is standing.

Maud, glad of the chance, slips from the room at this moment, and escapes to her own sanctum.

"Why, father, what lucky chance has driven you up to town?" says Dick, affectionately, and placing his hand on Penruddock's shoulder.

"No lucky chance, but the news of this duel that you have been fighting," says his father, gloomily. "Into what dangers have you been enticed?"

"Why, how came you to hear of it in your quiet country home?" says Dick, with some amazement.

"It matters little. I did hear, that is plain, and came up by the first train."

"Must have been that incorrigible Wilding," mutters Dick, below his breath.

"My time in this great city must be short," says Penruddock, not heeding him, "and I would speak with you seriously before leaving. When can I find myself alone with you? There is much that I have to tell."

"Any time; I am quite at your disposal. In an hour—half an hour," says Dick, readily. "First, I must see Wilding to explain matters; I had promised to dine with him to-night, but shall, of course, resign everything to devote myself to you. Where shall I meet you in half an hour? Where are you putting up—at the Langham, or Claridge's?"

"Claridge's. I shall expect you at the time you say. Do not disappoint me."

"You have my word," says Dick. "Well, I shall be off now. Good-bye, Mrs. Neville. You must not scold me any more, you know; I'm not proof against your displeasure, that is a positive fact. I shall drop in to-morrow, if I may, to tell you all about my adventure."

"Yes; do come, if only to see how thoroughly I can forgive," says Mrs. Neville, smiling; her heart is incapable of harbouring anger.

And the young man, smiling in turn, presses her hand, takes up his hat, and quits the room.

Penruddock, having made his adieux in more elaborate form, goes slowly down the stairs, and into the hall.

As he passes a room, the door of which is now open, a woman, tall and dark-browed, comes quickly forward, as though summoned by his footstep, and confronts him.

As his eyes light upon her, a ghastly change comes over him. He is white as a sheet, seems to shrink and grow smaller, and draws his breath heavily.

"Well, Penruddock," she says, in accents slow and distinct, appearing to enjoy his discomfiture; "and so we meet again! How pleased you look!"

"What has brought you here?" demands he, hoarsely, looking nervously around.

"Fate!" replies she, coldly.

"But here—what has brought you here?" asks he, as though unable to refrain from idle questioning.

The woman, bending towards him, lays her bony hand upon his wrist.

"To help you to remember!" whispers she, in a tone that makes him shudder, so much compressed hatred lies within it. "Have you forgotten? Fifteen years ago this month, Penruddock! Fifteen years ago!"

So saying, she turns abruptly, and enters the room again.

Penruddock follows her.

"Stay, woman!" he exclaims.

"Be not so eager," replies Esther; "we shall meet again."

By this time she has reached a door opposite to that by which she had entered that room, opens, and darts through it closing it quickly behind her

Penruddock would still follow her, but reaching the door through which the woman has gone, he finds it locked against him.

CHAPTER VIII.

A TRUE LOVER.

AFTER a momentary sensation of faintness, that follows close on Esther's disappearance, Penruddock rallies, and tells himself that her presence in this particular house is but one of the coincidences that will occasionally occur in all our lives, and that her wild allusion to objectionable dates has only arisen from the morbid qualities that go so far to make up her character.

By the time his son has arrived, and is ushered into his private sitting-room, he is himself again, composed, calm, and cold, and freer from foolish sentiment than he was an hour ago, reaction having set in.

He opens his subject, which has to do entirely with Dick's misplaced affection for Miss Neville, " so called," without any appearance of excitement or undue warmth, merely expressing in every possible way his disapprobation of the young lady to whom his son is so devoted.

When he has finished, Dick for several moments remains quite silent.

When rejected by Maud on the night of·the dance, he had given way to despair, but so many little things have occurred since then to encourage new hopes, that he has, on reflection, declined to be altogether disheartened.

Her love is not as yet given to another, and therefore she may be his some time in the happy undefined future.

"I regret that I must go against you in this matter," he says at length, quietly but decidedly.

He is standing on the hearthrug, his arms folded, and looking frowningly upon the carpet.

His father, standing opposite to him, with clouded brow, is regarding him anxiously.

" You speak like a child who is asked to relinquish a

favoured but dangerous toy," he says, contemptuously. "You, with your fortune and position to marry a girl penniless, nameless—nay, if report speaks correctly, even worse than——"

"That will do," says the young man, with a sudden gesture suggestive of passion. "Say nothing more, if you please. It is of no consequence whatever to me that she is poor and nameless, as were she possessed of all the wealth in Christendom, and owner of the highest title in the land, I could not possibly love her more than I do now."

"Sentiment in the young is admirable," says Penruddock, in a sneering tone. "It betrays amiability and good feeling. But even virtues may be carried to excess. Do you—pardon me—but do you mean to *marry* this young woman?"

"It would be difficult to say why, but who ever knew a man that wasn't annoyed when any one called the girl he loved a 'young woman'?"

"What else should I mean," he asks, with wretchedly-concealed ire, "if she will have me?"

"Oh! you need not entertain any anxiety on that point. They always have one," says Penruddock, contemptuously. "It is generally a complete 'take in' from start to finish." Then, changing his tone from one of unpleasant banter to that of authority. "Now look here," he says; "let us have no more of this. You can't marry her."

Perhaps as he speaks he forgets how the son inherits his own blood and temper to some degree.

"I shall be quite charmed if nothing more is said about it," says Dick, brushing carelessly some spots of dust from his coat; "but I shall certainly marry Miss Neville if I can induce her to accept me."

There is something in the quiet determination of his tone that impresses George Penruddock.

Going over to his son, he lays his hand upon his shoulder, and says more gently—nay, even with entreaty—"Think well of what you are going to do. This marriage will mean to you ruin, misery, unavailing regret."

" It means my one chance of happiness," says Dick, with a deep sigh, throwing up his head, and looking eagerly forward, as though in the distance he could see some sight that to him was full of sweetness and light.

"Can nothing move you?" asks Penruddock, unsteadily. " Not all the years gone by, in which I have lived, and thought, and speculated for you alone? Is this, after all that I have done, to be my sole return?"

" Dear father," says Dick, turning to him with quick and eager affection, "why try to make me miserable? I remember all—every kind word and kinder action ; and I would implore you in this, the most important act of my life, to give me your sympathy. When you know Maud you will better understand me, because you too will love her. To-morrow I shall ask her again to be my wife, and if she consents, which " (and here he looked and spoke very mournfully) " I strongly doubt, you will gain a daughter as loving as your son."

" Nay," says Penruddock, angrily, turning aside; " I want no daughter picked from the mire. Go, sir ! " pointing to the door. " I shall not again sue to you for either your love or obedience. Yet stay, and hear my last words, as you intend to go to-morrow to ask that girl again to marry you. I warn you I shall be there too, to explain to her the terrible injustice she will do you should she consent to your proposal."

"And I warn you," says Dick, calmly, but in a very curious tone, "that it will be extremely unwise of you, or any one, to say anything likely to wound or offend Miss Neville, even in the very slightest degree."

As the door closes upon his son, George Penruddock sinks heavily into the nearest chair, covers his face with his hands, and is overcome with emotion.

" And for this I have suffered, and endured, and sinned ! " he says, with a convulsive shudder. " Oh that it were possible to undo my wretched past ! But that can never be, alas !—that can never be ! "

*   *   *   *   *   *

When Dick leaves his father's presence, it is but to hasten to his rooms, and send a hasty but tender note to Miss Neville, telling her of his intention to call next day, and again entreat her to look favourably upon his suit.

Then he puts in a few lines about his father, very delicately written, saying that he also intends putting in an appearance at South Audley Street on the morrow; and while assuring her of his own lasting affection for her, implores her—as she feels even a poor sentiment of friendship for him—to pay no heed to any disparaging remarks that ignorance of her sweet excellence may induce any one to make.

After this follow a few more little sentences, put in rather incoherently, but, in all probability, the dearer because of their want of precision to the reader of them, and then he is hers "most faithfully, and with the entire love of his heart, Dick Penruddock."

It is a thorough love-letter ; one that might have been written a century ago, when love was a thing more sacred and more full of courtesy than it is to-day.

Maud, sitting in her own room, weeps bitter tears over it, and kisses it foolishly but very fondly, and tells herself again and again that fate has dealt unjustly with her in that it compels her to resign the writer of this gentle *billet doux*, and putting him entirely out of her life, leave him free to be gained and loved by some more fortunate woman.

And that she must so leave him is, perhaps, the deepest sting of all.

Esther, the nurse, coming in, finds her prone upon a sofa, crying quietly, yet very bitterly, and, full of sympathy, and a little frightened, comes over to her, and smoothes back tenderly the soft hair from her forehead.

To this fond and faithful woman, the girl will always be her child, her nursling.

"What is it, my lamb?" she says, bending down to her with deep concern. "What distresses you? All day long you have been fretting, and now, even as evening falls upon us, I find you weeping again! Why is this, my precious? What has happened?"

"It is nothing," says Maud, evasively. "A foolish fancy; and, besides, my head aches."

"Or your heart, perchance. Yet why? He has come back to you, that young Penruddock, safe and sound. Your conscience, therefore, must be free of offence. Saumarez has been true to his word, and has spared him; yet, in spite of all this, you are openly unhappy. The boy is alive. It is I should weep for that, not you."

"Esther," says the girl, suddenly, sitting up, and confronting her with flushed cheeks and angry eyes, "you must not speak thus—you shall not; and if you persist in hating him, I shall learn to hate you!"

"Ay, that will be my reward, no doubt!" mutters Esther, bitterly.

Her tone smites her listener to the heart.

"I was wrong," she says, with contrition. "How could I speak to you like that?" She slips a warm, soft arm round the woman's neck as she speaks, and Esther, turning, kisses her little hand with passionate love. "How could I hate one who has taken care of me all my life, and even saved me from death once, as you have told me? But of what kind you have not said. Death from starvation, was it?"

"No; from sudden death."

"Why have you never told me about that?"

"What?"

"You know what I mean—that rescue?"

"I shall some day."

"Why not now?"

"I shall wait till you are more sensible."

"I do not understand you."

"I mean, till you have learned to forget Penruddock, and to love another."

"Then I think I shall never hear that story," says the girl, very simply.

"Tut! Does love, think you, last for ever? Time will teach you more than that."

"It would take a very long time indeed to teach me to forget Dick."

"So you think now; but when a year has gone by, and he has forgotten you, and found a fresh idol, then you will come to believe in my words, and then you shall hear the story of your deliverance from death."

"I don't want to hear it," says Maud, wilfully, drawing back from Esther.

She was silent for a few moments, and then asked, in an anxious tone, "Are men really so fickle as you say, nurse?"

"Fickle, and worse! Cold and cruel!"

"But not Dick, I am very sure!" says Maud, with tears in her eyes and voice.

"He is his father's son, and will no doubt follow in his father's footsteps, notwithstanding that his mother was, really and truly, a saint upon earth."

"Was she?" eagerly. "Then I think he must be like his mother."

After which she falls to weeping again bitterly, with the little crumpled note, so precious to her, hidden in her small, feverish hand.

Her tears seem to drop like molten lead upon the woman's heart.

She gets up impatiently, and paces the room in a restless fashion, stopping at last close to the chair where her darling sits lamenting.

"Do not cry," she says, tapping the back of the chair with nervous fingers. "Why will you spoil your eyes and wear away your heart strings? What is it that ails you now? Tell your old Esther?"

"It is a hopeless wish," says the girl, mournfully; "but I want to be as other girls are—I want to have a father and a mother of whom I need not be ashamed. I want to be born in the same society as—as Dick's, and to be his equal. I don't want money; I only want to be raised above the finger of scorn. Oh, Esther, come near to me! I must tell it all to you! I never knew until to-day, when he seemed given back to me from the grave, how fondly, how truly I love him!"

"Alas—alas! that things should have gone so far!" mutters Esther, regretfully.

"When I saw him again, and felt his hands in mine, a great well of joy sprang up within my heart. It was as though he belonged to me, was mine for ever—as if nothing could ever part us again; yet it is all in vain."

"All is vanity," repeats the woman, dreamily.

Her thoughts seem far away, lost in dreams that belong to a curious past.

"To-morrow," goes on Maud, sadly, smoothing out the crushed note with tender fingers, "he is coming again to ask me to be his wife, and for the last time I shall say no. After that we shall be strangers for ever, and how shall I bear it? Oh, how bear it, and live?"

"Then marry him, if your heart is so set upon it," says Esther, sullenly.

"Do you think I would do him such an injustice? And, besides, I would not marry him against his father's will. I have still "—scornfully—"some pride left."

"How can you possibly know that Penruddock would seriously object?"

"By this letter, though the thought is well disguised, and by many other things."

"So, still proud!" says the woman, scornfully. "Yet the day is fast approaching when he will be compelled to lower his tone!"

"What do you say, Esther?" hastily cried Maud, wondering at those words.

"Nothing. Never mind me. Yet it kills me to see you unhappy, when I could help you."

"Help me! Oh, nurse, if you only could!" says the girl, in deep agitation, kneeling down before Esther, and leaning her arms on her knees while gazing with intense earnestness into the dark visage above her. "Sometimes your manner is so strange it makes me believe you are suppressing something. Dear nurse—dearest Esther, help me in this matter if you can ! Mr. Penruddock is coming here to-morrow with Dick. Help me to meet them. Oh, do, pray do ! You could not endure to see me miserable, I know, help me, then, dear Esther ; if only for the sake of your own peace, help me !"

There is a whole world of entreaty in the large blue eyes that gaze upwards through a veil of tears.

Esther, after a moment's hesitation, and fearful struggle with herself, makes a gesture as though resigning something that for years had been sweet to her, and, stooping, presses her lips fondly to Maud's white brow. Is she not as her own child— dearer to her than anything the world can offer? Shall she not, for her darling, relinquish her pet scheme ?

"Perhaps the time is come," she says, slowly. "Tell me, child, is Gilbert Saumarez in town ? "

"I don't know ; but you could find out. Why do you want that dreadful man, nurse ? "—with a blush and a shudder, as she remembers that last meeting with him, in which Esther had borne a part.

"Now lie down again, and try to sleep, or you will be in a high state of fever to-morrow, and unfit to encounter any one," says Esther, with authority, not answering her question. "And" —meaningly—"there is *much* before you—more than you form any idea of !"

CHAPTER IX.

ALL KNOWN.

NEXT morning, sitting in her own room, discussing the post and her chocolate, Mrs. Neville grows suddenly serious over a letter just opened, and which not only disturbs, but very greatly perplexes her.

It is from Mr. Penruddock, demanding an interview, and begging her to name an hour in which he may speak to her upon a subject of much importance, both to him and her.

There is no mention of Maud in the letter ; yet it so unmistakably means business in every line, that Mimi feels uneasy, and, ringing the bell, summons Esther to her aid—the woman having proved herself of sound judgment upon several occasions when Mrs. Neville had found herself in want of good advice, and knew not where else to look for it.

For two long hours she and Esther remain closeted together, at the end of which time Mrs. Neville, opening the door, comes out into the corridor with an air of open triumph and gladness in her whole demeanour, that contrasts rather oddly with the pink lids and heavy eyes that betray the fact of her having been crying bitterly. In her hand she bears a letter, which is addressed to George Penruddock.

Esther, going on to Maud's room, after some persuasion induces her to send a note to Dick, desiring him to come to South Audley Street at a particular hour—that is to say, at nine o'clock that evening.

*   *   *   *   *   *

The lamps are carefully lowered, the curtains drawn. There is sufficient light to discern objects, but hardly enough to read the features of Maud Neville, who, reclining in a low chair at the upper end of the room, sits idly gazing into vacancy, whilst swinging slowly to and fro a huge black fan.

Upon a table underneath Mrs. Penruddock's picture, two lamps are burning dimly.

Mrs. Neville is lounging in a solemn armchair, and is to all appearance enjoying life in its greatest intensity, which, to speak more plainly, means that she is slowly but surely falling into the arms of Morpheus.

The sound of a bell rings through the house ; there is a pause, and then the door opens slowly, and Mr. Penruddock comes in with the heavy, determined step of one who has a righteous cause to be adjusted, and with his countenance stern and white.

It is at all times a forbidding countenance, no one has ever thought otherwise, though strangely handsome, but to-night it is very nearly repulsive.

He advances to where Mrs. Neville (who was suddenly roused from slumber to a full sense of the situation) is sitting, but pauses on his way, and shudders perceptibly, as, looking up by chance, he sees that he is before the portrait of his dead sister-in-law.

Mrs. Penruddock's large pathetic blue eyes are gazing down upon him, as so often they gazed in life, sweet and earnest, and just now, as it seems to his distorted fancy, something more than all this.

Is it that he has grown superstitious within the last few moments, or do they wear a reproachful look, that thrills his whole being?

Is the beautiful face eager and expectant, as though she would demand at his hands the little one left to him in trust?

Recovering himself by a great effort, he goes up to Mrs. Neville, and says something formal to her about his gratitude for the interview thus granted.

He is perhaps going on to explain why the meeting was solicited, when the abrupt entrance of his son checks him for the time being.

A quick shade of anger crosses the young man's brow as he sees his father.

Instinctively his glance turns to where Maud is sitting, so far apart from the rest ; but she is so enveloped by the shadows falling from the lowered lamps, that he cannot distinguish her features with any clearness.

He would have gone over to her at once, but Mrs. Neville, by a sharp gesture of command, stays him, and brings him to her own side.

"Stay, Dick," she says, quietly. "Your place is here—as *yet !*"

So he stays by her, as in duty bound, though sorely troubled at heart.

"After all that I have urged, you have come," he says, coldly turning to his father.

"Yes; to say that which I told you yesterday I intended to say!" retorts Penruddock, stubbornly. Then, addressing Mrs. Neville, he adds, in a laboured tone, "It would make matters much easier if I might speak to you alone, without the presence of—Miss Neville!"

There is a covert insolence in the hesitation that he shows before pronouncing Maud's name that makes Mrs. Neville angry and indignant.

"If what you have come here to say refers to Miss Neville, it is both her wish and mine that she should be a listener to it," she says, slowly. "Therefore, do not hesitate, but commence at once, and let us hear, if you please, that which you have come hither to speak."

"That is as *you* desire, of course," Penruddock returns, calmly; "and, indeed, it is but little of your time I shall require. I would merely remark that I shall never, under any circumstances, give my consent to an alliance between my son and your adopted daughter."

At this, Maud, who until now has sat silent and almost motionless, starts into life.

She rises to her feet, and, though still keeping well in the shadow, turns to confront Penruddock.

"Reserve your disapprobation, sir," she says, in a voice low but distinct; "there is no occasion for it, still less for your consent to my marriage with your son. As he will himself inform you, I have already told him, and very distinctly, that such a union is utterly impossible."

Dick makes a movement as though he would go to her, but Penruddock detains him.

"You hear what she says?" he exclaims, eagerly. "She has refused you. Let it rest there. It is all at an end. Surely you would not press the matter? Have you no self-esteem? Have you no pride?"

"In this case, none," says the young man, sadly. "It is my happiness, my life for which I plead."

"But she tells me plainly that with her own lips she has rejected you."

"If," says Dick, earnestly, going up to Maud, and taking both her hands in his—"if she will also tell you, not only with her lips, but honestly and from her heart, that she does not love me, I shall then resign all hope of ever gaining her. I shall cease to weary her with my presence and my sincere protestations of affection, and leave her free to wed a happier man; but never until she has told me that. You may therefore spare yourself all further trouble on my account."

He pauses, as if overcome by emotion, and then goes on again, in a voice that trembles slightly, "I await my sentence. Maud, speak!"

But she does not speak. Twice her lips move as though she would unwillingly have given voice to some thought, but no articulate sound escapes her.

Presently she lifts her sad eyes to his as if in mute reproach, and then two tears gather within them slowly, and as slowly fall one by one down her pale cheeks.

"Dick, come here," says Mrs. Neville, nervously, her voice trembling.

He obeys her.

Pressing Maud's cold hands, he whispers hurriedly, "I shall wait for ever."

And then goes back to Mimi's side.

"If you mean to defy me in this matter," says Penruddock, who has overheard him, "you can take the consequences on your own head, and you know very well what those consequences will be. Henceforth you and I shall be strangers, and I will do my best to forget that I ever had a son. But I warn you that such mad marriages bring only grief and disgrace in their train."

"There shall be neither grief nor disgrace through *me*," says Maud, faintly.

She is still standing, and has her hand on the back of her chair as though to support herself.

"It is the first time," goes on Penruddock, remorselessly, not heeding the heart-broken interruption, "that a blot or stain has fallen on our house or name!"

"Silence, sir," cries Dick, furiously turning upon him; but no more can be said on either side, for at that instant the attention of all is turned upon the door, just inside which, upon the threshold, Esther stands, with one arm extended, as if she would demand silence.

There is something in her whole attitude and demeanour that is remarkably striking, and which engenders fear and expectation in every breast.

The looks of all are fixed on her as she comes slowly up the room, her tall majestic figure clothed in black, and drawn up to its full height.

Her manner is expressive of mystery and long-suppressed excitement. Of all present in the room, Mrs. Neville alone possesses a clue to her thoughts.

Silently and slowly she advances until she has reached Penruddock.

Here she comes to a standstill, and confronts him with gleaming eyes and parted lips.

"No blot, no stain upon your house or name? You dare say that! Have you lost all memory of the past? Does your conscience never speak?" she repeats, mockingly. "Is murder no crime? Have a care, Penruddock! And answer me, if you dare, this question—*Where is the child Hilda?*"

Penruddock starts back, his face growing livid. Yet only for an instant does he lose his self-control; rallying by a mighty effort, he says, glaring savagely at Esther, "This woman, this fanatic, lives but to torment me! Leave the room, I command you! Your idle ravings have nothing whatever to do with the subject we are now discussing. Begone at once, or I will force you hence!"

Esther pays not the slightest heed to that, but pointing

towards the picture, and gazing sternly on Penruddock, says, "See where her mother looks down upon you! Do not her eyes haunt you? Where is the little one, the little heiress of Penruddock, who stood so fatally in your way to her house and acres? Answer!—where is she?"

"She is dead—drowned, as all the world knows!" says Penruddock, gloomily, answering her against his will, as if in some-wise compelled to it.

"It is false!" cries Esther, triumphantly. "She is not dead! She lives! She is here to claim her own! Behold her, villain, and tremble!"

At this moment Mrs. Neville turns up to their fullest height the two lamps that stand beneath Mrs. Penruddock's picture; and Esther, holding out her hand to Maud, says, in a loud tone, "Hilda Penruddock, come forward!"

Obeying the gesture, not the words, which as yet she fails to understand, Maud comes slowly forward until she appears in the full glare of the lamps, and right beneath her mother's portrait.

Standing thus, silent and half-bewildered, she is so exactly like the beautiful painting above her, as to call forth an exclamation from Dick.

Mrs. Penruddock is dressed in cream-coloured satin; the girl is attired in cashmere of the same shade, trimmed exquisitely with old gold and some costly lace.

It would be a difficult, indeed an impossible, matter to decide which is the loveliest, the dead mother or the living daughter.

As the extraordinary likeness dawns upon Penruddock, he is completely overpowered, turns aside his head, and groans aloud.

Above even the startling resemblance to the mother, he sees in the grown girl the features of the little child so cruelly, though passively, done to death.

Again the whole terrible scene in the cottage garden flashes before him; again he watches, with cold persistency, until the tiny heiress meets, as he supposes then, and has till now believed, with her death.

He throws up his hands, as though to fling from him the hateful vision, and turns fiercely upon Esther.

"It is all a lie!" he exclaims, loudly,—"a cleverly-concocted scheme; but it shall not avail you much. It is an old story. Accidental likenesses have been ·tried before this, but an imposture always comes to light."

"Always! Yes, there you are right," returns Esther, with deep meaning.

, Maud, white as an early snowdrop, is clinging to Mrs. Neville, who has her arm round her.

Dick, at a little distance, is listening, with intense excitement, to the strange revelations now being made.

"Who ever saw the child again?" says Penruddock. "She was washed out to sea. All inquiries were made. No stone was left unturned to discover her; but it was too late. There was no one, not a living being, in sight when it occurred; no one saw the fatal accident."

"There you are mistaken. Two saw it," says Esther, solemnly. "You and I!"

"I was not present, saw nothing of it!" says Penruddock, hoarsely.

The ground seems slipping from beneath his feet. His parched lips seem barely able to form his words, and he with difficulty supports himself.

"You were present!" says the woman, relentlessly. "You stood inside the library window, and I saw you there, crouched as I was in the bushes at the other side of the river."

"In the bushes?" stammers Penruddock.

"Yes; I had come to get a glimpse of my darling at her play, and watched you as, with greedy eyes, you waited till the child crept nearer and nearer to her death."

Fearful is now the expression on the countenance of the wretched man.

"Without one word of warning, without one attempt to save

the innocent life left to your charge by a dying brother, you looked, with a cruel longing, to see her perish ! "

" 'Tis false ! " Penruddock, with very great difficulty, contrives to say.

" Though you never touched her, though the crime was a passive one, there was murder in your heart that day, as surely as you are shivering here before us all ! "

" It is all a fabrication ! " says Penruddock, feebly, wiping his forehead.

Then he glances, in a stealthy fashion, at his son—the boy for whom this horrible thing has been committed—to see if there be condemnation in his looks.

" Dick, do not believe it ! " he says, in a tone full of keenest agony.

He looks so old, so broken, that Dick is touched, and, going up to him, places his arm round his neck.

" I believe nothing against you, father," he says, tenderly; " be sure of that.   But pray control yourself, and let Esther tell her story."

" When the deed was done and the fatal plunge taken, you rushed to the water's edge," goes on Esther, who declines to address any one but Penruddock, gloating over the fact that he plainly cowers beneath her glance.   " But even then, at the last moment, a strong desire to save did not possess you.   Had you pursued your search to the bend in the river, hidden by the drooping alders, you would have seen the little white figure floating onwards whilst battling feebly with the stream.   You would have seen me running along the bank in wild pursuit; and you would have seen, too, the poor child drawn from the water by Gilbert Saumarez."

" Gilbert Saumarez !   He ? " exclaims Dick, in the utmost surprise.

" Yes ; he was a guest at the Vicarage at that time, as you, Penruddock, may remember.   But he shall himself tell his own story."

She beckons with her hand and Saumarez, who has plainly

been waiting in the ante-room, on receiving that signal, comes up to them.

"Captain Saumarez, tell us all you can of this strange tale?" entreats Mrs. Neville, with faltering accents.

"I have very little to tell; but it's all quite true," says Saumarez, after a swift glance at Maud's pale face. "I was fishing lower down upon the river on that day, the 14th of July, when, looking up, I suddenly saw a little child struggling in the water, and a woman—that woman there," pointing to Esther—"running along the bank. I jumped in, pulled the child out of the river, and saw that it was Hilda Penruddock, whom I knew well. Only that very morning I had been playing with her up at the cottage. I restored her to this woman, who represented herself to me as the child's nurse, and thought no more about it. I should of course have mentioned it in conversation at the Vicarage if I had had time; but, unfortunately, I had made up my mind to leave that day, and finding on looking at my watch that I should barely catch the up-train, I rushed home, seized my things, bade my friends farewell, and within an hour was steaming up to town. Four days afterwards I started for India, where, as you all know very well, I remained for years."

"But you knew Maud—you recognized her in town?" asks Mrs. Neville, in great agitation.

A suspicion of shame crosses Saumarez's face, darkening it for a moment.

"Yes, last year," he says, unwillingly. "I called here one day, and Esther passed through the hall as I entered. I knew her at once, and asked for the child. She was, I think, about to deny all knowledge of her, when Miss—Miss Penruddock, with whom I was not acquainted at that time, came out of some room, and, looking me full in the face for an instant, passed on. Her wonderful likeness to her mother, who was well known to me, struck me at once. I had heard of the adoption by Mrs. Neville of some strangely pretty child, and, as if by inspiration, the truth occurred to me. I accused Esther of it, and she at once, taken off her guard, confessed all."

"Then why did you not immediately speak?" demands Dick, coolly.

"It was no business of mine," responds the other, shrugging his shoulders.

"But, surely, you might have spoken," says Dick; "and it seems remarkable that you did not."

"No doubt I should, some time or other, have mentioned the circumstance, only that the woman had implored me to keep silence; saying that she had waited for years to have revenge on some one; and I really thought it a pity to spoil the planning and plotting that had lasted for so long."

"Yet you made love to my niece, knowing all that you did," says Mrs. Neville, gravely.

"In that matter, madam, I acknowledge I erred," says Saumarez, lightly, though he bites his lip. "But all is fair in love and war. I wooed her as a girl over whom a cloud rested, knowing her in my heart to be an heiress, and of irreproachable birth. Nay, hear the exact truth!" he says, with a somewhat reckless laugh. "I am not so rich as the world deems me; and thought if I could win Miss Neville, I might afterwards prove her to be Miss Penruddock, and so secure her fortune. But I failed. At first I thought only of the money to which she was entitled; but now, and always, I shall think that, were she penniless and unknown, the man who gains her love will be richer than any soul on earth. You believe me, I am sure?" he adds, turning abruptly, and most unexpectedly, to Hilda.

"Yes; I believe you," she says, earnestly; and then—very sweetly, struck by the extreme melancholy of his expression—she comes a few steps nearer to him, and holds out her hand. He takes it, presses his lips to it, hastily but fervently, and without another word quits the room.

"It is, I plainly see, an unnecessary question; but, for all that, I will ask if you have quite made up your mind that this ridiculous story is true?" demands Penruddock, angrily, addressing his son, upon whose countenance no disbelief can be read.

"Quite !" says Dick, readily, who has forgotten to think of anything beyond the fact that the stigma attached to Hilda's birth has been removed.

"Then you acknowledge her ? "

" As my cousin ?   Yes, certainly."

"Then, as certainly, *you* are a beggar !" says Penruddock, with a harsh laugh.

The young man starts as if shot, and puts his hand to his forehead.   For the first time he realizes what all this may mean to *him*.   By what right now shall he speak of love to the woman who is all in all to him, whose image occupies his heart.   Their positions are reversed ; *she* is the possessor of land and fortune; *he* is now the lonely outcast.

He draws a deep breath, and then rouses himself.   Going up to Mrs. Neville, he bids her good-night, in a low tone, that still does not falter.

"All this has been too much for you, and—my cousin," he says, gently, though without looking at Hilda.   "To-morrow, everything can be discussed more thoroughly ; but for to-night enough has been said."

"We shall see you to-morrow, I hope ?" says Mrs. Neville, anxiously.

"I think not.   It will be better not," says Dick, with a faint smile.   "I shall have many things to see to, and my father will, of course, require me."

At this mention of his name, Penruddock turns his head, and all present notice how terribly his face has changed within the last few minutes.

As if all hope has died within him, he looks crushed and broken, and very pitiable.

There is, too, within his eyes a somewhat vacant expression that contrasts very powerfully with his insolent demeanour of an hour ago.

" Eh, Dick ?—eh, lad ?" he says, in a confused fashion, putting his hand to his head, and sighing deeply.   "What are you saying of me ?   I heard my name——Don't believe them, Dick !

It is all false, every word!" Then, in a tone of eager, almost abject entreaty, he adds, in a whisper, "Don't *you* condemn me, Dick ! You have not the right to do that. It was all for your sake, Dick—all for you !"

"Come away ! Come home with me, father !" says Dick, hurriedly and anxiously.

A touch of deep pain, mingled with shame, mars the beauty of his features as he listens to his father's words, which are a confession of his guilt.

"Home ! Where is that *now ?*" asks Penruddock, vaguely, disregarding his son's effort to lead him from the room. "From the Castle to the Cottage—that is a fall, indeed ! And," sinking his voice, "I can't go to the Cottage, Dick— *the river is there !—always* the river !" with a strong shudder. "And it never ceases—it flows on and on for ever ! I can hear it always in my dreams at night !"

"Rouse yourself ! You are dreaming now, I think !" says Dick, who is as pale as death.

"No ; not now !" says the old man. He looks a very old man now indeed, so strangely altered are his features and mien. "It is too late now for dreams. If what she says be true, all is over, all is at an end !"

"The end is not come yet !" returns Dick, bravely, throwing up his head with a certain proud gesture that brings tears into the eyes of one who is watching him.

He closes one hand firmly, as though to defy misfortune, while into his face there comes a nobility, a sense of dignity, that perhaps it lacked before.

"*You* have still enough to satisfy every want," he says, addressing his father; "and as for me, the world is before me, and I shall conquer it in defiance of fate and evil fortune. All is for the best, and we should be thankful that the little one was saved. You *are* thankful, father, are you not? Say that you are thankful," he asks, with extreme earnestness.

It is as though he had completely and entirely dissociated

the love of his manhood from the delightful little companion of his earlier days.

"Yes, yes—deeply thankful!" says Penruddock, in a strange tone, hardly recognizable. "A weight is lifted from my heart —a load from my soul—that has lain upon them for many a year! Now it is raised, my heart feels lighter! But," looking helplessly around, "my *head* is bearing the burden now! It feels like molten lead! And there is a sound as of many voices—and——"

A deep groan escaped him; he staggered, and, but that Dick hastily caught him in his arms, would have fallen heavily to the ground.

CHAPTER X.

FORCED TO BE HAPPY.

It is two months later, and already Penruddock has lain for six weeks within his quiet grave.

For some days after that fearful seizure—consequent on the destruction of all those hopes he had purchased even at the price of crime—he had lingered in an unconscious state, knowing no one, hearing and seeing nothing, but sometimes murmuring, "The child! drowned—I might have saved her— but, no—let her go—all for my boy—all for my son!"

Then the fertile, scheming brain had come to a standstill; the heart, that in all its many years had known but one pure affection, had ceased to beat, and Penruddock was no more.

Mrs. Neville had called at Dick's rooms, where the dying man lay, every day during his illness, and had seen Dick and conversed with him many times, of his father's state alone—no other topic had been touched upon.

On two occasions Hilda had accompanied her, but on those days the young man had been either accidentally or wilfully absent.

Not once during all these long weeks had the cousins met.

They had never, indeed, seen each other since that last momentous evening in South Audley Street, when Esther's disclosure had made them change sides, and had changed the fortunes of both; so happily for the one, so disastrously for the other.

Yet, about that time, there was a policeman in that quarter who for many nights had kept a sharp watch upon a young man, well dressed but with his collar turned up to his ears—looking upon him as a possible burglar, for he would stand for an hour without flinching opposite a certain house, gazing upon nothing—so far as X 91 could see—except a faint streak of light that came from an upper window.

Finally, X 91 grew tired or ashamed of his suspicions, and, comforting himself with the thought that this eccentric young man was either a harmless lunatic or an admirer of the upper housemaid, let him gaze in peace.

*   *   *   *   *   *

To-day is too lovely for description. "The sun has drunk the dew that lay upon the morning grass;" the very birds are silent from excess of languor; the flowers droop and grow pensive beneath the heat, and all nature seems at rest.

> "The wind had no more strength than this,
> 'That leisurely it blew,
> To make one leaf the next to kiss
> That closely by it grew."

In the Castle, on this golden September morning, scarcely a sound can be heard. The inner world seems as lazy, as averse to action of any kind, as the world without.

Three days ago Mrs. Neville brought Hilda down to her birthplace; but the girl has refused to find comfort or pleasure in the the grand old Castle. Wealth has come to her, and, for the time at least, happiness has departed.

There is a pallor in her cheeks, a fountain of hushed tears in her expressive eyes, that goes to Mimi's heart; but having extracted a promise from Dick that he will not leave England without bidding them farewell, she can only wait patiently, if unhappily, for what is yet to come.

It is coming very quickly, that for which she waits—the solution of all her doubts.

Even as she and Hilda are sitting together in one of the morning-rooms, silent, but full of thought, a footstep sounds in the hall without, the door is opened, and Dick Penruddock stands hefore them, pale and haggard, but always the same Dick in one pair of eyes at least.

"I am very fortunate in having found you at home," says Dick, in his most formal manner. "I have come down here because I promised, and because I could not leave England without bidding you good-bye."

He takes Mrs. Neville's hand, and presses it warmly with a faint, a *very* faint, smile.

"*Good-bye?*" echoes she, in dismay, as though the fear of this hour has not been tormenting her for days.

"Yes; I am about to leave the country, never more to return to it!"

He has not dared to glance at Hilda after the first involuntary look on greeting her.

"But this is all so sudden, so dreadful!" says Mrs. Neville, who is at her wits' end. "What is your purpose in leaving? Where are you going?"

"To New Zealand—anywhere. I hardly know whither; and, indeed, it matters very little, so long as I get well away from the old world and all its associations."

"How you must hate the old world!" says a soft voice close to him, that has a suspicious trembling in it. "Do you mean to carry nothing from it but regrets?"

"Nothing!"—shortly.

"Is everything forgotten?" asks the soft voice again, even more tremulously this time. "Can you remember *no* happy hours?"

"My deepest regret," says the young man, with infinite sadness, "lies in the fact that I shall never be able to forget those happy hours."

Mrs. Neville, kind and considerate soul that she is, has stepped into the conservatory for the time being, therefore they are virtually alone.

"Dick!" says Hilda, looking and speaking very tenderly and very reproachfully.

"Don't!" says Penruddock, hastily. "Do anything but speak to me in that tone. It is more than I can bear. For weeks I have been training myself to meet you with proper coldness, and now, by one kind word, with one gentle look, you would seek to undo all my labour."

"And why, if I may ask, should you want to meet me with coldness?"

She is very close to him by this time, and has laid her hand upon his arm.

"There is no reason why I should tell you, because you know."

"I know!—what is it that I know?"

"Do not torture me."

"I have no desire to do that. But you have not yet said what it is that I know."

"Oh, cruel!" he exclaimed. "You know that you are rich now, whilst I have nothing, or next to it. I—in fact," says Dick, mournfully, "I am no match for you now, whatever I might have been before."

"But you are the same Dick as you were then," argues she, "except that you are a little more—I mean, a great deal more unkind."

"Am I?" says he. "It is very likely. Misfortune embitters us all."

"Won't you look at me, Dick?"

"There is no need to look at you. Your image is engraven on my heart. I can see you at every moment, and shall see you, go where I may."

"Nevertheless, look at me; it may soften you a little. Oh, Dick, I don't want this odious money; but I *do* want you. Now I have said it"—flushing crimson—"and you will not, I hope, think badly of me."

" I could never do that.　But it is impossible.　Do not let us talk about it."

His voice breaks a little.

" Then you refuse me ? "

" Yes ; because it is for your own good."

" No ; because I happen to have more money than you possess.　Let us have the truth, at all events.　Say that that is really what you mean."

" Well, then, *yes*, since you make me say it.　I could not be indebted to my wife for—for everything."

" No doubt you are right," says Miss Penruddock.　" Pride before all things, no matter how many hearts may be broken by it."

She means to be sarcastic, but only succeeds in being wretched.

" Mine is a just and proper pride," he says.

" Oh, very well !　Then it is not worth while, I suppose, to say anything more about it ? "

" No, indeed," he sighs.

" And you are quite determined to leave England for ever, and to go to New Zealand ? "

" Quite."

" Then," cries she, " since you insist upon it, I shall give this hateful money to a lunatic asylum, and, whether you like it or not, I shall go to New Zealand too."

" Maud ! " says Dick, in his overpowering agitation forgetting her real name.

" Yes ; I shall.　Nothing shall prevent me," says Miss Penruddock.

And here, we very much regret to say, she so far forgets herself as to place her arms around his neck and to burst into tears upon his breast.

So for the next few moments, at least, Penruddock's trip to the other side of the world is delayed.

He drops his hat, and encircling her fondly with his arms, for a full minute is quite ridiculously happy.

Then he checks himself, and, sighing deeply, says, " There must be an end of this. This will never do, you know," in a most miserable tone.

" Never ? " says Hilda, who has quite recovered herself, and in whose blue eyes a malicious twinkle may now be seen.

Does not victory already lie with her ? no wonder, therefore, that she rejoices.

" Come over to this sofa," she says ; " and as we must, to please you, give away our detestable, though rather comfortable income, tell me, which do you consider to be the most deserving of all the asylums ? "

At this point, Mrs. Neville coming in, and seeing them sitting together on apparently amicable terms, goes up to Dick, and kissing him on either cheek, tells him, without a word of warning, that he is a "dear boy," and as worthy as any one can be of her " dearest girl," and that she is happier to-day than she has been for a very long time, and several other things that are equally pleasant to hear.

All which so overpowers Dick that he has not sufficient courage to say anything that shall damp her satisfaction, and Hilda carries the day.

*   *   *   *   *   *

They have been married now for four weeks, and are in Italy, or Egypt, or St. Petersburg, or somewhere—we really have, at the present moment, quite forgotten where.

At all events, we may safely say that, be they where they may, they are two amongst the very happiest mortals the world contains.

ZARA.

"Peste! how the sun burns!" she said, breathlessly, as she ran lightly up the flowery hill, her bare, brown, shapely feet scarce touching the earth as she went. A lithe girl, softly formed, and lissom as "Dian, chaste and fair," with red-brown hair, and radiant lips, and eyes like deepest midnight. As she ran, one slender hand was tightly clenched. In it lay all her worldly wealth. A tiny wealth indeed—but for it she had worked and slaved, and *starved*, that it might buy for her the one thing upon the earth she loved. The one thing, too, that clave to her! She lived alone; no kith or kin laid claim to her.

She gained the top of the hill, and pushing aside the vines and straggling roses that hid a small gateway, ran through it, and up to a man, who, stretched upon a bench, was staring lazily at the white flecked ocean far down below in the curved bay.

"See, it is here; I have brought you the money," she said, panting with eagerness and her swift coming. She held out to him her open hand with the coins lying on the soft palm. " Now give me my Damma," she said, her voice trembling with suppressed delight.

" Too late," said the man, slowly.

" But how? The Signor promised me. It is a bargain," flashed she, advancing a step. Hot anger flamed into her eyes and deadened the sweetness of her lips. "Is it, then, too little a sum, this ? Has your master repented ? Eh ?" Dismay and scorn fought for mastery in her tone.

"Nay, then, Zara, come and see how it is," said the man, with some compassion. Rising languidly to his feet, he led her to the brow of the hill, and bending over, motioned her to follow his gaze to where the rocks shone white and cold in the dazzling sunlight, a hundred feet below. Upon them, inanimate and cold as they, lay stretched her only friend, her playfellow.

It was nothing but an old goat after all, so old as to be scarcely worth a thought. But ever since Zara's soul had pierced the haze of infancy, it had romped with her, suckled her, been to her the fondest mother the little waif had ever known, and now it was lying there, crushed, mangled, broken upon the cruel rocks. She scrambled down to it, by help of heather and tufts of strong coarse grass, and, reaching the spot, stretched herself beside the dead thing, in speechless grief.

There was blood upon the soft white hair; the face to the heart-broken child looked full of reproach ; some pale-blue flowers were in its drooping mouth, stained, too, with crimson. It was the last fatal mouthful, with death hidden in its treacherous sweetness.

Two or three stars had already crept into the sky when she rose and went silently back to the cave in the huge rock she called her home. Upon her threshold a man met her.

" Who is the master here? " he asked, impatiently.

" I am, and mistress too," returned she, lifting defiantly to his her large, grief-laden eyes. The one thing she loved was dead ; her heart felt dead, too ; and then—she had so many reasons for hating her own kind.

" St——that is bad," said the man, with a shrug, "for I believe him dying. And *you*—you are a child, you will know nothing."

She passed by him brusquely and entered the cave. Upon the rude pallet that served her as bed, lay a young lad, fair skinned, golden-haired, with blue eyes wild and vacant. He

tossed his arms above his head, and screamed to her in shrill
accents as she drew nearer. The demon of fever had him in
his grasp, and made a cruel jest of his weakness. He shrieked
so loudly, and played such fantastic tricks with his emaciated
hands, that for the moment he drove the dead Damma from
the girl's thoughts. She knelt beside him and pushed the hair
from his damp brow. The touch soothed him. His voice
sank, and presently faded away into a shaken quavering verse
of song that rose feebly, and died and rose again amidst the
echoes of the stony roof.

"At his chanting again," said the man contemptuously, from
the doorway. "He must be better. So!—it is well we were
on our way."

He approached the bed and looked down on the sick boy.

" Come, get up," he said, touching the fever-exhausted body
—slim and nerveless as a willow-wand—with his foot—not
over-roughly, but still with his foot. The boy groaned as if
racked with pain, and an agonized expression desolated his
face for a moment. It was more than Zara could bear. She
sprang to her feet and held out her hands imploringly.

"Give him to me," she said, a divine pity in her voice. "He
is ill—dying perhaps. He will be but a burden to you. Give
him to me."

The man hesitated, and glanced at the doorway, through
which the sky was peeping. Already night had fallen, and it
was essential he should reach the town, towards which he had
set his face, before daybreak. And of late the boy *had* been
in very truth a burden ; lagging here and there by the wayside,
and too languid to sing before the wine-shops the merry lilts
and lays that had so often earned them their supper, and a
sleep upon the scented hay. Again he glanced at the boy,
and marked the deadly pallor of his cheek, the purple ring
beneath his lids.

"For the price of a meal you may have him," he said,
coarsely, lifting his shoulders and laughing scornfully.

Swiftly she unwound from her waist the strip of coloured

linen that encircled her, and drew from it the coins that were
to have given her Damma. It was her whole fortune; not a
centime would remain in the cave with her when this was gone.
She was freely offering for the purchase of this stricken lad, this
stranger with the wandering eyes, blue as gentian, and the
yellow locks, wet with fever's poison, all her worldly wealth.

"Take them," she said, holding out the coins to the man,
who eyed them hungrily. "They were to buy Damma, but
she is dead. I saved and saved to buy her; a whole year it
took me, and this morning, when I went with the money in my
palm for her, they could only show me where she was lying
dead and cold upon the rocks. She was only a goat, look you,
but she was my all." She threw out her hands with a little
passionate gesture of despair.

"Here, give them to me," said the man. He clinked the
coins in his hands, and then laughed aloud:

"I doubt if a dead goat isn't better than a sick boy," he said.
"But——"

"Hush—he wakes to sense," she said, seeing a change in the
forlorn face beneath her. She pointed with a slender finger to
the doorway. "Go," she said. "To see you will distress
him; I can guess so much. Go, before he knows you."

The man scowled, first at her, and then at the boy: "Well,
a bargain's a bargain," he said. "I wish you luck with
yours."

"Go," she said again, imperatively, her eyes on the face that
was slowly struggling back to consciousness. She waved him
once more towards the aperture in the rock that served as
entrance. The man bowed his head and passed through it, and
out of her life for ever.

But the boy for ever stayed in it, and grew to be the heart-
string on which all her griefs and joys were founded. For two
careless, happy years the kindly cave sheltered them. They toiled
together, they sowed and reaped, tended their neighbours' brown-
eyed oxen, and tied their glowing corn. They gathered the
flaming poppies, and sang their songs at eventide, until the

maiden moon arose to wake the world to sensuous light. Then *his* voice, soaring heavenwards with ever increasing passion (as though crying aloud to the angels beyond the blue, to give him place in their choir), would silence hers, and overawe her by the majesty of its purity. Through the valley his voice would ring, and he himself, rising half unconsciously, would fling wide his young arms to the crescent moon, in a rhapsody of joy.

At such moments Zara, with all her heart in her eyes, would crouch at his feet, and worship there the beauty that lay resplendent in his face, pale with inspiration. *He* thought of the singing that thrilled him, she thought alone of him; and ever she would draw nearer to him, and touch his hand, and lightly pass her lips across it, thus trying mutely, nervously, to call him back from his unseen fires to the prosaic earth she trod.

They were but boy and girl together—brother and sister— and not even her own heart told her with what a mad affection she clung to him. There was unspeakable happiness in her life. They were *together;* all day long he was in her sight, and what should part them? Another world might lie beyond those purple hills, but why seek it? Those amongst whom they lived, died contented year after year, without having solved the secret those hills hid; then why not she and Lillo?

So went day by day, and though the boy grew pale at times, he showed no longing for a wider life, and his songs, though they took a sadder tone, spoke of nothing that could startle her from the restfulness of her false security.

One night, when the woods were all aflame with the magic of the moon's rays, the boy sat alone, until the serene calm of the night entered into him, and woke his muse to life. Then high, sweet, and pure, his voice rang forth through the rustling trees, that now seemed to grow silent beneath the witchery of his music.

A stranger, passing through the valley below, had heard the splendour of his voice as it rose bird-like, and cleft triumphantly the clear, warm air. To him it seemed that some one invisible was imbued with a gift from Heaven. Entranced he stood and listened, until the last note died lingeringly away ; then he came nearer, and searched the scented wood until he came face to face with this new Marsyas.

A simple boy half naked, and beautiful as one of those fair early gods who had turned Arcadian shepherds for the easier wooing of their earth-born loves. A very Apollo in rags, he found him seated on a fallen pine, with dreamy, wistful eyes, and petulant mouth.

With gentle words and promises of coming glory he enticed and bought him, until the lad rose, dazzled, staggering, and held out his hands to him, as one imploring guidance, and swore to surrender himself to him body and soul, if he would but take him with him whithersoever he might go, and give him a chance of seeing realized even *one* of the fair visions he had conjured up.

There were more words, an assurance or two, and then the lad went down, half mad with the intoxication of it all, to tell Zara that he was going from her into the unknown world.

"It means fame, wealth, honour," said the lad with glowing eyes, in which the fatal fever of 'ambition was already lit.

"It means death," said she slowly, gazing at his hectic cheeks fired with eager hope ; but he laughed her to scorn, and taking her in his arms, kissed her fondly once, and whispered to her of many things,—of how he should come back to her rich, famous, renowned ; but she answered him never a word. Then he thrust her angrily from him, and held out his hand to his new friend, and went eagerly up the hill with him to the new life for which he panted—the world that was to be won by his gift of song.

At the foot of the hill stood she, until the shadows hid him, and then she smote her hand upon her breast until the tender flesh ached, but no cry, however small, broke from her parched lips.

*   *   *   *   *   *

Wearily, heavily, went the day, and now it was eventide ; and just such a tide as when he left her, five long years ago. Only

the vaguest tidings of him had reached the quiet village all that
time, though the world had rung with the fame of the new and
marvellous tenor. Zara had blossomed into perfect woman-
hood, and had been sued and sought by many, in vain,
Her great eyes had widened upon most matters best left alone
in the little, gossiping, idle village to which she belonged. But
though the world's mire had fallen upon her white soul, she had
kept herself pure for very love of Lillo—that strange fair boy
whom she had bought, one summer long ago, on an evening
such as this.

What an evening it was ! Earth, sky, sea, all blended into
one harmonious whole by the soft grey mist that, rising from
the trembling ocean, pushed ever inland. The girl, struck by
the glory of the scene—in its setting of red and gold and purple
dyes, borrowed from earth and heaven—stood silent amidst the
deepening shadows of the woods, listening to the river song
below : what was it saying? why was it ever calling, calling to
her, as it rushed in its mad haste to the illimitable ocean ?

She raised her hand to her brow to shut out from her the
dying rays of the hot sun as though they hurt her. The corn
was waving high around her. She stood in a scented bed of
poppies and blue cornflowers and perfumed weeds, all whispering together as the light wind went and came their way. Ay !
on such a night indeed he went ! The remembrance, like a
stab, wounded her poor heart and made it bleed afresh. She
clenched her hands and turned her dark eyes moodily to the
glowing sky, but she never said to herself that she would learn
to forget. Nay ! let *him* forget : women were born to be the
sad thralls of cruel memory.

She turned her head a little and saw him standing beside
her—a tall, slender figure, careworn, travel-stained, with dust
upon his sunny hair, and with hollowed cheeks and eyes full of
a horrible brilliance. He was changed almost beyond recognition, but she knew him. With a quick, glad, mournful cry she
went to him and laid her hands upon his shoulders.

"You—*you !*" she cried, with a passionate outburst of relief and joy ; and then she checked herself. "You are a little tired, dear heart," she said next, with a studied suppression of all surprise or excitement, though her heart beat as though it would rend her vest.

"Ay !" said he, querulously. He did not touch her or seek to return the caressing pressure of her soft brown hands. "Tired? ay—to death."

"Come home, then," she said, gently, leading him towards the old cave where once he had found shelter and an escape from servitude. At the word "home" he shuddered and shrank from her, and petulant tears, born of past joys bittersweet, rose to his feverish eyes. At this a deadly pallor crept over her face, but still she clave to him.

"Come," she said again, this time perhaps a little sternly, though still with deepest love, and he followed her. Alas ! how bare to him looked the cold walls, the scanty comforts, the meagre supper !

With a shiver of disgust he flung himself upon a rude bench and muttered that he was cold—cold.

She lit some wood with deft fingers, and poured him some goat's milk into a vessel, which he drank ungratefully, and then silence fell between them.

"Why don't you speak ?" cried he at last, angrily. "Why don't you jibe and jeer at me like the rest? Where is the fortune Fate had in store for me, of which I boasted to you so many times? There is *no* fortune—none. I come back to you beggared, empty-handed, a mendicant——"

"Nay, dear, but you *have* come back," she interrupted, softly, stroking his hand. There was glad triumph in her tone.

"Because I had to," retorted he sullenly, as though eager to disenchant her and show himself in his worst colours. "As long as *life* was mine—the world's friendship, beauty's smiles, wine, colour, light—do you think I ever thought of this hovel or of you ? I tell you a thousand times *no !* And yet," regarding her curiously, "you, too, are handsome—but—not as *she* was. *Her* eyes burned through me, until they drew my heart from out my very flesh and laid it writhing at her dainty feet. She held my soul within her palm; yet she, too, when the blight fell, cast me from her!"

In his excitement he tried to rise, but she, kneeling at his feet, restrained him.

"Forget all that," she said, faintly, a cold, sick feeling, she knew to be despair, rendering her voice low and indistinct. "Tell me how it has been with *you.* Tell me of yourself— yourself *alone,*" hurriedly. "We heard of your singing, even we here in this hidden village. It came to us as a strange breath from a strange land, telling us of your triumphs. Ah! but it was hard to think we could not witness them!"

"Yes, yes, I sang," he said, hoarsely; "I sang until all other voices were silenced, until the world listened. It was a victory unparalleled—a triumphal march all through. Gold flowed at my feet, princes held out their hands to me, all men bowed speechless before the magic of my voice." He stood as one inspired. His cheek flushed: for the moment his glad young youth came back to him, pure, unsullied. "There were the crowded houses," he went on in a low rapt tone, speaking as one who sees some sight to other eyes unseen, "the lights, the music, the *hush!* and then the clapping of hands, the shouts. I go forth to them: flowers fall around me, I bow—I feel my-self a god—and she——" All at once his manner changed, his head lowered, the *young* look vanished from his face. "And then one night," he said, wearily, "something seemed to snap *here,*" smiting his breast. "I felt a strange apathy—some blood came—I forget——" He sank back again upon the bench as if exhausted.

"You are safe now: it will be well with you yet," whispered she, caressingly. "Here, amongst these quiet hills, you will regain your health, your strength, your voice. It will come again, sweeter, fuller than of old—and you will rejoice in it, and go forth again to your world—to——"

Her own voice failed her. Her head sank upon his knees

A sob burst from her dry lips—but he was lost in the beatific vision she had raised.

Presently, some thought occurring to him, he started, and remembered her.

"Are you married?" he asked nervously, as though in fear of her answer.

She raised her head slowly, and looked at him. Something in the strength of her gaze troubled him, because his eyes drooped before hers.

"Married—ay—to a dream!" she said at length.

*   *   *   *   *   *

He sickened, and grew weaker, hour by hour. The old fever was upon him again, mingled with that other consuming fire, slow but deadly. Day after day she nursed him, with a secret delight in her recovered possession that overpowered all other thoughts. Not once during this sad week did slumber fall upon her eyelids, not once did he cry aloud unheard. Her name was for ever on his parched lips. In his delirium he cried aloud for Zara—Zara—always Zara; until in her tired soul she rejoiced, and told herself the new life had not torn him altogether from her, and that the new love was forgotten. With hungry fear she listened to his ravings, for the sound of some fresh name unknown to her, that should tell her whither his thoughts wandered—but she never heard it.

At length upon the eighth day consciousness returned to him, and as towards evening she bent over him, striving to wet his dry lips with cooling drink, she raised her eyes and saw men standing in the doorway; no vagrants these, but clad in costly garments as becomes the minions of the rich.

"It *is* my lord!" said one of them, screwing up his eyes and bending forward, to cast a searching glance upon the languid Lillo. With a quick movement, suggestive of apprehension, Zara stepped between the bed and the door, and spread out both her hands.

"Your business, sirs?" she asked, with frowning vehemence.

They had come, they said, for the Signor Lillo (by which

14

name, no doubt, she knew him), to convey him to Florence by the Duke's orders.

"Stand back, you cannot have him. He is ill, *dying !*" she cried, threateningly waving them from her.

"It is a command," said the first man, shrugging his shoulders and coming a step nearer.

"But I tell you he cannot go—you shall not have him," she protested wildly. "He is mine—my own. I *bought* him."

At this they laughed a little, and then explained to her. His true birth had been discovered. He was no longer a waif to be wafted hither and thither on Fortune's wind, but a scion of an ancient house. His friends, the Duke himself, required his presence. They had been many days searching for him, and now at last had found him. No doubt she would be rewarded—the family was old and wealthy——

The fury that flashed into her eyes checked them there; they fell to mumbling, and at last were silent.

"In his need," she said with slow scorn, drawing her magnificent figure to its full height, "you all forsook him. When he was crushed and humbled to the earth," pointing her trembling fingers to the brown floor, "you all turned from him. He was beaten down by you and your masters, trodden upon, wounded to his heart's core, and then—*then* he thought of *me.*" She threw out her arms with a gesture of unutterable pride and exultation. "He came back to me of his own accord. He is mine now for evermore. He has done with you, and yours. He will not return to you. He told me so himself—he—the very night of his home-coming. He spurns you. He will stay here amongst the hills that sheltered him when first he came. What are your gauds and your briberies to a hurt soul like his? I tell you he will not go back to the world whence you came."

Her eyes sparkled, her whole frame dilated : she defied them with a high courage, sure in her belief that she was speaking as he would have her speak, and that, in very truth, he was hers for ever.

A slight movement on the pallet behind her caught her

attention; eagerly she turned to it. The sick man had raised himself with difficulty upon his elbow, and was holding out a shaking, transparent hand—*not* to her—to the group in the doorway !

"Nay! Heed her not—she lies!" he cried shrilly, in a voice strangely loud and clear. "I am not hers. I renounce her. Take me away from this horrible place to life—a new life—and freedom. I go !"

He dropped back upon his pillow. He had indeed gone to a new life.

*   *   *   *   *   *

Zara, as though stricken to stone, stood motionless; gazing on the stiffening clay, an awful expression on her rigid features.

"He is dead," she said, without meaning. Her eyes were fixed immovably on the pale corpse, yet it was not the thought that never again would his voice strike on her ears, or his eyes show recognition of her coming, that had brought that stony look to her face. He had died repudiating her; with his last words he had appealed to strangers to *save* him from *her*—from *her* whose very heart's-blood would have been freely poured for him. In death as in life he had been ungrateful ! A sudden sense of the *uselessness* of all things came to her like a flash !

They sought to take his body from her, but at first she resisted; it was her last feeble protest.

"He is mine—I bought him," she said again, foolishly; and then, wearily, "Nay, take him. He *would* go. You all heard him."

So she moved away; and then they lifted him, and made great moan over him, and carried him reverently, as befitted the going of one who, though in rags and in death, could still lay claim to an old name. With much pomp and ceremony they bore him from her sight, up the high hill, and far, far away.

Then she, too, stirred from her dream; she sighed, and cast one long lingering glance on the tiny cloud of dust, that was all that remained to her of the gloomy procession on the hilltop. She moved a step or two, and wondered idly at the strange sweet fairness of the summer evening. Then she went swiftly towards the rushing river, that to-night seemed singing its weird song with expectant glee, and thought how loudly it was calling—calling! How clear it was, the music! A siren's song—a longed-for lullaby. Like a tired child she stretched her arms to it, and sank softly, lightly, gladly, into its embrace.

VIVIENNE.

She was, without doubt, the prettiest girl in all the country round—small and slight, and beautifully made, and of a nature the most lovable. Imagine a face that possesses no colour except when its owner blushes, but is fair and calm and sweet as a summer evening, with large brown eyes that frown, and smile, and sparkle, and show in a thousand ways the character of the girl.

Her mother, the Honourable Mrs. De Vere, left a widow two years after Vivienne's birth, clung to the child with passionate intensity, and spent her life endeavouring to shield her from all those little griefs and troubles that beset the path of childhood. And so far she had fully succeeded; for although, at the time I write of, Vivienne had passed her twenty-second birthday, she still retained, both in mind and manner, all that careless gaiety and freshness which belong alone to extreme youth; in fact, a complete system of perfect spoiling had left her, as she now was, the most impulsive, the most passionate, and withal the most perfect darling—to my eyes—this world has ever seen.

Just a few brief words about myself, and then I will continue my story.

My name is Guy Hamilton, and I am Vivienne's cousin— about three years, perhaps, her senior. At a very early age I lost both father and mother; indeed, so young was I, that I have not the slightest recollection of either of them; and, my guardians having desired that my education should be carried on abroad, I saw very little of any of my relations until my return to England, on the event of my coming of age.

Arrived in London, and being well known as the possessor of considerable estates, I was speedily admitted within the circles of the best society; and here for the first time I beheld my cousin Vivienne.

Flushed and sparkling with the triumphs of a first London season, she seemed to my enraptured sight the personification of all things lovely. I was her willing slave upon the spot; and from that moment until now she has been, and always will be, to me, the one woman upon earth.

The county in which we resided was generally very gay, much given to balls, croquet parties, pic-nics, &c., and with some of the finest hunting and shooting to be found in England. But somehow of late very few balls had enlivened our vicinity, some families being in mourning, some having gone abroad, and others having excellent reasons of their own for indulging in a quiet season.

It was now September, the summer being almost gone, though enough of its sweetness remained to remind us of what we had lost, and Vivienne, her mother, and I were standing one day or the terrace, overlooking the garden below, when our eyes were attracted by the appearance of a mounted groom riding slowly up the avenue.

"The Castle March groom," cried Vivienne; "run, Guy, and see what message he brings from Flora."

I ran down, and, confronting the man, received from him a tiny note in Lady March's handwriting, which I flourished triumphantly on my way back.

"An invitation," cried I, with mock enthusiasm—"an in-vitation—I'd swear to the envelope;" and I held the letter at a very respectful distance from me, while I gazed with rever-ence at its soft pink cover.

"Nonsense!" Vivienne said, the little face flushing; "it is a great deal too early in the season for any ball, and you know she hates morning parties; but—will you give it to me, Guy, you torment?"

"What will you bet, then?" insisted I, still holding the letter high above my head, simply for the sake of seeing her try to reach it; "in gloves, for instance—half a dozen, or a dozen?"

"Half a dozen that it is no invitation," she said, and I gave her the letter. She opened it impatiently, glanced through it, and then read aloud—

"DEAREST VIV,—We have at last decided to give a ball on the 30th—that is, before Blanche leaves us, to reconcile her to our parting; so get up your prettiest dress, and do try to make your ugly little self look lovely if you can. Love to the mother and Guy, who, of course, will both come to take care of you; and tell the latter that I have just got down some extra capital champagne, expressly for his use.—In awful haste, ever yours,

"FLO."

"The darling!" said Vivienne, clapping her hands with delight as she finished the letter. "Oh, I'm so glad. What dress shall I wear, mamma? I think I'll go and make my choice," and she turned towards the house.

"I hope you don't forget that you owe me half a dozen pair of gloves," cried I, as she sprang through the low French window into the drawing-room; "but——"

"Don't you wish you may get them?" sounded strangely like the answer I received, as she disappeared within the house. And here I think it only justice to myself to add that I never did get them.

In her hurry when leaving, Vivienne had dropped the letter, and it fluttered to my feet; mechanically I stooped to pick it up, and, carelessly turning the page, I perceived a postscript written at the other side. It ran as follows :—

"P.S.—I very nearly despatched this without telling you that my brother Cecil—my favourite brother, you know—will arrive here on the 29th, delightfully bronzed, and altogether decidedly Indian, I hope. In fact, I picture him, in my own mind, as quite a hero for my ball.—Yours, F. M."

I followed Vivienne, and, showing her the letter, whispered jestingly that this perhaps would prove another lover to add to her long list; but all the time upon my heart most heavily there lay a sad and unaccountable misgiving.

*　　*　　*　　*　　*　　*

The Castle March ball-room was by far the handsomest room in the county, and on this particular night of which I write was crowded almost to inconvenience both with rank and beauty; but Vivienne, with her bright bewitching loveliness, was undoubtedly the belle of it.

After the first waltz, which she danced with me, was ended, I resigned her—reluctantly, be it said—to the arms of a young squire, and went to do a few duty dances at the top of the room.

An hour passed thus, and, having charitably spent this time endeavouring to persuade three antiquated damsels that theirs was the style of beauty I particularly affected, I began to think that I might once more claim a dance from Vivienne, and forthwith commenced a slow though eager search all through the room, looking for the little form so dear to me.

At last, in the embrasure of a window I beheld her, flushing and lighting up with animation as she talked with a dark and very handsome man, who, standing beside her, leaned negligently against the side of the window, which opened to the ground. He was speaking, and both in look and tone there was evident admiration.

"So I am quite forgotten, Miss De Vere," he said. "Well, I think that a little too hard, considering that I once had the honour of saving you from a heavy fall from an apple-tree, when you were about so high," placing his hand not quite a yard from the ground.

She laughed.

"I never should have known you," she said—"you are so changed; and then, remember, it is such a number of years. Why, at that time I was only a mere child; and now——" she paused.

"Well, and now?" he asked.

"Oh, now," she answered, archly, "I am quite an old maid, you know; and, considering how age does dim the sight, I surely may be forgiven a little forgetfulness."

"An 'old maid,' are you?" he said, ignoring the latter part of her sentence. "Well, all I can say is I never saw an 'old maid' before. Shall we finish this waltz?" and he moved a little forward as he spoke.

She also rose, and, turning up her large brown eyes to his with an expression half shy, half laughing, lurking in the soft darkness of their depths, she murmured gaily—

"You will understand—without telling—that I hate flattery in any form—in fact, it always rouses within me every particle of the bad humour I possess—no small share I can tell you; but that last little compliment of yours was so charmingly disguised, that really, on the whole, I rather think I liked it—there!"

"Did you?" he whispered softly, passing his arm round her waist, and bending low to look into her face. "I am glad of that; but I would far rather you liked me;" and then they moved away, and were lost amongst the throng of dancers.

He is very like his sister, I thought sadly, as I passed over with difficulty and by slow degrees to the other side of the room, where some half-dozen men of my acquaintance stood discussing the girls and the dancing.

Handcock of the 14th was holding forth as I came up to them, and the subject on which he was enlarging arrested my attention in a moment.

"How lovely Miss De Vere is looking this evening!" he was saying. "That scarlet in her hair is awfully becoming."

"Ah, show her to me," said one of a new set of fellows who had only arrived at the barracks a few days before, and consequently knew little or nothing of the neighbourhood, pushing forward eagerly as he spoke—"that's the girl who has refused the entire county, isn't it?"

"Pretty nearly," returned Handcock, who, as report went, had been very hard hit himself in that quarter. "Look, there she is, all in white, with the scarlet geranium in her hair.   Do you admire her?"

"Admire her?" answered the other, with a hearty burst of enthusiasm.   "Egad, I should rather think I do; why, she is perfectly lovely.   Who is the fellow dancing with her?"

"Captain Verschoyle," I said, slowly, perceiving they were at a loss for an answer.

"Verschoyle, did you say?" exclaimed a fair, sinister-looking man, whom I had not perceived before, but who now came quietly to the front of the group.   "Cecil Verschoyle?   Ah, by Jove, yes; I knew him in India.   When did he return?" appealing to me.

"He arrived here yesterday, I believe," I said.   "He is come home on leave; the climate was destroying his health."

"Ah, yes," he returned, slowly, and a cold, sneering expression crept up over his face; "yes, I should think he did find the climate rather warm—not to be wondered at, considering the name he made for himself out there."

"A name?" lisped a young ensign.   "Lucky dog! Wish to Heaven I could make myself a name!   How did he do it?"

"In a way that I don't envy, and that I wouldn't advise you to go in for," the other answered, coldly.   "I wasn't on the spot myself—only heard it from some other fellows.   It was a bad business altogether—running away with the Major's wife being the principal feature in it, I believe.   It created an awful sensation, I can tell you; and what added to it was the tragical end of the story, the woman herself dying three days after the elopement.   Mind," he went on, looking round, and seeing the expression on our faces, "I cannot vouch for the exact truth, not being myself an eye-witness.   I was only told it by others; and such things are better kept dark."   With which wholesome advice he turned and left us.

I thought in my own mind that, if such was his opinion, an open ball-room was hardly the place in which to discuss it; and, looking across the room at the handsome, open, and thoroughly well-bred face before me, I could not in my heart connect it with the story I had just heard.

The man had reasons of his own, I concluded—mean, pitiful ones they must have been—for wishing to blast Verschoyle's reputation in the eyes of the world; and if so——but here Handcock broke in upon my meditation.

"An ugly story," he said, "and one made uglier by the telling. In my opinion, the fellow who could, in an open ball-room, tell a story so calculated to ruin the character of any man, must be at heart a blackguard."

I acquiesced with a nod, and two hours later, the ball having broken up, we went home.

On the Friday morning following (Wednesday had been the night of the ball) Captain Verschoyle called, and paid us what seemed to me an unconscionably long visit. Before leaving, he arranged a riding party, to take place the next day, to see some ruins a few miles off. On Sunday he accompanied us home from church—Monday he called again ; and so on for a month—never a day passed without bringing Cecil's handsome horse and his rider to our door.

His coming—I saw at last—was Vivienne's heaven, his voice beyond all music to her ear, and in her eyes I read that she at length loved him, with all the passionate tenderness of her most loving nature.

"So ran the world away," and it was a day towards the close of October, warm and bright as the middle of June—what is commonly called a "pet day,"—and Vivienne, taking advantage of the weather, had driven over in the morning to see the Laytons, some friends of hers, but had signified her intention, before leaving, of being home to luncheon; and I, having nothing better to do, strolled out with dog and gun to get a stray shot at a partridge.

However, the birds proving shy, or being myself in no humour for shooting, after about two hours' ramble I turned slowly homewards, and, entering the low French window of the drawing-room, I flung myself on a couch half hidden from the room by falling draperies.

Tired out, far more in mind perhaps than in body, I had lain there for about half an hour or more, when the door opened suddenly, and Verschoyle entered, but without perceiving me; and, as I was in no mood for talking, but on the contrary very much disinclined for it, I made no sign, but lay as I was, half asleep from the heat of the weather and my own dull thoughts.

I think I must have dozed, for the next thing I remember hearing was Vivienne's voice in the hall, and Verschoyle starting to his feet from the large arm-chair in which he was lounging, with an exclamation of pleasure, and a smile that made his handsome face still handsomer.

In another moment she was before me, and Verschoyle met her in the centre of the room.

"Come at last, darling," he said, gaily. " You cannot fancy the relief to my feelings, as I was quite certain young Layton had eloped with you," and he stooped to kiss her.

But at the word " elope " Vivienne's face had darkened, and now, putting her hand suddenly against his breast, she drew herself back from the proffered embrace, thus by the action revealing at once that something unusual had happened.

"Vivienne," Verschoyle said, hurriedly, "Vivienne, my dearest, what is it? " and as he spoke he placed his own hand over the tiny gloved one, still lying so heavily upon his chest.

Glancing at her face, I could see that it was as white as death, and that her eyes shone dangerously; but her voice was low and steady, and the quivering of her lips alone showed how deeply she was agitated, and how rapidly her breath both came and went.

"About India," she said—"I have heard all that story. Answer me, Cecil, answer me: is there one word of truth about you and Mrs. Grey ? "

"Who has dared," Verschoyle broke in fiercely, as his face flushed a deep red and a heavy frown crept over it—" who has dared to poison——"

"That is not the question," she interrupted quickly, speaking low, but vehemently. "I will have 'Yes' or 'No.' Was there any story about you and that woman?"

"Yes," he answered. "But listen to me, Vivienne, for one moment. You cannot understand—let me explain;" and both his voice and manner grew passionately imploring.

But it was too late; the unlucky admission on his part had roused within her breast all the passion of her nature, and, starting violently back as though stung, she cried bitterly—

"'Yes'—is that your answer? Good Heavens! what fools some women are! And you have dared to say you love me—have asked me to be your wife—have kissed me!"

"Great Heaven!" he entreated, still holding her little hand tightly between his own, "won't you listen to me, Vivienne? For my sake, for both our sakes, hear me now."

But she resolutely drew her hand away, and, raising herself to her full height, said coldly—

"Hush!—not another word;" then moving a little to one side, she drew back the skirts of her dress with a movement at once cold and decisive, and so left open his passage to the door.

The action without the words was in itself sufficient, more than if she had spoken volumes; and, seeing it, he accepted his fate without further pleading. For one moment—a second perhaps—he looked as if he would have spoken, then simply bowed, and walked haughtily out of the room. For such I felt at once was the spirit of the man, that he would not sue a second time for mercy even from the woman for whom his heart was breaking.

Vivienne never stirred from the position in which he had left her, until the closing of the hall door told her that he was indeed gone, and for ever; then she raised her head, and oh the look of hopeless misery on her sweet young face! I could not bear it; and, springing forward, I caught her in my arms and pressed her dear head close down upon my breast.

"My darling," I gasped, "for the love of Heaven, don't look like that. Think of your mother. There may be some happiness for you yet;" and so on, a few passionate words I murmured, feeling all the time that they were falling on deaf ears. It seemed to occasion her no surprise, my sudden appearance there at that moment; she only clung to me a little wildly for a minute or so, and then said wearily—

"He is gone, Guy—I shall never see him again!" and so turned to leave the room.

She went a few yards, then paused, and, coming back to me—

"Dear Guy," she said, with a little faint attempt at a smile, infinitely sadder to me than all the tears that could be shed, and, putting her arms around my neck, she drew down my face to hers, and kissed me, and so went quietly away.

From that day Verschoyle's visits ceased, and his name was never mentioned amongst us—from which I concluded that Vivienne had told her mother the entire story.

Mrs. De Vere looked troubled and careworn, and followed her daughter's every motion with eyes full of tender love and pity; while the poor child went about her usual daily occupations, never omitting a single duty, never forgetting or neglecting, but always with the same sad and lonely look upon her face.

She read, she walked, she superintended her garden, she fed her swans; at times she was even cheerful; but she never laughed, and very seldom smiled.

*　　*　　*　　*　　*　　*

It was Tuesday evening—that is, the evening of the day, one week back, on which Vivienne and her lover had parted—and, being chilly, we three were sitting round the fire in the drawing-room discussing my departure to my own home, which was to take place on the following day—for the poachers had become troublesome, and my steward required my presence for many reasons—when a bustle and noise were heard in the hall, and, the door opening suddenly, Cummins, Lady Flora's maid, came hurriedly into the room. She seemed much agitated, and her eyes were red, as if from excessive weeping.

"Oh, ma'am," she began, hysterically; when Vivienne sprang to her feet, crying, "Cecil!" with pallid lips, and in a despairing tone, showing—Heaven help her, poor girl!—the one thought that occupied her mind from morning until night.

"Oh, Miss De Vere," Cummins went on, turning at once towards Vivienne, "Mr. Cecil—the Captain—about four hours ago, riding by Horts Wood, the poachers fired at him, and it seems——"

"He is not dead?" Vivienne moaned, interrupting her.

"They mistook him for some one else," the woman went on, never heeding her question, and weeping bitterly all the time. "The ball entered his side, ma'am, and——"

Down came Vivienne's little white hand heavily on her shoulder, shaking her roughly.

"He is not dead; speak—speak!" she cried, fiercely, almost mad from suspense.

"No, miss," Cummins answered, turning quickly round, and frightened by the girl's face into speaking concisely, "but the doctor says there is no hope, and he has been calling for you, miss, for the last half-hour, and please 'em, my lady says——"

But what my lady had or had not said was quite lost on me, as Vivienne suddenly left the room, and I followed quickly to order the carriage, knowing well that her intention was to reach poor Cecil's side without a moment's delay.

Returning to the drawing-room a few minutes afterwards, I found Vivienne there before me, a dark shawl thrown over her white dress, and both her hands clasped within her mother's; so they both stood, neither of them speaking until, the carriage being announced, I took her down and put her into it.

Giving the word to the coachman, I sprang in after her, and, Cummins sitting opposite, we set out in silence for the Castle. The distance was but a short one, about half an hour's drive perhaps, but I pray Heaven I may never again in all my life spend such a thirty minutes.

When at last we did arrive, we found the door wide open, and Vivienne, springing to the ground, without waiting for any assistance, ran up the steps and entered the hall, which was but dimly lighted and quite deserted, having over it that indescribable look of desolation and gloom which too surely betokens the approach of death.

Throwing her shawl on the ground, Vivienne continued her way up the stairs, while I followed a few yards behind, and on the first landing came face to face with the old doctor of the district, who attended all the families for miles around, and had known her from her birth.

"My dear," he said, speaking slowly and kindly, and putting both his hands upon her shoulders, "I cannot allow any excitement; it will only increase the suffering, and can do no good."

"You need have no fear for me," she said, in a quiet, self-possessed tone; and, seeing the calm expression of her face, he gave a satisfied nod, and took her across the landing to the door of the chamber.

But here her courage failed her, and, turning to him, she caught his arm, whispering piteously—

"His face?"

"Is quite uninjured," he made answer, understanding her question at once. "Take courage, child;" and, opening the door of the room, he motioned her to pass through.

As he was about to follow, I stopped him, and asked, hesitatingly—

"How long?"

"Perhaps four hours—perhaps only two," he replied, with a mournful shake of the head; and then we two passed into the apartment where Cecil Verschoyle lay, surely dying.

What Vivienne first saw was Lady Flora kneeling by the side of the bed, her lips pressed to her brother's hand, which hung slightly over the edge of it; but, seeing Vivienne, she rose, and tottered to the other side of the room, where Lord March received her in his arms.

Cecil was lying with closed eyes, his face deadly pale, and seemingly in a deep lethargy when we entered; but Vivienne's approaching step aroused him, and, languidly opening his eyes, now growing dim with the sad touch of death, a glad smile of recognition overspread his face, and—

"My darling," he cried, faintly, stretching out his hand—"my darling, I knew that you would come."

"Oh, Cecil, Cecil, that this should be our meeting!" poor Vivienne moaned, leaning over him and pressing her lips passionately to his.

"I am glad you are come so soon," Verschoyle went on, his eyes brightening as he spoke; "because I could not die or be at rest, until with my own lips I had told you all the fatal story that separated us."

"Hush, Cecil, hush, my dearest," Vivienne said; "I want no explanations now—I only want your forgiveness for ever having doubted you."

"Vivienne," he said, slowly and impressively, "when I tell you that I can have neither peace nor happiness until I have told you this story, I am sure you will listen to me, my dear." He paused for a moment, with a faint gasp for breath, and then continued—

"I saw a good deal of her in India, more perhaps than was usual, but she had no friends out there except myself and her husband. Well, he is dead now, but this I must say, that for the year I saw them together only one word could express his conduct, and that is—brutal. She bore it all in silence, poor little woman, being naturally timid and unaccustomed to harsh treatment; but one day—it was in the presence of somebody —he struck her savagely across the mouth, and this, even for her meek spirit, proved too much.

"Having no relation that she could appeal to in that foreign country, where she was far away from home and friends, she came to me and begged me for Heaven's sake, and on her bended knees, to take her to Colonel Kearney, who lived about two hundred miles up the country, and whose wife she had known in happier days. Of course I raised her from the ground, promising to do all she wished in this unhappy business, and left her for the time to obtain leave of absence for a few days. This was easily procured, and that very evening she came away with me secretly, not daring to let any one know of her resolution.

"That, I remember well, was Monday evening; on Tuesday, passing through a village, she caught the cholera, which was raging in that place; and on Wednesday she was dead."

Here he ceased, his voice failing from exhaustion and intense emotion, but presently he whispered—

"This is the entire story—you believe me, Vivienne?"

"Yes," was all she answered, and for some little time there was silence in the room.

At last he broke it, turning slightly towards her and speaking very painfully and sadly.

"I am dying, Vivienne—dying. I feel it, my darling. It is very young to die, is it not?—when I am only twenty-nine, and we might have been so happy together, you and I."

No answer from Vivienne, save the tightening of her hand on his, and a low choking sob that told but too plainly of the blank despair fast settling down upon her heart.

Verschoyle spoke again, hurriedly.

"Vivienne, my own, you must promise not to grieve too much for me when I am gone. Promise me that when the first great grief is over you will cease to think of me with sadness; though still," he added, with a little wistful smile, "I would not wish that you should quite forget me."

"Oh, Cecil, don't!" she cried suddenly, with bitter pain. "Oh, my darling! my darling! is there nothing I can do to keep you with me? Am I quite powerless? Can nothing be done to save you?"

"Nothing," Verschoyle answered, subduing her in a moment by the utter calmness and resignation of his tone. "You must only try to remember, as I do, that all things are ordered in love and mercy."

Again there was silence in the room, broken only by the irregular and laboured breathing of poor Cecil, and an occasional sob of utter despair from Vivienne.

About half an hour was passed thus, and it must have told fearfully on Verschoyle, for when next he spoke his voice was much changed. All life seemed gone from it; and it was almost in a whisper that he murmured—

"Raise my head a little higher, Vivienne, and brush my hair from my forehead; I feel so tired—so tired."

Gently and lovingly she passed her hand beneath his neck, and, raising his head, placed it with great tenderness upon her bosom. A smile of almost perfect happiness, although mingled with much sorrow, illumined his face for a moment, and—

"Kiss me," he said, softly.

With a sigh she stooped and kissed him, and presently he went on—

"Poor Flora! she, I know, will miss me greatly. My poor little sister! But I leave her to you, Vivienne, my own, to cheer and comfort her, when I am gone."

"And who in all this world can cheer or comfort me?" she cried, passionately, bending and laying her fair round cheek to his.

Another hour passed slowly, an hour of smothered agony and intense stillness, his head reclining on her bosom, and she with both her arms clasped closely round his neck, as though by her feeble grasp to shield and keep him from the inevitable.

At length, when suspense was becoming unbearable, he opened his eyes, and gazing wildly round for a moment, whispered anxiously—

"Vivienne, are you still with me? You have not left me, my darling? How dark it has grown! Put your face close to mine, that I may once more see the eyes I love so well. Hush, hush, my sweet! don't sob like that. Kiss me once again, and say good-night, and so may Heaven ever guard and keep you, my only love."

These were the last words he ever uttered. A little time after that, glancing towards the bed, I saw that his face had changed terribly; and turning anxiously towards the doctor, I found that he too had perceived it, and was hurrying swiftly and noiselessly across the room.

He bent over the bed; and, seeing him, Vivienne put up her hand with a warning gesture.

"Hush, you will wake him," she said; "and he is sleeping so peacefully now."

The doctor turned and motioned me to come to him, shaking his head mournfully the while; by which I knew at once that poor Verschoyle could no longer be numbered amongst the living.

"Vivienne," said I, taking her by the hand, "come with me, my dear."

"No, no, Guy," she answered, "I cannot leave him now. If he should wake and find me gone——"

"Oh, Vivienne," I whispered, in despair, "cannot you understand?"

For a moment she gazed at me wildly, then turned her eyes slowly on poor Cecil's face, and the next instant she lay as if dead within my arms, and so I carried her from the room.

*   *   *   *   *   *

I opened my desk this afternoon, and, taking from it the foregoing manuscript (written just two years ago last autumn), I read it every word. It is dusk when I have finished reading, and, turning to the fire, I sit, slowly pondering many things.

Presently the door opens quietly, and Vivienne enters the room; she is a little slighter, a little paler, a little sadder perhaps, but to me as lovely as of old. She comes across to the fireplace, and, kneeling on the rug—

"It is cold," she says, and holds her hands up to the blazing heat.

Still pondering, I take one of the little hands between my own, and, as is my usual habit when they are cold, chafe it softly and lovingly. In a minute or two she sits down on the carpet altogether in her old cosy fashion, and leans her head against my knee.

I place one arm round her neck, still holding her hand in mine, and then I put into words slowly and earnestly all that I have been thinking.

"Vivienne, I know that you can never love me as you loved him; but this I also know, that your friendship is more to me than the love of any other woman, and I think that I could make you happy. My darling, I need not say how much I love you, for that you know already; but I ask you now to be my wife, and if your answer should be 'Yes,' then I can ask from Heaven no higher happiness on earth; but if it should be 'No,' then I will bid you, your mother, and old England a long farewell, and try to find some peace in a distant land. So now, Vivienne, give me my answer."

But she gives me no answer—neither word, nor look, nor sign, though I wait for many minutes, silently hoping against hope; and at last I continue—

"Well, then, I will go."

"No, no, Guy!" she cries, suddenly, breaking into bitter tears—"you must not leave me! Whom have I in all the world but you and mamma? And, losing one, how can I like——"

"Hush, hush, my darling!" I implored, hurriedly. "I will not go. It was unmanly of me so to threaten you. There, I swear I will not leave England; but you must let me go to my own home for a few months, until I can come back calmly to my little sister without any fear of troubling her as I have troubled her just now; though, Heaven knows, Vivienne, I would not willingly pain you, my dear; so to-morrow I will take a kiss, and bid you good-bye, and return to you again after a little time."

"Nay, Guy," she says, softly, raising herself quietly, and putting her arms around my neck, "if it will make you happy, take the kiss now, and stay with us for ever."

And so, in perfect peace, I hold my own within my arms at last—at last.

A FIT OF THE BLUES.

"HE is abominable, Aunt Jemima!"

"He is a most godly man," says Miss Jemima.

They are sitting out of doors under the shadow of the branching limes, and in full view of the tennis-ground.

"He is an insufferable bore!"

"It is his mission to talk on one subject; he is a devoted friend of 'the cause.' He is the apostle of temperance. Mark that modest but brilliant speck of blue upon his coat. Becoming, but not conspicuous."

"Mark the mole upon his nose. Conspicuous, but not becoming!"

"Don't be irreverent, Dorothy. As you cannot understand him, at least be silent."

> "The Blue Ribbonite
> Is a new light;
> With most folk
> It ends in smoke,"

chants Dorothy, undismayed. Never mind, auntie; there is at least *one* point on which I cannot wrong him. He is, you must allow, perfectly hideous."

"Ah! look not to the outward seeming," says Miss Jemima, piously. "It is the heart—the heart alone, that one should study."

"I don't believe Mr. Giles has one," says her niece, confidently. "Tom and I are fully agreed that if he was dissected there would be a large hole in his left side, but no heart."

"Tom is extremely flippant! I can see no sign of grace in Tom. He is your cousin and my nephew, so I would willingly think as leniently of him as possible, but I doubt he lacks grace. And you are certainly wrong about dear Mr. Giles: would that all had hearts as pure as his! I will let you into a secret, Dorothy. It is my most earnest desire that you should wed Mr. Giles. He is a good man and true, and would help to lead a young and thoughtless girl like you into the right way."

"I have no particular objection to the right way," says Dorothy, mildly; "but I think, if I am to start for it direct, I should prefer another guide."

"Tom, for example!" says Miss Jemima, sharply. "Oh Dorothy, what a pit you are digging for your own feet! A young man who thinks brandy-and-soda preferable to spring water, and who despises his good soup unless he has a glass of madeira after it!"

"You used to like your madeira too, auntie, until Mr. Giles came to stay with us; and I have heard you say very kind things now and then about your claret at luncheon, and your champagne at dinner."

"I blush to remember it all," says Miss Jemima. "Alas! why will not people see the virtues that lie in coffee and tea, and that excellent, if slightly trying, drink called lemonade? When my nose has got accustomed to it, I know I shall love it dearly."

"I know I sha'n't," says Dorothy.

"Well, well, youth is headstrong."

"And age isn't, I suppose. Is that why Mr. Giles has taken to weak drinks?"

"Poor man! he really drinks little or nothing," says Miss Jemima.

"Nothing is nearer to it," says her niece. "Jane tells me that when she brushed out his room this morning, she found the zoedone and gingerbeer he begged for so hard last night lying quite untouched upon his table."

"Poor soul! he takes no care of himself," murmurs Miss Jemima, sadly.

"I told Tom about it, and he says it is evident he takes the utmost care of himself. Tom says zoedone and all such stuff are poison. Are they, auntie? He says, too, that if you had given him a dash of brandy in them, Mr. Giles would have drunk them all."

"Do not quote that reprobate to me," says Miss Jemima, indignantly. "Brother's son though he is, I have the very lowest opinion of him. If you are bent on marrying that scamp, Tom Delmege, all I can say is, Dorothy, that I wash my hands of you."

"I don't know that I want to marry any one," says her niece. "Oh, look, auntie—what a splendid serve! Ha, he has won that game! Of course he would, you know! Tom can handle a racket, if you like! Not as some people I could name, who hold it as if it was a frying-pan."

"Mr. Giles has better things to engross his attention than a mere frivolous amusement like tennis. Oh, Dorothy, why will you not sift the wheat from the chaff?"

"Am *I* one of the better things, auntie?" says her niece, mischievously, laughing behind the large fan she is waving indolently to and fro, as though to coax a breeze to her out of the scented pinewoods beyond. "Thank you, dear! I always felt you thoroughly appreciated my many virtues, no matter how silent you might have been about them."

"Tut, you saucy girl!" says Miss Jemima; but a smile that will not be forbidden curves her lips. Truly this niece of hers is out of the common sweet. Oh, that some good wind would blow her inclinations the way of Mr. Giles! As her thoughts get to this point, the gentleman in question may be seen advancing towards them across the sun-smitten grasses. The very daisies seem to bow their little heads at his approach. Perhaps they are afraid of the huge foot that supports his portly person. He is a tall man, stout as he is tall, and what is commonly known as smug-faced. He has a huge unsightly mole upon his fleshy nose. His eyes are sunk with fatness. One might deem it likely that oil and wine had been the ingredients used to raise that imperial gloss upon his ruddy cheeks. But the very name of wine is as an abomination in the ears of the Blue Ribbonite. Offer him a glass of even that meek marsala, and see how he will recoil from you, as though a demon lies within your tankard. He has a plausible manner, saintlike, smooth. A "beautiful manner," says Miss Jemima Browne, who, having fallen a victim to his doctrines some months ago, has been very uncomfortable ever since. The soul of hospitality, she nows feels that, if true to her principles, she is offering with every glass of wine to her friends the chance of eternal damnation. Perhaps there have been years in her life when Miss Jemima had felt happier than in these last six months, when what she fondly believes to be her true duty has dawned upon her.

"My dear Dorothy," she says to her niece, as the sanctified Mr. Giles draws nearer, "oblige me by being civil to him. He will want you to go for a walk with him, my dear. Go! I —I don't feel as if I could converse spiritually with him to-day. Loss of sleep last night, general debility, rheumatism, neuralgia, dyspep—— "

She gathers up her crewel-work with quite juvenile alacrity, and vanishes round the corner with a speed to which rheumatism is unknown.

"It is my firm opinion she hates him," says Dorothy, looking after her wrathfully; and, indeed, there is a celerity about the elder Miss Browne's movements that suggests the idea of fleeing before the foe.

Dorothy makes the best of unpleasant circumstances. She greets the fat Mr. Giles with becoming civility, and even consents with a sigh to accompany him to the lake, half a mile away, where the swans float gracefully. This will take her from Tom and his society, and though she has not altogether arranged with herself her feeling towards Tom, still she knows she is sacrificing something, as she turns towards the distant lake. Tom and she are cousins, and have laughed with each other, and quarrelled with each other, since time immemorial, and just lately they have taken it into their heads to be almost in love with each other. "Still," as Dorothy said to him when he pressed for an engagement, "there is no knowing what, or who, may turn up, so it is as well to keep oneself free."

By this you will see that the engagement has neither been ratified nor even partially arranged; which fact is to Tom Delmege a bitter grievance, Miss Browne junior being as lovely as she is fascinating, and an heiress into the bargain. Not (to do Tom justice) that her money has anything to do with his affection for her.

Of late, he has been sorely exercised in his mind about the attentions that Mr. Giles—the apostle of temperance—has showered upon Dorothy: attentions favourably regarded by Miss Jemima, who has brought herself to that pitch of admiration for the apostle that she might easily be said, in vulgar parlance, to "swear by him."

Just at this moment Tom Delmege is in a towering rage. All the afternoon guests have departed. It is nearly seven o'clock, and still Dorothy and Mr. Giles are off the boards. He is on the very verge of suicidal despair, when the gleam of Dorothy's white gown, shining through the trees, restores him to sanity, but not, I regret to say, to his temper. She is accompanied by Mr. Giles, looking smoother, more rubicund, more sanctified than usual.

Tom advances towards them, fell determination in his eye. Dorothy, who is a careful girl, marks his eye.

"Ah, *you* Tom!" she says, with the utmost *bonhomie*, much experience having taught her that there is great virtue in the first word. "So glad you haven't gone yet. I was afraid I should have missed you, I have been so long away. We are awfully late, aren't we?"

The very audacity of the way in which she acknowledges

her crime reduces the angry Tom to silence. He is still inwardly boiling with rage, but hardly knows how to let off the steam.

"The descent of evening was amazingly sudden ; down it came upon us like—like an avalanche, or—or a feather bed ; soft, you know, but confusing," says Mr. Giles to Tom, with a smile replete with brotherly love. "We weren't thinking of it, you see. We—we were thinking of something else "—with a godly chuckle. "Did *you* ever lose yourself, Mr. Delmege, in a pleasant abstraction of that sort ? "

"No," says Tom, "I didn't ! I always have my senses quite about me. I seldom lose anything, except perhaps my patience—or my temper ! "

"Hah !" says Mr. Giles, with a pious sigh, "to lose either of those is sad, very sad. It is that terrible thing called Temper that creates most of the crimes that disgrace our morning papers. It leads to violent language, manslaughter, murder—— "

"Ay, murder !" says Tom, glaring at him. "It often leads to murder. I—I feel *right down* murderous at times."

"My dear young man," says Mr. Giles, "you should try to conquer all such degrading feelings. It is with pain and loving regret I have of late very frequently noticed the growth of this mental deformity, that threatens to uproot all the grace that doubtless lies dormant within you, though as yet, I grieve to say, belief in it must be an act of faith. Try, try to conquer your wicked self, when you feel the fit coming on you."

"I feel it coming on now," says Tom, advancing towards him. "It is coming on—uncommon strong, too. I have seldom felt it so bad. Who spoke of murder a moment since, eh ? " He brandishes his fist and dances up to Mr. Giles.

But that worthy evades him. He jumps nimbly to the other side of the flower-bed, full of glowing geraniums, that stands between them, and stares at him in an imploring fashion that savours strongly of fear.

"My good friend, my dear Mr. Delmege!" he pants unctuously, "control yourself. Murder is a fearful thing. You don't mean to tell me that you—— "

"Yes, I do!" says Tom, furiously. "That's precisely it. I'm dying to be at somebody—*at you!*"

He flies across the bed to him. Mr. Giles, having grown a pale yellow with ever-increasing fright, springs away from him. And now commences a most undignified race round and round the innocent flowers.

"Speak to him, my dear Miss Dorothy! Exercise your influence, the sacred influence of beautiful woman!" shrieks Mr. Giles, when passing her; whereupon Dorothy makes a faint sign to Tom. It is particularly faint, as she is so convulsed with laughter behind her fan that she can scarcely breathe. Tom, though still revengeful, obeys it. He pretends to trip over the gnarled root of a beech-tree growing near, and Mr. Giles, taking advantage of the supposed check to his adversary, steps hastily on to the walk, and may presently be seen mounting the balcony in such hot haste as soon puts him out of sight.

"Oh, Tom, how could you!" says Miss Browne junior, now giving freedom to her mirth. "Oh, you bad boy! Did you see his face? You are better than Banting to him, or Anti-fat. He will be quite slim to-morrow. Poor old soul, what a fright he was in!"

"Coward!" says Tom, contemptuously. "And so"—regarding her with angry disfavour—"this is your last conquest, is it?"

"Conquest, dear?" says she innocently, as though not understanding, and being quite athirst for knowledge.

"Yes, exactly; *conquest,*" says Tom, uncompromisingly. "It is excellent English. Don't you understand it?"

"Oh, of course! I see what you mean *now,*" says Dorothy as though just enlightened. "But what a silly remark of yours! No wonder I didn't grasp its meaning at first."

"Well, I hope you are proud of him," says Tom, bitterly, "now you've winged him."

"Every bird that flies isn't game," says Miss Dorothy, demurely. "The capture of a barn-door fowl could hardly be considered sport."

"You may jeer at him now," says Tom, who in truth is in a most abominable frame of mind. "But you certainly laid yourself out to secure him. You have spent with him the greatest part of this day, at all events."

"By auntie's desire."

"Auntie is very convenient," says Tom.

"Do you know, Tom," says Miss Browne junior—oh, ever so sweetly!—"that if I didn't know you as well as I do, I should at times call you rude? Yes, really!"

"I dare say, even with knowing me, you call me a good many other objectionable things, at times," says Tom.

"I don't," says Miss Dorothy, tenderly. "I never call you anything but Tom! There is no harm in that, is there?" She peers up into his half-averted face with the prettiest grace in the world. Tom gives way partially.

"What were you saying to that fellow all this time?" he asks, gruffly. "I sat here, like a fool as I am, for a good hour, waiting your return. What could you have been saying to him, or he to you?"

"He was telling me about his lecture the other night in Cloughmore."

"Where he advocated the cause of temperance in the most intemperate speech ever known."

"You were there?" asks she, surprised.

"Yes; I went to hear your hero. He *did* make an exhibition of himself! It's my belief," says Mr. Delmege, in high disgust, "that he was as drunk as a fiddler."

"Tom, you ought to be ashamed of yourself!" says Dorothy. "Poor man, he won't even look at anything."

"He looks at you," says Tom, gloomily.

"I'm not spirituous liquor. Though he did say something to-day about my society being very intoxicating," says Dorothy, with a sigh, and a side glance at Tom.

It must be confessed that Miss Dorothy, in spite of her many virtues, is *un soit peu coquette.*

"I must beg of you," says Tom, vehemently, "to spare me a repetition of that old reprobate's sayings and doings. Believe in him as much as ever you like yourself, but don't expect *me* to be hoodwinked too."

"You are wilfully prejudiced. I am sure he is at least quite sincere. He is a thoroughly good man, auntie says."

"And of course auntie knows! And you and she sit at his feet, and make a demi-god of him, and believe in every word he says."

"He talks very well," says Dorothy.

"He is a blatant ass," says Mr. Delmege.

"It is such a pity, Tom," says his cousin, "that you permit yourself now and then to be so excessively vulgar."

"Yes, isn't it?" says Tom, with a derisive laugh. He is growing more and more miserable every moment. "Come," says he, "what has your paragon been doing of late? How has he been forwarding his cause—his precious cause, that is so dear to his soul?"

"He has been adding converts to his army," says Dorothy, with precisely the air Mr. Giles himself would have used on the occasion.

"An army of babes and sucklings! It is the most preposterous nonsense on earth," says Tom. "Those who sign his pledge are either old maids who never drank more than pump-water in their lives, or little children whose chief nourishment is milk."

"Your assertions are so extreme," says Dorothy, who is secretly much amused and decidedly sympathetic.

"Are they? Let us test them. Who was his last recruit in the village to-day?"

"Little Barny Kelly, aged five," says Miss Browne, demurely.

"Ye gods!" says Mr. Delmege, with a sarcastic laugh.

"I'm so fond of him," says Dorothy, softly.

Tom starts as if stung.

"Of him!—of that viper!"

"Oh, he's not that, Tom. He is the gentlest creature; he——"

"Don't talk to me about him. He is, in my opinion, the meanest, the most unworthy of his sex."

"You can't understand him if you talk like that. He is considered quite a pattern of goodness. He always does what he is told, and——"

"What *you* tell him, I suppose," with a sneer.

"Yes, always. I never met any one so obedient or so lovable."

"Good Heavens!" says Tom, growing livid; "what am I to hear next—that you love him?"

"Yes, indeed; and that he loves me. Why not?"

"Why not, indeed!" says Tom, with a terrible laugh. "Love away, by all means; but, as sure as you are there, I'll have his life!"

"What! the life of a poor little child of five years old— poor little Barny! Oh, Tom, I did not think you were so bloodthirsty!" And Miss Browne junior, as though quite overcome, lets her face fall gracefully into her pocket-handkerchief.

"Barny Kelly! Why, I thought you were talking of Mr. Giles!" says Tom, taken aback. Then he perceives that she is giving way to emotion, because her shoulders are heaving ominously, and she resolutely refuses to let her face be seen. "I'm awfully sorry if I have said anything to offend you," he says with deepest contrition, seizing her unoccupied hand. "I wouldn't, you know, for the world. Dorothy, Dorothy darling, speak to me! Let me look at you!"

"Well, for one moment only," says Miss Browne, in a stifled tone; and, as he slowly withdraws the handkerchief, she lets him see a charming face bright with laughter.

"Let us be friends," she says, gaily. "You know, Tom, you are delightful, but very absurd. Say you are sorry for the suspicions that made you accuse me of—of—you know—with Mr. Giles."

"Flirting with him?" says Tom, who scorns subterfuge. "I may be sorry for my suspicions, because they hurt me inexpressibly; but I cannot think they are unjust. You certainly are far nicer to him than you need be, and I think it very disgraceful of you."

Miss Browne knows better than to take any notice of such a speech as this, when peace is half arranged.

"Dear old bear!" she says, with a delicious little smile, and the tenderest pat of her cool fingers upon his flushed cheek. Having administered this medicine, she proceeds to perfect her cure. She slips her hand, in the simplest, most confiden-tial manner in the world, through his arm, and draws herself close up to him. What man worth calling a man could resist all this? "Do you know, Tom," she says, gently, "I quite like being scolded by you; it does me more good than any-thing. Come now, and let us have a nice long chat, just like one of those we used to have before that horrid old bore, Mr. Giles, came to stay with auntie."

In this speech she ignores, with a beautiful entirety, the fact of her having rather run up the "horrid old bore" only a few short moments ago. Tom is not proof against so much and so sweet a wiliness; yet he makes even now a desperate effort to maintain his position.

"I haven't any time for a chat," he says, glancing at his watch. "It is seven all out. I must get back to my dinner."

"Why not dine here? I am sure auntie would——"

"Are you?" interrupts he. "I'm not. No, thanks; I won't stay to-day. Cold shoulder makes a poor repast."

"She wouldn't make you unwelcome, if you mean that."

"No; but she would talk at me all through dinner; and, besides, too much of Mr. Giles would make me a hardened criminal. I should find myself at Kilmainham in no time."

"Still, there would be *me*," says she, with a touch of coquet-tish reproach.

"There would," says Tom, thoughtfully; "there is always you. But for that, I should have gratified my taste for travelling long ago. And yet, do you care whether I go or stay? Look here, Dorothy, I am coming over to see you to-morrow at three o'clock."

" Are you?" says Dorothy, innocently. "That is very good of you."

" It is about something particular—very particular ; something that must be settled at once and for ever," says the young man, earnestly. " I can bear the suspense no longer. Remember—at three o'clock. If I fail to see you then, I shall know you have avoided me on purpose."

" But why, Tom ?" asks she, casting a shy glance at him from under her long curling lashes. "What is this mighty thing you are coming to say to me ? Tell me."

" To-morrow you shall know. It is about—that is—" stammers Tom ; " that is to say, I mean—to——"

" Propose to me ?" says she ; after which graceless speech she drops her fan, and rushes away from him into the house, laughing all the way.

Tom—smiling, too, in a grave fashion—saunters off to the stables to find his horse.

As he disappears round the corner, a large fat shiny face protrudes itself carefully from behind the clump of laurustinus near which Tom and Dorothy had been standing.

" So," says Mr. Giles, thoughtfully following his face into the open walk, "it was well I stole back—that is, returned. To-morrow, at three, the mad Tom has arranged to meet my *bew*teous Dorothy, for the felonious purpose of entrapping her into an engagement, and inducing the silly maiden to enter with him into the bonds of matrimony. Hah ! hum ! ho !"

Mr. Giles, as though lost in some secret communing, strokes his flabby chin with a large and careful hand, and turns his eyes upon the ground. This is against his principles, as he usually turns them up to the skies in a rather embarrassing way that makes the beholder wonder if they will ever revert to earth again or go straight heavenward, leaving only those sickly yellow-white balls in their place. Just now, however, there is no beholder, so there is no theatrical effect. Mr. Giles stares earthward. The ignoble mole on his nose seems to grow bigger and more oppressive as the moments fly, and his imaginings come to a head.

At last he lifts his gaze. There is the light of a noble purpose in his watery eye.

"It is plainly my duty," says he, in a gentle soliloquy, "to baulk the intention of this godless young man. It is—it *must* be part of my mission to separate that guileless maiden from the clutches of the unbeliever. Clearly it has been appointed that I should use any ingenuity I may possess in this vile weakly body" (oh, the pounds of flesh upon it, and the tons it weighs !) "to circumvent the plot so carefully laid for to-morrow. 'At three o'clock,' said he. 'Blatant ass.' Hah ! 'Drunk as a fiddler.' Hoh ! 'Old reprobate.' Hum ! hum ! And so he will 'have my life,' will he ? Or shall I have his Dorothy ?— which ? Sweet Miss Dorothy, I will save you from affiancing yourself to one so utterly beneath you. I will even permit you to ally yourself with another who, though doubtless above you in many respects, is yet sufficiently humble-minded to be willing to share with you your ample fortune ! "

He bows his meek head upon his spreading breast, and moves cautiously away, lost in exalted thought.

Already the desired morrow has arrived, calling itself by its new name—to-day. It is a charming morning, all blue and gold, and merry with the music of many birds.

"Ah ! a day in which to uplift ourselves, and rejoice with a righteous joy !" says Mr. Giles, at breakfast, beaming upon Miss Browne and Dorothy. "May I be permitted to inquire, Miss Dorothy, as to what you are going to do with yourself to-day ? "

"Eh ? " says Dorothy, somewhat puzzled by the extreme suavity of his tone. "Why, nothing, I should say."

"Hah ! Good—very good," says Mr. Giles, rubbing his hands with quite a saintly glee, and smiling at her blandly over a plate piled high with buttered toast. "I shall, then, with a clearer conscience, be able to trespass on your time. My busy life, spent in forwarding 'the cause,' and shedding the true light and blue ribbons on all around, knows but few idle days. This is one of them. I would, therefore, gladly employ it in gazing upon the beauties of Nature, in pondering upon the manifold charms of this gracious earth of ours. In short, I would ask you, my dear Miss Dorothy, to take me to that island you spoke of yesterday, from which one may behold so grand a view of the surrounding neighbourhood."

"Dinish Island?" says Dorothy, somewhat aghast. The island in question is one of the chief objects of interest in that part of Ireland where she lives, but it is a long way from The Towers, the residence of Miss Jemima Browne. It is a troublesome island, too—only to be got at with the aid of a ferryman, who is anything but constant in his attentions at the point of embarkation. "It is so far away," says Dorothy, "and the day is so warm, and——" .

"Oh, not too warm," says Mr. Giles. "What season can compare with the joyous summer?

> "Summer has come again,
> Tra la la, tra la la!"

It would be impossible to describe the amount of godly urbanity Mr. Giles throws into the exceedingly ill-tuned voice he employs to chant this gay refrain. "We should, my dear young lady, revel in the glad sunshine, fit emblem of a perfect nature—all warmth and tenderness."

He looks consciously down upon the remains of the buttered toast, as though modestly aware that such a nature as he has described is all his own.

"Dear Miss Browne," he says to the maiden aunt, "add your persuasions to mine, and induce your niece to accede to my request."

"It is the very day for a trip of the kind," says Miss Jemima, eagerly. "Do, my dearest Dorothy, take Mr. Giles to Dinish.

It will occupy an entire morning and afternoon going there and coming—oh, *do* take him, my dear Dorothy!"

There is agonised entreaty in Miss Jemima's voice and eyes as she gazes imploringly at her niece. What on earth shall she do if anything interferes with this blessed chance that has cropped up of disposing for a whole morning of this good, *good* man? Dorothy, receiving the agonised glance in full, takes pity on her. She agrees instantly to Mr. Giles's proposition.

"But we must start immediately," she says, "as I must be home again by three sharp. I—I have a pressing engagement."

"Certainly, certainly!" says Mr. Giles, blandly.

The ponies being brought round to the door, they start for the ferry in half an hour or so, leaving Miss Jemima upon the stone steps, bowing and scraping an adieu to them, with the light of a glad content upon her face.

"It is quite ten to one, you know, if we find Micky Maguire, the ferryman, at his post," says Dorothy, as they draw near the end of their destination. "He is very seldom at his post. Ah, I have maligned him! There he is, by the greatest good luck."

"Such good luck," says Mr. Giles.

Micky, who is a tall Celtic lad of about seventeen, with a twinkling eye, seeing them approach, looks not only willing to ferry them anywhere, but quite as if he had been expecting them long years ago.

Stepping out of the phaeton, Dorothy and Mr. Giles walk slowly towards the boat, whilst George, the groom, whipping up his ponies, starts for home again.

"Do you know," says Dorothy, in a pained tone, to Mr. Giles, "once or twice during our drive here, I fancied I noticed the smell of brandy! Did you? I do hope George is not growing unsteady."

"Dear me! I hope not. I hope not, indeed!" says Mr. Giles, with much concern. "I must speak to him. I shall bring the artillery of my eloquence to bear upon him. I have seldom," with charming diffidence, "known it to fail. But there is something disheartening about George's nose! Have you noticed his nose? Red—terribly red!"

They step into the boat. Half-way across from the mainland to the island Dorothy's face grows distressed again.

"There," she says, leaning towards Mr. Giles, "I noticed it again! didn't you? The smell of that horrid brandy, I mean. Oh, I hope it isn't Micky Maguire!"

"I hope not, indeed," says Mr. Giles, with a severe glance at the unconscious Micky; "but I have my doubts—strong doubts. Oh, how thankful I should be that Providence directed my steps to this brandy-ridden spot!"

They have reached the island now, and are stepping ashore; Mr. Giles, with heavy gallantry, assists her to *terra firma* with so mistaken an ardour as almost brings her into his arms.

Righting herself with a sudden vehemence, she steps back from him on the gravelled shore, and frowns slightly.

"Again I am distressed by that abominable thing!" she says. "Surely there is brandy somewhere!"

"Do you know," says Mr. Giles, with the hesitating air of one just awakening to a curious fact, "I begin to think *I* must be the delinquent. I have a dry throat, a *very* dry throat—a sad affliction, dear Miss Dorothy—and, oddly enough, the lozenges I use for the relief of it smell of brandy, though I need hardly say to *you* that they have nothing in common with that most pernicious liquor."

"Ah," says Dorothy, "what curious lozenges!"

"Very, very curious," says Mr. Giles.

Dorothy's gaze, a little puzzled, wanders over the water, and marks the ferryman rowing away from them to the shore that is quite half a mile off.

"You told him what hour he is to return for us?" says she, carelessly.

"Yes, oh yes," says Mr. Giles.

It is a really charming little island; and for some time Dorothy occupies herself in showing its beauties to Mr. Giles. But he has grown singularly dull and distrait. He seems totally unimpressed by the charms of his surroundings, and presently Dorothy finds, to her infinite disgust, that he has even ceased to *pretend* admiration for aught but her, and is busily employed demanding her hand in marriage.

To refuse a man is a simple matter enough ; but things grow difficult when the man refuses to accept his "No" with a proud submission.   Mr. Giles declines to receive it at any price.

" You will think it over, dear girl," he says, confidently, with a fat squeeze of her hand.   "Oh, yes; believe me, you will think it over."

" I sha'n't," says Dorothy.

But he consigns this determined remark to the winds with a wave of his obese fingers.

" You will," he says, " and I sha'n't think the worse of you later on for this maidenly shrinking; comfort yourself with this assurance.   An inward conviction tells me that Nature has framed us for each other. So thinks your good aunt—*our* good aunt, I might say now," with a deep chuckle.

" You may say what you like now, or then, or any other time," says Dorothy, indignantly, " it will make no difference whatever to anybody concerned."   Here she glances at her watch, and finds it is long after two o'clock.   Good gracious ! why doesn't Micky come ?   She fixes her gaze earnestly upon the far-off shore, and after a bit makes out the boat, but, alas ! no Micky.   Oh, miserable boy !   Oh, perfidious ferryman !

Turning her back resolutely upon the good Mr. Giles, she seats herself upon the grassy sward, and, taking her knees into her embrace, gives herself up to a secret reviling of Fate.   But Fate is impervious to her reproaches; it takes no heed. Slowly, with leaden heels, the minutes go by, until three o'clock is reached, and then it is astonishing with what rapidity they fly. Dorothy's discomfiture is indescribable when she discovers that five o'clock has been reached, and still no tidings of Micky. Her heart dies within her.   Oh, what will Tom not think ?   Of course he had arrived at The Towers at three o'clock, the hour he had appointed to meet her. to—to—to tell her that he loved

her; and what will be the result when he finds her absent—
wilfully absent, as he will certainly think? He will imagine her
as happy, and enjoying herself with this most hateful man
beside her, who, regardless of her misery, is keeping up a con-
tinual chatter on matters absolutely repugnant to her! Oh, the
horror of being chained against her will to this small island!
Is there no chance of escape? And yet, how different would
be her imprisonment, if only Tom had been the one ordained
to share it with her!

All at once it dawns upon her that no place would be altogether bad with Tom by her side. She goes still further, and
declares to herself that there are few people preferable to Tom.
Another half-hour of vain waiting, and she willingly, nay tear-
fully, admits that there is nobody in all this wide world who
could dare presume to place himself in a category with Tom.

And possibly, all this time, while her heart is full of his
image, he is believing her false! It is terrible! She feels that
a very little more waiting will reduce her to the verge of weeping. She stirs impatiently.

"I think," says Mr. Giles, blandly—"that is, it has just
occurred to me, my dearest girl, that you appear a little uneasy.
About that 'pressing engagement' you mentioned this morning,
eh? Dear, dear, how remiss of me to forget it! I hope it will
make no difference. This boy's non-appearance is most remarkable. Shall I haste to the other point of observation, and
see if there be any signs of him?" He rises to his feet with
much alacrity as he says this.

"Yes, go; go to—go anywhere you like, and stay there,"
says Dorothy, who is now in a frame of mind not to be described.

"I fly to obey your commands," says Mr. Giles, with affectionate ardour and a beaming smile. "But I sha'n't be long.
Don't—don't, my dearest girl, let anxiety for my safety prey
upon you in my absence."

Quitting her side, he skips coquettishly round the corner.
But she has hardly had time to congratulate herself on his

disappearance, when he returns to her again with even a jauntier air than that with which he left her. It is indeed with quite a rollicking air he re-seats himself beside her.

"Vain was my hope," he says. "Our boatman continues obdurate. Sighs and tears are wasted upon him. He comes not. Fortunately, however, my sweet girl, the evening is fine."

He has dropped upon the bank close to Dorothy. She draws away from him with rather a suspicious air.

"Yes," she says, slowly, staring at him ; and then—"You've been having another lozenge, eh?" she says, very quietly, but in a peculiar tone.

The charming yellow of Mr. Giles's complexion becomes, on the instant, a brilliant saffron.

"I have," he says. "Sharp nose, eh? Those lozenges are the most remarkable things of the day."

"Just my idea," says Dorothy. "May I see one of them?"

"Dear girl, how unhappy it makes me to be obliged to refuse even so small a request of yours!" says Mr. Giles, mournfully. "A moment since, and I would have complied with it, although—you remember what I told you about my dry throat —the compliance would have left me speechless."

"The want of compliance would be more likely to have that effect," thinks Dorothy to herself.

"But the fact is," continues the apostle of temperance, playfully, "that, like a greedy schoolboy, I ate the last of my goodies just one minute and thirty seconds ago. If I had known another little bird was pining for one, I should——"

"If you mean me," interrupts Dorothy, coldly, "pray cease your regrets. I feel certain your lozenges would be most hateful to me. It is six o'clock, and auntie will be greatly distressed at our prolonged absence. Where *can* that boy be? You are sure you told him the exact hour he was to return here for us?"

"I gave him the most minute directions," says Mr. Giles, with a twinkle of his small black eyes. "But, clearly, he is not to be depended upon. Young men, my dear Dorothy, are always disappointing. You'll find 'em so throughout your life. It is the men of mature age, whose senses have been—hah! here comes our recreant Micky, our knight of the oar. Better say nothing to him, my dear Miss Dorothy. Leave me to administer to him a wordy chastisement."

"It could hardly be worthy enough," says Dorothy, starting into life and gazing wrathfully upon the late Micky, who is rowing leisurely towards them with a face innocent of guilt.

"Hah, very good, very good!" says Mr. Giles. "Wordy—worthy; quite a play upon words."

Then Micky ships his oars, the boat grates upon the beach, and presently Miss Browne, too indignant to address him, is seated in the stern, with Mr. Giles beside her. Soon they reach the opposite shore, but having told the groom early in the day that they would walk home, there are no ponies at the point to meet them. The walk is performed in comparative silence, Dorothy being too depressed and angry for conversation, Mr. Giles too hungry. As they approach The Towers, Tom Delmege is to be seen upon the balcony, with knitted brows and folded arms, in the attitude Napoleon is popularly supposed to have used during his journey across the Alps. Something in the brows, or the arms, disheartens the good Mr. Giles.

"I think I shall enter the house by the side door," he says to Dorothy with some haste. "Pray remember me very kindly to your excellent cousin, who I see is awaiting you. What a cheerful countenance is his! Ah!"

He sighs, beams fondly upon her, and after a last glance at Tom, who has now raised his head and is steadily regarding him, makes a rather undignified exit round the corner. On goes Dorothy to her fate. She knows by Tom's eye that a battle is imminent, and being a thoroughly good girl, with a fair conscience, she determines to fight it out with him inch by inch.

"Well, here I am," she says to him brightly, in the cheerfullest of tones, as a beginning to the hostilities.

"So sorry you hurried yourself," says Tom, taking his cigar slowly from his lips and dropping it over the balcony.

"I didn't," returns she, sweetly. "Don't make yourself uncomfortable about that. Have you forgotten that you told me you would be here to see me to-day at three? I didn't forget it, and quite meant to be back, but you see I wasn't."

"Well, no," says Tom, "you weren't." He has altogether declined to look at her up to this.

"That careless boy, Micky Maguire, never brought the boat to meet us until an hour ago. So stupid of him, wasn't it?"

"Was it?" says Tom.

"There is something about your tone, Tom," says Miss Browne junior, with dignity, "that suggests the idea that you do not believe I am adhering strictly to the truth. If that be so, say so, but don't stand there glowering at me."

"I am glowering at nothing," says Tom, indignantly. "But I wonder you have the—the cold-bloodedness to come here and speak to me at all after the disgraceful way in which you have been going on with that old Giles."

This is coming to the point with a vengeance.

"It wasn't my fault that I was late," says Dorothy.

"Why did you go with him at all, gallivanting off to a desert island with a man old enough to be your father? I'm ashamed of you."

"But, my dear Tom, what was I to do? Control yourself a little, and let me say one word, at all events. Poor auntie, as you know, suffers so dreadfully from lowness of spirits when left alone with Mr. Giles, that, out of sheer pity for her, I took him off her hands this morning for a little while."

"*A little while!* From twelve to seven 'a little while!' Oh, this is too much! I'm glad you found the time slip away so quickly; shows how thoroughly you enjoyed yourself."

"Don't be absurd, Tom," angrily. "You know very well that I detest that man. It is to me a positive misfortune that auntie *will* invite him here off and on."

"Then let me congratulate you on the excellent fortitude with which you endure your misfortunes," says Mr. Delmege, with what he fondly believes to be fine irony. But Dorothy will none of it.   She smiles superior.

"There are few things so unbecoming as a sneer, unless well done," she says, calmly ; "and forgive me, if I say, my dear Tom, that you haven't the nose for it !   If I were you, I should give up trying that sort of thing."

"I shall give up more than that," says Tom.   "Belief in you, for one thing."

"Because I took a walk to oblige auntie ? "

"Because you choose to prefer that old reprobate to me. Because you permit him to make love to you.   Because——"

"Oh, Tom !"

"Well, *doesn't* he make love to you ?   Tell me honestly, now, what he was saying to you all this morning and afternoon and "—with increasing wrath—"evening !"

"You are so violent that really I don't know what to say to you.   Come into the drawing-room ; we shall at least be beyond the observation of passing grooms and stable-boys."

This is an able move, meant to change the current of his thoughts, but it fails.   Mr. Delmege once in the drawing-room resumes the attack with undiminished vigour.

"Well," he says, "do you mean to tell me he spoke no word of love to you to-day ? "

"If he did, what does it matter ? "

"It does matter.   Did he propose to you ? "

"Perhaps you don't quite know how rude you are," says Dorothy, at bay.

"Silence, or a refusal to answer, gives consent," says Mr. Delmege, furiously.   "So it has come to this, has it ?   Well, I wish you joy of your Blue Ribbonite.   Take care he doesn't make *you* feel rather blue in the long run.   A man with a long-tailed coat, and a mole on his nose ! Well, I gave you credit for better taste ! "

"That was good of you," says Dorothy, who is now fully as angry as he is.   "I never expected you to give me credit for anything. It is really quite too kind of you. Anything else to say?"

"No, except good-bye. I'm going abroad. I'm—I'm going at once—this minute!"

"Don't let me detain you," says Miss Browne.

"I shall travel—to the ends of the earth. I'm very fond of travelling."

"That's a good thing," says Miss Browne, cheerfully. "Where may the ends of the earth be?"

"I shall go to India first," declares he, disdaining to take notice of her question, "and from that—anywhere! Plenty of big sport in India; and besides that, it possesses one great advantage. There is "—with immense bitterness—" a paucity of women there!"

" Mrs. Evans is there," says Dorothy, placidly. Mrs. Evans was an old flame of Tom's. " If you happen to meet her, give her my love. I always thought her such a nice girl."

"So did I," says Tom.

"And so pretty."

"Lovely."

"Such eyes!"

"Such lips!"

"And such a heavenly temper!" says Miss Browne, with growing enthusiasm. Now, as the Mrs. Evans in question had a temper of the worst description possible, this last remark leaves Mr. Delmege somewhat stranded.

"At all events, she wasn't a flirt," he says, with accumulated scorn.

A pause ensues—a terrifying pause. Then Dorothy slowly advances on the foe until she is several feet nearer Tom than she was before. This tactic reduces him to that state commonly described as " shaking in one's shoes."

" What do you mean?" asks Miss Browne junior, in an awful voice. " What do you mean by that?"

" Nothing, oh, nothing!" mumbles Tom, now thoroughly subdued. What on earth possessed him that he should make that unfortunate remark?

"Yes, you did," says Dorothy, still horribly calm. "Don't deny it." She advances even closer, and brings her foot down with a little thud upon the floor. Tom makes a backward movement that places a gipsy table betwixt him and the enemy.

"You meant every word of it," says Dorothy. "You called me—*me*—a flirt!"

"I did not," says Tom, faintly.

"Don't contradict me," says Miss Browne, with a second stamp and a few more steps that bring her up to the table. "You did mean it; but now you are ashamed of yourself, and —no wonder! Come here, if you dare, and say it all over again! Come out from behind that table, Tom Delmege; it sha'n't protect you!"

"I won't," says Tom. He seems to cling to his table as a last resource. Miss Browne, very justly incensed by this point-blank refusal to obey her command, makes a final move. She puts out her hand. No doubt she only meant it for a tragic gesture, but Tom understands it otherwise. To him it represents a desire to take him prisoner. He makes an awkward lunge to one side, which so startles Miss Browne that she trips, comes suddenly against the table, and sends it heavily to the ground. It is covered with little glass and china gimcracks, so that a most resounding crash ensues upon its fall, followed a few moments later by the sounds of hurriedly approaching footsteps in the hall.

"Aunt Jemima!" exclaims Dorothy, in an awe-stricken tone; and turning suddenly towards the upper door, she flies precipitately from the spot.

Tom (being the man) of course loses his presence of mind, and only recovers it when too late. His attempt at a retreat is rendered abortive by Miss Jemima, who, entering the room in mad haste, catches him in the very act of making his escape.

"Good Heavens! what has happened?" cries she, gazing in dismay at the ruins lying at her feet. "My Chelsea cup in atoms! My Dresden vase in bits! Oh, Tom Delmege come here! Where are you going, Tom Delmege, in that disgraceful hurry? Come here this moment, sir, and confess that this is your act!"

With a movement full of wrath, the old lady points to the *débris* upon the carpet, and to the gipsy table that, lying prone upon its side, looks as though it were kicking up its heels in a most unseemly manner. Poor Tom, with a most woe-begone countenance, creeps slowly back into the room, and on his bended knees, and, with flushed cheeks, proceeds to pick up the broken bits of glass and china beneath a perfect volley of abuse. Abuse, too, to which he has no claim. But though he tries to hate her, there is sweetness in the thought that he is enduring it all for Dorothy. He is still crawling about the carpet, and Miss Browne is still giving him her opinion of him in no measured terms, when a servant enters the room.

"Micky Maguire is below, miss, an' wants to see Miss Dorothy."

"Let him want," says Miss Jemima, still fuming. "Oh, my precious porcelain! Oh, goodness gracious! look at my best bit of Valérie! Would its own mother—I mean its own maker —know it! Tell that miscreant, Micky Maguire, that Miss Dorothy will never again see him after his treatment of her to-day."

Tom pricks up his ears.

"Av ye plase, Miss Jemima, 'tis myself has come to explain all that," says a second voice at the door; and enter Micky, much dishevelled from hard running and mental disturbance.

"Go away, Maguire! It is of no use your trying to excuse yourself," says Miss Jemima, sternly. "I have the whole story straight from Mr. Giles's own lips."

"Then humbly beggin' yer pardon, miss, ye couldn't have it from a greater blagguard," says Micky, with the utmost mild ness.

"Connor, remove this boy," calls Miss Jemima, vehemently addressing the departing servant.

Just at this moment the upper door is gently pushed open, and Dorothy, looking as innocent as a dove, appears upon the threshold.

"Dear me! who threw down the table?" asks she, looking with deep horror upon the remains of the Chelsea. "Was it you, auntie? or was it—oh, Tom!" Her reproachful glance at Tom is shortened as she catches sight of Micky in the background.

"You here!" she exclaims. "Go away! I cannot think, Maguire, what brings you here after your disgraceful carelessness this evening."

"If ye'd on'y let me spake, miss," says Micky, nervously twisting his old "caubeen" round and round upon his fingers. "Sure, 'twasn't my fault at all, at all. 'Twas the ould gent as done it."

"Mr. Giles didn't make you late," says Dorothy.

"Fegs, an' that's just what he did, miss; that very same, bad luck to him!"

"Boy!" says Miss Jemima, severely, putting up her glasses and subjecting him to an awful stare, "recollect yourself!"

"That's what I'm doin', miss. I'm recollectin' as hard as I can. An' here's the very words he said to me. Says he, 'Come for us at sivin o'clock,' says he. 'Not a minyit sooner,' says he, 'or be the powers I'll have the life o' ye,' says he."

"Boy!" says Miss Jemima again, in a strident tone, meant to re-conduct him to the paths of truth.

"But when did he say all this?" asks Dorothy, bewildered.

"Airly this mornin', miss. Before iver ye started, he come to me to tell me to be ready for ye at the landin' place, an' 'twas thin he said thim very words. I didn't misthrust him then, miss; but when I heard a while ago that ye were mad intirely wid me for bein' so late, it sthruck me that the old vagabone was playin' some game."

"Boy!" says Miss Jemima, but rather more faintly this time, "have a care!"

"A what, miss? No thank ye, miss. It's too airly for thim

foreign wines ; an' Father Jerry would be the death o' me if he heard of it. But, indeed, Miss Dorothy, 'tis the solemn truth I'm tellin' ye about that ould gent wid the mould on his nose. Did ye iver hear, miss, that moulds is very onlucky? Faix, they are so, miss, an' I'd have ye take care of him. Have nothing to do wid him, Miss Dorothy. Any one wid a mould can bring down the divil's own disasthers on any one that vexes them."

"I must request, boy," says Miss Jemima, weakly, "that we have no cursing and swearing here. And—and how are we to know that your words contain truth ? It was only a moment since that Mr. Giles was deeply regretting to me in the most flowery language the unfortunate delay caused by your carelessness."

"Bring me face to face wid him, miss ! He promised me a shillin' for me day's throuble, an' divil a rap have I seen yet. Whin he was lavin' the boat I inthroduced me hand to him, miss, an' he said, 'The ould hag above would see to it,' manin' yer honour's self, miss; an' axin' yer pardon for repatin' it, 'tis me own belief, miss, as he'd been dhrinkin', for he smelt very sthrong."

"Oh, Heavens ! " says Miss Jemima, sinking into a chair. "What is this I hear? Have I lived all these years to be called 'an old hag ?' Oh, my dear Tom, won't you see me righted ? Won't you chastise that villain ? That wolf in sheep's clothing ! Oh, my poor Dorothy, to what a fate I was hurrying you ! "

Just at this most opportune moment the door is softly opened, and Mr. Giles puts in a fat face aglow with loving smiles.

"Am I welcome ? " asks he, with his most playful air, appealing to Miss Jemima. But that maiden has lost her faith in smiles, however heavenly. She turns upon him.

"Monster ! " cries she, shaking her hand at him. "Avaunt ! Out of my sight, villain ! Away—away ! "

"Eh ? What ? How is this ? Has my dear friend taken

leave of her senses?" demands Mr. Giles, changing colour as he sees Micky.

"It means that we have discovered your creditable little scheme to cause a breach between me and my affianced wife," says Tom, promptly, drawing Dorothy's willing hand through his arm. Tom is a young man of a ready wit and many resources, and is always up to time.

"And where may *she* be?" asks Mr. Giles, in a tone that strikes Tom as being insulting. He makes a dash forward, but is seized by Dorothy.

"Here!" she says to Mr. Giles, answering his question by a motion of her disengaged hand that indicates herself. Tom is still struggling, but Miss Jemima has also added her strength to Dorothy's, to prevent his falling on the foe.

"We know all about you now," pants Tom. "This boy, Micky, has just informed us of your baseness, you infer——"

"Thomas! beware!" says Miss Jemima. "Do not be a partner with him in vice. Keep from evil words. Go, man!" to Mr. Giles; "I can't hold him much longer. Go! whilst your skin is whole upon your body."

"This is sad—very sad!" says Mr. Giles. "The old Adam breaketh forth again. Oh, how degrading are the effects of alcohol!" He groans dismally, and, making a cautious movement towards the door, runs almost into the arms of the upper housemaid.

She is a pretty girl, but at this moment without her temper. She gives the benevolent Mr. Giles a vehement shove that sends him tottering back once more into the drawing-room.

"See here, mum," says she, advancing towards Miss Jemima. "Look at this here, which I found under his bed this morning." She casts a withering glance at Mr. Giles, and holds up for general inspection a large black object. Alas for the apostle of temperance! Alas for the Blue Ribbon! It is a brandy bottle. "*I'll* teach you to chuck me under the chin again!" says she, shaking it angrily at Mr. Giles.

He is growing very yellow. But he makes a last feeble effort to support his cause—*the* cause.

"There is such a thing as martyrdom!" he moans, lifting his eyes until only the whites of them can be seen. This, on his part, is a foolish proceeding, as it dims his vision for the moment, and in that moment Tom gets him. Breaking loose from his gentle chains he falls upon the foe, and when next Mr. Giles's eyes return to earth it is to find himself in mid-air, flying down the broad staircase at a speed hitherto unknown to him. Despite innumerable bruises, however, he picks himself up off the hall mat, and beats a hasty retreat from The Towers, never to return.

The housemaid and Micky Maguire, filled with deep joy, retire to the lower regions. A silence falls upon the three left alone in the drawing-room. It is broken by the butler.

"Dinner is served," says he, in the sonorous voice with which Nature has endowed him. It acts upon Miss Jemima like an electric shock. She bursts into tears.

"Tom," she says, plaintively, "I am quite unstrung. I am ill, Tom—very ill. Something is weighing on my breast." As if unconsciously she detaches the Blue Ribbon from her dress and holds it out to Dorothy. "Perhaps it is this, my dear! It reminds me of that bad man. Put it carefully away somewhere, where—where I can't see it. And, Tom, I feel very weak; I think I should like a—er—just a thimbleful of champagne—but no more, *no more!*"

MONICA.

To any one coming direct from all the luxury and beauty of the old Court above, naturally this little cottage room looks small and poverty-stricken, yet there is a pathetic tenderness about it, too, born of a woman's hand—a touch of gentle refinement that shows itself in the masses of old-world flowers, carelessly and artistically put together, that adorn the one table and the two brackets, filling all the tiny apartment with their subtle perfume.

The windows, opening to the ground, are thrown wide open. Outside, the garden lies panting in the sunshine. There is the sad lowing as of many cows in the far distance. All the land lies quivering in its heat. A faint useless little breeze comes lazily into the room, ruffling the ancient curtains that are drawn closely together in a vain effort to exclude the sun.

Poor Mr. Norwood, with a praiseworthy determination to seem quite the contrary, is looking the very picture of misery. He has been dragged from his sanctum and his beloved " Aldines, Bodonis, Elzevirs," to interview, or rather be interviewed by, a fashionable young man fresh from town, who, though his nephew, is to him an utter stranger.

Conversation for the last five minutes has been growing more and more languid. Now it threatens to cease altogether. The host is at his wits' end, the fashionable young man is looking distinctly bored. It is therefore with a glance full of rapture, and a nobly suppressed sigh of extreme relief, that Mr. Norwood hears a step upon the gravel outside, that comes quickly nearer.

It is—it *must* be—Monica, to the rescue !

Now one of the windows is darkened : a figure, stepping airily from the bright sunshine beyond to the room within, parts the curtains with both hands, and gazes inquiringly around.

As her glance falls upon the strange young man, it alters from expectation to extreme surprise—not confusion, or embarrassment of any kind, but simple, honest surprise, visitors at the cottage being few and far between, and as a rule exceedingly ill to look at.

The strange young man returns her gaze with generous interest, and a surprise that outdoes her own. For a full half minute she stands with a curtain held back in either hand, and then she advances slowly.

She is dressed in a gown of Oxford shirting—very plain, very inexpensive. It has a little full baby body that somehow suits wonderfully the grave childish face above it with its frame of light-brown hair so like the colour of an unripe chestnut. Her eyes are blue as the heavens above her; her mouth a trifle large perhaps, but very serious, and very sweet. One cannot but believe laughter possible to her, one cannot also but believe she has found self-communion on many occasions a solace and a solemn joy.

"Come here, Monica, and let me make you known to your cousin, George Norwood," says her father, very proudly. The pride is all concentrated in his daughter. In his soul he deems a king would be honoured by such an introduction.

At this she comes closer, and places a small slim hand in her cousin's.

"I should have known, of course," she says, as though following out a certain train of thought. "I heard you had come to the Court."

"You must be good friends with him, Monica," says Mr.

Norwood, nervously. "He is your only cousin, you know—except Julia."

"Yes "—she is smiling now—"we shall be friends of course!" Then more directly to the man who is still holding her hand, as though he has actually forgotten it is in his possession, "As my father likes you, it follows that I shall like you too."

"Ah!" says George Norwood, with an answering smile that renders his face quite beautiful, "then I owe your father a debt of gratitude I shall not easily repay."

Mr. Norwood has been getting nearer and nearer to the door by fine degrees. Monica, without seeming to notice this, says gently:

"Go back to your books, papa. I will take care of—of—my cousin."

At this Mr. Norwood beats a thankful retreat, leaving the two young people alone.

"Why did you hesitate just now?" asks George, suddenly. She has seated herself on a very ancient sofa and is regarding him thoughtfully.

"When?"

"Over my name."

"Because I didn't quite know what to call you. Your being my cousin does not prevent your being a perfect stranger —and a stranger, I suppose, ought to be called Mr. Norwood."

"If you call me that, I shall be unhappy for ever," says George Norwood. "Besides, you can't, you know, because I shall certainly never call *you* anything but Monica."

"Oh! at *that* rate!" says she, smiling again.

Presently, as he stands upon the hearthrug, he lifts his eyes and fastens them upon a portrait that hangs above the chimneypiece.

"What a charming face!" he says. "What a complexion —and eyes!"

"Yes, it is lovely! It is my grandmother. Don't you think the mouth and nose like papa's?"

"The very image!" says George Norwood. He doesn't think it a bit, but seeing she plainly expects him to say it, he does his duty like a man. "It is a perfect face! But the eyes—they are your own surely."

"Are they? Do you know I never look at that picture without feeling *bitter!*" She laughs as she says this in a way that precludes the idea that acrimony of any sort could belong to her. "It was the only thing my grandfather left papa. He made a particular point of it in his will, that it should be given to him. When he had carefully cut him off to a shilling, he bestowed upon him an oil-painting—wasn't it munificent? The eldest son's portion to be a mere portrait, while the second and third son's *children* should inherit *all!*" Then, as remembrance comes to her, she reddens, and grows for the first time confused. "I beg your pardon," she says, softly; "I had forgotten you were the child of the second son."

"Don't mind about that," says Norwood. "In my eyes too it was a most iniquitous will."

"Papa was very glad to get this portrait of his mother," says Monica, hastily. "He adored her. She did all she knew to make grandfather destroy his first will, and leave everything, as was only right, to my father. She gained her point too, but when she died, he forgot his promise and everything, and betrayed the dead, as you can see." She makes a mournful gesture towards the room that so painfully betrays their poverty.

"My father as the second son was badly treated too," says Norwood, anxious, he hardly knows why, to create a feeling of sympathy between them.

"Not *so* badly. By leaving the property to you and Julia, the daughter of his third son, on condition you marry each other, he provided for both the children of the younger sons. For me he did nothing. He never forgave papa's marriage. You will marry Julia of course?"

She is regarding him seriously, and he laughs a little and colours beneath her gaze.

"I dare say," he says, lightly. "It would seem a pity to throw away ten thousand a year; and if I refuse, she gets all, and I am in the cold. As I am heartwhole, I may as well think about it; that is, if she will have the goodness to accept me."

"She will," says Monica, with a certain meaning in her tone. "If she refused she would be left penniless too, it would all go to you, and she is fond of——" She pauses. "I dare say you will get on very well together," she continues, hastily. "And as you are heartwhole, as you say, it really cannot much matter."

"What can't matter?"

"Your marrying for money."

"And if I was *not* quite free—if my heart owned another tie—how then?" asks he, with an anxiety to know her opinion that astonishes even himself.

"Then it would be disgraceful of you, and contemptible," returns she, seriously, but without haste. Perhaps she thinks she has spoken too severely, because presently she smiles up at him very softly and kindly. And then, after a little bit, he says good-bye to her, and goes out into the gleaming sunshine, and all the way up to the grand old Court (that may, or may not, be his as his will dictates), and carries into it, not the face of the cousin who reigns there, and whom it is expedient he should marry, but a soft vision, glad with eyes that shine like sapphires, and sunburnt hair, and a smile grave and sweet and full of heavenly tenderness.

*　　*　　*　　*　　*　　*

It is a month latter. Thirty days—as cruelly short, as days will ever be where happiness reigns supreme—have taken to themselves wings and flown away.

It is now high noon; already the day begins to wane. The god of light grows weary; "Tired Nature halts." The streamlets are running wearily, as though fatigued with the exertions of the day, now almost past. "It is the earth's siesta—even the bee flags in his deep and dull monotony."

All the morning George Norwood has toiled assiduously after his cousin at the Court; has followed from greenhouses to conservatories, from conservatories to orchards, the woman he has been taught he must marry, if he wishes to keep up his good fellowship with the world to which he has so long been known. Now, when evening is descending, he has escaped from his duty, and has flung himself with deepest, intensest relief at the feet of the woman he ought not to marry, with whom indeed marriage will mean social extinction.

He met her half an hour ago in this little shadowy valley, where the dying sunbeams are playing at hide-and-seek amongst the branches of the trees, and where a tiny rivulet is lisping and stammering as it runs lazily over the pebbles.

Monica, having thrown aside her huge white hat, is sitting on a little mound, with her back against a beech-tree. She has taken her knees into her embrace, and just now is looking at her cousin from under heavily-lashed lids, that seem barely able to support themselves, so languorous is the hour, and so contented her spirit.

Her companion can scarcely be said to be looking as free from care as she is. There is a slight suspicion of weariness in his eyes; his manner, which as a rule is of the *débonnaire* order, is somewhat tinged with a depression very foreign to it.

"Anything the matter with you?" asks Monica, at last.

"Yes; any amount of things."

"Well—go on—say them all over—it will do you good," suggests she, sympathetically.

"Not for worlds—at least, not for many reasons. It would bore you; it wouldn't cure my case; and, besides," with a half laugh, "my worries are of the kind difficult to put into speech."

"That means they are nothing but fancies."

"Does it?" Then leaning back and placing his hands behind his head, he turns his eyes slowly upon hers. "I wish I had never come down here," he says, deliberately.

"What!" cries she, leaning towards him. "Has Julia

proved unkind? or is it kind—— Won't she marry you? Or will she?"

"Nonsense!" says Mr. Norwood, gruffly. "I wasn't think-ing of Julia."

"No? Then why are you sorry you came to the Court?"

Norwood at this regards her fixedly. "I wonder," he says, in a curious tone, "whether you really don't *know*, or whether you are an accomplished coquette!"

"Don't know what?" asks Monica, opening her large earnest eyes to their fullest, and looking at him with such sweet and honest surprise as awakes within his breast the deepest self-contempt. How *could* he have doubted her, for even one short moment. "To be a coquette," she says, in a little dignified tone, "requires, I believe, practice. There is nobody down here except the rector and Sir John Frere."

"Sir John Frere?" apprehensively.

"Yes. He is toothless and seventy-five. The rector is hairless and sixty-one!" With this she very properly turns her back upon him.

"Thank goodness!" says Mr. Norwood, devoutly. He feels affectionate towards both these old men — in spite of their shortcomings, and in spite of the fact that he has never seen either of them. "I beg your pardon very humbly," he says, after a pause, full of eloquence.

No reply.

"Monica—speak to me."

"I will not," says Monica, giving herself the lie direct.

"Oh! but you *are* speaking," declares he. "I am awfully sorry I said that, because it was as absurd as it was unpardon-able."

"As you acknowledge it to be unpardonable, you can't well look for my forgiveness."

"Nevertheless, I do," exclaims he, boldly.

"Well, then, say at once I am not a coquette."

"Certainly you are not. You are an ang—You are all you ought to be. You are——"

"That will do," says Miss Monica, with a mischievous glance; "you will overdo it if you go on any further. And now don't let us quarrel any more. Tell me what you were doing all the morning."

"Lounging, after Julia."

"Happy man! I do so love that old Court; and I suppose she took you through the gardens? If *only* my grandfather had behaved properly, and left it to papa! Instead of which, here we are, playing second where we should be first."

"Well, it's nearly as bad for me," says the young man, moodily; "*I* was brought up in the belief that, as your father was not in it, I was to be the heir. And see now where I am."

"You will be all right when you marry Julia," says Monica, with the friendliest encouragement. But this encouragement falls through.

"Oh, I dare say," says Mr. Norwood, ungratefully, and with increasing gloom.

"But you *can't* be badly off. You must have money now, too," says his cousin, with a swift glance at his clothes, which are irreproachable.

"Not enough to keep me decently. My mother left me £700 a year."

"£700 a year!" says Miss Norwood, severely. "I think no young man could possibly require more than that. You have only yourself to think of—no other expenses—no grown-up daughter to dress and keep."

"Well, I could hardly have that, you know," says George Norwood, apologetically. "I won't be twenty-six until next month."

"I was thinking of papa—if he had £700 a year, how happy we should both be!"

"No—you would instantly want more."

"I am sure not. That would give him all he requires—'a house full of books and a garden of flowers.'" She makes her quotation with a sweet wistful smile that goes to his heart.

"And you—what would it give you?" he asks, earnestly.

"Me! Oh, I should be happy enough in his happiness," replies she, lightly. "'The garden of flowers,' you see, would be as much mine as his. *Now,*" she says, with a little irrepressible sigh, "he hasn't even enough money to buy some of the books in which his soul delights."

"What are they?—I mean, their names?" asks he, eagerly, *too* eagerly.

She raises her soft eyes to his; there is gratitude in them, but stern resolve too.

"No, no," she says. "Remember what you said a moment since—your income is not sufficient for yourself. You shall not waste it upon us."

"I don't think it is quite a civil thing to remember every word a fellow says," returns George, reproachfully.

"Well, we won't go into that," replies she, quickly. Then, as though some hidden force compels her to return to the subject, she says, "Tell me how you get on with Julia?"

"Very well," impatiently. "She will look all that is satisfactory at the head of one's table. There is consolation, no doubt, in that thought, as "—bitterly—"I suppose I *must* marry her."

"Oh, why say *must?*" gently, and with a glance at him from under her long lashes. "It is not a hardship, surely?"

"Perhaps I shouldn't have thought it so a month ago."

"She is young, handsome; that is all one requires, is it not?"

"Not quite! There is something else, I think—*many* other things; but, above and beyond all, the essential grace that makes life—that is, *married* life—sweet; I mean sympathy."

"She hardly knows you yet," says Monica, deep but suppressed pity in her eyes. "By and by it may be different." Knowledge of Julia makes her confess to her secret soul that small hope for him lies in a nearer acquaintance with the cousin he needs must marry.

"In six months more it must all be settled," says the young man, restlessly. "Julia up to that time has everything. It will

then depend upon me whether she will still have everything or
cnly half."

"You are sure she will accept you?"

"I am afraid—I mean," colouring hotly at his mistake, "I
think she *will* do me the honour to be my wife."

"You think rightly. She will not resign the property. Only
yesterday she told me she could not live without it. In six
months, then, she will still have everything, and—*you into the
bargain!*"

Almost as these last words escape her she repents them, and
growing pale to her very lips, turns her head aside, and becomes
painfully anxious about an insignificant tear that a straggling
briar has created in her gown.

"I am not so sure of that," says Norwood, unsteadily.
"Monica, look at me. Nay, you *must*," trying to compel her
to return his gaze, which has grown impassioned.

He has taken one of her hands in his, and is trying to draw
her nearer to him.

"Release my hand," she says, in a low tone, yet with so much
authority, that at once he obeys her. There is a strange flash
in her beautiful eyes that warns him to dare nothing further,
and yet makes his pulse throb madly. What a strange proud
glance it is, and yet what grief, what anguish it contains!

"I am tired," says the girl, wearily. "I will go home—yes,
you may come with me; but for the future"—she pauses and
resolutely, but with evident difficulty forces herself to look at
him—"for the future you must promise me never again to forget——"

"I promise you faithfully," interrupts he, quickly, "I shall
never forget!"

She sighs.

Presently, turning to her almost as they reach the cottage,
he says, "Are you going to the ball at the Grange to-morrow
evening?"

"No."

"But you told me you were asked."

"So I was. I am not going, nevertheless."

"Why?" There is terrible disappointment in his tone.

"If you must know," she says, gently, "it is because I have not got a gown good enough."

"That dress you wore at the Court last evening—— "

"Is a fossil—almost an heirloom. The whole county knows it by heart by this time. No! pride forbids my exhibiting myself in it again."

"If you asked your father——"

"I should have one at once—at the expense of his being even duller than usual for a month afterwards. He would give me every penny he possesses, would probably sell some of his dearest possessions—books—to get me a few yards of muslin, in which to enjoy myself for an hour or two. Do you think I *should* enjoy those two hours, knowing that? What purgatory they would mean !"

"They would indeed !" he says, reverently, gazing at her fair loving face with unaffected admiration. He does her full justice, and understands perfectly the loyal affection that could find no happiness in a pleasure secured at the expense of a beloved object. Then he wonders why Julia, who has more money at her command than she quite knows what to do with, has had no thought for the poor little cousin in the cottage; and then I am afraid he thinks bitter thoughts of the woman he ought to marry.

"You must come to see me the day after the ball, and tell me all about it," she says, lightly. "Second-hand to hear of it will be better than nothing."

"Yes, I will come," he says, absently; but it is plain his thoughts are roaming, and that he is thinking of something far removed from the soft evening scene that surrounds him.

*   *   *   *   *   *

The morrow passes ; the day dies. Night comes on apace and covers everything. At the Grange the fiddles are sounding, bright forms are moving to and fro ; the air is heavy with the breath of dying flowers. It is eleven o'clock, and the ball is well begun; the music grows sweeter, fainter; fans are waving gently.

Down in the cottage a girl is standing in a white gown at one of the open windows, and is gazing eagerly and with sad straining eyes at certain lights, that two miles away can be seen distinctly through the still haze of the summer night.

Yes, he is there of course; and happy and regardless of everything but the moment. It is most natural, is it not? What is there else for him to think of? She, herself, how dearly *she* would like to be there too! She glances at her gown and tells herself that almost she might have gone—and then she shrinks within herself, and refuses to confess even to her own heart that it would have been agony to her to have appeared badly dressed before—before—oh! *many* people!

She sighs impatiently, and the tears gather in her eyes, and blot out the lights shining gaily so far away; they blot out too a dark figure that, advancing rapidly through the few shrubs, enters the second open window, and, crossing the room, is at her side before she has time to recognise him.

It is George Norwood of course—a little flushed from his run, and with his hair slightly ruffled, and with the gladdest light possible in his handsome eyes.

Monica, moving backwards, involuntarily seizes the curtain with one hand and stares at him almost affrightedly. Her attitude reminds him of that happy moment when first he saw her. Before he has time to speak, she recovers herself and says, with a poor attempt at coldness:

"What has brought you here?"

"You know," replies he, calmly; "an overpowering desire to see *you*—to hear your voice again. Your face was in every corner, smiling at me—your voice was clearer than the band, and called me incessantly. I have come!"

He sinks into a chair with all the air of a man who intends to make it his resting-place for the remainder of the evening.

"Where is Julia?" asks she, reproof in her voice, unmistakable gladness in her great gleaming eyes. She has got a heavy spray of scarlet geranium in the bosom of her white gown. It rises and falls nervously, as she stands before him, trying vainly to be stern and angry.

"I don't know—I don't care. Dancing, I suppose."

"Go back to her. I won't have you here. Go back to her *at once !* "

"I won't."

"But I desire you," exclaims she, with a little stamp of her foot.

"Of course, if you turn me out, I shall have to go," says George Norwood, without showing the faintest symptom of an intention to depart ; "but I certainly sha'n't go to Julia—I've had enough of Julia."

Monica's breath comes a little quickly; she lifts her hand to her soft rounded throat.

"You ought to be with the woman you mean to marry," she says, slowly.

"I entirely agree with you," says Norwood, with the utmost vivacity. "But that wouldn't drive me back to the Grange. I shall never marry Julia."

"You don't know what you are saying," says Monica, shrinking still farther from him.

"I do. Quite well. I ought to have said it before, but to-night I have made up my mind. If you refuse me, I shall never marry any woman—*never !* My darling, don't shrink from me ; say you love me, *say it*—Monica, *say* it."

"No—no. You must be mad," says the girl, as, white as death, with both hands she keeps him away from her. "It is £10,000 a year. You *shall* not do this thing. In the morning you will think——"

"As I do now," interrupts he. "And as I thought yesterday morning, and every morning during the past week—that I love you better than my very life—to say nothing of filthy lucre."

The pressure of the hands that repulse him is not so strong now. Emboldened by this sign of coming weakness, he goes on with renewed spirit :

"We shall be poor, you know; but you said once you thought £700 a year quite enough to live on. You can't go back of that *now*. You said also that it would be a disgraceful and contemptible act on the part of any man to marry one woman when he loved another. You can't get out of that either, and I am not going to look either disgraceful or contemptible in the only eyes I worship."

The hands have grown quite reasonable now, and indeed have slipped from his chest to his shoulders.

"Monica, I am yours, whether you like it or not. You must try and make the best of me," he says, very humbly. "My beloved, I can only promise to be a good husband to you till death us do part!"

"Do not talk of death," she whispers, tremulously.

"No? Shall we not pray that we may die the same day, and be buried in the same grave? But living or dying, my own darling, every thought of my heart will be yours."

The hands have slipped a little higher up, and now, with a faint but heavy sigh that is almost a sob, she twines them round his neck and lays her soft cheek against his.

(You must imagine a good many asterisks here, and then we go on.)

"How was Julia looking?" asks she, presently. They are now sitting close together—very close indeed—upon the patriarchal sofa that certainly has seen better days. But if it were satin and down they could not be more contented with it.

"Very handsome," replies he, with the most satisfactory indifference. "'Icily regular, splendidly null' sort of business. No soul, and too much flesh. My angel, you have saved me. To think that only for you I *might* have married her; should, to a moral certainty, you know, as I didn't know what love meant then."

At this juncture there is no mistaking he knows what love means now.

"If you should ever be sorry about this," says Monica, nervously.

"Nonsense, darling; you know you are miles too good for me. I hope *you* will never be sorry, that's all;—Monica "—wistfully, "are you certain, *positive*, that you really love me ?"

"I am as sure of it as that we are sitting here," says Miss Norwood, solemnly.

A further demonstration that they now *really* know what love means !

"Do you know, I'm awfully hungry," says George, presently, without the smallest shame, or recollection that people in novels never eat anything when filled with the tender passion.

"Are you? Do you know so am I, but I didn't quite like to say it," confesses she, naïvely. "The servants are in bed, I am afraid; but there is cold chicken in the pantry, and——"

"Let us go for it ourselves," says George. "As we are going to set up housekeeping on a limited scale, the sooner we learn how to lay a table and help ourselves the better."

"I don't believe there is any sherry," says Miss Norwood, blushing generously; "but there is "—with considerable hesitation—"beer."

"If there is one thing on earth I love, it is beer," says George Norwood.

"There now," murmurs she, reproachfully. "And just this moment you told me you loved only me."

"And so I do, you and you only," declares he, fervently.

More asterisks !

"The key of the beer is always kept behind this picture," says Monica, pointing to the oil-painting of her grandmother he had admired on the first day of his arrival.

"That's a good thing to know," returns he, laughing.

"Well, take it down for me, now; it will be a lesson. You will know exactly where to go for it next time."

She laughs too as she says this, and drawing him up to the chimneypiece, points to where the key hangs behind the picture.

Was it fatality, or was it awkwardness? As he puts up his hand, he touches the painting, and the string that supports it snapping suddenly, the picture falls heavily to the ground—so heavily that the back parts from it, and leaves it rather a dilapidated object on the hearthrug.

But something else is on the hearthrug too! A piece of yellowish parchment, tightly folded, has slipped from between the picture and the frame. George and Monica, both stooping to pick up her grandmother, see this paper at the same instant. She, being the woman, is naturally the most curious, and therefore the swiftest to snatch it.

"Now," she says gaily, putting it behind her back, "what do you say it is—a legacy or a hundred-pound note, or mere padding to keep the portrait steady?"

"Mere padding," guesses he.

"A fairy gift," declares she.

Then they stoop over the lamp, and examine it cautiously.

When Norwood has opened it, and read two or three lines of the writing it contains, he utters an ejaculation, and turns to Monica with eyes bright with excitement.

"What was the date of our grandfather's will?" he asks, eagerly. "I mean, how long before his death was it written and signed?"

"Three years," says Monica, gazing at him in wonderment.

"And this is dated six months before his death," says he, with something in his tone that resembles awe. "This is another and a later will, Monica, and it bequeaths *all to your father!*"

*   *   *   *   *   *

It was quite true. I suppose the old man when feeling sickness come on him—that first attack of paralysis that suggested to him the possibility of death—had repented him of the betrayal of his promise to the wife, dead and gone for seven long years, but green still in his memory. To leave *all* to the son of her heart—the first, and therefore the dearest babe that had lain upon her bosom—was her prayer. And the father, though estranged from this son for many reasons too numerous to mention here, had succumbed as a husband should to the love of his youth, and had sworn to her that justice should be done.

Yet it was gall to him, the doing of it. Gladly would he have got out of the promise given to the dying woman, but even though the grave closed upon her, she had a hold over him, born of memories when spring was glad with flowers, and the sun shone, and all was youth and love.

And yet the gall rose to the top; and after a bit, so strong was it, that he looked about him for a way to fulfil his promise to the dead and yet work his own desire. He would make a new will—so far she was obeyed, poor soul!—leaving all to the eldest son, whom he so deeply detested, and it should be given into his own hands, but in such wise that he should be none the better by it.

His mother's portrait was made the medium. Behind it, in between the wooden back and the picture, the old man in secret hid the will that vexed him, and in the first document that suited his pride he inserted a codicil, leaving portrait, concealed will, and all to his eldest son.

Yet Fate is strong, and Time brings all things to perfection.

Julia, when matters were made clear to her, took it all very badly. Having a very good income of her own, and an implacable temper, she refused to be comforted, and went abroad to Egypt, or Tangiers, or somewhere, and may now be married to a swarthy prince for all I know.

Pretty Monica has married her lover, and when last I saw ner was teaching her little son to "Ride a-cock horse to Banbury Cross" on his grandfather's knee.

DR: BALL.

HE was a very little man, with a cherubic face, and a large soul, and nothing at all awe-inspiring about him. His eyes shone through his glasses anxiously, as though in eager search of any good that might be lying about amongst his parishioners. He thought no evil of any man, and, in truth, no man thought evil of him.

He had been twenty years a curate, but had never sighed for higher wage or betrayed a hankering for the flesh-pots of Egypt. Contented he was and happy amongst his ungrateful old women and surly old men. He went to bed at eight o'clock, or half-past; he never went into society; indeed, there was hardly any into which to go in the benighted Irish village in which he lived. He knew as little about the subtle changes that creep now and again into fashionable life, as the South Sea Islander.

Dulcinea—a charming girl of eighteen, and a great heiress, his friend and godchild—would often walk down to his cottage to see him, but he would seldom go to her. He would never dine from home, but sometimes he would take from Dulcinea's hand the cup of tea she had ready for him at all hours of the day, knowing it to be his one carnal delight.

His Rector was old and infirm, and for the most part resided in Italy. In fact, the little Doctor did all the work of Inchinabagga, which was the somewhat outlandish name of his parish.

Dulcinea, with an unpardonable play upon his name, had christened him her Candy-ball : saying in excuse that she had a right to give him any name she pleased, because he had given her hers—which did not please her—at the font, many winters ago now. .

"Yet, after all, I don't think my sobriquet suits you : candy-balls are such *hard* things," she said, tenderly, as she walked with him up and down his little garden-path one morning in mid-winter, hugging his arm the while. "I'm sure I have nearly smashed all my teeth with them over and over again. And you, with your tender heart, could never hurt me or any living thing. I know—and Gerald says it too—that you are the best and dearest man in all the world."

Having exploded this little shell, she waited somewhat anxiously for the result.

"Now—now—I am afraid you have been writing to Gerald again," said the Doctor, stopping in his walk and regarding her with what he believed to be severity.

"Yes, I have," said Miss Vane, promptly. "Isn't it good of me to tell you the truth out quite plainly? I'll tell you something else, too. If you say even one small scolding word to me, I shall run away from you, and you sha'n't see me again for a week."

"Dear me, dear me, this is terrible!" said the Doctor, almost tragically.

Now, Miss Dulcinea Vane, besides being an heiress, was also the Bishop's ward. And the Bishop was sternly desirous of doing his duty by her—which meant turning a cold shoulder on all needy young men who paid their addresses to her. Their name was Legion, so that the poor Bishop had by no means a good time of it.

There had come nothing serious of it all, however, until about six months ago, when Gerald Wygram had descended upon Inchinabagga as if from the clouds. He said he had come for the fishing, which was excellent in the neighbourhood; but having seen Miss Vane one day in the Curate's garden, his desire for trout suddenly died a natural death, and his desire for something else grew into a mighty longing. He was a tall young man, handsome, and, worse than all, eloquent. He talked Dulcinea's heart out of her body, before she woke to the knowledge that she had a heart.

There was absolutely no fault to be found with him beyond the fact that he was the fifth son of a by-no-means wealthy baronet. This was a sin past forgiveness in everybody's eyes except Dulcinea's. She was reasoned with, expostulated with, *threatened.* All to no good.

The Bishop in a long letter—exquisitely written and perfectly worded—finally *commanded* Miss Vane to cease to think again of this Gerald Wygram (this clerk in the Foreign Office, with a paltry stipend) for even one moment! To which Dulcinea sent a meek reply, to the effect that as usual her guardian's behests should be obeyed to the letter. She would indeed *never* think of Gerald Wygram again for that insignificant portion of time called a moment, but daily, hourly, until the family vault claimed her for its own. Whereupon the Bishop wrote to Dr. Ball, as her spiritual adviser, begging him to bring her to a proper frame of mind, and to see, generally, what was to be done.

It was wonderful how little *could* be done; and Dulcinea would promise nothing. So Sir Watkyn Wygram, Gerald's father, was written to; and he, though mightily amused at the whole affair, took the law into his own hands, and ordered Gerald to leave Inchinabagga without delay.

There were certain reasons why it was best to obey this order, and so, with many kisses and vows of eternal constancy, the lovers parted. They felt their constancy might be put to the test, as Dulcinea was barely eighteen, and, by her late father's will, was not to come of age until her twenty-third year. Five years to wait! An eternity to an impatient heart! A month's trial having proved to them that life without each other was an earthly Purgatory, they resolved to try one more expedient to soften the man in the apron and the long silk stockings.

"What is terrible?" asked Dulcinea of the Curate as they walked up and down the garden.

"This correspondence with Gerald, when you *know* the Bishop——"

"Well, I won't do it again," she said. "It would be a stupid thing to write to him, wouldn't it," continued Dulcinea, innocently, "when I can see him every day?"

"*See* him!" Dr. Ball stopped short again, and gazed at her over his glasses. "Why, you don't mean to tell me that——"

"Yes I do, indeed. He is staying down at the white cottage just like last spring. He says he has come for the fishing."

"Fishing in January?"

"Well, if it isn't for that, it is for something else. And you can't think how nice he is looking. And he is so fond of you! Do you know you were the very first person he asked for."

"Did he now!" said the Doctor, with a broadly gratified smile. Then he recollected himself, and brought himself back to a proper frame of mind with the help of a dry little cough. "The Bishop and Sir Watkyn will be greatly annoyed," he said.

"I don't care," returned Dulcinea, rebelliously. "What fault can the Bishop find with him?"

"He is not your equal, my dear."

"I hope you are not growing worldly?" said Dulcinea, with a severity that to the poor Doctor sounded very terrible.

"But he is *very* poor, my dear," he said, faltering, and feeling himself the most worldly creature on earth.

"And is his poverty the only thing against him?"

"The Bishop has other objections."

"Oh! I know all about that," said she, with superb disdain. "I know he has been meanly trying to spy out some trumpery little peccadilloes belonging to poor Gerald's Oxford days. It is my belief the Bishop did far worse himself when *he* was at Oxford. I hate a spy!"

" But, my dear——"

" And if Gerald was a little bit wild at college—I—I think it was *delightful* of him ! I can't bear goody-goody young men. I should quite despise him if I thought he had never done anything he oughtn't to do."

" Dulcinea, this is horrible !" said the Doctor. " If your guardian——"

" I know my guardian," with a contemptuous shrug of her pretty little shoulders—" and you would, too, only you are too good to fathom his schemes. Do you think a real Christian would forbid two people to be happy? No, you don't. A real Christian would help them to be happy. And "—turning to him suddenly, with a quick, radiant smile—" you *will* help us ? " She spoke with an amount of assurance she was far from feeling, but determined to play her last card with a high courage. " You will go to the Bishop yourself, and plead for us. He respects you (it is the only sign of grace about him) ; he will listen to you, and you will bring us back word that you have succeeded. You will give us that bad old man's blessing ; we shall fall upon your neck and embrace you, and then you will marry us."

" Stop—stop," said the Doctor. " I daren't do this thing. The Bishop's face is set against Gerald, and——"

" Then you are to set your face against the Bishop's and turn his in favour of Gerald. Yes, you must indeed ! Oh ! my dear godfather, you have never refused me anything in all my life ; do not begin to do so now. Tell him I am sick, dying——"

" But, my dear girl, I never saw you looking better."

" Never mind, I shall *get* sick ; tell him, too, that Gerald is such a regular attendant at church, and that——"

" I *can't*, Dulcinea. All last spring, Sunday after Sunday, I missed his head in the Rectory pew, where he was supposed to sit."

All the pews in the church at Inchinabagga were so built that only the heads of the parishioners could be seen, staring over them as if impaled.

"Perhaps he *was* there, but sitting low," said Dulcinea, mendaciously.

"No. He wasn't sitting there at all," said the Curate, sorrowfully. "He was up at South stream, at Owen's farm, fishing for trout."

"Well, even if he was," said Gerald's sweetheart, boldly, "surely there was some excuse for him. Sundays should not be good fishing days, and on every one of those you mention the trout were literally jumping out of the water, and crying to be caught! He told me so. Why, the Bishop himself would have gone fishing on such days."

"I must request, Dulcinea——"

"Well, if he wouldn't, he would have been dying to go—it is all the same," said Miss Vane, airily. "Come, you will go to the Bishop—you will do what you can for us, won't you?"

"What "—nervously—"am I to say if I *do* go? Mind, I have not promised."

"Say that Gerald is worthier of me than I am of Gerald. That will be a good beginning ; be *sure* you say that. Make me out a most perverse girl, of whom you can get *no* good——"

"Dulcinea," said the Doctor, with mournful reproach, "in all these years have I failed to show you the graciousness of truth ?"

"Oh! but what is truth in comparison with Gerald!" said Miss Vane, with an impatient gesture of the right hand.

Quite overwhelmed by this last proof of the uselessness of his ministry, Dr. Ball maintained a crushed silence.

"You will say just what I have told you—won't you?" asked Dulcinea, anxiously.

"I shall say you have certain faults I would gladly see amended," said the Curate, sadly ; "but I cannot bring myself to malign you, Dulcinea, and, of course, the Bishop knowing you—though slightly—must have formed an opinion of his own about you."

"He is such an old bore," said Miss Vane, irreverently,

"that I don't believe he could form an opinion on *any* sub·
ject." In which she wronged the Bishop.

"I must beg you won't speak of your Bishop like that," said
the Curate, earnestly. " He has been of much service to the
Church. He is a great and good man. Well," he continued,
with a sigh, after a pause, "I will go to him and intercede for
you. I shall write and ask him for an interview—but I doubt
if good will come of it. And what shall I do there, in a
strange place, amongst strange faces, after all these years?"

In truth, it seemed a terrible thing to him, this undertaking.
He would have to leave his home, for the first time these ten
years, and go beyond his beloved boundary, and launch himself, as it were, upon the world.

But he wrote to the Bishop, nevertheless, asking for an
interview, without stating the object he had in view, and
received a very friendly letter from that dignitary in return,
who, indeed, was a very kindly man, *au fond*, and most wilfully
misunderstood by Dulcinea. The Bishop granted Dr. Ball
the desired interview with pleasure, and begged he would
come to the Palace early in the ensuing week, not on business
alone, but as a guest for a day or two.

On the Monday following Dr. Ball rose betimes, and having
shaved himself with extra care, and donned his best clothes
(oh, that he should have to call them so!), he started for the
cathedral town in the heaviest snowstorm they had known
that year.

On entering the episcopal drawing-room he found there, not
only the Bishop and his wife, Mrs. Craik, but a goodly company of guests. He was at first bewildered by the lights, and
the fine small chatter, and the *frou-frou* of the silken gowns,
and in his progress up the room fell over several chairs and
tables. But presently he came to his senses and a comfortable
ottoman close to his hostess—a handsome woman with great
kindly eyes and a delicious voice.

He saw that she was pouring out tea, and that every one was

drinking it. He saw, too, that there was a good deal of cake going about, and thin bread-and-butter, and some delicate, wafery little things he had never seen before. He glanced at the ormolu clock on the chimneypiece behind him, and saw it was nearly six o'clock. "And a very reasonable hour for tea, too," he said to himself, complacently, and ate a good deal more bread-and-butter, and told himself the tea was excellent. He looked round him and beamed through his glasses at the pretty girls in their charming gowns, and declared them to his heart a sight worth seeing. Two or three of them, struck by the benevolence of his smile, smiled back at him, so that his satisfaction was complete.

Then a dismal, booming sound came from the hall. The Doctor started on hearing it, and nearly dropped his cup of sèvres.

"The gong," said a little woman near him, getting up with graceful languor from her chair.

"First bell! Who would have thought it was so late?" said a tall, pretty girl. "How time does fly sometimes!" The Doctor, in a vague way, had noticed that this last speaker had had a young man whispering to her for the last half-hour.

Then, as if by magic, every one seemed to disappear. They melted away through the open doorway before his very eyes. *Where* were they going? To their rooms? The little Doctor— who had been puzzled by his afternoon tea, an entirely new custom to him—now grew mildly speculative and somewhat bewildered. Seeing the signs of hesitation that enshrouded him, the Bishop went up to him, and laid his hand upon his shoulder.

"You will like to go too," he said, kindly, "after your long drive." There were no trains in those days to or from Inchinabagga.

"Certainly, my lord," said Dr. Ball, mildly; "but where?"

"Why, to your room," said the Bishop.

"Ah! to be sure," returned the Doctor. Then he shook hands with the Bishop, rather to that good man's surprise, and would probably have performed the same ceremony with Mrs. Craik, but she had disappeared.

The lamps were lighted everywhere, and a tall servant in powder handed him a silver candlestick at his bed-room door, to which haven he had conducted him. Inside, the bed-room fire was burning brilliantly, and the Doctor, sinking into an arm-chair, gave himself up to thought. He meant to arrange his speech about Dulcinea's engagement to be delivered to-morrow, but somehow his thoughts wandered.

"Evidently they dine early"—(they took this form at last)—"*Evidently.* I suppose they thought *I* did too, but I depended on getting something here. A mutton chop now, or even a little bit of cold mutton with my tea—it *is* a long drive, as he said himself. Not that it mattered really. They had all been kind, *most* kind; Mrs. Craik especially. Beautiful woman, Mrs. Craik. He was a little, perhaps—well—a little hungry certainly, but a good night's rest is better than meat or drink; and he had often been hungry before when on a long day's tramp; and better be hungry and receive such a kind reception as had been accorded him, than—than——"

The fire was splendid, and the wax candles burning here and there were full of sleepy suggestions. The Doctor roused himself by an effort, and spread his hands over the glowing coals, and enjoyed the glorious heat, and almost forgot the mutton chop. When he had bobbed nearly into the flames, and recovered himself many times, it occurred to the little Doctor that another and a final bob might land him in the cinders; so he pulled himself together heroically, and rose from his chair. He yawned gently. How quiet the house was! No doubt every one was gone to bed. Had he not heard the Bishop say they were gone to their rooms, and for what—after tea—except for repose? He was tired. He, too, would go to bed.

Then the good little gentleman knelt down and said his evening prayers. He prayed most sincerely for the Bishop in spite of that missing chop, and calmly, with a conscience de-

void of offence, began to make preparations for his couch.   If
he had any doubts about the earliness of the hour, he put it
down to an episcopal rule that all should retire at an appointed
time, and so found it good in his eyes.   To his primitive mind
(a mind that had never wandered from a strict belief in the
customs of the earlier part of the century), a dinner at half-
past seven was a thing unknown.   If he had heard of any
such absurdity, he had forgotten it.   As I have told you, he
was as dead to all innovations that had taken place, since
"Sailor Billy" was king, as the babe unborn; and yet it was
the sixty-fifth year of the nineteenth century.

Finally he kicked off his boots, and crept gladly into bed.
It was a bed so comfortable that in two minutes he was sound
asleep.   He was indeed just entering into a beatific dream
where his poorest old widow had received provisions sufficient
in quantity to last her for several years, when a sound rang
through the room, driving sleep affrighted from his lids.   *Where*
had he heard that sound before?   The gong! the gong!
What! morning so soon!

He sprang up in bed, and looked vaguely round him.   As
he did so, the door opened, and a young woman entered the
room.

"Eh?" said the Doctor, staring hard at her.   He felt he
was at a disadvantage in his night-cap, and could not help
wishing at the moment that the tassel would not dangle so
insanely.   He wished, too, that some more intellectual remark
had risen to his lips, but the wish was productive of no good.
The young woman stared at him in return with undisguised
wonder, but from speech she refrained.

"Eh?" said the Doctor again; then, remembering that she
had refused to make reply to this monosyllable before, he
struggled with himself, and added some words to it. - "What
is this?" he said, confusedly.   "What hour is it?   Does his
lordship rise before *daylight?*"   He bobbed the tassel at her
as he said this.   A most confounding tassel! of abnormal
stoutness and unparalleled length.   The maid went down before

it. She drew nearer to the door, and laid her grasp, as a precautionary measure, upon the handle.

"Lawks, sir," she said, "whatever are you lying a-bed for? Dinner will be served in two mingits?"

With that she darted into the corridor outside, and fled from the "mad gentleman" to the safe regions below.

"Dinner?" repeated the Doctor to himself, in a dazed tone and then, "Bless me!" He had not even time to repent him of this rash oath, as he called to mind the bare two minutes left him; and springing from his bed, he plunged into his clothes again.

With all the haste he made, however, he did not succeed in being less than ten minutes late as he entered the drawing-room. All the other guests were there, but were fortunately arguing busily over a huge portfolio of Italian views. Mrs. Craik was standing on the hearthrug somewhat apart. With a deep blush and a very distressed countenance, the Curate advanced towards her.

"Ah, Dr. Ball! As I said before, it was a long drive," said the Bishop, graciously, leaving the group near the portfolio to come up to him. "Confess the truth, now; say you fell asleep before your fire. I often do it myself—often."

"It was hardly that, my lord," said the Doctor, to whom even prevarication was hateful.

"Ah, ah!" said the Bishop, laughing. "Did any one ever, I wonder, confess to those forty winks? You were tired though, eh?"

"I *was* tired," said the little Doctor, simply. He might have let it so rest, but his conscience pricked him. In leaving the matter thus, was he not leading his host and Bishop astray? His little, round, guileless face assuming even a deeper tinge of red, he turned to the Bishop again.

"The fact is," he said, earnestly, "that when at home, I dine early, and take my tea, when—when *you* take *yours*. Then after a couple of hours' reading I go to bed. Having no reading with me to-night, and feeling fatigued, I went to bed straight.

I did not understand about the dinner, my lord. That is *actually* how it was. I beg, madam," turning to Mrs. Craik with the old-fashioned courtesy, that all his years of poverty and seclusion had not been able to steal from him, "you will try to forgive me for having had the misfortune to keep you waiting."

The Bishop had suddenly found some fault, or some remarkable virtue, in his shoe-buckle. He bent obstinately over it. Only his wife, however, could see by the shaking of his shoulders that he was convulsed with laughter. She launched at him a withering dart from her usually mild blue eyes, then pulled her satin skirts aside, and beckoned to Dr. Ball to sit down beside her.

"You must not think you have kept us waiting for even one moment," she said, with extreme sweetness. "I don't believe dinner is ready even yet; cook is *so* unpunctual!"

Even as these words passed her lips the footman announced the meal in question in an aggrieved tone suggestive of many abusive words addressed to him by an irate cook. Nevertheless, I feel sure Mrs. Craik's kindly fib was forgiven her in the highest courts of all.

After dinner the Bishop led Dr. Ball into the library, and with a cheery, " Now, let me know how I can help you," threw himself into a lounging-chair, and prepared to listen to some small parish trouble.

Thus addressed, all the Curate's wits at once deserted him. In a mean, paltry fashion, they fled, leaving him utterly stranded. He had meant to be more than ordinarily eloquent about Dulcinea's love affair ; but now, brought face to face with the foe, he found himself barren of words. Yet speak he must ; and so, boldly, curtly, tersely, he stated his mission, and expressed his hope of obtaining for Dulcinea permission to marry the man of her heart.

To say the Bishop was astounded would be to say little. He was so amazed that he leaned back in his chair, and for some minutes was incapable of an answer. Then he began a diatribe about fortune-hunters, and his duty as a guardian, and Dulcinea's wealth, and her general impracticability. When he had got so far he paused, and looked at the Curate, as if for a further lead. But Dr. Ball was sorely in want of a lead himself. He was in fact frightened out of his life. It seemed such presumption to sit there, and argue with his Bishop! What *was* he to say? Silence was impossible with the Bishop sitting there staring at him in expectant impatience; speech seemed equally so! At last his lips unclosed, and some words unbidden rose to them.

"She is such a very *good* girl," he murmured in a dull, heavy tone, hardly knowing *what* he said. Could anything be tamer more meaningless? He felt his cause was lost.

"Yes, yes, no doubt," said his lordship, testily, somewhat put out, he hardly knew why, by the Curate's simple remark. "I have hardly had an opportunity of sifting her character *so* far, as she has obstinately refused of late every invitation sent her by Mrs. Craik. But I am glad to hear you speak of her so favourably."

Again he paused, and looked expectantly at the Doctor, who felt the blood mount surging to his brow. Oh, for the tongue of a Demosthenes to sing his dear girl's praises! It was denied him! His very brain seemed dry as his parched lips. Yet speak he must.

"I never met so *good* a girl," he stammered again in the same heavy, impressive tone, his shamed eyes on the ground. Good gracious, was he never to get beyond this lukewarm formula?

"No doubt, no doubt," said the Bishop, with growing discomposure. "The fact that she *is* so admirable a girl as you describe her proves to me that there is all the more reason why I should feel myself bound, as her guardian, to look after her and her interests, and shield her from all harm—from *fortune-hunters* especially. And this Mr.—ah—Wygram seems to me nothing better than one of that class."

Then he looked once more questioningly at Dr. Ball, as

though defying him to take up the cudgels *here*. It was a piercing look this time, and utterly wrecked the small remaining wits the poor little Curate still possessed. He sank deeper into his chair, and thought longingly of the fate of Korah.

" He is such a *good* young man," he said at last, not feebly as one might imagine, but with more than ordinary loudness, born of his distraction. Alas ! alas ! why did Dulcinea choose a broken reed like him to be her lover's advocate ! Oh ! where were the chosen. honeyed words he had rehearsed in secret for this fatal interview ? He sat covered with self-reproach, a sight to be pitied.

" Eh ? " said the Bishop, with a start, stirring uneasily in his chair. Something in his companion's mild but persistent praise seemed to rebuke him. Here was a man who thought of nothing but the grandeur of moral worth ; who looked upon position, wealth, social standing, as dross in comparison with it ! He, the Bishop of the diocese—who should be an example to his flock—sitting here, dealing altogether in worldly topics, such as the worth of money, was brought to bay by a poor curate who was mildly but righteously insisting on the worth of *goodness*.

"You know him intimately, of course," said the Bishop, after a short pause, alluding to Gerald Wygram. "You can give me an honest sketch of him as he appears to you. I have faith in you judgment ; you have seen much of him, no doubt. As guardian to Miss Vane I am desirous of looking well into both sides of the question. Her happiness should be a first con-sideration. Now," leaning one elbow on the table and looking fixedly at the devoted Curate, "give me your exact opinion of this young man."

A deadly silence followed. Now or never the unfortunate Curate felt was the moment in which to break into laudatory phrases about Dulcinea's lover. But none would come. He opened his lips ; he tried to focus his thoughts. In vain !

" I think I never met so *good* a young man," he said, in a tone so solemn it might have come from the dead. To the Bishop the sound was earnest, to Dr. Ball it meant despair.

"Indeed, indeed!" said the former, who was fond of reiteration. He said it impatiently, and got up, and began to pace the floor. He was a good-hearted man, and something within him seemed to warn him against forbidding the happiness of two people praised by the best man in his diocese. "It is a great responsibility," he said, striding slowly up and down the room. "He—this Mr. Wygram—has a bare subsistence, *no* prospects; and *she* has close upon £5,000 a-year. She ought to marry a title. Her father was bent on it; he as good as said so to me just a month before his death. This, that you speak of, is not a thing to be lightly done. But you give me such a high character of Mr. Wygram—you have bestowed indeed such unqualified praise on both him and Miss Vane—that you make me hesitate about refusing my consent. Who am I, that I should take it upon me to make or mar two lives? You have no doubt in your mind about their suitability to each other, have you? You, who know them, you think highly of *both?*"

Again the Bishop leaned towards him. Again that concentrated gaze fell upon the luckless Curate. Again he felt that he must speak when speech was denied him. The Bishop was waiting. Oh! the agony of *knowing* he was waiting.

"I believe it would be hard to find two such *good* young people," he said at last; and then he covered his face with his hand, and felt that now indeed it was all over, and that he was on the verge of tears.

There was a long silence. Then—"Well, well, well," said the Bishop—"I promise you to think it over. Worth, such as you have ascribed to this young man, should count before anything." It really did seem to the Bishop that Dr. Ball had uttered unlimited words of commendation about Gerald Wygram. "And he is of good birth undoubtedly. That is always something, even nowadays. Yes, I'll think it over. When you return home, Dr. Ball, which "—courteously—"I hope will not be for some time yet, tell Dulcinea from me, that I shall come and stay with her at the Hall very soon for a day or so, to talk all this over, and that I shall ask Mr. Wygram here to study him a little, before giving my final decision. Tell her too "—with a kindly smile directed at the astonished Curate—"that it was your hearty praise of Mr. Wygram that induced me to look into a matter that I cannot still help considering a little imprudent.

"This will be good news for Dulcinea, my lord," said the Curate, finding his voice at last when it was too late. But *was* it too late ?

"I hope it will continue to be good news all her life," said the Bishop, with a sigh. He knew he would be glad to get rid of his guardian duties, and for that very reason was afraid to get rid of them. "But now for another topic," he said, cheerfully, laying his hand on the Curate's shoulder. "You know the Rector of Dreena is dead, and——" In fact he offered our little friend a rectory, with an income that quadrupled his present salary. But the Doctor shrank from him when he mentioned it.

"Nay, my lord," he said ; "give it to some better man."

"I couldn't," said the Bishop.

"Give it to some better man," repeated the Curate, earnestly. "I could not leave my present place, indeed. They could not get on without me ; they are, for the most part, so old and so cross. I beg you will leave me there, with my old men and women. They all know *me*, and *I* know them ; and it is too late for me to start the world afresh, with new faces and new interests."

The Bishop said nothing further then, but he took his arm, and led him into the drawing-room, where presently he drew his wife aside, and told her all about it. After which, Mrs. Craik made a great deal of the little Doctor, and treated him delicately, as if he was of extreme value—as indeed he was.

At the end of two days he went home, and told Dulcinea all the news, and she, on hearing it, took him round the neck and kissed him tenderly.

"I *knew* it," she said. "I *felt* it. Something told me you were the one person in the world to win my case for me.

Dearest, sweetest, *loveliest* Dr. Ball, how shall I thank you?"

"My dear, if you only knew," faltered the Doctor.

"I *do* know. Don't you think I can appreciate you after all these years? You are so clear, so convincing. You can come so directly to the point. You can say so much that is *good.*"

"I can, indeed," groaned the Curate, desolated by dismal recollections. "The little I *did* say was *all* 'good.'"

"I'm sure of it," gratefully. "Your fluency, you know, is your great point. How I should have liked to have heard you parrying successfully every one of that horrid old Bishop's attacks upon my Gerald! But, indeed, it seems to me that I *can* hear you—running through all his good qualities (and what a number he has!) in that nice, eloquent, self-possessed manner that belongs to you."

"Dulcinea, hear me," said the Curate, in desperation; and then and there he made his confession. But he failed to convince Dulcinea; she steadfastly adhered to her belief that his eloquence alone had won the Bishop's consent.

"And really he can't be such a *very* bad old man after all," she said, "or he would not be capable of appreciating real worth such as yours—would he, Gerald?" For Mr. Wygram had stolen up to them in the twilight and secured the Doctor's other arm. Miss Vane looked upon his right one in the light of a fee-simple property.

"It is the one redeeming point in his character," said Mr. Wygram, promptly. "And another thing, Dulcie: nobody shall marry us but Dr. Ball. Eh?"

"Nobody, indeed," firmly.

"My dear girl, nonsense!" said the Doctor. "You must have your Rector, if not the Bishop himself. And—of course, by-the-bye, being your guardian, it *will* be the Bishop. I am a mere nobody. It would not do at all; and you the most influential—that is, at least, the largest proprietor in the country round!"

" You may call yourself a 'nobody,' or any other bad name you like," said Dulcinea, earnestly, "but I can tell you this, *no* one but you shall ever make me Mrs. Gerald Wygram."

"Nothing shall alter that decision—not even the *Arch-*bishop," said Mr. Wygram, emphatically.

The Doctor protested, but in his soul I think he was pleased, and went to bed that night as happy as—I was going to say a king : but, indeed, I believe he went there ten times happier than that care-laden mortal.

And the morning brought him news.. The old man, his Rector, lay dead in an Italian town, and the Bishop had appointed Dr. Ball as his successor. "So you need not leave those happy old men and women who call you pastor," wrote the Bishop, kindly—almost tenderly.

So it was as rector, *not* as curate he made his dear girl Dulcinea Wygram.

BARBARA.

I MUST introduce myself as Barbara Challoner. I am just nineteen—have said farewell to my foreign boarding-school about a year—and am now living at Laxton Grange with aunt Priscilla, all alone. My aunt Priscilla is an old maid of about sixty, harsh, stern, and unforgiving, though prosperous and well-to-do, being possessed of a thousand a year and a handsome house surrounded by much good land. For myself, I am an orphan, around whose birth hangs a faint—and not altogether reputable—halo of romance and mystery. To throw some light on this obscurity, it will be necessary for me to go back some years to the days when aunt Priscilla was younger—and, let me hope, pleasanter of aspect than as I remember her.

She had one sister—my unknown mother—who, according to report, was more than beautiful. For the truth of this, however, I cannot vouch, as I simply know she did not bequeath to me—her only child—any of her vaunted loveliness.

My handsome mother, being many years younger than her sister Priscilla, and more desirable in every way, was much sought after by her kinsfolk, with whom she spent many months of the year, they for the most part residing in the north of England, while my grandfather's home was situated in the south.

During one of her long absences it so happened that my aunt Priscilla was wooed and won by a gentleman who had come to reside in the village, principally, it was believed, for

the fishing season, he being a genuine disciple of old Izaak
Walton—at least he had so far won her that they were engaged
to be married. The day was named, and everything was in
preparation for the great event, when, at the appointed time,
my luckless mother returned to act as bridesmaid on the occasion. Her coming sealed Priscilla's doom, as her lover, who
had ever admired my aunt's *dot* better than herself, now proved
faithless for a fairer, tenderer face. To see my mother was to
love her. Finding himself, therefore, unable to fulfil his promise to his earlier love, and lacking courage to confess his
disaffection, George Challoner threw himself upon my mother's
tender mercies, and implored her to fly with him. He was an
extremely fascinating man, both in appearance and manner,
and she, being young and inexperienced, was no match for
his superior worldly wisdom. She unfortunately returned his
attachment, and, after many entreaties and coercions, was pre-
vailed upon to consent to his proposition, and leave her home
with one who was to her, comparatively speaking, an utter
stranger. So one day, she being missed from the Grange and
the stranger from the village, it became generally known that
an elopement had taken place.

One may readily conceive what confusion, despair, and rage
this discovery caused at the Grange, as my aunt had been
thoroughly and sincerely devoted to her handsome though
recreant adorer. A private marriage took place—so it was
declared—as my father feared, through a more open avowal of
his nuptials, to displease a near and wealthy kinsman, supposed
to be lying on the bed of death, and who had his own plans
laid out for his heir's future, in which a moneyed heiress bore
a conspicuous part ; while my mother, though rich in beauty,
was without further and more substantial dowry.

Therefore the affair was hushed up and kept as dark as possible ; but, before three months had expired, and while the
wealthy kinsman was still hovering upon the brink of the grave,
my father was killed by a fall from his horse, and seven months
afterwards my mother died in bringing me into the world. So

totally without support was she at the time of my birth, that, but for the intervention of my aunt Priscilla, who came forward to receive me from her dying sister's arms, I should have been thrown a helpless infant upon the wide world.

How often have I since wished that she had not come forward! For, though thoroughly conscientious in her treatment, she cared not for me, and, as years passed on, avoided my society so persistently as to render me almost morbid through want of companionship. The chances of friendships outside my home were but small—Lady Janet Stapleton, the Rector, and Piers Ormond, a lad some seven years older than myself, being the only creatures my aunt would tolerate inside her walls.

Of these, Piers, being the one who more nearly approached my own age, attracted me most; and on him I lavished all the growing love and tenderness of my thwarted childhood, until the decree went forth that banished me to a foreign school, far from the few pleasures that went to make up the scanty joys of my life.

Then followed my home-coming in the character of a grown-up young lady, to whom the ways of English society were as yet new lessons to be learned. I was shy and reserved in manner—in appearance small and slightly made ; my complexion, a pale olive, was set off by eyes large and dark—perhaps too large for the sad little face to which they belonged. Interesting I might have been ; beautiful, or even pretty, I certainly was not.

The second day after my return, I well remember, was a Sunday. We went to church, my aunt and I; and, sitting in the old-fashioned pew, I spent my time endeavouring to peep over the high sides and see what I might of those who had once been neighbours to me. In the pew opposite to ours sat a young man—alone. Of course it was Piers Ormond. I knew him at once, in spite of the alterations time had worked in his appearance during my seven years of banishment. He was tall, rather thin, and unmistakably handsome. The mouth

I so clearly remembered was now partially hidden by a heavy yellow-brown moustache, while his cheeks and chin were clean shaven. His hair seemed darker, his face longer and more determined than of yore ; but his eyes—they could not change. They were the same as when I last saw them, as blue, as tender, as lovable as ever.

After service, as we went slowly towards our carriage, I said to aunt Priscilla—

"That was Piers Ormond, was it not, who sat in the opposite pew ? "

"Sir Piers," returned my aunt, somewhat coldly. "His father died the year after you went to school."

"Oh !" I answered, and wondered in my heart whether a title would necessitate a line being drawn between him and me.

The next day he called, and, by the open frankness and warmth of his greeting, made me know it was indeed my old friend who was restored to me. He was so unaffectedly glad to renew our acquaintance, so clearly anxious to bridge over the years that had divided us, that even my natural shyness gave way, and restraint—with him at least—vanished, never to return.

So began a second bond more dangerous than the first— a chain that linked us, lightly indeed at first, but that grew and strengthened as the days went on, until at length my inner self confessed that to break it would mean death to me. Thus passed the happiest, peacefullest days of my life—days that seemed destined to endure for ever, until, as autumn deepened into winter, and winter once more burst forth into spring, the first blow fell that roused me from my dreams and made me know my gorgeous castle was but a castle in the air.

* * * * * *

"Barbara," said my aunt one morning early in April, "I wish you would gather some spring-flowers, and put them in the west bed-room. I expect your cousin Lettice to-morrow."

"My cousin Lettice !" I exclaimed, laying down my work and gazing at my aunt in blank amazement.

"Just so.   Why do you look so surprised?"

"Because I never knew I had a cousin Lettice."

"Nor an uncle John either, I suppose?" curtly.   "Well—you have; and she is coming here to-morrow to spend some months with me.   As I wish her visit to be an enjoyable one, I beg you will lay aside—at least for the time being—the constrained and unpleasant manner you reserve for my benefit, and make yourself as kind and obliging as you can."

I passed over this sally in silence, and asked presently—

"What kind of girl is she, aunt Priscilla?"

"Very beautiful, accomplished, and prepossessing," my aunt replied, with gusto; "well-born and well brought up, she is fit to adorn any society.   I was in the North just before your return from school, and there saw her last.   She struck me as being the most elegant girl, both in appearance and manner, I had ever seen.   But she is somewhat peculiar in her ideas, and her father and I both think it high time she should settle."

"But how?" I asked, fighting with the anxiety that was devouring me.

"By marriage, decidedly," said my aunt, in her cold, hard tones.   "And, as I see nowhere so excellent a *parti* as Sir Piers Ormond, I have invited her down here to make a conquest of him if possible.   She of course is quite ignorant of this design; and I fancy so handsome and charming a young man as Sir Piers will be irresistible even to a London belle. You see a good deal of him, Barbara; therefore I hope you will assist me in this plan, by withdrawing yourself from their society whenever occasion offers, and so throw them as much alone together as may be."

I felt so stunned and bewildered by this revelation that I could make no reply.   Was my aunt human, that she should impose upon me such a command?   "Beautiful, accomplished, elegant"—the words were surging through my brain.   How was I to live when my Piers had married this fascinating girl? How was I to endure the loss of my best and dearest friend?

For I had no doubt that my aunt's wishes would be fulfilled, and had worldly wisdom enough to know that Piers wedded would be widely different from the Piers I had hitherto known and loved. Mechanically I rose to my feet.

"Are you going to pluck the flowers now?" demanded my aunt, without raising her eyes.

"No—they will be fresher if gathered to-morrow morning," I found composure to stammer.

"True," she replied; and, without further questioning, I hastened from the room to my own chamber, where I flung myself upon my bed, and made a vain endeavour to think calmly and dispassionately of the news I had just heard.

The next morning, after breakfast, I started to gather the cowslips and primroses and violets destined to adorn my rival's room. Before I had gone very far I met Piers coming towards me.

"You see I cannot keep away from you," he said, smiling. "I was making tracks for Laxton as hard as I could—now I will go your way, if you don't object. Indeed I think I shall go whether you object or not." Then he put his hand under my chin and turned up my face. "Why so dejected on this beautiful morning, my nut-brown maid?" he said, regarding me curiously.

"Do I look so very dismal?" I asked, making an effort to smile, and failing miserably.

"Yes," he said. "Now tell me the cause?"

"It is really nothing to signify. I know you will think me very foolish, but I was vexed and put out by something aunt Priscilla said to me yesterday."

"Aunt Priscilla again!" groaned Piers. "I verily believe you have aunt Priscilla on the brain! What a tartar that woman is! Why, Bluebeard himself would sink into insignificance beside her! Of what has she been accusing you now?"

"She has not accused me of anything. But I have news for you. My cousin Lettice is coming to us to-day."

"And who is your cousin Lettice?"

"She is uncle John's daughter, who lives in the North—in Cumberland, I think."

"But surely her coming did not bring to your face the lachrymose expression that distinguished it just now ?"

"No, of course not ! I told you it was something aunt Priscilla had said to me."

"Well, what was that ?"

"I would rather not tell you."

"Nonsense, Barbara ! I insist upon knowing !'

"It is not worth repeating."

"Let me be the judge of that. I really wish to hear it."

"Indeed I cannot tell you !" I returned, imploringly. " Do not ask me. I would not tell you for the world !"

"A heavy price ! Well, never mind ; I dare say I shall find it out for myself. How long does your cousin intend staying with you ?"

" For several months. And aunt Priscilla says she is 'elegant, accomplished, and beautiful !'"

"What a paragon ! We sha'n't know ourselves presently in this stupid neighbourhood. I suppose she will break all our hearts. Do you think, Barbara, this northern goddess will deign to smile on me ?"

"I rather think you will have all her smiles," I said, as carelessly as I could, "as you are the only gentleman she will be likely to meet."

"You forget Ford of Leithly—he is an eligible."

"I doubt if he would suit a town-bred young lady. Moreover, I am reserving him for myself."

"When I have gone over to the enemy, I suppose you mean ?" said Piers, casting a quick glance at me, and bringing down his teeth sharply on his under lip—a sure sign that he was angry. "How excellently you have arranged everything, Barbara—and beforehand too ! I had no idea you were such a diplomatist. And so you have told off the faultless new comer to me ? Allowing her to be as handsome as you say she is, that is really good-natured of you. Probably she will prove so irresistible that I shall end by marrying her."

"It is more than probable," I rejoined, quickly, though I felt half choked, "and so aunt Priscilla said when—that is—I mean——"

I stopped, hopelessly confused.

"Oh, that was what aunt Priscilla said, was it?" murmured Piers, coldly, stroking his long fair moustache meditatively, while keeping his eyes well fixed upon me.

"Yes," I returned, coldly.

"And did that vex you and put you out, Barbara?"

"I believe I was silly enough to say so a little while ago," I answered, icily. I felt that I was growing pale, and dreaded lest he should see how my hands were trembling.

"And why should it vex you, Barbara?"

I felt my wrath rising at his pertinacity, which seemed to me positively cruel.

"I wish you would not ask me any more questions," I cried, pettishly. "I hate being cross-examined in this way. You know you are the only friend I have, and, if you marry, of course I lose you. Therefore it is only natural I should feel some regret about it. And, if Lettice Neville is as handsome as they say she is, no doubt you will marry her, and—and there is an end of it."

"Indeed I never will, my Barbara," he said, softly, taking both my ungloved hands and holding them closely in his own —"no new face, however lovely, could have power to fascinate me. I care but for one little girl in the world, and that is Lettice Neville's cousin."

Here he stooped and pressed his lips tenderly and warmly to my hands.

"My darling child," he said, "how cold you are! Your hands are frozen! Come for a brisk walk—that will bring back the vanished roses to your cheeks. I would have this rare exotic see my wild-flower at her best. What a pity she cannot content herself where she is, Barbara! She will ruin all our pleasant walks and happy *tête-à-têtes.*"

"Ah, wait until you have seen her!" I returned; but dejection was no longer to be detected in my tone.   My eyes were sparkling, my whole face was full of joy, my heart was lighter than the softest down.

*   *   *   *   *   *

I reached home about half-past two, and heard, to my consternation, that my cousin had already arrived.   We had not expected her until the dinner-hour; but, for all that, I knew my aunt would blame me for not being present to bid her welcome.   How much angrier still would she be, did she but know with whom I had spent the wasted hours !

I ran upstairs hurriedly to my room, changed my clothes with frantic haste, and, coming down again, reached the drawing-room, where I found my aunt stiff and disagreeable as usual.   She raised her head as I seated myself, but scarcely had she commenced to give me the scolding I knew was in store for me, when the door was thrown wide open and our new visitor came in.

My cousin was dressed in something fawn-coloured, trimmed very fashionably with silk of a darker hue; a plain linen collar was round her neck, and at her throat was a tiny bow of crimson ribbon.   Her hair was a light brown, her eyes were a soft, pure violet.   Her complexion was clear, though rather pale—her mouth sweet and lovable, but rather too large to be strictly perfect.   Her feet and hands were small and aristocratic; her figure was tall and slight; and she had a certain trick of shrugging her shoulders, with a little protesting frown, and casting a swift side-glance at one, when disagreeing, that was absolutely fascinating.

She came towards me at once and held out her hand.

"You are Barbara," she said, in a very sweet voice; and then—"I suppose, being cousins, we should kiss."   As she spoke she stooped a little—she was considerably taller than I was—and left a soft impression upon my cheek.   In spite of all I knew—in spite of all I might yet have to know—just then, as her lips touched me, I felt I loved her.

On the second morning after my cousin's arrival she and I

were sitting alone in the breakfast-parlour, conversing—that is, I was listening while she was chattering pleasantly, and telling me charming stories of the great world I so earnestly longed to see. Suddenly, rising from her seat, she craned her neck eagerly in the direction of the window.

"Who is that?" she exclaimed. "I have just seen some one tall and handsome, and positively distinguished-looking, pass by; and they told me, when coming down here, that I should not find a man in the neighbourhood."

"I suppose it was Sir Piers Ormond," I said. "Is he coming in?"

"I hope so. He went towards the hall door. Sir Piers? Who is he, Barb'ra?"

"A baronet, and a very rich one too," I answered, conscientiously. "He lives near here, at Ormondsgrove."

"Is he a friend of yours, Barb'ra?"

"Yes."

"A very great friend?"

"Of course. I have known him all my life. It is impossible but we should be friends."

"That counts for nothing. People I have known all my life I find generally detestable and interfering. I mean, is—he—your—lover?"

"I don't understand you," I replied, reddening painfully; and then the door opened, and Piers came in, followed closely by my aunt Priscilla.

After that, conversation became general, and I was glad to find myself sinking into insignificance, when aunt Priscilla asked Piers if he would accompany Lettice out riding.

"I shall be more than charmed," said Piers, cordially. "It will be quite a new sensation to escort a young lady about these quiet roads. Shall I put a horse in training for you, Miss Neville, or——"

"No, thank you. I have brought down my own mare. I never go anywhere without Tatters; she is part of myself. 'Love me love my Tatters' is my motto. I do hope you will like her when you see her, Sir Piers."

"Considering the conditions, I feel a rising adoration for her already," answered Piers, returning with interest the half-laughing glance she had bestowed upon him during her last speech.

"Oh, I don't care to prejudice you in her favour beforehand!" said she, gaily. "My Tatters requires no backing. However, you shall judge for yourself presently. But Barb'ra must come too. Won't you, Barb'ra?"

"I do not wish Barbara to learn riding," put in my aunt, coldly.

"Oh, nonsense, Prissy! That is mere prejudice on your part. What is she to do the long summer through, unless she can get a canter now and then? She will die of *ennui* in this stupid place. Sir Piers——"

"I really wish, Lettice, you would not interfere with my arrangements," said aunt Priscilla, severely.

"Only this once," begged Lettice, directing a winning smile at my grim guardian. "You know, Prissy, nobody ever denies me anything. It makes me ill directly I am thwarted, so beware! I shall order my man to send Barbara down a habit."

"I will take every care of her, Miss Neville," said Piers, eagerly ; and so it was settled.

The provoking innocence of any participation in my aunt's hopes for her future welfare displayed by Lettice on the foregoing and other occasions was so refreshing that, but for the increasing uneasiness that at this time possessed me, it would have afforded me the utmost amusement. As for Piers, I know it caused him the very keenest delight. Indeed there was something exquisitely pleasurable in seeing all the plans so carefully laid down ruthlessly annihilated by the very hand of her for whose well-being they were formed.

At length, as the weeks—counting from my cousin's arrival —grew into months, and, as yet, her great object appeared no nearer its fulfilment, even my aunt began to lose patience ; and one evening, to my consternation, she spoke out plainly on the subject that lay so near her heart.

It was once more June, warm and drowsy-sweet, when we three—Lettice, my aunt, and I—sat together in the gathering dusk to watch the falling of the dewy night.

"Lettice," said my aunt, suddenly, and without any preamble, "I wish you would make up your mind to marry Sir Piers Ormond."

"Marry Sir Piers Ormond!" repeated Lettice, turning widely-opened eyes upon my aunt. "My dear Prissy, what has come to you? Surely your mind wanders? I have never even thought of such a thing!"

"Then I wish you would think of it. He is everything most desirable; well-born, rich, handsome, and of your own age— what can you require more? He has clear ten thousand pounds a year; and you, with your extravagant habits, should hesitate about marrying a poor man."

I fancied there was some hidden meaning attached to this last remark, but my cousin's quick and nonchalant reply at once dispelled the idea.

"You make me shudder," she said, with her peculiar shrug. "Do not let us even talk of poverty. Because I do not agree to marry one rich man is no reason why I should condemn myself to misery for life. Love in a cottage would kill me in six months."

"And yet," I put in, dreamily, "I think if I loved any one, I would not care whether he were rich or poor."

"Fortunately there are very few of us with ideas so romantic and high-flown as yours," said my aunt, in a tone that was meant to wither. "I wish, Barbara, when you condescend to open your lips at all, it would be to utter sense."

"I do not think Barbara high-flown," averred Lettice, kindly. "I only think her ignorant. She does not know—she can have no idea what it means to be really poor. Now I do; because I have two friends who obstinately married 'for love,' without any money to speak of, and who now, I firmly believe, repent their bargain—though, to do them justice, they have never said so. Poverty, Barbara, means no carriages, no horses, no box at the Opera, one silk dress in the year, no society, and gloves by any one in the world but Jouvin. To me, I honestly confess, the picture is not inviting."

"Then why not think of Sir Piers?" said my aunt.

"Because, dear Prissy, it is absolutely necessary he first should think of me, and because I verily believe he has delivered every spare inch of his heart into another's keeping long ago."

What was she going to say next? I literally shivered as I waited for her coming words.

"What do you mean?" demanded my aunt. "To whom has he given his heart?"

"I hardly like to give utterance to my suspicion, being but a stranger amongst you," said Lettice, with wild mischief; "but Barb'ra—she is such an old friend of his—she knows—don't you, Barb'ra?"

"Indeed I do not," I answered, huskily, actually trembling with fear at her rashness, yet unable to direct a warning glance towards her, lest my watchful aunt should intercept it.

"Don't you, dear?" she murmured, innocently. "Then probably I am mistaken, and, after all, Prissy, he may be eligible."

"I should hope so," said my aunt, severely. And she got up, and we all went indoors, letting the dreaded subject rest. But often, during the remainder of the evening, I caught my aunt's cold eyes directed towards me, in such a manner as I felt boded me no good.

* * * * * *

Three days afterwards—how well I remember the day!—I was coming quickly along the balcony, intending to gain the drawing-room, when, just as I reached the open window through which I meant to enter, I saw the door of the room unclose, and my aunt and Sir Piers walk in together. Hating to meet Piers in my stern guardian's presence, I drew back hastily, and, the hanging curtains entirely concealing me from view, I waited breathlessly until they should have reached the upper part of the room before making my escape.

But suddenly Piers spoke, and his words rooted me to the spot.

"You wish to speak to me about Barbara?" he said.

"Yes," returned my aunt—and I thought her tone was peculiarly hard and forbidding. "There is something connected with her birth that it is most necessary you should know. You must pardon my mistake, if it is one, but I have feared of late that between you and her a foolish attachment may be springing up; and, knowing what I do, I think it only right to check it at the outset."

Here there was a faint pause, but Piers made no rejoinder.

"You may perhaps have heard," went on my aunt, "of the peculiar circumstances attendant on the marriage of my sister, Barbara's mother—how she ran away from her home with George Challoner, how they were privately married, and how he received his death hurt three short months afterwards. Well, all such reports are true, except in this one matter—there was no marriage."

"Ah!" The exclamation came as though forced from Piers's lips. As for me, hardly understanding all that was said, I only grasped the curtains tighter in my hand, and waited with passionate impatience to hear what should come next.

"There was no marriage," repeated my aunt, distinctly, and with cold emphasis. "They left this house towards evening, were obliged to travel all night—so that it was impossible any ceremony could then have taken place; and the very morning after the elopement George Challoner—who, as you know, was utterly dependent upon the will of his uncle—was summoned to the supposed death-bed of this relative. He found the old man seemingly at the last gasp. He was hurried to his bedside to receive his parting words, and the dying man, who had his heart set on uniting his nephew with a certain heiress—a ward of his own—demanded of him that he would give his oath to marry this girl. George Challoner refused, declaring that his heart was already given. Upon this the old man, starting up in bed, asked with angry vehemence if he were irrevocably tied by the laws of matrimony to this unknown love, and on being answered in the negative, desired him, on pain of disinheritance, to give him a written agreement that until after his—the uncle's—death, he would not wed her. It was a solemn moment, and the request a strange one, coming from the lips of one who was considered unlikely to survive till the coming morn; everything around bespoke the near approach of death. On the one hand were poverty and enforced toil and honour—on the other, affluence, an oath that could not be many hours binding, and dishonour. George Challoner hesitated, and then was lost. He signed the paper in the full belief that the next day would release him from his bond; but time proved doctors and nurses in the wrong, as the uncle rallied and outlived the nephew, while, with that terrible oath on his soul, the latter did not dare pledge himself by law to my ill-fated sister. Therefore Barbara was not born in wedlock."

My aunt ceased, and no sound came to break the horrible stillness. My brain felt surging—my sight grew almost dim—a strange flavour of blood was in my mouth. Mechanically I put up my hand, and found I had bitten my lip severely. Some of the blood had gone between my lips, a drop was trickling slowly down my face. Hastily I wiped it away, and the action roused me. There must have been a pause within also, as, when next I heard a voice, it was Piers's responding to my aunt's last sentence.

"You mean that she is illegitimate," he said. "Poor Barbara —poor little girl!"

I could not see his face, but his tone was full of infinite pity; nevertheless the pity, just then, to me was torture.

"I speak as much for the girl's sake as for yours," went on my aunt in her hard, metallic way, "lest any thoughtless understanding might arise between you."

"Thank you," he said; and I could not judge from his voice in what spirit he had received her intelligence.

I could endure no more. I crept away noiselessly, as one half dead, dragging myself like some wounded animal to where

I could wrestle or—if only fortunate enough—die alone with my misery.

Behind the summerhouse was a small enclosed, well-hidden plot of grass—a cherished retreat with me in my earlier days. Thither I went, and, flinging myself upon the ground, face downwards, buried my head in my hands, to shut out if possible the very light. I would not think. I lay there battling fiercely with the self within, that strove to master me and compel me to review my situation in all its new-found horrors.

How long I might have thus lain I know not, had not a voice close to me startled me into animation.

"Barbara!" called Piers.

I sprang to my feet, and stood with my back turned towards him.

"Barbara, what are you doing?"

"Nothing," I answered, shortly.

"Well, then, don't stand there with your back turned to me. You are forgetting your good manners."

"Do not speak to me!" I said, shuddering at the lightness of his tone. "Go away and leave me. I am not well—I want to be alone."

"What is the matter with you, Barbara?"

"I have heard all!" I returned, in an accent meant to be cold, but which I felt was only heart-broken.

"I guessed as much," said Piers, gently. "Well, and if it be so, what can it matter to you and me, dear Barbara?"

"To me!" I cried—and for the first time I turned and looked into his face.

"Barbara"—he was evidently shocked and pained at my expression—"don't look at me like that. Child, what thoughts have you been thinking? Your face is white as death, your lip is cut and swollen, your eyes—Barbara, you must not let them keep that expression at your age."

He put his hand over my eyes and forced down the lids upon them. I sighed faintly, but made no further protest, for I felt weak, and his very touch was dear to me. Involuntarily

I leaned against the strong arm he had placed around me. Feeling me yield so far, he drew me closer to him, and encircled me warmly.

"Think of what you are doing," I said, with a faint, wan smile. "Think of all you have just heard. I am nameless— a mere waif upon the world. How can you bear to have me near you now?"

"My dear child, I wish you would talk sense," he returned, giving me a little shake.

"Am I not talking sense? I am; I was never more sensible in my life. I fully understand everything, and in what way it affects me. Indeed I wonder myself how I can feel so clear, because it was a shock to me—I may tell you that—a terrible blow—one that never—— But I shall live it down, I dare say, in time, as others have lived such heartaches down before me. Still, in the meantime, to make my task easier to me, will you promise me something?"

"What am I to promise you?"

"To let me see as little of you, for the future, as is possible."

"And why, Barbara?"

"Because "—I hesitated, and then went on recklessly, "I am so degraded now, so humiliated, that it little matters what I say or leave unsaid; and so I will confess that I like you so well—nay, I love you so dearly—that to see you every day and feel myself unworthy of your affection—even could you ever have brought yourself to love me—would be greater misery than I could endure!"

"But suppose I had brought myself to love you already, Barbara; how would it be then?"

"Oh, that is impossible!" I cried, passionately. "Nothing so cruel could occur. You must forget you have ever seen me; you must help me to forget. There is a barrier, an insurmountable wall, between us; do not let me hear your voice at the other side, lest I should ever be tempted to call to you to come and make the vain effort to cross it."

" All walls can be climbed, Barbara; and my effort would not be vain. I can do wonders in the way of scaling. You may remember, even as a small boy, how ingenious I was about it; and now, with such an end in view—— Whenever you call me, Barbara, I will come."

" That will be never," I answered, sadly.

" Then I shall not wait to be called!" he cried, putting his arms around me again, and pressing my head down upon his breast. " I will come now—this moment; I will hear of no barrier. You were mine, by right of your own words, when you said you loved me. Who shall dare to say there is a wall between us two?"

" I dare," I said, with mournful earnestness.

" Then I shall have to punish you terribly. No, Barbara; you are my property now, and no earthly consideration shall induce me to surrender you. It is selfishness on my part, if you like; but, having known you all my life, I find I cannot now do without you. You are my wife, and as such I will hold you against yourself, Miss Priscilla, and all the world. Look up and smile at me again your own dear smile—my treasure, my darling, my life!"

He kissed me warmly between each tender word. It was the first time his lips had ever pressed mine, and for the moment I was utterly happy. A little later I had torn myself from his embrace, and stood a few yards from him, flushed and miserable, but quite determined.

" This is madness!" I cried. " Have some thought for yourself. Do you think that under the circumstances I would consent to be your wife—that I would bring such a blot upon your name? I love you too well for that."

" And so you will refuse me and make me miserable? Surely you love me too well to do so?"

" You are talking only folly," I said; " while I am doing the best I can for you. I will never consent to be your wife!"

" Then I will marry you without your consent. I always get my own way, you know, Barbara, in the end; so it is as good for you to give in gracefully first as last.   My wife you shall be, sooner or later!"

"How can you be so cruel?" I demanded, with tears in my eyes.   Was my strength failing me in my sore need?   Was I indeed giving in, as he had said I should?

"Cruel!" cried he, gaily.   "Yes; I am the veriest despot. Have I not shown you how I can level even insurmountable walls by a bare word?   I am a tyrannical king who, having once placed his foot upon your territory, claims every inch of it.   Nevertheless, I can be gentle too at times, and am now ready to hear any conditions you may wish to make—my queen!"

"A sorry queen!" I returned.   "Well, hear the conditions attached to your marrying one so far beneath you.   I will have you leave this place to-morrow.   I will have you go to London, Paris, Vienna, for one year, during which time you shall neither see me, write to me, nor, if possible, think of me."

"Twelve long months—oh, 'cruel Barb'ra Allen,' make it four!"

"No; it must be the twelve."

"Say even six?"

"No—no!"

"Then make it eight—though even that will break my heart."

"No—twelve."

"You will have your pound of flesh—then be it so.   What day will to-morrow be—the 20th of June?   Then, Barbara, if next year I am not by your side, be it fair weather or foul, on that self-same day you may call me recreant, coward, traitor— what you will.   Is that our agreement?"

"It is," I whispered, with white trembling lips.   "Perhaps during that time you will see some one prettier and brighter than me to love; some one who, though she cannot love you more fondly, will have no blot upon her birth, no stain to render her unworthy of your affection.   And I hope you may!" I cried; and then I burst into a passion of tears.

For fully five minutes I sobbed unrestrainedly on Piers's breast, with his cheek pressed against mine. He did not speak —he attempted no word of consolation; but every now and then in mute sympathy his lips sought my forehead. Presently he spoke.

"That is right," he said; "those tears will do you good. Cry on, my little Barbara, and let all painful memories flow from you. It is fully understood between us now, my darling, is it not, that when I return it will be to claim my wife?"

"Oh, if you should ever regret it !"

"Nonsense ! Surely at twenty-six a man should know his own mind? There will be nothing to regret. You are making a grand romance out of nothing. Besides, nobody knows anything about this business but your aunt Priscilla, and she will not betray her own niece. Now, before you send your knight into exile, you must give him some love-token to hold sacred until his return."

"If I gave you anything, it would help you to remember me."

"Barbara, you should have been a Roman matron, instead of a quiet, though extremely hard-hearted, little village maiden. Well, give me a kiss, at all events; that is not tangible and will linger only in my memory."

I kissed him twice, sadly, passionately, as one might kiss one's dead ; and so we parted.

This was June ; in November Lettice left us; and I, beyond all others of the household, missed her bright merry ways and ready laughter. She was indeed a universal favourite, and my aunt became even more than ordinarily sour and hard when she was gone. Whether my aunt ever guessed the real reason of Piers Ormond's abrupt departure, or of the increased reserve and coldness of my manner towards her from that day, I never knew for a certainty, though later events made me imagine her cognisant of the truth. But, as with his defection her schemes for Lettice died, so her interest in Piers died too.

In December she fell ill—not seriously or painfully, but day by day she weakened perceptibly, and no doctor could do her good or give a name to her ailment.

"It is a general break-up," she said to me one evening, when in one of her softer moods ; "my mother died just so."

"You must not talk of dying, aunt Priscilla," I returned, feeling a strange pang at my heart which was neither love nor anguish, yet was a curious blending of both ; for she was the only one in the world who in some way belonged to me or had ever befriended me, except my Piers.

She was right, however. Before Christmas came she was lying dead and cold in her own chamber.

The week before she died I was sitting in her room one night, watching while I thought she slept, when suddenly she spoke.

"Barbara, open my drawers," she said, in a strange weak voice—"here is the key—and give me the small bronze box you will find in the corner. I wish to give you something."

I obeyed her ; and, having handed to her the small box and the bunch of keys, she opened it, and, drawing from it a soiled and folded paper, held it out to me.

"That is the certificate of your mother's marriage," she said, slowly, but without glancing in my direction.

"The what?" I gasped, putting out my hand blindly and grasping one of the bed-posts to keep myself from falling. It must have been my intense anxiety to hear her corroborate her words that alone kept me from fainting—so great a shock did this announcement cause me.

Reluctantly and half nervously she turned and regarded me unsteadily for a moment or two before replying ; and it was then for the first time I guessed she knew why my manner towards her of late had been so cold.

"The copy of your mother's marriage certificate," she repeated. "Yes, she was married, child. Why do you look at me so wildly ? Take the paper—it is yours."

I took it mechanically, but did not open it.

"If I have done anything to wrong you, Barbara, will you

forgive me?" she asked presently, in a low, quavering voice. "If I have caused you any unhappiness, I now repent it. On my dying bed I ask your forgiveness—will you grant it?"

Vaguely I wondered whether she knew how cruelly she had made me suffer—how keen had been the torture of the past months. The remembrance of it all was very close to me at the moment; but above it, helping me to holier and more merciful feelings, there floated a great joy and relief and thankfulness not to be repressed.

"Yes," I said—and even to myself my voice sounded foreign and far-distant.

"Then why do you not kiss me?" went on my aunt, querulously. "You are hard and cold, Barbara, or you would be gentler to the dying."

"I am not hard or cold," I cried, suddenly; "but I was thinking—thinking. I will kiss you, aunt Priscilla, and forgive you too. You have told me to-night the thing I most longed to hear."

That night week she died; and when, some days later, her will was opened and read, it was found she had left me the house and grounds and five hundred pounds a year. The remainder of her income was to go to her " niece and god-child, Lettice Neville." Whether she meant in this way to make me amends for all the injuries I had sustained at her hands I never knew.

I was glad to find the old place still mine—glad that there would be no necessity for me to seek new scenes and fresh faces—to lose sight of all the pleasant recollections and tender memories that thronged my childhood's home. Though to me it had not been the happy place it should have been, still all that made life most precious had come to me there— all the friends I had ever known were in and around Clayton. It would have been almost death to me at this time to have been obliged to quit the spot endeared to me by ties of long years' standing. Here I could still wait and watch for the hour that would bring back Piers to my expectant arms. And oh, with what different hopes—with what different emotions—I now longed for his return ! Now indeed I might with pride and gladness become his wife—might feel myself worthy to bear his name.

The weary months crept on in almost utter solitude to me. Now and again a few scraps from the outer world reached me, causing my sleeping blood to rush with unwonted fervour through my veins. Sir Piers was on his way home from Vienna—Sir Piers was in London—Sir Piers and Lettice Neville had renewed acquaintance at the Russian Ambassador's ball. Such little vague reports kept warm my weary heart.

I had no confidant, and was very lonely. Even to Lady Janet Stapleton, who, I knew, loved me, I could not confide my sentimental story ; though I felt the dear old lady would sympathise with me and indulge me in my fancies as much as I could desire. My secret was my own, and close in my own breast I kept it ; so that it happened that from kind Lady Janet's pen came the first tidings of my lover's faithlessness.

The news arrived in a little harmless, delicately - scented note, begging me to spend the following day with her. " But I cannot wait so many hours "— so ran the middle of the letter—" to tell you my last bit of news (you know what an inveterate old gossip is your friend), so scribble it down here. My nephew Gordon writes, telling me of your cousin's engagement to our handsome neighbour Piers Ormond. There —is not that astounding ? But perhaps you know it already, as without doubt she will wish to let you hear the first of it. It is an excellent match for her, as you will see, and it is pleasant to think of young people settling in this quiet spot. However, it may be all or half a fabrication. Gordon says it is not a positive thing, merely an *on dit ;* but they are always together at balls, kettledrums, and in the Row—which of course looks particular. Come to-morrow, my love, without fail, if only to cheat me into the belief that I am still youthful," &c.

The doubt expressed towards the close of her letter kept

me from despair. I clung to it. I neither could nor would believe in the truth of this report; even against the promptings of my heart I strove to check the fears that threatened to destroy me. He was much with her—what more natural? Was she not my cousin? Surely he would like to hear some news of me. It was an *on dit* merely. The world was always given to marrying people, with or without their consent; and the fact of their being a good deal together in public would easily give rise to the idea in their case. Thus I tried to console myself. When off my guard, contrary thoughts would rise, and overwhelm me while they lasted.

Meantime the days grew into months, and summer was once more at hand. It was the 19th of June—gorgeous, glowing June—and the very air was full of fragrance. The atmosphere was almost too heavy and drowsy for enjoyment; the flowers drooped and languished under the oppressive sun. All around was peace and lazy content—I alone was miserable.

It wanted only a few short hours to the day that should have been to me the happiest of my life. But now I felt no exquisite joy at its approach, no tearful ecstasy, such as I had believed I would experience as the hour drew nigh to unite me to my beloved.

Only that very morning the Rector had been up with me, and had added keener agony to my already bleeding wound.

"Will your cousin reside here?" he asked. "She is naturally gay. I hardly think Ormondsgrove will suit her."

" Sir Piers has a house in town," I answered, with admirable composure. "Is the marriage then arranged ? "

"Well, so we hear ; but one cannot always depend upon the chit-chat of one's friends. I suppose, however, marriage will be the end of it."

" Nothing more natural," I returned, carelessly.

As the next morning came, in all its golden splendour, it found me waking. I had not slept all night, and turned with a groan from the first faint streak of dawn, as it came rushing into my room. I rose, and, strolling into the garden, paced restlessly to and fro, waiting until the breakfast-bell should summon me indoors. Bitter were the thoughts that attended my languid steps. I was feeling cold and weak from want of sleep and exhaustive memories. Suddenly, raising my head, I found myself face to face with—Piers Ormond.

Could it be he? I half feared my senses had misled me, more especially as he made no advance, but stood regarding me with a keen silent attention. At length he broke the spell that was fast overcoming me.

"Barbara, where is my welcome?" he said.

"Welcome?" I echoed, foolishly, putting up both my hands to my head in a vain endeavour to recall my wandering recollection. Then, the one thought uppermost in my brain gaining sway, I cried aloud, "Why should you ask a welcome here? Go back to Lettice—she no doubt will give you one as warm as you can desire!"

"Barbara!"

The word came with such angry vehemence, with such utter amazement from his lips, that involuntarily I raised my head until our eyes met. His, dark and stern, almost burned themselves into mine, as though determined to read the inmost workings of my heart. At once I knew it was my own Piers who had come back to me—but what an angered, disappointed Piers! My glance fell beneath his; I grew frightened, confused; I held out my hands to him, murmuring piteously—

"They told me so. In the end I could not help believing—they all said it, not once, but many times."

"What have they told you?" His tone was still harsh and unbending. He took no notice of my poor outstretched hands.

"That you were engaged to Lettice—that you were to marry her at once—that you were going to bring her down here."

"What base lies!" he cried, fiercely. "Who has dared so to meddle with my name? And you believed them, Barbara—you could not keep faith with me for even one short year?"

Had I regained him only to lose him again—a second time

through my own folly? I grew sick and faint. The fingers he had disdained to touch fell heavily by my sides.

"They told me so—they—they——"

I felt my body sway helplessly for a moment or two, and then I fell forwards and lost all consciousness.

When I came to myself, I found I was seated on one of the chairs in the summerhouse, supported by Piers. He had evidently been bathing my forehead with water—a small stream ran through the garden—as I could see a glass upon the table, and my brow felt moist and cold. I raised myself and pushed back my hair vaguely.

"Are you better now?" he asked, gently; and then, as though shocked by what he saw, he added, "Barbara, how thin you have grown!"

"Have I? I have not been very happy of late, and I have been too much alone. Yes—I am better now, thank you."

"Can I do anything else for you? I suppose it was all my fault—I fear I spoke too abruptly."

His tone, though kind and gentle, still seemed to me to lack the old tender consideration and fondness; and, chilled by the contrast, I quietly put his arms from me, and, rising, walked over to the table.

"You must not blame yourself in any way, Sir Piers," I said, calmly. "It was mere nervousness at seeing you so unexpectedly that upset me for the moment. I feel quite recovered now. Have you breakfasted? If not, perhaps you will come in and join me at mine."

"In a few minutes," he replied; "but first I want you to answer me one or two questions."

"Certainly."

There was a long pause. I laid my hand upon the table to steady myself; but I knew, if the silence lasted much longer, I should not be able to control the tears that trembled beneath my downcast lids.

"Barbara, look at me," he said, suddenly.

I did as I was desired, and, looking, saw I was forgiven.

His face was full of such earnest entreaty, such tender love and longing, that a great peace, long unknown to it, fell upon my beating heart. He held out his arms, slowly, imploringly; and, with a little faint sob, I ran and threw myself into them. When I had recovered my composure, I said—

"So it was all untrue about Lettice?"

"So untrue that your cousin is to be married in two or three months to a man in the Guards—an ugly fellow, but rich and good-natured—I give you Lettice's own description. It is rather a romance too, as he has been attached to her for years; but that wise young woman thought fit to wait until his handsome expectations had been safely realised."

"This is your news," I said; "now hear mine. But first guess what I am going to tell you."

"If you had asked me that question two minutes ago, when you stood over there by the table, looking so dignified and so unlike my own Barbara, I should have said, 'Probably, Miss Challoner, you are about to be married.'"

"Well, and so I am, am I not?" I asked him, with a shy laugh. He laughed too, and of course kissed me.

"But still you have not discovered my news," I said; "and you are so stupid that probably you never would; so I will tell you. When aunt Priscilla was dying, she gave me a small piece of paper neatly folded; and what do you think it contained?"

"Snuff," answered Piers.

"Don't be absurd!"

"Peppermint lozenges, then—I know she had a weakness for those delicacies."

"No, no—it was the certificate of my mother's marriage."

For a few moments he was speechless with surprise; then he said—

"So it was all a lie?"

"Yes; she wished you to marry Lettice, and feared you cared for me. She thought such a story as she told you would effectually prevent your ever thinking of me again as—in that way."

"What a miserable old sinner!" began Piers, but I placed my fingers over his lips.

"Hush!" I said, checking him quickly. "She is dead; and, after all, she has done us no great harm, as now we are together again."

"Still I cannot forget she has robbed us of one good year of our lives," he remarked; "and, Barbara, whose fault is it that your poor little cheeks are so thin and wan and your small brown hands so fragile?"

"I will soon recover my strength, now you are come to cheer me. You will see what a different Barbara I shall be in six months."

"I hope so; but, to ensure it, you must come with me to summer climates and very different scenes, my own darling. You can marry me at once, I suppose, Barbara?"

"What—this instant?" I cried. "No, I think not, because I have not had my breakfast yet—and I am literally starving."

"So am I," said he. "I do hope Trimmer has something nice for us. Come in, Barbara; and as we appease the pangs of hunger we will discuss our wedding tour."

*   *   *   *   *   *

A month afterwards we were married very quietly—for many reasons. Lady Janet, however, declaring it would be downright shabby if my dress was not everything of the most desirable, I consented to be covered with as much satin and tulle and Brussels lace as Worth thought fit to furnish. Lettice condescended to desert her cherished Guardsman for a day or two, and came all the way from London to be my solitary bridesmaid; while Hugh Grantley, Piers's cousin, was our "best man," and Lady Janet's brother, old Lord Lindley, gave me away.

It was a very successful wedding, though—or rather because—it was a very small one, and everybody was in charming spirits; while I gained considerable credit for the very excellent manner in which I comported myself during the ceremony

When we had fairly bidden adieu to all our guests, and were driving rapidly towards the nearest railway-station, Piers turned to me, and, ceremoniously taking my hand—

"Madam," said he, "permit me to congratulate you. You have actually been through a most trying 'situation,' and yet have omitted to shed a single tear!"

ONE NEW YEAR'S EVE.

To Miss Kathleen Blake, *Derrygra, Galway.*

"Tomakin, Edinburgh, Dec. 22, 1883.

"My Dear Kathleen,—Here I am at last, after *such* a journey! If I had only known about it, I should have stayed at home, so that now I am rather glad I didn't know. That means that I am pretty comfortable, and quite charmed with all my surroundings. We are *of* Auld Reekie though scarcely *in* it, being perched upon the outskirts of it in a quite too charming' house. When I jumped out of the carriage the night of my arrival, and stood in the small outer hall waiting for the bell to be answered, and peered curiously through the glass doors into the larger hall beyond, where a goodly fire was burning, I felt as if my lonely journey had not been for nothing after all. There were two large shaded lamps, that cast a rose-coloured flame upon the polished floor—the big fire I have already mentioned—and somewhat farther back a dark oak staircase that faded off into gloom.

" Then a man threw open the door, and in another moment I found myself wrapped in the glow of the crimson lamps, and following my conductor obediently across the hall and down a passage, and round a corner, and into a recess, and goodness knows where, until we came to a—compartment, shall I call it? At any rate it was an antique in the way of ante-rooms, and a door in some obscure corner of it being thrown wide, I was ushered ceremoniously into a brilliantly lighted room beyond.

"I never saw so many corners in any room before in all my life; and it was full of men, and a few women, and several dogs, all more or less in reposeful attitudes. There were no pink lamps in this room, and though it was singularly bright, I think it was only the enormous pine logs on the open hearth that lit it. Lady Janet rose to welcome me, and was as gracious in her reception of me as Nature permitted.

"I felt a wee bit shy at first, and hardly knew what to say. But they were all very good to me, and the women said some pretty things about our picturesque, if somewhat unpleasant, land. One of them gently pushed me into a luxurious chair, and, unrequested, deprived me of my sealskin. Another administered to me my tea. It was sweet and strong, and such as my soul loveth. Oh! Katty, the very smell of it made me long for you, and our little cosy chats at home. Surely no sister ever loved another as I love you! I said 'Yes,' and 'No,' to all their pretty speeches, as eloquently as I knew how, but I was, on the whole, silent, and spent my time trying to learn by heart all the different warlike weapons that adorned the walls of this strange room. I wondered how many arsenals in how many countries had been robbed to decorate them and the ceiling of it. There were rifles, dirks, broadswords, pistols, Indian daggers, boomerangs, clubs, spears, assegais, *everything* except (I regret to say it!) the simple and gentle shillelagh.

"Lady Janet has really been quite extraordinarily kind to me, and has given me to understand that she hopes I will forget that she was only my father's step-sister, and try to think of her as his very real own one. I have promised to do all that in me lies in this direction.

"And now, Katty, a last word. Don't let George come to Edinburgh. What's the good of it? I like him; but liking isn't loving, and I don't think I *want* him to love me. I've known him such a time, and when one has grown up with a person it makes all the difference. And the fact of his being a baronet doesn't count a scrap! And he is always looking at me so exactly as if he felt certain I should have him after all, that he aggravates me. I want you to understand that I esteem George and all his solid qualities quite as much as you and mamma do—only that he worries me.

"Now, there is a man here who doesn't worry me. He calls himself my cousin, because he is a nephew of Lady Janet's; but really he isn't our cousin in any way. He is tall, handsome, distinguished. One likes him at a first glance. He is a little light and frivolous, perhaps, but very enjoyable; and—he fancies *me!* a *great* charm! After all, most women's likes and dislikes are bound and governed by the fact that somebody else likes or dislikes *them.*

"Let that be as it may, however, I confess I find a modest amount of pleasure in Darnley Bruce's conversational efforts, and in his near vicinity. I wish I had you in the next room, Katty, that I might go in and bore you a bit with my fancies; but as it is, I can only do it on paper—a more merciful way, as you can escape it if you will, with the fire so close at hand.

"Good-bye, my darling sister; and be *sure* you dissuade George from paying that visit here to Lady Janet he has so often threatened since I mentioned my determination to accept her last invitation. A kiss to the dearest of mothers.—Ever your own, "NORAH."

To MISS BLAKE, *Tomakin, Edinburgh.*
"Derrygra, Galway, Dec. 26, 1883.

"DARLING NORAH,—Look out for squalls! Because he has *started!* The mother having read your letter to me, let out the whole affair without meaning it. She told him how you were enjoying yourself, and what delightful people Lady Janet had gathered round her, and that there was one man in particular whom Norah seemed to have found especially interesting. You know what mamma is when she once begins! He had a flowing account, I can tell you. I gave her a some·what severe kick (we were at luncheon), which she bore like a martyr at the time, but for which I had a lecture afterwards. George was up in arms in a moment. I could see that by the glitter of his eye, and the increased suavity of his manner. I write this thus hurriedly, to give you timely warning of his advance upon you. I was quite mad with poor mamma about her want of discrimination in mentioning to him your modern Darnley, and she, when I explained matters to her, professed to be equally mad with herself. But, to be candid, I didn't believe her. I know that in her soul she favours George, and would gladly see you Lady Blake. And I cannot wonder. George, to my thinking, suits you down to the ground; and I don't believe one bit in your hero with the romantic name.

"Dear Norah, don't stay *too* long with that pompous old woman and her nephew, or I shall do something desperate.—Ever your loving sister, "KATHLEEN."

Christmas had come and gone, and a New Year was at hand. To Norah Blake the past three weeks spent in her aunt's Scottish home had proved far from unpleasant, though it had been with a doubting heart she had accepted the invitation. There had been moments, indeed, which were altogether pleasant—moments with which Mr. Bruce had had a good deal to do. He had fallen into her life at once, from that first hour when he saw her enter the firelit room, tall and pale, and faintly smiling, and had found himself a little later on rather wrapt up in the arranging of her movements, and almost of her thoughts. He had begun by declaring he would make her visit a pleasant one to her, and had ended by finding that it would be a pleasant one for him.

She was fresh, delightful, even a little amusing; one forgot to yawn when with her—one forgot a good deal, indeed, that one might better have remembered, perhaps, were the truth told. But to be able to forget successfully at times is a very comfortable gift.

The first few days had gone charmingly, and others might have followed as smoothly but for a new element that was thrown into their midst, in the person of the stalwart, solemn young Irishman, Sir George Blake. To Norah, even though his coming had been foretold to her by a faithful sister, his sudden descent upon all the surrounding frivolity had been something of a shock. At times in her quiet home in Ireland she had found him now and then a trifle oppressive; here he was immeasurably more so. He was, yet he was not, her lover. He had, indeed, gone as far in that direction as she would permit, and had certainly conveyed to her the impression that he fully intended to go farther. He had not in actual words asked her to marry him, but there was not a shadow of doubt that he meant to do so on any occasion that might happen to strike him as being favourable to the possibility of his receiving to his question the answer he desired.

He was calm, methodical, by no means an ideal lover, but he was very good-looking, and there was a standing solidity about him that carried its own weight and compelled her at times to think more of him than suited her.

As for Darnley Bruce, he was altogether different. He was as light as the other was solid, and knew more of the world's ways in his thirty years than Sir George would have discovered in a lifetime. He was a tall, dark man, with an appealing, half-subdued manner that hinted at love-making, but that seldom overstepped the limit or made *himself* uncomfortable. He was, Norah told herself, everything he ought to be, and she gave herself up unconditionally to the enjoyment of his perfections, and the arrangements he made for her *bien être.*

Chistmas had been an effective time, and Norah, in a new gown that had shown off all her many points, had been conscious of a universal admiration. strange as it was exhilarating Mr. Bruce had looked at her in a very appreciative fashion, and even Sir George's quiet glances, that always seemed to her half full of disapprobation, had not had power to damp her inward satisfaction or her open delight at the fitness of things generally.

And now it was the eve of a New Year! To-morrow would see it dawn! They were all a little depressed in spite of many efforts to the contrary, and Lady Janet was undisguisedly sleepy. Sir George, the only guest that night, tired perhaps of listening to Norah's soft laughter as she sat apart with Bruce, had taken an early departure—almost immediately, indeed, after dinner; and at nine precisely Lady Janet rose from her couch, and declared her intention of seeking her maid forthwith and the virtuous couch that was to follow on that damsel's administrations. Norah, a little dismayed at the idea of having so early to seek a repose in which she was of no need, rose too.

"You need not come quite yet. You may stay a little longer dear, and entertain Darnley," said Lady Janet, with drowsy good-nature. "But don't sit up *too* late. See to that, Darnley." She smiled at them in a listless fashion, and then faded sleepily away.

Norah glanced ruefully at her companion. "That means half an hour's grace, no more," she said, "and I do hate going to bed until the spirit moves me. The way aunt Janet speaks makes one feel as if one was a baby!"

She laughed, but there was unmistakable vexation in her mirth.

"Well, don't do it," said Darnley. Then he looked at her suddenly as though some thought had just occurred to him. "It is New Year's Eve," he said, "and the city will be illuminated, and there will be rejoicings of a rather unique character in certain parts of it. You, who live so far from us and our customs, should know something of our lower classes. Lady Janet is in bed, and the world lies before us. Let us play truant for once. Put on your ulster and the hat that you least esteem, and let us sally forth in search of knowledge."

"I don't think," said Norah, hesitating, "that I much care for knowledge. There should be something else."

"There will be adventure. Cannot even *that* stir you? There will be the certainty that, if discovered, condemnation will fall upon our heads. There is the thought that the estimable Sir George (who plainly regards you with open dis-approval) would look with scorn upon our conduct. And——"

"Yes—let us go," interrupted she, lightly, flushing and lifting to his, eyes that burned with a quick yet sombre fire.

A few minutes later she stole down, wrapped in a warm fur cloak and gently hooded, and together they stepped across the hall with its pink shaded lamps, opened the hall door for themselves, and, unknown to the household, emerged into the dulness of the night.

Her letter to her sister, a few days later on, described rather accurately what she saw and felt that night, and the strangeness of the circumstances that were to have such an effect upon her after life.

"I was told that up in the old town at the market cross, under the shadow of the Iron Church, all the poorer people assembled to 'proclaim' the New Year. Of course few of the eminently respectable class, of which we form two units, had ever witnessed their rites or ever meant to! The way was all uphill, as slippery as glass, and thronged with people, who were making noise enough to break the drum of one's ear. I was glad I had on my warm cloak, as it was colder far than anything except ice-pudding.

"The mist was below us, and looked much as the moon might look to those who had got above it, being all luminous with a pure white brilliancy that came from the electric lamps of the railway station hidden somewhere in the depths. Above us was the black outline of the old town and the Castle rock. Everything reasonable seemed all at once *miles* away, and I was beginning to have a strong fit of repentance, and a mean hankering for my bed-room fire, when—I was rewarded for all my temerity. Oh! Katty, I *wish* you had been with me. I hardly feel sorry for *anything* when I recall it! There was the pitch darkness of the night, the surging, trampling crowd somewhere near, the gaunt houses creeping away up into the ghost-like mist like so many giant cliffs; and all and everything lighted up in the true demoniac style by the red and green and orange fires that flamed up at the corners of all the streets.   The effect was indescribably weird, and to add to it one could see vaguely, through the smoke of the fires and the cloudy mist, the great tower of the church with its clock lights.

"And then suddenly there was a great silence—a silence that seemed to me louder than all the tumult that went before it.   I thought I heard the beating of all the hearts around me. The fires grew on the instant brighter and brighter; they sprang up as if to reach the sky; their lurid tongues pierced and flamed through the murky darkness, and then, all at once, some clock tolled the hour.   What hour I did not then know; but as the last sound of it died on the air, there arose from the multitude a shout, such as I, at least, never heard before!   It rang and echoed through the night, and then it ceased, and the fires died down mysteriously, and the smoke and the mist met each other and swept over everything, and even the yellow lights in the church tower grew dim.   It was all very eerie, but exciting, more than I can say."

So far, Norah's letter could explain matters; but no farther. The mist, indeed, came down upon her and Bruce, and the thought of home ran at last very high within their breasts. When the final toll of the bell had sounded on their ears, they turned, as if with one mind, and sought to escape the turmoil around them.   They ran, indeed, a little, and at last paused breathless in a small side-street that struck Norah as being remarkably solitary for even that time of night.   But in truth she had been so entertained that she felt as if only a few minutes had elapsed since she left Lady Janet's drawing-room.

It was a quaint old-fashioned street in which they found themselves, and it might have been a city of the dead, so still it was, so replete with an unbroken calm.   Norah, pausing, glanced at her companion, and then burst out laughing.   It was the gayest laugh imaginable, and the lightest-hearted, but it echoed with such a cruel clearness through the deserted street that it at once sobered her.

"Why, where are we?" she said, glancing somewhat timidly

to the right and left. "Who could imagine we had only just emerged from that noisy thoroughfare! Why, it might be miles away now, so—so *singular* is this quiet that has enveloped us. Where are all the people to whom this street means home? Have they, too, joined the madding crowd beyond?"

"More probably they have gone to bed," said Bruce, laughing.

"To bed!" She started violently. "At *this* hour!"

"Why, what hour do you think it is?" asked he, a little surprised at *her* surprise.

"Ten, perhaps?" faltered she, nervously.

"*Ten?* What do you think the shouting was about just now? Have you forgotten that it is the New Year's Eve? It is—twelve," said Bruce, reluctantly, taking out his watch and pretending to examine it beneath the light of the street lamp.

"Oh, no!" said the girl in a horrified tone. She clasped her hands, and a look of passionate distress darkened her face, and deepened the curves of her beautiful lips. "I forgot everything—the hour, the occasion, the meaning of it all! But we must get home; that is the principal thing now," she exclaimed, turning to him with a pitiful attempt at composure. "What would Lady Janet say if she heard of—of this?" Then another horrible thought striking her: "How shall we get in? The servants will be all asleep."

"That will be right enough. I have a latch-key; but——" he was glancing eagerly around him, and stopped short in his sentence.

"But what?" sharply.

"I confess I don't quite know where we are," he acknowledged with a rather forced laugh that unnerved her even more than his assertion. All at once she seemed to lose faith in him : it was he who had brought her into this scrape, and now he seemed unable to get her out of it. A little swift anger flamed into her eyes, and deadened the sweetness of her lips.

"Come," she said, coldly; "we must walk on at all events until we meet some one who can tell us where our home lies."

The mist had cleared away a little, and the stars were

coming out in the dark blue vault above them. A light wind arose, and softly buffeted her cheeks as she walked eagerly on, entirely silent. Almost at the end of the street a figure came towards them. It was light here, because of a gas lamp, and they could see the face of him who thus advanced towards them. It was the curate of their aunt's parish—a spare, lean, unprepossessing man, to whom Norah had not been altogether gracious in small ways, having from the commencement of their acquaintance resented a tendency on his part to discover in her certain charms and graces. He was a good man, but, like many of his class, narrow. He was now hurrying to the side of a dying bed, and as his small eyes fell full on Bruce, and then wandered from him to Norah, he paled and dropped his glance, and, with bent head and an exaggerated pretence of being ignorant of their nearness that served to heighten the hideousness of the situation, passed beyond them into the darkness.

Norah bravely repressed the tears that fought for mastery, but Bruce could feel that she was trembling. Her downcast lids hid her eyes, but he could see that the pretty mobile lips, erstwhile so prone to laughter, were now possessed by melancholy. He smothered an unmentionable word or two that rose to his lips, and were meant for the curate; but to her, to comfort her, he could find nothing to say. That he was passionately grieved for her, his own soul knew, but he could not put that grief into words.

And now the sullen mist that had overlain the town, covering it as with a shroud, was quite all gone, and the stars were twinkling gaily in the sky. The night had grown quite bright, and "there, where the moonrise broke the dusky grey," one saw soft luminous clouds that crossed and dimmed the majesty of Dian for the instant, only to leave her fuller of beauty when she stole from beneath their embrace.

They had turned down one street and walked up another. But they did not know where their steps were taking them. Two people only had they met, and both were useless. It

was horrible, this perpetual going on without any knowledge
of the end, and with the ever-increasing desire for somebody
who could give them information—that somebody who never
came! Again a clock sounded in the distance. It struck the
half-hour.

"This is growing too terrible," said Norah, stopping short
and pressing her hand to her heart. "It cannot last, or it will
kill me. Oh! think of something!"

Even as she spoke, the sound of rapidly approaching footsteps
came to them. Norah almost ran to meet them, and presently
could see the man to whom they belonged standing out clearly
from the intense darkness behind him. And as she saw him
she came to an abrupt standstill, and turned eagerly to Bruce,
who had joined her. Her heart seemed to cease beating, and
she knew that her face was growing, not only white, but cold.
Who was it? What fanciful resemblance was this? Surely
Fate could not do her so base a turn! Even as she stood and
stared blankly at him, with parted lips and wide, horror-stricken
eyes, the figure emerged into the fuller light of the near lamp,
and stood revealed as Sir George Blake.

Norah made a sudden retreat—a sharp movement suggestive
of the idea that for a moment she had dwelt upon the possibility of being able to hide herself behind her companion.
Then she conquered the undignified desire, and as a means of
proving that she had never intended it, she went ostentatiously
forward and confronted Sir George as he stood rigidly upright
in the centre of the street. Only for an instant, however, did
he so stand: the inexpressible pain he suffered then was subdued almost as it came to life. He recovered himself wonderfully, before Bruce had time to notice the shock he had sustained, and at all events before Norah had realized the entirety
of it. He was ghastly pale, but his voice as he spoke was
perfectly under control.

"Ah! so you *too* ventured out to see the ceremonies," he
said, addressing himself exclusively to Norah. "Not altogether
so good a thing as one had been led to believe. But we have

all lived long enough to allow for exaggerations. Are you on your way home?"

"If you can *only* tell us that," said she, with a poor attempt at unconcern. She tried to laugh, but failed, and was unhappily conscious of her failure. She was miserable, and looked it. "The fact is," she said, breaking down a little, "we have lost our way."

"An awkward time to lose it," returned he, with a pale smile.

"*So* awkward that, if you *can*, I hope you will help us," said Bruce, with a frown. He had not quite liked the manner of Sir George—a manner that had distinctly ignored him.

"Yes, help us," said Norah, in a low tone. Blake saw the dewy brightness of her eyes as she spoke, a brightness that hinted at tears not very far away.

"If you will follow me," he said, coldly, still addressing Norah, "I think I can lead you to a stand where one cab, at least, may be found.

They followed him as culprits might, and got their cab. That he had asked for no explanation of her extraordinary appearance there, at that hour of the night, struck cold upon the girl's heart. Yes, he had condemned her. Without a word, without giving her a chance of clearing herself, he had condemned her! It was hard! He declined a seat in the cab, and went away from the door of it after carefully putting her into it, without a spoken good-night, and with no courtesy indeed beyond the iciest bow and the very faintest lifting of his hat. Her drive home was one of unbroken silence, and when she got safely to her room without rousing a member of the household, she flung herself upon her bed and burst into a passion of tears.

*   *   *   *   *   *

Next morning Lady Janet was closeted for a considerable time with a very early visitor, who would take no denial. As he took his departure she rang her bell sharply, and demanded that Miss Blake would come to her *at once*. Miss

Blake came; not without some trepidation, her conscience being anything but calm.

And then it all came out. Lady Janet, in some mysterious fashion, had been made aware of last night's escapade. Her niece had been seen at *midnight* in the streets of Edinburgh with Darnley Bruce. It was horrible, shameful! She declined to say who her informant was; she only asked if the information was true. *Was* it true? She sat in judgment, and gazed at the terrified girl with a cruel sternness.

"Yes," said Norah, faintly. There was a great deal more she could have said, but if her life had depended upon it then, she could not have framed more than that little damnatory affirmative. The thought that it was George—*George !*—who had betrayed her, was so indescribably bitter, as to render her foolishly dumb.

Lady Janet, too, was apparently deprived of speech by the openness of this small avowal on the girl's part. Only for a short while, however, and when speech returned to her she made good use of it—perhaps to make up for lost time. She stormed, she scolded, she reproached, and through all said very many nasty things.

"If it had been any one but an engaged man," she said at last, looking at the girl with contemptuous eyes.

"*Engaged !*" The word fell from Norah's lips with startling rapidity. She looked fixedly at Lady Janet. That she was thoroughly roused now was quite plain to the elderly woman.

"Yes, engaged. Did you not know it? Had he not the decency to tell you? He has been engaged for more than a year to a Miss Prendergast, a girl of no family, but with a large fortune. Darnley is a man of expensive tastes, and is bound to marry some one who can help him to gratify them. He could not afford to marry a poor girl."

"You should have told me all this before; you, my guardian for the time being," said Norah, in a choked voice. "It never occurred to me that he was not heart-whole; that there was an honourable reason why he should be regarded as

different from other men; men without a tie. To my mind
he is as much married as though the words of our church had
been read over him."

"Were he married or single there is no excuse for your
conduct of last night. Were you *mad* to do such a thing?"

"I am not thinking of last night. I am thinking of all the
other days. If he *is* engaged to that girl I am very sorry
for her," said Norah, slowly. Had her words been brilliantly
eloquent she could not have further conveyed to her hearer
the depth of her contempt for the man in question. "As for
last night—I don't know how it happened. It was wrong,
foolish, mad; but I will not admit that I meant any harm.
Me sole fault lies in the fact that I deceived you, but even
then I thought you would not so very much care if no one
knew of it but you and I and Mr. Bruce. It seemed such
a simple thing—and—I did not think George would have told
you."

"It was not George!" exclaimed Lady Janet, impulsively,
and then checked herself; but it was too late. She had explained everything. The curate's gaunt face rose before Norah,
and she told herself she almost knew the very words in which
he had told his tale.

"It is a most distressing affair altogether. I'm sure I don't
know how I am to explain it to your mother," went on Lady
Janet, presently.

"*That* trouble I can at least spare you," returned Norah,
haughtily. "I can go home and explain it to her myself."

"Well, perhaps that would be the better plan," said Lady
Janet, slowly. She rose from her seat as she said this, and, as
if a little afraid to look at the girl, moved noiselessly from the
room.

For a long hour Norah sat there silent, almost motionless,
until a step in the ante-room outside compelled her to raise
her head, and see that it was Darnley Bruce that had entered
the room and was now standing before her. She rose involuntarily.

" My aunt has just told me," he began, with a little amused air, "that she has been criticising, somewhat unkindly, our very harmless adventure of last evening. Has her criticism vexed you ?"

"Certainly," said Norah, gravely.

"Then let it do so no longer. Let us make the impropriety of these prudes—proper." He hesitated and laughed lightly. "If a girl were to walk abroad at any hour with her affianced husband, very little would be said—isn't that so?" he asked, still smiling.

"I don't know," replied Norah, regarding him steadily with large expectant eyes. Unconsciously she afforded him encouragement.

"Place *me* in that position, Norah," said he, quickly. "Tell me that I shall one day be *your* husband." A sudden fervour fell into his usually nonchalant voice. His face changed and grew singularly earnest. The smile died from it.

" *You !*" she said. She looked at him strangely for a minute or so, and then her eyes fell to the ground. "And how about Miss Prendergast ? " she went on very gently, her closed lips growing full of meaning. He coloured warmly.

"You have heard, then," he exclaimed, quickly. "That was a folly—a madness I have recovered from."

"She is pretty—an heiress ! "

"She is not your equal. And it is all over now. A week ago I wrote to her to—to absolve her from her promise to me."

" A week ago ! "

" A full week. And now I am free to wed you, Norah."

Did she shrink from him as he eagerly approached her ?

" *Only* a week," she said, raising her hand reflectively to her forehead. "And before that ? " Her pause here was so slight, that if he had meant to explain matters, his hesitation in doing so went almost unmarked. "It is all very strange," she finished, with a deep sigh.

"Strange that I should change my fancied admiration for

another to my strong love for you? It would have been stranger had I not done so. And now you will take pity on me," said he, smiling fondly. "You will name our wedding day—a *near* day. You will marry me, Norah?"

"Oh! as to that," she answered, gravely, "that is impossible!"

"Impossible!"

"Quite—*quite* so!"

"I don't think I understand," said Bruce, making a strong effort at composure, but growing extremely pale. "Do you mean to tell me that after all that has passed between us you now mean to reject me?"

She looked at him steadily and very coldly.

"After all *what?*" she demanded a little haughtily, her clear eyes darkening.

"After all our happy hours spent together. Hours in which you drew my heart from out my body and made it yours. Will you destroy that heart?"

"Ah!" she said, gently, "I do not think I shall destroy it. A month ago it was hers: to-day it is mine: to-morrow——" She paused, and ran her slender fingers, with an absent air, along the edge of the antique cabinet near her.

"This is trifling!" cried he, angrily. "I tell you that for your sake I have thrown up fortune, and now you say you will have nothing to do with me. I have given up that other girl to gain you."

"I am sorry for that other girl," replied she, a sudden flash in her eyes.

"You need not," returned he, with a bitter laugh. "Believe me, she requires no commiseration. She was *glad* to be released. She cares for me quite as little as you do."

"I am sorry," she said again, but this time she looked at him, and he could see that there was genuine kindly regret in her glance. It was a glance fatal to his hopes, yet it seemed to moisten his parched soul.

"You will have pity," he entreated, laying his fingers lightly on her arm. "What is it that stands between us? What has that old woman said? What is it you can't forgive?"

"There is nothing—*nothing!*" she declared, eagerly. "I forgive—I don't know even what it is I have to forgive. It is only"—her voice sank a little and she half turned away—"that now I *know* I could never have loved you. There, *go*," she whispered, hurriedly, a moment later, as steps could be heard outside drawing nearer and nearer to the door. "Go before Lady Janet comes to question, to learn that you—you asked, and I had nothing to give!"

He straightened himself, and with a swift glance at her—a final glance—quitted the room by the upper door. As he did so the lower one was opened and some one came in. After all it was not Lady Janet—it was only Sir George Blake.

Norah started and turned a vivid crimson. It was the first time he and she had met since that terrible moment last night, when she had found herself face to face with him in the middle of the deserted street.

"Lady Janet tells me you are thinking of returning home," he began, hardly looking at her. "I fear she has been unwarrantably severe with you. But it will be wise to make allowances. To go back now in such hot haste to Derrygra seems to me to be the very height of folly."

"She has left no alternative," said Norah, making a little impulsive gesture with her right hand, that conveyed the impression that all things had come to an end between her and her hostess. "She was too angry to be reasonable. She was not so much unwarrantably severe as unpardonably *rude!* Of course, I shall go. Kathleen at least understands me, and mamma always *knows.* I am not afraid of their verdict. As for Lady Janet, she has behaved abominably."

She turned suddenly to him, with her red lips apart and her eyes all aglow.

"What was it all but a *mistake*," she cried, passionately. Not for all the world could offer would she have confessed, even to herself, that the desire to clear herself with him was the uppermost thought in her heart. "My mind was so occupied—I was so interested in the people—the scene—the strange weirdness of the effects—that I forgot everything. But," haughtily, "forgetfulness is not a *crime !*"

"No," said he, meditatively, his eyes on the carpet. "And, as you say, you were interested."

"In the people—the whole scene," she repeated, impatiently. "But Lady Janet would not listen. She herself had so much to say, that she gave me no room to say anything. There are indeed two or three things she said that I shall find it difficult to forget." She drew herself up, and through her soft eyes there shot a flame of undisguised anger.

"She will be sorry for them herself, by and by. I think, perhaps, she is sorry for them even now," said Blake. "Sometimes, too, she speaks of things that are not quite understood by her. Perhaps——" He hesitated, and then went on : "Perhaps she spoke to you of Bruce's engagement?"

"Yes."

"She does not know the truth about that affair. Bruce is no longer engaged to be married. He has broken off any ties that bound him to Miss Prendergast. He is a free man."

"You have been speaking to him?" said the girl, regarding him fixedly.

"Yes." He looked past her, out of the window, and frowned slightly. "You see," he said, slowly, "in a measure I feel bound to look after you—your interests—your *happiness !* It was with a visible effort he made this speech, yet his voice was unbroken, and his gaze was not lowered.

"It is very good of you," said Norah, a faint inflection of sarcasm in her tone. "And what is it you want to do for me now ?"

A short silence followed on her question. Then—

"Bruce loves you," said Sir George, slowly. Receiving no answer to this startling assertion, he felt himself bound to look at her, and saw that she was standing motionless upon the hearthrug, her hands clasped before her. She was very pale.

To him that loss of colour told its own tale. She did then love Bruce in return, and that foolish pallor was but Nature's tattler that flew to betray her secret !

"Yes, he loves you," he went on, speaking now very rapidly. "He is a man of good position, of excellent family; he is a man with many friends !" He broke off abruptly, and came a step nearer to her. "I have been assured," he said, "that the dearest wish of his heart is to make you his wife !"

Norah moved as if involuntarily, and raised to his a very pale face wreathed in a cold, disdainful smile.

"All that, I know," she said, "He told me everything just before you came in."

Sir George started violently.

"So soon !" he exclaimed. "Then it is all over, and I might, at least, have spared myself—*this*.

"Do not regret it," said she, with an ironical intonation. "You have taught me how elegantly you can plead another's cause."

"I think it was *your* cause I was advocating," returned he, a little wearily. "I had seen Lady Janet, and had listened to her angry remarks about you. I had combated with her prejudices in vain. It occurred to me you must be troubled, distressed, about all this, and then a way out of your difficulty presented itself to me. I knew how he loved you; I guessed how you loved him. I at once felt that an engagement between you would simplify all things. I knew, too———"

"What a great deal you seem to know !" interrupted she, contemptuously. "Even a great deal more than what actually *is*. As for me, I do not love, and I shall never marry Mr. Bruce. He quite understands that. He is gone. It is unlikely I shall ever see him again."

"You *refused* him ? "

"Yes, yes ! Why will you make me repeat it ?" cried she, with some suppressed vehemence.

For a long time neither of them spoke. Then she raised her head and sighed heavily. She turned her eyes to his.

"Will you leave me?" she murmured, in her gentlest tone.

He rose at once to obey her.

"You *meant* to be kind, I suppose—I *believe*," she said, in a low voice. "And I thank you. But you have given me many things to think of, and—I would wish to be alone!"

He moved away from her down the room, but as he got to the door he paused and looked back at her, his hand upon the handle.

"If you won't marry him, will you marry me?" he said.

She let her arms fall to her sides.

"Oh! George," she cried.

"Well?" said he, looking at her. Perhaps what he saw decided him, because he dropped the handle of the door and went back to her.

"Well?" he said again, but in a very different voice this time, being now in full possession of her trembling hands.

"I know I shouldn't have been there last night," she confessed, humbly. "But I did so want to know what it was all about."

"And now you know," said he.

She blushed hotly beneath his grave glance and the indirect meaning of his words.

"Yes, I know——" she murmured. "And after all it wasn't so *very* much. I didn't care about it. You will believe *that?*"

"I will," said he, tenderly. "I understand *all*. And, as you say, there was nothing so very much in it after all."

"Still I should not have gone," whispered she, penitently, lifting to his face lovely, plaintive eyes. "It was wrong of me, *very* wrong. Think, George! Consider *well* what I have done. The world is sometimes unkind, and what will people say?".

"That is my affair," said George Blake, as he bent down and sealed his forgiveness with a kiss.

NURSE EVA.

A WARM, bright day in golden June; a crowded park; a rushing of dainty wind soft and pure, such as one seldom feels in this smoky London of ours ; and over all a brilliant sun, grown drowsy now, as it seeks its rest, and sinks languorously into the fond arms of evening.

The stream of carriages is growing thinner ; the Princess has disappeared.   One young man, riding a handsome chestnut in a somewhat careless fashion, as though his thoughts were elsewhere, quits the Row, and turns towards the ugliest thing in creation.   Having reached the Albert Memorial, he passes through the gate a little further on, and finds himself presently in the midst of a hopeless jangle, composed of cabs, hansoms, drags, and so forth.

Something in the jangle disagrees with the chestnut's temper. She starts, throws up her sleek head into the very midst of her master's day-dreams, makes a false step, and comes heavily to the ground, flinging her rider, with a horrible crash, right under the wheels of a passing carriage.

It is all done in a moment.   There is a cry from the bystanders, a vain attempt to make a clear space, and then a senseless form, soiled and disfigured with dust and blood, is raised by half a dozen rough, if kindly, hands, and conveyed to the nearest hospital.   They pull the bell, and the door being opened, they enter with their ghastly burden, and lay it down within the hall : it is all that remains of the careless, gay young man, so full of happy life, who had left the Park only a short time ago.

The house-surgeon, passing through the hall at this moment, casts a sharp glance at the unsightly object on the bench.

"What is this?" asks he; and, coming nearer, bends over it. His face changes. "Good heavens! It is Sir Rawdon Dare!" he exclaims, in a horrified tone. "Send the matron here at once. See what has happened," he says, presently, as a tall, handsome woman comes hurriedly up to him. His tone, though low, is agitated.

"An accident," says she, stooping, in turn, over the prostrate baronet.

"And a very serious one. It is Sir Rawdon Dare. Is there a special ward?"

"One empty."

There is a touch of curiosity in her glance as she examines the death-like features beneath her.

"Let him be taken there. It is impossible he can be conveyed to his own house in his present state."

"It is a chance whether he will ever be conveyed there—alive," says the matron, turning away to give her orders.

"There is another thing," says the surgeon, detaining her. "He must have a careful nurse. You can recommend one from the wards?"

"Certainly," says the matron, pausing as if to consider. There is a good deal of kindly interest in her compassionate, if somewhat austere, face, as she gazes at the poor crushed figure; just as kindly, however, would she have looked at him had he been the veriest beggar that crawls our streets. "There is Nurse Eva," she says, hastily; "she can undertake the case. She is both careful and sympathetic."

And now the wounded man, mercifully oblivious to his pain, is carried by experienced tender hands to a small private ward, and laid upon a bed. The doctors cluster round him. A young woman in hospital cap and apron comes quietly into the room, and stands beside the bed. She glances earnestly at her patient.

Surely that poor blood-bestained creature can have no life in him? There is a long pause; then one of the doctors, who has been stooping over the senseless figure, lifts his head.

"He is not dead—yet," he says. There is little or no hope in his tone.

After a long sleep, as it seemed to him, the sick man woke. He lay silently gazing at the four white walls of the small room in which that strange sleep had taken place, but without wondering why he was there. Thinking, as yet, was too great a task; and so he put it from him. The window was open, and beyond, in the outside distance, there was a waving of green branches, and from still farther on there came to him the subdued roar of unsubdued populace. Inside there was some very curious furniture—or, at least, so he thought it, as his languid glance travelled over it—a huge branch of crimson roses on a small table, a wicker chair, and a girl.

The girl's head was turned from him towards the window. Her body also slightly bent in its direction. It occurred to him that she must be lost in thought. The idle way in which her hands lay upon her lap helped him, too, to this conclusion.

As he watched her, a little sooty sparrow perched upon the window-sill, and looked at her knowingly out of his small eye. She rose, found some bread-crumbs in a funny little cupboard, and returned with them to the window. Of course, when she got there the bird was gone. She seemed in nowise disconcerted by this, but sat down and fell back again into her former thoughtful attitude, and then presently not one but three little sparrows came and carried away some of her donation. She had not glanced at the bed when getting her crumbs, believing her patient to be dozing; but he, watching her with newly-opened eyes, had seen her face.

It was a revelation! It was beauty perfected! He lay quite still after he had seen it, dwelling with a drowsy pleasure on the remembrance of it until some minutes had gone by, and then a growing desire to see it again took possession of him. He felt still so weak and tired that he shrank from giving his voice sound, so, to attract her attention, he clutched feebly at the bedclothes, and then made a sorry effort to tap upon the quilt.

In a moment she was alert and eager. She came quickly to him, and bent over him.

"Why, this is good news," she said, in a low, exquisitely soft voice, and with a smile. "You are beginning to be yourself again, are you not? No, do not answer; I know what you would say; I understand you quite."

She laid her hand with a soothing touch upon his forehead; she settled his pillows, and then, going to the door, pressed her fingers on a knob in the wall outside. This brought the house-surgeon to her in a few minutes.

"Come," said he, cheerily, nodding at the patient, "this is well; you are to be congratulated, nurse. Our patient is getting on, eh?—eh?"

He said "eh?" a good many times in a pondering fashion, and then took the nurse aside and whispered to her in quite a confidential manner. As he did so, it occurred to Sir Rawdon, in quite a feeble inconsequent way not to be accounted for, that he hated the house-surgeon! Nurse, he had called her. With that face—a nurse! Of course she wasn't a lady, poor thing; but with those little white slender hands to be—a nurse! And with that charming figure and that high-bred— "No, no, thanks, old man, nothing more. See you by and by at Lady Stanhope's. Look out, Alys: those bull-terriers are often treacherous"—and so on, again falling into the old delirious state, and babbling ever of this Alys, whose name had been so frequently on his lips all through his illness.

The nurse was at his side again directly.

"You must expect these little relapses for a while," said the surgeon with encouragement, patting her kindly on the shoulder.

Then there came a week when he felt much stronger, and could lie contentedly gazing at his nurse with certain recognition in his eyes, and no fear of its slipping away from him.

"When may I go?" he asked her suddenly one morning, when she was giving him his breakfast. His question was somewhat ungraciously put. He was, indeed, a little querulous at times; but she, accustomed to the vagaries of sick people, didn't appear to mind it.

"Not for a short while yet," she said. She spoke to him with the intonation one might use to a fractious child, and with a lenient smile. " Are you tired of us already ?"

"Not tired of you—no."

"But you want to get back to the other life? Of course it is only natural." Did a faint, faint sigh escape her here? "Your friends want to get you back there too."

"It is hardly that," said he, quickly. "It is more—that I want to feel myself—*myself* again. A *man !*—I am sick of coddling, and physic, and so forth."

This, too, was ungracious, and he knew it when the words had passed his lips. He glanced at her furtively, to see if he had offended her; and though he would have been miserable had he succeeded in paining her, he was still angrily disconcerted at finding she had taken no heed whatsoever of his petulance.

"It is a matter of indifference to her whether I am pleasant or the reverse," he said to himself, with a frown.

"I am afraid you must be content with us for a week or two longer," she said, brightly. "But that should not be so great a hardship to you. In your present state, how could you be better off *there* than *here ?*"

She was looking frankly into his eyes, and the beauty of her expression killed his small touch of rancour.

"I should be worse off," he said, flushing warmly; "I should be without my nurse."

"No; we supply nurses to private cases. You would probably have had one in your own home as good as I am," returned she, calmly.

"Still, it wouldn't be you," said he. Then, "Do you like the life here ?"

"Yes."

There was as much No as Yes in this answer, and it puzzled him.

"It is a hard life," he said.

"Most lives are hard," returned she, sententiously.

This checked him for a time, but the demon of curiosity having made him his prey, he was compelled to go on again.

"What is your name?" he asked.

"Nurse Eva."

"I know that. I shall never"—gratefully—"forget that. But your other name, I mean."

It had tormented him inconceivably in his sick moments to think it might be Smith or Jones.

There was a short but eloquent pause. When it had gone by she turned and looked him fairly in the face.

"I have no other name," she said, icily.

She got up from her seat, and moved towards the window.

"I beg your pardon, I'm sure!" exclaimed he, horror-stricken with shame at his mistake. "I assure you I didn't mean it—I——"

"If you excite yourself you will have a relapse, and not be able to leave us even as soon as I have said," interrupted she, with increasing coldness. "Think of the misery of *that*, and compose yourself."

A suspicion of scorn in her manner checked further speech on his part. He turned on his side and feigned slumber. But he could not get her face out of his thoughts. That last little touch of hauteur had become her. Strange to say—for one in her class—it had *suited* her, had seemed to belong to her of right! What a brute he was to ask her such a question! Surely she had a right to her own secrets; and yet—yet he wished now her name had been honest Jones or Smith, and that she had been able to say so.

But he had angered her, and could not sleep without her forgiveness. He was still so weak that sleep at all times was essential to him.

"Nurse," he said, presently, in a tone that reminded him of the days when he was a schoolboy and in disgrace.

" Well," said she.

"I'm very sorry I said *that*," mumbled Sir Rawdon from beneath the bedclothes; " it was abominable of me."

He had now evidently come to the point when a good sound caning was reasonably to be expected.

"You want me to say I forgive you," said Nurse Eva, softly, coming up to him again and looking down upon him. " Very good—I say it. Now go to sleep."

" You don't *look* as if you forgave," protested he, anxiously. "If you could only know what I feel about it! You must think me so contemptible—and you so kind to me, and——"

" If that is all, be comforted. I do not think you contemptible," returned she; and even as she spoke a sweet soft smile overspread her lovely face, falling like a healing sunbeam on the repentant invalid. With a sigh of relief he closed his eyes, and sank into a refreshing slumber.

Then came a day when his nurse entered his room with a very jubilant air. Perhaps it was rather too jubilant an air.

" Rise, prisoner," said she ; " the hour of your release has arrived."

He answered her with a reproachful glance, but no word.

She laid the little breakfast-tray upon the table near, and began to busy herself with its contents.

" It seems a shame to give you any trouble now I am so strong again," he said. " And yet—I like to see you doing that."

" You like to see me getting your breakfast ready. A very sensible fancy."

" You misunderstand me," he said, hastily, and then stopped abruptly. It was difficult to go on with those large clear eyes fixed coldly upon him. And, after all, what was it he wanted to say ? Yet the very repellency of those eyes only made some vague unanalysed feeling within his breast the more unendurable.

"Eva," he said, suddenly, with a vehemence that suggested hidden passion.

She laid her tiny teapot down slowly, without a suspicion of agitation, and turned her eyes fully upon his.

"*Nurse* Eva !" she said, with indescribable dignity.

She then gave him his tea, and arranged the tray as carefully as ever before him. If her hand trembled a little, she took very great care it should not be seen.

As for him, he seemed dissatisfied with all she gave him, and toyed discontentedly with his food, and finally told her, almost rudely, to take it away from him.

"This is foolish," she said, gravely. "You will want strength for your removal. Try to eat something."

"The very thought of my removal takes away my appetite," retorted he, sullenly, rejecting with angry persistence the little dainty trifle she sought to press upon him.

Then the surgeon came in again, and felt his pulse, and asked a question or two, and went through the usual formula.

"All going on as well as we could wish," he said at last. "You have, indeed, made a wonderful recovery, my dear Sir Rawdon. Give you my word, there was a time when—eh ?— eh ? Well, and so the carriage is to be here for you at twelve? Hah ! glad to run away from us, eh ?—eh ? "

" Is it safe for me to move to-day ? " asked Sir Rawdon, languidly. There was no languor, however, in the deep anxiety of his eyes. "I don't think I feel so well as I did yesterday."

"Eh ? what ? Pouf !· nonsense, my dear sir !" said the surgeon, gaily. "Invalid's tremors, nothing more. I tell you, you are getting out of our hands more hopefully every moment. We shall be ashamed to prescribe for you soon."

"Perhaps if my going were to be postponed until——"

"Not at all—nothing of the kind. The very change will do you good," said the surgeon, cheerily. "Come, come now— speak to him, nurse."

" But supposing I should have a relapse—that would be un-pleasant," said this remarkably careful young man.

" Eh? How is this, nurse?" said the surgeon, somewhat perplexed by his patient's pertinacity.

As he appealed to her, Sir Rawdon raised himself slightly on his elbow, and appealed to her too—with his dark eyes. Her glance, passing from the surgeon's face to his, rested there for a moment. There was entreaty, longing, hope, and some-thing far more than all these in his gaze. She turned away from it slowly, but resolutely.

"There will be no fear of a relapse," she said to the surgeon, in cold measured tones, her eyes bent upon the ground. " It is better, *far* better he should go to-day, as arranged."

A swift change altered the expression of Sir Rawdon's face. Whereas before it was almost humbly imploring, it was now proud and stern.

"To-day, then, be it, by all means," he said, in a decided tone. " The sooner the better;" after which he sank back with an angry jerk upon his pillow.

The surgeon laughed a little, and presently went away. The nurse busied herself in tidying the already scrupulously tidy room.

"In what mad haste you are to get rid of me!" said Sir Rawdon at last, finding the silence unbearable. How cold, how calm, how unfeeling she appeared with that beautiful un-readable face of hers·!

"You see I have your interests at heart," she said.

" Mine?"

"Yes. Do you forget how you were pining for your freedom only a short two weeks ago? Now it lies before you."

"You are ungenerous," he said. Then more slowly, " A fortnight is a long time. One may learn many things in it."

"True. *You* have learned to get well," said she, quietly.

"More than that!" He flushed a dark red, and held out his hand to her, " I have learned besides to——"

He paused with terrible, unmistakable suddenness. The

colour died from his face, and a quick pallor succeeded it. His
very lips grew white, because of the severity of his mental
struggle. What was it he had been about to do? To tell this
nameless girl—this worse than nameless girl, who was ashamed
to declare aloud her honest appellation—that he loved her!
To ask her to be his wife! He, a Dare, and the head of his
house! His hand sank once more to his side, he breathed
heavily, and at length, without looking at her, turned his face
away from her to the wall. Here a bitter strife took place
between his heart and him, but when it was ended his heart
remained the victor, and he roused himself, and looked round
for her.

Of her, however, he found the room empty. During that
short but violent battle with prudence and affection, in which
prudence had been slain, she had left him—had vanished, as it
were. In her chair sat a probationer, a young woman with
pale eyes and a snub nose, and a generally affected air. He
had seen this probationer before, and had amused himself at
odd moments counting the number of aspirates she could drop
in half an hour. She spoke with a little snuffle in her throat,
and was otherwise in many ways most hateful to him.

Now, the knowledge that Nurse Eva was never absent from
him for longer than thirty minutes at a time became an intense
consolation to him. She would soon be here, and that odious
young woman would vacate her chair, in which it seemed a
positive sacrilege that she should ·be allowed to sit. But the
minutes crept on, and the half-hour grew into an hour, and the
hour into two, and still the probationer sat on, and Nurse Eva
made no sign.

The dragging hours were at first a bore to him, and at length
became intolerable. And when the probationer rose, and declared it was time for him to rise, as the carriage would soon
be here, and when a nurse from another ward came to assist
her, he was almost rude to them both.

But time was inexorable and wore away, and at last the
carriage was announced, and two or three of his friends and

relations came in to congratulate him and help him down to it. The house surgeon was present also, looking really pleased at his recovery. To him Sir Rawdon turned with a somewhat hurried air, and an amount of passionate anxiety he vainly tried to conceal.

"Where is Nurse Eva?" he said, his voice trembling slightly; " I cannot go until I bid her good-bye, and thank her—thank her for—— "

He stopped, and cleared his throat huskily.

"I'm afraid you can't see her to-day," said the surgeon, cheerfully. "She has been somewhat overworked of late, you see; so when she asked the matron, a couple of hours ago, to give her a holiday to take a run down to Putney, or somewhere, you may be sure she got no refusal. The matron—indeed we *all* think a good deal of her, and she did seem pale and fatigued, poor girl, when she came down from your room about ten o'clock. I'm glad the day is so fine, both for your sake and hers. She said, by the bye, that you were so thoroughly con-valescent that you would require her services no longer. She seemed to me in bad spirits—a little overdone, no doubt."

"No doubt," said Dare. He said even this with difficulty. Of course he understood it all! That brutal hesitation of his! What woman but would have taken fire beneath such an insult? His manner in itself was unbearable, presupposing as it did that if he uttered his proposal it would of a surety be accepted. With what sweet dignity she had behaved! She had uttered no taunt, had looked no scorn. She had only withdrawn her-self, and taken measures to insure herself against the annoyance. of ever being face to face with him again.

But it should not end here. Of that he was determined. He would at least see her once more, and compel her to believe· that when his craven wavering had drawn to a close he knew himself to be hers, body and soul. He got down to the carriage some way, and was driven home.

But he was a good deal knocked up by the exertion of re-moving, and suffered a slight relapse that kept him to his bed for a week or so. The old familiar scenes were now, too, changed to him, and touched him as being barren and wanting in many ways.

When he rallied a bit, and found himself in possession of a little of his former strength, the first use he made of it was to drive straight to the hospital. He was shown into the matron's room, where he thanked her courteously, if a little absently, for the care conferred upon him whilst under her roof. After that he said casually that he thought he should like to thank his nurse also. It was with a paling cheek he said this, and with eyes downcast.

"Nurse Eva?" said the matron. "Oh, she left us quite a fortnight ago. We were all so sorry to lose her, she was such an excellent nurse. I am sure you too, Sir Rawdon"—with a smile—"will have a good word for her on that score."

"Left!" It was all Sir Rawdon could say.

"Yes; almost the day after you did."

"You know her address perhaps?"

When he asked this, he felt like a drowning man grasping at a straw, and he knew the straw would fail him.

"No," said the matron, regretfully. She thought him a very kind young man. Gratitude, as a rule, is not an overpowering passion with the many. "But do not fret about that," she said. "I am sure she understood that you would wish to thank her. Yes, she was an excellent nurse—so sympathetic; we were sorry to lose her."

Sir Rawdon rose to bid her good-bye.

"I suppose Dr. Bland would not know her address?" he said.

"No, I am sure of that. She went away very suddenly—for family reasons, as she told me—and left no word with any one as to where she was going. Good-bye, Sir Rawdon; so glad to see you so thoroughly restored," &c.

Sir Rawdon, returning her farewell, told himself he was not so fully restored as she kindly imagined, and that his strength was by no means what it used to be.

It is a year and a half later, and Christmas Eve. There is no suspicion of invalidism about the tall, handsome young man who, sitting in a first-class carriage, with a rather bored expression on his face, is being whirled swiftly northwards. He had checked his journey by spending one day in Edinburgh, and had felt it dull in the extreme. Even now, when he is hastening on to Aberdeen, the stupidity of his lonely stay there has not quite worn off. But he is always dull now, he tells himself, with a disdainful shrug of his broad shoulders, and grows moodier and moodier, until, his journey coming to an end, he finds himself on the chilly platform, with two gleaming carriage lamps awaiting him. The drive is a long one, and bitterly cold. The change from it to the soft, brilliant warmth of a huge hall, hung with many skins and bristling with antlers, is almost more than he can endure with fortitude. As in a dream, he follows the servant across the hall—rose-lit from two large shaded lamps upon the dark oak staircase beyond—and valiantly suppresses a desire to stay beside the huge log fire for ever.

But the servant mercilessly marches him onwards, and presently he finds himself in a long, low, many-cornered room full of people, all more or less in the reposeful attitudes that border upon sleep. There is a soft, sweet subdued hum of slumberous voices, a tender tinkling of delicate china, the music of many spoons. There are no rose-lamps in this room ; nothing but the leaping light of a glorious fire that renders all things clear as day. The divan-looking lounges are covered with tartan, so are a good many of the men, and only a few of them have their nether limbs covered.

Sir Rawdon, still unthawed, stares idly round him. There is a pretty girl in a voluminous arm-chair, who nods brightly to him—Miss Adair ; and another crouched picturesquely upon the bearskin rug before the fire, who stops her chatter for an instant to gaze at him curiously; and——

Good heavens ! who is that? Who is that sitting over there, with *her* face, *her* figure, the very hands of *her !*

A slender creature, reclining in a low chair, and clad in an exquisite tea-gown—all satin and old lace. She is smiling. One arm, half naked, but mittened to the elbow, is lying gracefully across the arm of her lounge as she leans towards her neighbour ; the other is trifling idly with a huge white fan.

Even as Dare gazes at her, spellbound, she laughs, softly, merrily, at some remark made to her by her companion—a red-headed young Scotchman. The laugh somewhat restores Sir Rawdon to his senses. Alas ! *she* had never laughed ; her lovely face had always been tinged with a deep. melancholy. What madness possessed him to make him think he saw again before him the one woman he had ever loved—the only one he ever should love ? And to dream of meeting her here, of all places ! A hospital nurse as a guest at The Towers, in that gown, that——

"Dear Sir Rawdon, so glad !" says his hostess—a tall handsome woman—at this moment, coming languidly forward with a smile and a graceful gesture. "So nice to see you again."

Sir Rawdon murmurs something to the effect that he is positively overpowered with joy at the idea of seeing *her* again ; but his words sound vague and unmeaning—to himself, at least—and his eyes are not his own to deal with ; they wander incessantly to the low chair and its lovely occupant, and will not be controlled. Who *is* the owner of that tea-gown ?

"I think you know everybody," says Lady Dalruth, at the end of a long sentence, not one word of which he heard.

"Not quite all. I have not the happiness of knowing your pretty friend on the hearthrug, or—or the lady in the low chair over there."

"No? Well, time will cure that. The latter is my cousin, Miss Monteith. You would like to be introduced to her? Come then."

"Evelyn dear, let me introduce to you Sir Rawdon Dare," she says, a moment later.

Miss Monteith, turning slowly, lifts her eyes fully to Sir

Rawdon's, and, after a calm comprehensive glance, makes him the very faintest salutation.

If he had ever seen this girl before, it is certain that she shows no recognition of ever having seen him. There is no surprised start, no faintest blush, no betraying pallor. Her little bow is cold in the extreme, but nevertheless civil. She answers his rather agitated remark with the utmost composure; it is some ordinary thing about the beauty of the scenery round, and hardly requires any acknowledgment save a bare "yes," to which she confines herself. If, indeed, some wild freak of Fate has suddenly changed the Nurse Eva—for whom he has been so persistently searching during all these past interminable months—into this stately repellent girl before him, she is so clad in an impenetrable armour of reserve that he cannot pierce it.

And, after all, *is* it she? Could even Fate play such a trick? Is not all this rather some cruelty of his imagination, born of his long dwelling on one engrossing desire?

Once or twice during the evening he tried to speak to her; but though she always answered him very gently, still her manner was so cold as to check on every occasion further conversation.

Dropping into the background after a last defeat, he finds himself close to an old beau, a certain Sir Harry Loune, who is well known to everybody and to whom everybody is known.

"Wouldn't look at you, eh?" says this old gentleman, with a chuckle. "Don't take *that* to heart; more than you have got the same tale to tell. She won't look at any one, not even at the best *partis*. Pretty, isn't she? Good form, eh? Thing of the season next year, I shouldn't wonder. Lady Dalruth wanted, right or wrong, to introduce her this year, but she wouldn't hear of it. Seems to shrink from publicity. No wonder, too; beauty has made itself so dooced vulgar of late," says the old gentleman, with a shrug of disgust.

"Yes?" says Dare, calmly, but his look is in itself a question.

"She's charmin'—charmin'," goes on Sir Harry, when he has refreshed himself with a pinch of snuff, "and mysterious as she is lovely."

"Mysterious?"

"Rather, my dear boy! Mustn't say a word about it, you understand; but when she was about eighteen, her father, Sir Pagan Monteith, you know—eh—what? Don't *want* to know? Ha, ha! Very good indeed! Well, he wished at that time to force her into a marriage with a most dilapidated person—an earl, notwithstanding—quite old enough to be *his* father. Girl wouldn't hear of this sacrifice at any price, and when pressed to it by angry parent, bolted—no one knows where, unless Lady Dalruth may. For three long years she remained incognita. Odd affair, isn't it? Nobody can explain it."

Dare thinks *he* could. Again the belief that Miss Monteith and his sweet nurse are one is full upon him; but he refrains from making his thoughts known to this old gossip.

"Why can't she say where she was, eh?" says Sir Harry, in a distinctly aggrieved tone; "this deadly silence is very injurious to her, eh?"

"Why should it be injurious to her?" asks Sir Rawdon, fiercely.

He turns upon the old baronet with open wrath in his dark eyes. It is insufferable to hear her name bandied thus from lip to lip. And yet—*Her* name? *Whose* name? If he lets this madness overpower him, what will the end be? What has that haughty beauty over there to do with his gentle nurse? Seeing Sir Harry's look of amazement, he hastens to change his tone.

"She looks too proud to be a subject for calumny," he says, confusedly, almost apologetically.

But the old scandal-monger has found him slow, and in nowise a kindred spirit; so he hobbles away from him to where Lady Dalruth is standing. Dare, too wearily disturbed in mind to find amusement in his present surroundings, follows his movements with idle, uninterested eyes, but presently is attracted by something he hears him saying to his hostess.

"Left him at the point of death," said Sir Harry, unctuously, "as *he* thought; but it was nothing of the kind. Gordon recovered almost immediately. One of the Gordons of Clayne, you know. Fellow who upset him was a cousin, and thought to come in for the property, d'ye see?"

"One of the Gordons of Clayne" is a bosom friend of Sir Rawdon's, so naturally he pricks up his ears.

"What *did* happen to him?" asks Lady Dalruth, looking interested.

"Oh, a mere trifle! Nothing vital, at all events. One fellow told me it was a broken clavicle; another a fractured humerus; but I haven't the faintest idea what either means."

"You should ask Evelyn for a translation," says Lady Dalruth, with a merry laugh.

Miss Monteith, who had been listening silently to the conversation, turns her eyes upon her. Is there entreaty or simple indifference in her glance? If entreaty, it comes too late; Lady Dalruth does not even see it.

"Miss Monteith?" asks Sir Harry.

"Yes. Didn't you know she has studied medicine, surgery, and all the rest of it?"

"You terrify me," says Sir Harry, with mock horror.

"That is quite a correct feeling for the occasion. She is really terribly learned. Aren't you, Evelyn?"

She smiles at the girl, as though in pleasant appreciation of a jest that is known to them alone. But Miss Monteith's return smile is forced and very faint.

"Learned? no. But I really *have* some taste for that sort of thing," she says, quietly; and then turns away, as if anxious to terminate the conversation. In so doing her eyes meet Dare's. There is a pause, in which each regards the other with a strange anxiety. Then the blood slowly mounts to Miss Monteith's brow, until all her lovely face is dyed a warm crimson. Her breath comes quickly; she wavers; then, with a last defiant, contemptuous glance, she moves away and sinks into a chair at the opposite end of the room.

But to Dare there is no longer even a chance for doubt. Just so had she looked at him when, in a moment's passion, he had called her "Eva" in the hospital, and she had coldly corrected him ; just so, no doubt, her large, scornful eyes had rested upon him during that last fateful hour, when he had half declared his love, and had hesitated—and been lost.

With a terrible sinking of the heart he tells himself that he has sinned past forgiveness in her eyes.

The next morning all the world is clad with snow. The soft, white, fleecy carpet is covering the land far as the eye can see, and is lying heavily on branch and bough. The Christmas bells are chiming merrily. A soft grey mist is trembling between earth and sky. Over all, the merry sun is shining gaily. It is indeed an ideal Christmas morn.

Luncheon has come and gone, and they are all standing before the glowing fire in the billiard-room discussing the costumes to be worn at a fancy-dress ball, to be given in the neighbourhood some time in the ensuing month.

"One gets so tired of the art rags and the past centuries' gowns," says Lady Dalruth, dejectedly. "Oh, for something new, something *bizarre*, out of the common ! I'm sure I don't know what is to be done about Evelyn. She and I are quite worn out trying to imagine a costume that all the world hasn't seen a hundred times before. The anxiety has robbed me of my honest sleep for a fortnight past, I have so set my heart on making her a success. But each of my ideas only seems more crude than the last. Dear Sir Rawdon, *do* suggest something."

An uncontrollable impulse takes hold of Dare. He glances at Miss Monteith, to find she too is looking full at him, that dreamy touch of scorn that had offended him last night now wide awake within her large eyes. It spurs him to his half-determined purpose.

"Why not try the dress of an hospital nurse ?" he says to Lady Dalruth, pale but smiling. " I don't recollect having ever seen it at a ball before, and I think the pretty little cap and apron would suit Miss Monteith admirably."

"Sir Rawdon! What *can* you know about hospital nurses?" says a pretty girl from the opposite side of the hearthrug, with an amused laugh.

"Didn't you know I was in hospital for many weeks—summer before last—when I smashed myself up?" returns Sir Rawdon, distinctly. "I don't think I shall ever forget the kindness I received there; and at all events I know I shall never, under any circumstances, forget—my nurse."

"Ah, gratitude is a charming virtue!" says the pretty girl, with a second laugh. "Was it *her* cap and apron you were thinking of just now?"

"Yes; they are indelibly imprinted upon my brain." Again he glances at Miss Monteith. If she has grown a little whiter it is at least only perceptible to a lover's eyes.

"Do you know, the costume *sounds* well," she says, quite calmly. "Let us think of it, Mirabel," turning to Lady Dalruth. "It is the one thing you desire—out of the common."

Lady Dalruth's answer is a little confused. Miss Monteith looks full at Sir Rawdon, her eyes dilate, and—

> " Oh, what a deal of scorn looks beautiful
> In the contempt and anger of her lip ! "

With a little passionate movement of the hand, unseen by all but him, she crosses the room with slow, graceful step, and disappears through the doorway.

It takes Sir Rawdon but a moment to invent some idle speech, that leaves him, too, free to quit the apartment without arousing suspicion of the real motive of his departure.

Finding himself in the hall, he comes to a standstill, and asks himself what it is he means to do. He cannot forget that last glance of hers, or the passionate anger contained in it. He feels he would give half his possessions to be able honestly to hate her, but yet knows, by the sheer impossibility of his being able to do this, that he *loves* her.

As he stands irresolute, one of the footmen passes through the hall. Then and there a sudden resolution comes to Sir Rawdon. He will go to her, tell her all—lay bare his heart to her, and, if it must be, hear from her own lips the "No" that will blast his life for ever. *Anything* will be better than this crushing suspense.

"Where is Miss Monteith?" he asks the man as he goes by.

"In the library, sir. Saw her go in there just now."

Opening the library door he enters the room, and finds himself alone with her.

She is standing at the far window, and, with a little start, acknowledges his entrance. He would have gone to her, but with a certain impulsive eagerness she too moves and meets him half-way. That her late anger is still warm within her eyes is known to him at the first glance.

"So—now you know me," she says, defiantly, "are you satisfied? Is your curiosity satiated?"

"I knew you from the first moment. Was I likely to forget?"

"That is the bitterness of it," she says. "Are those three sad years of my life never to be obliterated?"

"From *my* mind, never! The few weeks I claim out of them were the happiest of my life."

"What brings you to me now?" demands she, suddenly. "Is there more you would still learn as to the why and the wherefore of my going into hospital as a nurse? I warn you I shall give no explanation."

"I do not desire one," says Dare, humbly; "I know all about it. Your father's tyranny; your escape from a marriage with that vile old man; your life in hospital—everything. Do you hate me the more because I know all this?"

"Hate you—no!" There is studied contempt in the curl of her lip. "Hatred is a strong sentiment; what I feel for you is only indifference."

She goes back to her former position in the window, as though to terminate the interview. But he having "cast his all upon the die," makes one more effort for dear life. He follows her there.

"Even the worst criminals get a fair hearing," he says. "Let me plead my cause."

"No. It would be waste of time."

"At least tell me of what I stand accused."

"Listen, then !" exclaims she, turning to him with flashing eyes. "When unkind Fate sent you to that hospital a year and a half ago, and you saw me there day after day, a mere nurse, and—as you believed—unknown and obscure, you deigned to fancy yourself in love with me. Your momentary infatuation went even so far, that as the hour approached that was to put an end for ever to our intercourse with each other, driven by some puerile impulse, you deemed it even possible to declare your love, and offer me your name. But when it came to the point, you *quailed ;* you drew back your half-uttered words ; you shrank from allying yourself with one beneath you. *My* feelings were as nothing to you. Knowing myself scorned, rejected, without being afforded so much as the poor gratification of being able to refuse you, I left the room, hoping, *praying* I might never see your face again. Do you think," with a painful sob, "I shall ever forgive all that ?"

"Hear me."

"I will not. If your life and heart and title were all at my feet now, I——"

"They are at your feet."

"Then I reject them," returns she, with vehemence.

"As you will. But at least you shall listen to what I have to say in my defence," says Dare, with dignity. "That morning of which you speak—my last in the hospital—I truly meant, as you say, to tell you of my love."

"*Meant !* And then—you hesitated."

"I did," says Dare, simply. "My name and the honour of my house is dear to me. Is it a crime beyond forgiveness that I should have paused before offering that name and honour to a woman who, though the most beautiful and lovable in the world, was still—unknown ?"

"Why should you seek to excuse yourself?" interrupts Miss Monteith, haughtily; "I know all that."

"There is, however, one thing that you do *not* know. You saw that I did battle with myself that morning, but you did not wait the termination of it. Love and duty fought a hard fight, but when it was over, you—that is, Love—had won the victory; I raised my head again to tell you all—to *beseech* you to be my wife, but you were gone. Later on I searched for you everywhere; I advertised, all to no purpose. For eighteen months I sought for you—in vain."

Her face is turned away from him now, but a faint sound, that is either a sigh or a protest, escapes her.

"About all this you must believe me or not, as you will," says Dare, quietly. "I have only my simple word to give you, but it is at least a word that has never yet been dishonoured. Will you not say *something* to me?"

"All I have to say has been said long ago. I cannot forgive you," says Miss Monteith; but as she says it she bursts into tears.

"I will not accept such words from your lips," exclaims Dare, with deep agitation. And then all in a moment his arms are round her and his cheek pressed to hers.

"Beloved," he says, "have pity upon me! Just think of it! You who have a name as old as mine, can you not understand the struggle I endured?"

"I can," murmurs she, sadly; "and—yes, I honour you for it. But——" Here her voice fails. "Oh, if you could only know what I suffered!" she says, sobbing bitterly.

"I do know it. It was just *half* what I suffered," returns he, gravely. "Oh, darling, put an end to my misery *now—here!* Of the two I am the more to be pitied, because if you still prove unkind my unhappiness will last for ever. Eva, speak to me."

"Evelyn," corrects she, softly.

"Ah, of course. But you must remember how long you have been 'Eva' to me. What an eternity lies in that year and a half! The very length of my wretchedness should buy my pardon."

"You are a special pleader," whispers she; and then she makes him a present of a little arch smile, and a tender glance from under her drenched lashes.

"Tell me you love me," persists he.

"I cannot—yet. There is first something——"

"Nothing that shall separate us," declares he, stoutly.

"There may be. Who—who was that 'Alys' you were always raving about during that dreadful time when you were ill?"

"Alys! My sister, of course!" says he, triumphantly. "Had a letter from her only yesterday. She has been in India with her husband for the past four years, or probably you would have seen her at the hospital during that lucky time when I was ill. Now, what have you got to say?" He is fast waxing into the wildest spirits.

"Nothing," returns she, demurely; "so now let us go back to the others."

She makes a movement as though to go to the door, but he seizes her.

"Oh, yes, there is something!" he says, "and you sha'n't go without confessing it. Now then—you will marry me?"

"Yes."

"Soon?"

"Ye—es."

"And you are sure you love me?"

"As sure as sure can be!" says Miss Monteith, solemnly with a shameless disregard of maidenly reserve.

A ROSE DISTILL'D.

"But who is she? and where has she come from?" asks Mrs. Vyvyan, with uplifted brows and a slight acerbity of tone. She actually lays down her novel (the third volume, too) as she says this, as though honestly desirous of information, or scandal.

"She is a widow, I hear," replies her brother, lazily. He yawns, and pulls with languid affection the ears of the small terrier sitting on his knee.

"Oh! of course; they always *are* widows," said Mrs. Vyvyian.

"Well, why shouldn't they be? Fellows *will* die, you know. By-the-bye, did you hear about Fred's parsnips? He——"

"Never mind the parsnips. Fred" (Fred is her husband) "is always making an ass of himself about one thing or the other. Tell me what else you have heard about this new-comer."

"About Mrs. Stamer? Not much. She has taken The Holmes, it appears, and has one little daughter. I know nothing more of her, and I shouldn't have known that if Daventry hadn't regularly button-holed me, and made me listen to him."

"How odd it is! That sort of woman has *always* only one child, and it is *never* a son. Why don't they have two? and why not a boy, sometimes?"

"Sometimes they have. I know a widow who has three little sons."

"A widow in society, no doubt. But this Mrs. Stamer has apparently no connections, no antecedents (that can be safely introduced), in fact, *nothing !*"

"She has money ; and the best place to be had now in the neighbourhood."

"I suppose "—fretfully—"she will expect us to call."

"Let her expect, and don't call. Why should you ? Stay at home, and so avoid this grievance."

"But if everybody else calls, I sha'n't like to feel I am the one ill-natured person in the parish. Why on earth can't she say who she is, or mention a cousin, or a sister, or an aunt ? Charlotte Grynde saw her yesterday, and says she is too pretty to be proper."

" If ugliness is a patent of respectability, Miss Grynde is all one could possibly desire," says Captain Blackwood. "She is, beyond all doubt, too proper to be pretty."

"Charlotte is trying, certainly, but I think she is a good soul," says Mrs. Vyvyan, carelessly, of her " dearest friend," "Stamer—Stamer. It is a good name enough, but perhaps assumed."

"'What's in a name?'" quotes her brother. "We have all heard about the rose, you know, and considering what we have heard she must be superior to any rose. If her surname was Brown, Jones, or Robinson, it wouldn't take the lustre out of her eyes, or add an inch to her nose—which I hear is pure Greek. By-the-bye, she has got the most questionable christian name."

" How questionable ? "

" It is almost improper," says Captain Blackwood, with a faint laugh. The day is warm, and laughter of the pronounced sort is beyond him. " She calls herself ' Audrey.' It sounds stagey, doesn't it ? A woman who respected herself wouldn t go round with that name, would she ? It's so disgracefully out of the common."

"A *name* signifies very little," says Mrs. Vyvyan, severely, who doesn't like being ridiculed even by a pet brother.

"Look here, Pussy," says Captain Blackwood: "don't you be the first to taboo this poor little woman. She is only your own age, I hear, twenty-seven" (Mrs. Vyvyan is thirty-two), "so don't be hard on her. No doubt she has had bad times enough, without our coming down heavily upon her."

"I sha'n't do anything, of course, until other people move," says Mrs. Vyvyan, much mollified by that happy allusion to her —or rather Mrs. Stamer's age. The *other people* mean the Bishop, Mrs. Bishop, and Lady Mary Gore.

"And don't be too hasty even then," advises her brother, who is a good-natured young man, some three years her junior. "By-the-bye, talking of haste, I would take three inches off her tail, if I were you. You shouldn't delay another hour."

"Off *whose* tail?" startled.

"Gilly's. These Irish terriers don't look the thing with tails."

"Oh! the dog," says his sister, in a relieved tone. "I thought you were speaking of——. I don't understand dogs, but take off Gilly's tail if you like, only—don't hurt her."

"Here comes Charlotte the Grynder: so I'll retire," says Captain Blackwood, glancing down the avenue through the open window. "She has got on her new black silk, so she means mischief. I won't have any tea this evening, thanks, unless you will be so good as to send it to the library. And, Pussy, a last word: if you really want to make your friend thoroughly happy, just expatiate on what you have heard of Mrs. Stamer's beauty."

A sound outside, a well-known semi-masculine step, and Captain Blackwood flies to regions dull—but inaccessible.

In spite of its many spinsters, society in Pullingham is eminently good-natured. Just now it is grieving excessively at having to hold back the right hand of fellowship from the stranger at The Holmes. But as The Larches have not gone to see her in their landau, The Elms have not dared to show her the light of their countenance in their phaeton; and so on in the lesser degrees of pride, each member shrinking from the initiative in this matter.

At the end of a week, however, things come to a climax. The Bishop, a wonderfully unworldly man as bishops go, waking to a sense of the situation, drags himself away from the contemplation of his strawberry beds, and persuades Mrs. Bishop to put on her best bonnet, and come with him to make a formal call at The Holmes. This, poor woman, she does in fear and trembling: Lady Mary Gore has not as yet signified her intention of visiting the new-comer, and Lady Mary is own sister to a duke! Supposing Mrs. Bishop should be putting her foot in it! Awful thought!

She feels a little faint, but having donned the bonnet in obedience to her lord, ascends the Noah's Ark they call a coach, and drives away with him to call upon this unknown woman who may or may *not* (here the feeling of faintness returns) be respectable : she almost weeps, and certainly scolds all the way there, and finally arrives just in time to meet Lady Mary departing.

Yes, there *is* balm in Gilead! Again, the sun shines, the flowers emit the sweetest perfume. All is changed. She presses Lady Mary's hand affectionately, and murmurs "how glad she is to see that dear Lady Mary *too*" (the "too" heavily emphasised) " has espoused this poor creature's cause, and has not gone over to those who seem bent on ignoring her presence in the county."

Lady Mary nods and blinks, and gives it as her opinion that the " poor creature " is absolutely charming, and goes on her way rejoicing, with a large smile upon her broad, ugly, lovely old face.

After the Bishop, Mrs. Vyvyan calls, and after that there is a rush from minor quarters to see the pretty widow, who has dropped down amongst them, as if from the skies.

They find her very good to look at; *so* good that somebody says she cannot be bad, her face is so angelic; yet every one, in his or her secret heart, feels that there *may* be something in her past not altogether—well—you understand : and this adds piquancy to the acquaintance, though all would have died rather than confess it.

There is one great charm about Mrs. Stamer. She is always at home, and always to be seen, so every one can gratify his curiosity about her. She is ever to be found seated in a huge rocking-chair in her drawing-room, with the windows open (it is hottest, brightest June), an immense peacock fan in her little jewelled hand, and a very tiny child at her feet.

She is dressed in deepest mourning—not crape exactly, but heavy black for all that, relieved here and there by some handsome jet, and old lace frillings at the throat and wrists. The child is in mourning, too : yet she tells every one she has been a widow for a little more than three years. On her left hand, as in duty bound (this is Miss Grynde's remark, not mine), she wears a plain wedding ring ; on her right two magnificent diamonds, worth a small fortune. Miss Grynde is further of opinion that diamond rings of such value on a widow of unknown fame—are not respectable !

Pullingham is festive : it is even lavish in its hospitality. Invitations to stately afternoons, pompous dinners, and frivolous evenings have been showered upon Mrs. Stamer—all in vain. She has politely declined to join the dance in any form whatsoever. Indeed, she lets it be understood that she means to abjure gaiety, and devotes herself exclusively to the cultivation of her child.

The child is a decided feature in her programme. There have been, and there are, pretty children in Pullingham, but anything so ethereally lovely as the little fairy who calls Mrs. Stamer "mamma" has never yet been seen there. She is a minute thing of five years, with yellow hair that encircles her like a cloud, and out of which gleam dark eyes and crimson lips, a complexion like a veritable white rose, and a wistful expression that must have come with her from her own domain of Faerie.

"To-day, being just a trifle cooler than its fellows, Mrs. Vyvyan drives her ponies down to The Holmes, and entering the shaded drawing-room there, literally lays siege to Mrs. Stamer, who is looking as slender and cool and calm as though the heat is not 90° in the shade, without even one sighing breeze to relieve its intensity. The flowers are drooping; the streamlets run slowly; gentle Zephyrus has forgotten the earth!

"You *must* come to us this evening," says Mrs. Vyvyan, impetuously. "You must indeed. Why, you have been here for a full month, and never put in an evening anywhere. It is almost uncivil of you."

"Oh! not uncivil," says Mrs. Stamer, gently.

"Well then, unkind. We wish to make you one of us, and you won't have it," says Mrs. Vyvyan, who had been the first to traduce her and the second to adore her. Besides, to-night I want you."

"There are so many others," says the pale widow, with a faint smile. "In your charming circle a stranger—such as I am—cannot possibly be missed. A stranger, however, who feels your kindness deeply, and hardly knows how she can repay it." This last with extreme grace, and a soft, undulating movement, and a sweeter smile.

"I know," says Mrs. Vyvyan, briskly. "There is nothing to repay: but if *you think* there is, come to me to-night. It will be an early party; so early that I will ask you to bring the little one with you; my May and Edith will look after her."

At this, a faint little plaintive voice that seems to come from the mother's feet makes itself heard. The child has been sitting on a low footstool buried in one of Mrs. Molesworth's charming tales, but the last sentence spoken has become English to her. She rises and throws her bare soft arms around her mother's neck.

"Oh, mamma, *do, do* take me! I have never bèen to a real party, and I want to play with Edith." Mrs. Stamer is not proof against this solicitation.   It was indeed a lucky hour when Mrs. Vyvyan thought of asking the child.

"But my pet——" begins the widow, faintly.

"Say *yes*," entreats the golden-haired elf with authority—at which Mrs. Vyvyan laughs.

"You *will* come," she says, hopefully.   "That is right. Dulce," to the child, "I owe you a debt of gratitude.   The fact is, the General is to be with us.   He is staying with the Claremont people, and he is such a charming man, I should quite like you to meet him."

"I will come to you," sighs Mrs. Stamer, unwillingly.   It is terrible to her to emerge from her seclusion, but she feels, in this instance, it will be too unfriendly to refuse.   And if she has to live her life amongst these people, the sooner she accepts their ways the better, if only for her child's sake.

"Now that is right," says Mrs. Vyvyan ; and she presses a little kiss upon Mrs. Stamer's pale cheek as she takes her departure.

As Mrs. Stamer enters the reception rooms at the Grange, she finds them fuller than she had anticipated : where all these people can have come from is the first thought.   Pullingham, in her eyes, had not appeared large enough to contain one-half of them, yet, after a careful scrutiny, she confesses to herself that no face here is unfamiliar.   Every one seems a little surprised, and a good deal glad to see her.   Her child is caressed and petted to her heart's content, until May and Edith Vyvyan carry her off bodily.   The hostess rustles up to Mrs. Stamer, and makes much of her, and says something about George ; whereupon Captain Blackwood asserts himself, and takes Mrs. Stamer to the upper end of the room, where a window opens upon a scene replete with moonbeams and a shimmering lake.

Somebody is singing.   The voice is not loud or powerful, but it is sweet, and it thrills one's soul only to hear it.   Mrs. Stamer sighs profoundly, and, sinking into a low chair, tells herself she may probably be happy here for an hour or two.

The moon is streaming in upon her; the gardens below are all aflood with its light; the tiny wavelets on the lake seem to be sobbing and swaying through very ecstasy, so loving is the touch Diana gives them. A faint glimpse of the distant ocean, sparkling and scintillating in the clear rays, can be caught through the branches of the tall firs, that stand out jet black against the pallid sky. The perfume of many flowers creeps up, to render a perfect scene more perfect, and Mrs. Stamer, leaning back in her seat, with eyes sympathetic turned upon the lovely light, adds to it another charm. Captain Blackwood is not talking; for this she is secretly grateful. He is contenting himself with a prolonged survey of the faultless face beside him, that, calm and quiet as marble, yet suggests such possibilities of passionate feeling.

Then the song comes to an end, and a little murmur of admiration follows it; *that* dies away, and after it comes a fluttering : at the lower end of the long room there stands the entrance door, and Blackwood, glancing in its direction, says, lazily :

"The Claremont people at last, *and* the General!"

Mrs. Stamer, thus roused from her reverie, turns to her companion. "*The* General," she says, with a slight touch of amusement in her tone; and then, as if impelled by some absurd curiosity, she rises and glances down the room to where the last comers stand talking to Mrs. Vyvyan.

A tall, soldierly-looking man with clear-cut features, a heavy moustache, and very mournful eyes, is most conspicuous amongst the group. He is grave to a fault; but now, even as she looks, he smiles, and his smile is full of beauty, and transforms him in one instant from middle-age to youth.

"He is younger than one would expect in a General," says Captain Blackwood, without any particular interest in his tone, "though real live Generals, to tell the truth, are few and far between in Pullingham. He—by Jove!"

He is barely in time to catch Mrs. Stamer in his arms, as she sways forward and falls in a dead faint—caused by the heat, no doubt.

It is the simplest thing in the world to get her out of the room, and upstairs to Mrs. Vyvyan's bed without a sensation of any kind. One or two of the women guests, seeing what has happened, go with her, and as for the rest, they know nothing of the mishap that has befallen the mistress of The Holmes until several hours later.

Time flies. The General is naturally the hero of the hour, coming fresh from Afghanistan. By and by the young people take to dancing in the grand old hall, and the General—who has laughingly declined to trip it unless he can find a partner of his own age—and what woman will acknowledge to that?—steps out on the balcony, and gazes thoughtfully upon the sleeping garden. All is peace !—a great calm has fallen on the world. It seems almost as if ever-ready sin has sunk to rest : the lake ripples; the moonbeams shiver; the flowers sleep; no sound comes to move the intense quiet of the hour. But what is this ?

A little form—is it angel or fairy?—comes slowly up to the General across the stone balcony. Pausing near him, it lifts its large eyes confidently to his face. It is the child Dulce, who has grown wearied with her play, and would fain be at rest within her snowy bed. He can touch her if he will but put forth his hand. Involuntarily he does so, and, drawing her to him, gazes into her small face.

As he does so, his own changes : a heavy pallor shines through the bronze an Indian sun has laid upon his cheek. Raising her he takes her impetuously to where the light from the many lamps within must fall upon her, and illumine her baby features. *Who* is she like ?—*Who?*—alas ! too well he knows. His breath comes with painful rapidity, a film gathering before his eyes shuts out from them the little face he wants to see.

"Your name, child, your name?" he says, hoarsely, so

hoarsely indeed that the words are lost to her. She shakes her head wearily, and looks with the sleepy but uncertain interest of a moment upon the gay scene within. The General's eyes are wild, yet, strange to say, the child betrays no fear. She only nestles a little closer to him, and slips an arm round his neck, and lays one of the fairest heads in Christendom upon his shoulder.

"I am tired," she says. "I wish mamma would take me home."

"Where is your mother?" asks he, eagerly.

"In the drawing-room," replies the child, as her little head grows heavier. "If you see her, call her."

The General casts a piercing glance around the room. He can see nothing that may alleviate the uneasiness that has full possession of his breast. "Tell me your name, my little one," he says, gently.

"Dulce Stamer," replies the drowsy fairy. After which confession, she sinks into placid sleep within his arms.

Finding a seat near him, the General slowly takes possession of it. It is deep in the embrasure of the old-fashioned window, and is hidden from the room by curtains that hang heavily. Here he sits nursing the child contentedly : with infinite care he so disposes the little rounded limbs and dainty body that her sleep may be the sounder. With unspeakable tenderness he gazes upon the silken lashes and rosy lips, through which the breath of life ebbs and flows calmly, evenly.

So an hour passes, and then the curtains are parted, and Mrs. Vyvyan, looking in, stares at the tableau that presents itself to her view. A veteran and an infant! If incongruous, it is at least charming.

"General!" she whispers, with a low laugh. "Is it *so* you have been entertained? Who made you a nurse to-night?"

"She came to me of her own accord," says the General, somewhat proudly; "she gave herself into my keeping with the most flattering trust. If you don't want her, don't take her from me. I have seldom been so happy as I have been to-night."

"That is very sweet of you," says Mrs. Vyvyan; "but I must let you off duty now. Dulce's mother waits her. She is going home."

"Then, let me take her to her carriage," says the General, strangely loth to surrender his little friend to any one.

"No, no," says Mrs. Vyvyan, earnestly. "Mrs. Stamer has not been well, and so wants to get away quietly. A strange face might upset her." So saying, she stoops, and, lifting Dulce with the utmost gentleness, bears her away from the General.

"Did you enjoy yourself, darling?" asks Mrs. Stamer, as she and the child are rolling home swiftly beneath the light of the quiet stars, through the scented lanes, heavy with dew and moonshine.

"Yes, *so* much," says the little one. "But I went to sleep; and he was very good to me, and nursed me *so* comfortably."

"Who did, darling?" she asks, indifferently.

"The strange man."

"*What* man?" cries her mother, with as much force as though some one had struck her. A passionate throb takes her heart; all her pulses beat tumultuously.

"The tall, thin man," says the child, simply; "they called him the General!"

"Ah!" says Mrs. Stamer. She inhales her breath quickly, making a sound like a sob, and leans back in the carriage.

It is now next day; and again Apollo is on high, saluting the earth with his fire. Last night the General slept little, but asked many questions. He had kept one of the Clares (on their return from the Grange) in the smoking-room until an unconscionable hour, probing him unmercifully about The Holmes and its inmates, until the poor young man's lids fell down over his eyes. Then the General, seeing no more was to be gained from him, generously sent him to bed. But bed for the General that night meant nothing less than torment.

Something had happened to wake within him memories of

a past, now three years old. He had not been General Steyne then, but a colonel, and life at that time had shown him its sweetest and its bitterest sides. He had been wrong then, he knows that now—he had been wrong, indeed, all through, but only discovered his error when too late. And last night—a few hours ago—a little baby face, a tiny rose-tinged thing, framed in a glory of hair, yellow as uncut corn, had raised within him a demon of remorse and longing that will not be laid.

This morning, breakfast is a mockery to him, so unnerved is he by his long vigil. He fidgets secretly, whilst the others eat their kidneys and toast, and laugh over last night's proceedings; and, when decency allows, he rises, and, finding a hat, walks quickly down the stone steps of Claremont, and turns eagerly in the direction that leads to The Holmes. Yes. Now at once, and for ever, he will get rid of the gnawing anxiety, the consuming hope that has been destroying him for hours; and when he has walked two miles, and his heart has begun to beat feverishly, he comes face to face with Mrs. Stamer, at her entrance gate.

For a long minute they gaze at each other in a silence that may be felt. The General breaks it. "I was not mistaken, then," he says, in a low tone.

"No? and what then?" asks Mrs. Stamer, in a cold, clear voice, full of defiance. She raises her eyes proudly to his, though in very truth her soul is fainting within her.

"After three long years of incessant search, to find you here —of all places—unawares!" he says, gazing earnestly at her. He seems lost in astonishment, he cannot, though the doing so would be a relief to him, avert his eyes from the fair but wrathful face that returns his glance so steadily.

"Well, you *have* found me," she says, still defiant; "and now what have you gained by your discovery?"

"Not much, perhaps, in your eyes; but to me this accidental meeting has brought comfort that is almost overpowering. I have *seen* you—you are alive and well. It is a great deal. You cannot, of course, understand *how much*—and besides all this,

I have held the child in my arms! She slept *here*" (laying his hand upon his heart with a rather simple gesture). "She had her little arms around my neck : she was *happy* with me."

"My daughter told me you had been kind to her," says Mrs. Stamer, coldly. She speaks as one might who is acknowledging a small kindness done to her by an acquaintance of a day. The settled distance of her manner cuts him to the heart.

"It was nothing," he says, his colour rising, his voice growing tremulous ; "nothing to you, at least ; but it filled me with a joy I have not known for years—for three long years. I can still feel the pressure of her little head."

"Dulce was grateful to you," says Dulce's mother, icily. "I regret she cannot thank you in person."

"'Dulce.' She was Audrey once," exclaims he, quickly.

"I changed all that when I changed——many other things. Dulce suits her best—*my sweet !*" As the last words fall from her lips they soften them, and her whole face grows alight with the rapturous glow born of the most eternal love of all !

"May I not see her?" asks the General, very humbly. "Surely I have *some* claim to——"

"She belongs to *me*," says Mrs. Stamer, interrupting him with some passion. Is there not fear mingled with it? She turns aside from him, as though his presence is no longer tolerable. .

"You are in mourning," he says, quickly, bent on detaining her for even one more precious minute.

"Sombre colours become those who are widowed," replies she, with her eyes on the ground.

"But the child?" exclaims he, in deep agitation. "Last night I noticed it—she, too, is in mourning."

"It is only right she should be so ; she has lost her father," says Mrs. Stamer. She moves away from him to where the giant elms are throwing dark shadows on the grass, and soon is lost to sight amidst their gloom.

Looking older, greyer, the General goes down the dusty road, lost in saddest thought. Coming to a stile, he steps over it, and enters a field, green as emerald, at the side of which a little stream runs gurgling with tremulous glee, as it rushes to meet the great ocean, that lies in a white mist far below. A mighty fir uprears itself in the corner of this field, and, leaning against it, the General gives himself up to the most miserable reflections, when a sound comes to him: a fresh, sweet sound, that thrills him to his heart's core, and uplifts it to know that even for him there is joy upon the blessed earth.

It is a child's voice singing; and the child herself is coming to him across the sunlit sward, with her dark eyes all aglow, and her lips parted, and her hair flying behind her, like a golden glory. She has crimson poppies in her hands, and is holding them close to her little bosom, as though filled with love for them, as she speeds along. She has escaped from nurse, and in the delicious sense of freedom is chanting aloud a merry lilt.

But even as the General gazes upon her, a change passes over the little face. As if to prove that ever pain must mingle with our dearest gladness here, the child pauses in her happy run, her song ceases. The small face puckers ominously; and, sinking on the ground, she bursts into a flood of tears.

In a moment the General is at her side, has lifted her in his strong arms, and is asking her what has happened. He presses her tangled yellow head against his breast, and betrays such genuine grief at her mishap that the child is half consoled. He may be unlearned in childhood's ways, yet it is with a touch that a woman might have envied, because of its gentleness, that he sets about discovering the damage done.

Dulce is not shy. She has ceased crying; and now, lifting her angelic eyes to his, she points sorrowfully to her little rounded bare leg, as though demanding sympathy. It is a small affair, after all—the sting of a venomous nettle, that has raised a pink flush upon her tender skin. The General stoops and kisses the soft injured limb with the greatest tenderness.

He even removes the shoe and sock from her foot, with a view to ascertaining whether or not the wicked nettle has penetrated through the strong kid.　Then with an awkwardness unrivalled, he draws on the sock again, and after a fierce and protracted battle with it, reduces the button of the shoe to subjection.　Dulce is delighted with him.　She has quite adopted him by this time, and is sitting, without the slightest regard for decency, with her arms tightly clasped round his neck, and her cheek rubbing its velvet softness against his.

"Does he know mamma?　Does he love her?"

The General flushes.　"Yes, he has seen mamma.　Does *she* love her?"

"Oh, yes.　Mamma is beautiful and must be loved.　She, Dulce, loves her most, though, when she is crying; and she is often crying, poor mamma.　Then Dulce comforts her. Mamma says she is her only comfort."

"And Dulce's papa?"

"Papa is dead.　Mamma has said so.　He is buried, down, down," pointing to the ground.　"But mamma told her only yesterday that she must love him always, even though she may never see him till she goes up to Heaven.　He was the best man that ever lived," says Dulce, sweetly, as if repeating an old lesson, looking straight into the General's abashed eyes.

"He was *not*," says the General, suddenly, losing his head.

"But he *was*," declares the child, indignantly, regarding him with a sudden accession of disfavour.　"Mamma says so."

"Mamma!"

"Yes, my mamma—and she knows.　You knew him too," says the little one, with all a child's singular astuteness.　"Tell me about him; was he big?——Tall?"

She has forgotten her anger of a moment since, and is now gazing at him with one of her sweetest smiles.

"Yes," says the General.

"And with grey hair, like yours," stroking his grizzly locks.

"Yes, just like mine.　He was old, too," says the General, with a touch of ill-suppressed bitterness.

"Had he nice eyes, like yours?"

"Very like mine, my angel."　And then the child tightens

her arms about him, and entreats him to come home with her to her own house, and she will show him her pretty garden, and her ducks, and her little soft yellow chicks, and the rose that has bloomed upon her own tree.

But the General declares he cannot come to-day; some other time. He breaks off abruptly in the middle of a sentence, and bends his head upon his breast. Growing frightened, the little one tries to raise it, and she sees that tears are running down the General's cheeks, and that he is crying.

To-day, as usual, Mrs. Stamer is sitting in her huge rocking-chair, wafting her big fan to and fro. Her lids have drooped slightly over her eyes in true drowsy fashion; the action of her wrist grows languid; she is in full enjoyment of an afternoon as sultry and free from air of any kind as one living for years in the far East can possibly desire.

Yet there is a faint curve about her perfect lips that is hardly happy, a touch of pallor in her soft cheeks that suggests mournful, nay, even hateful thought.

"General Steyne," says a servant, opening the door suddenly, so detaching her from a painful past as to bring her to a yet more painful present—to judge by the cloud that covers her fair face.

But the servant's eye is on her, and so she forces herself to rise, and bow coldly to her visitor, and say "How d'ye do," as quietly as if the heart in her body is not beating wildly, madly with surprise and indignation, and something else, perhaps.

"Then the servant vanishes; and as he does so her enforced courtesy vanishes too, and with passionate contempt and anger she turns to the General.

"*You!* And here!" she says. It is as if she would gladly have said much more, but that her strength is insufficient for her. She is literally consumed by the emotion that is making her bosom rise and fall tumultuously.

"I couldn't help it," says the General. It is a perfectly puerile excuse, and at the least very humble—*so* humble that it would have disarmed most women's anger. Unhappily it has only the effect of increasing Mrs. Stamer's.

"That you should *dare* to seek me," she says, with a little gasp, "to even *look* upon my face again : to——"

"It was that that brought me," interrupts he, eagerly. So eagerly that, for the moment, he appears almost a young man. "To look upon your face once more—for the last time, perhaps. That I am unworthy to do it, I know; but I risked everything, even your anger. It was an overpowering desire; I could not conquer it." He speaks somewhat incoherently, and when his voice fails him, there is a pause.

"Now that you have gratified your desire, I shall be glad if you will go," says Mrs. Stamer, drawing her breath in a somewhat laboured fashion. She is standing always, and has one hand upon a chair near her, as though to steady herself. Her face is white as death, her eyes are all afire.

"Audrey ! have you forgotten all ? " cries he, in anguish ; " all our happy past, You used to say you were happy then. Must my one crime be as a curse upon my whole life ? Is pardon impossible ? "

"Quite impossible ! "

"Could you not *try* to forgive ? "

"For what ? " she asks, sternly. "To love again—to be again undone ? *No !* I have wisdom now, where I had only childish trust before. Unheard, you condemned me. Another's voice, the voice of a common slanderer, was more precious in your ears than mine. You believe me false to you—*false !* How can I forgive or forget *that ?* You have sown ; you now reap ; and all is at an end between us."

"Even memory ? " asks he, despairingly. "Are there *no* hours you can look back upon, and wish——"

"I *never* look back," cries she, vehemently, putting up her hand as though to ward off some fatal blow. "*Never !* I *will* not."

She is strangely agitated. She betrays a forced determination not to be won over by any argument, however specious.

"If, then, for the future I am to be nothing to you," says the General, in a low tone that he strives hard to reduce to calmness, "tell me—what of the child?"

At this a terrible fear takes possession of her. Her lips part, but no sound comes from them. She looks at him with a dumb entreaty in her beautiful· eyes that amounts almost to agony.

Will he take the child from her? Has he the power to do so? Will he cruelly deprive her of the little creature who has been to her for years as her very heart's blood? Must she live without the sweet companionship that has grown necessary to her, the fond baby kisses that have rendered her sad life not only bearable but almost to be desired?

"You will not take the child from me!" she says, in a dying tone. Her face grows absolutely grey with fear—involuntarily she lays her hand upon her throat, as one might who is in danger of suffocation.

"No, no, no," says the General, vehemently, her evident distrust of him causing him even keener anguish than what has gone before. "The child is yours. I surrender all claim, no matter what it costs me. I owe you so much. I will do nothing to wound you. You have suffered enough at my hands already. I shall do whatever you wish in the future. It rests in your own hands. If you tell me to go now, I shall obey you."

"Then go," exclaims she: and his face changes perceptibly.

"And if you tell me never to return—if you think that will be for your happiness," his voice trembles, "you shall *still* be obeyed!" Though he has forced himself to utter the words, they are almost unintelligible. Is she merciless, or has she indeed lost all love for him? Has his one act of unfaith destroyed for ever the hold he once had upon her heart?

"It will be better so," she says, her tone uncertain. She has risen to her feet, and is staring at him with yearning eyes. Is this indeed to be the end? Is she by two or three words to drive him for ever from her presence? How tall he looks, how

grand, how soldier-like, and—he is her husband—and once—
once she loved him wildly. The General, drawing himself up
to his full height, which is magnificent, walks to the door.
Has he not given his word to obey her?

In this world how many great things hinge upon a bare circumstance! But for an interruption he might have gone forth
and never looked again upon the face dearest to him. Even
as he opens the door, Dulce comes rushing in with flying hair,
and sparkling eyes, and happy crimson lips, glad with smiles.

"Oh, nurse told me you were here," she cries, as she pre-
cipitates herself upon the General, and impounds him on the
spot.

"It is my general," she says, glancing over her white, rounded
shoulder at her mother, who seems turned into stone. The
child is in a very rapture; she throws her little arms around his
neck and smothers him with kisses.

"I guessed you would come. I told mamma I had asked
you, and that I thought you would come: and you see," with
a triumphant glance at her pale mother, "I was right."

"Quite right," says the General, very gently. "Yet you see,
Dulce, my coming has been of no use. I must go now, even
as *you* come."

"No, no," says the child, hospitably. "Mamma, ask him to
stay and have tea with us."

"I can't stay, indeed," says the poor General, hurriedly.

"Mamma, make him," cries the anxious little voice. "I want
to show him my new chickens."

"I shall be glad if you will stay," says Mrs. Stamer, in a
stifled tone. The sight of the child in his arms, with her pretty
cheek pressed against his, is almost more than she can endure.

"There!" says Dulce, slipping out of his arms. "Now you
must stay—and I shall run and tell Jackson to bring the tea at
once."

In a moment she is gone. The General looks with some
embarrassment at Mrs. Stamer, and sees that she has covered
her face with her hands, and is crying silently, but passionately.

In a moment he is at her side, at her feet. " Audrey, Audrey," he cries, imploringly. " Would it be possible to forgive ! "

" No, no," sobs she, bitterly, but her voice is not unforgiving.

" Our whole lives must be influenced by this moment," says General Steyne, solemnly. " I implore you to think. I know I am unworthy of pardon, but if——"

" Memory would come between us," whispers she, sadly.

" *Nothing* shall come between us ! If so blessed a thing could happen, as that you would take me back into your heart, no earthly power should separate us again."

He waits with beating pulse for her reply. Lifting her streaming eyes to his, she says, "You are really sorry ? " It is a foolish question, but very womanly, and it fills the General with contrition.

" Alas ! " he says, mournfully, " need you ask me that question, my beloved ? I doubt if even the great joy of being forgiven by you—if that joy be mine, Audrey—can altogether blot out the recollection of these three past miserable years, during which remorse has been my companion day and night."

" I will drive out that companion," murmurs she with quivering lips, yielding to his sweet caress. " My husband, now that I am your own again, all evil thoughts will fly from yor ."

" Here comes tea ! " cries Dulce, dancing into tue room before the solemn footman, who is following her with the tray.

" Is it ? " says her mother, with a tremulous smile. " Good child ! Now, will you go and tell cook that General Steyne will dine with us at half-past seven ? No, Jackson, no, I want Miss Dulce to take the message herself."

UNWIN BROTHERS,
THE GRESHAM PRESS,
CHILWORTH AND LONDON.